Praise for
Don't Say We Didn't Warn You

"A story that's so weird, it has to be true . . . keeps our attention in
a chokehold."

—*The New York Times*

"[Ariel Delgado] Dixon's chilling and evocative debut features two
sisters whose traumatic history bonds them and shapes their adulthood."

—*Ms.*

"A badass queer thriller."

—*Autostraddle*

"Haunting at times, this book will linger with you for days to come
after finishing it."

—*Debutiful*

"Dixon's skillful pacing, brilliant structure, and creation of menace through exacting description keep the reader gripped. Like a wire being stretched, the mounting tension has to snap and the ensuing whiplash flings around unpredictably."

—*PopMatters*

"Consistently and devastatingly intriguing . . . A coming-of-age rife with destruction."

—*Kirkus Reviews*

"Two sisters navigate childhood trauma in Dixon's chilling, complex debut. . . . The layered story lines and Fawn's shocking actions pay big dividends. Readers will be eager to see what the author does next."

—*Publishers Weekly*

"Eventful, complex, admirably structured, relentless, and spooky."

—Joy Williams, author of *Harrow*

"What a striking literary arrival! Ariel Delgado Dixon is a prose stylist with a rare talent marked by atmospheric rhythm. This distinct tale of two sisters, crawling with tension, will carve its way into your dreams."

—Kali Fajardo-Anstine, author of *Sabrina & Corina*

"The high, subtle tension in Delgado Dixon's fiction arises from the precision of her language. However wild the situations her characters find themselves in—and they find themselves in some wild ones indeed—her control never falters. She's a master of cold light and moral ambiguity, a new, uncompromising voice."

—Camille Bordas, author of *How to Behave in a Crowd*

DON'T SAY WE DIDN'T WARN YOU

DON'T SAY WE DIDN'T WARN YOU

A Novel

ARIEL DELGADO DIXON

RANDOM HOUSE | NEW YORK

2023 Random House Trade Paperback Edition

Published in the United States by Random House, an imprint and division of Penguin Random House LLC, New York.

RANDOM HOUSE and the HOUSE colophon are registered trademarks of Penguin Random House LLC.

Originally published in hardcover in the United States by Random House, an imprint and division of Penguin Random House LLC, in 2022.

Library of Congress Cataloging-in-Publication Data
Names: Dixon, Ariel Delgado, author.
Title: Don't say we didn't warn you: a novel / by Ariel Delgado Dixon.
Description: First edition. | New York: Random House, [2022]
Identifiers: LCCN 2021016784 (print) | LCCN 2021016785 (ebook) |
ISBN 9780593243527 (trade paperback) | ISBN 9780593243510 (ebook) |
Subjects: LCSH: Sisters—Fiction. | Teenage girls—Fiction. |
Problem youth—Fiction. | Psychological fiction.
Classification: LCC PS3604.I9285 D66 2022 (print) |
LCC PS3604.I9285 (ebook) | DDC 813/.6—dc23
LC record available at https://lccn.loc.gov/2021016784
LC ebook record available at https://lccn.loc.gov/2021016785

Printed in the United States of America on acid-free paper

randomhousebooks.com

1st Printing

Book design by Susan Turner

For my mother

So much in modern life that can be enjoyed,
once one gets over the nausea of the replicate.

—SUSAN SONTAG,
*As Consciousness Is Harnessed to Flesh:
Journals and Notebooks, 1964–1980*

I

ON THE STREET WHERE YOU LIVE

I

My sister always had fixations.

A certain star celebrity, a certain song or food. Anything consumable. She would go at it full tilt for a week or year, however long it took to bleed dry all mystery. She said things that made my mother and I look past her and at each other. Once, driving home from a tearjerker, Fawn mused aloud from the backseat. She couldn't understand why everyone went on and on after someone died. She was staring out the window, holding her thumb up to the moon. Didn't they get tired of acting like they were sad? When were you allowed to forget?

It was 2003, and everyone was obsessed with suspicious packages. When the first human appendage appeared—an elbow, somebody's elbow—I was almost touched. I could hardly believe something so glamorous could happen to us, here in our town.

A postwoman found the limb stuffed inside a duffel bag after nearly running it over on her route. From the raised interstate that cut through Deerie, some culprit had flung away a host of body parts while zooming upstate or down, someone who clearly had no idea there was a rotting hamlet beneath the overpass. The easy off-ramp into town had not yet been built, and the world below appeared as coarse, uninhabited woodland, the scant lights of remaining houses no more than reflections in the window glass. Probably, it seemed like an excellent place for body parts to be tossed, if that was the sort of thing you were trying to do. When the second body part appeared, it came for us. As was her way, Fawn took to it and would not let go.

It began with the dog. He was given to us as a bribe by an ex-boyfriend our mother spurned, and though it was not the first ex to take the tack of wooing her through her children, this bait was extravagant. Fawn claimed him, and I didn't argue. He came with the name Peanut Butter.

Fawn and Peanut Butter went out for a walk together one morning, the dog nosing around the usual detritus swamped under the highway, when he locked on to one duct-taped bundle. Some sixth sense must have made Fawn think twice. She brought it home under her arm, took the parcel into her room, and shut the door behind her. It might have remained her secret to do with as she pleased, but because our mother was in New York, as she often was, I was left in charge. On this authority, I stormed into Fawn's room to complain about one thing or another and found her sitting straight-backed at the end of her bed in deep concentration. Her dresser had been cleared but for her prized puppy figurines, and the bundle had been set there, a desk lamp shining over it like an incubator. It was as if she were waiting for it to hatch.

Naturally, and out of earshot, I called my best friend, Zeke, and told him to come right over. I liked my odds when it was two against one.

While I waited for his arrival, I allowed Fawn to expound on her new mystery item and asked a dozen follow-up questions meant to lull her into a state of compliance. She gazed at the taut sheen of plastic.

"What should we do with it?" she asked. The bundle looked complete, like a small wet boulder. "What could it be? What are you?"

The utility door at the street level heaved open. Zeke always took the stairs up to the loft two at a time in a swift, sneakered bound. Fawn swung around and I held my hands up.

"Just wait," I said. "Okay? Don't get all crazy. Don't—"

Zeke banged at the door, and in the time it took me to flick open the lock, Fawn had wedged a chair under the knob of her door. I could hear her pacing, cursing her error in judgment. She shouted through her barricade that I was a traitor, a liar, that she was going to call our mother.

"Does she have a phone in there?" Zeke asked. He had ridden over on his bike, and the heat had glazed him pink, ears and all.

"You don't have a phone in there," I shouted back to Fawn.

"You can't take it," she said. "It's mine."

"Could be drugs," Zeke said. "Maybe it's a big brick of drugs."

"It is not drugs," I said.

I had anticipated an escalation such as this. For a while, Zeke and I puttered around the kitchen, made snacks with dramatic flourishes, anything to drum up noise and convince Fawn it was safe to emerge. The moment she peeked out, I strong-armed my way in with Zeke on my heels. He snatched the duct-taped bundle from her dresser and tossed it into the air like a baseball to test its heft. It was almost too easy.

Zeke held the package up to Peanut Butter, who had been sequestered in Fawn's room and was now wagging around our feet, grateful for guests. "What do you smell, boy?"

"Don't talk to him," Fawn said. "He doesn't like strangers. He bites."

"Zeke is not a stranger," I said. "Zeke is Zeke."

The dog licked the package and drooled.

"Maybe it's a head," Fawn suggested. "There was a chicken that lived without a head for a whole year. They fed him milk down his neck-hole, but he choked on a corn kernel and died."

"Congratulations," I said. "You are disgusting."

I knew Fawn was looking for an angle in, to shift the situation in her favor. She plucked at soft splinters in the doorframe. "No one listens to me, but I was the one who found it."

Fresh in our minds were the news reports of the forsaken elbow. I remember the reporter from the local station, the shape of her mouth, coral lipstick, how titillated she was by her first big break. Still, dismemberment was always in our midst. Objects were tossed off the highway in a steady and unremarkable hail. Out of the blue, tricycles rained down, split bags of fetid trash, shipping pallets, smashed bumpers, suitcases, couch cushions, roof tile. Once, a whole toilet. Another time, a bass drum. Wigs were surprisingly common. There was even the sawed-off shotgun Zeke's brother had supposedly found the summer before. He said he hid it in the woods. He would never say where. Zeke and I agreed. It was like living at the bottom of a landfill. Fawn's precious bundle was just more junk.

If I doubted this, I was bolstered always by Zeke's confidence. I trusted him to have answers. He was on his way to becoming an Eagle Scout. He was CPR-certified. I wanted desperately to be in love with him and it was not for lack of trying. It would check a certain box I'd never again have to worry over. That day, he was wearing pre-distressed cargo shorts and a hideous striped polo almost certainly shopped off the mannequin, courtesy of his mother, SUNSET BEACH FOREVER stitched across his chest. He liked to dress how he thought Californians dressed. Fawn was still limping through the beginnings of junior high with her baby face, friendless and strange, but Zeke and I were almost free. It was the summer before our senior year.

Behind our huddle, a shatter of glass.

Fawn was standing over a pile of fresh shards. She took one

of her puppy figurines in her fist and held it high above her head. "Don't make me do it again."

The bundle was in Zeke's hands. I could see his fingers itching.

"Don't," I told him. "She's showing off."

"Okay, then," Fawn said, and smashed her favorite dachshund to the floor. "How about now?"

"You're just breaking your own stuff," I said.

"Just give it to her," Zeke said. "It's trash. Who cares?"

"I care." I shot him a look and he bowed his head. It was one-on-one again.

Fawn selected another puppy from her collection and this time pitched a Doberman at the wall behind us. The glass head of the dog skidded across the hardwood. Peanut Butter barked and retreated promptly to Fawn's closet. He curled himself over her pile of shoes and buried his nose in a moccasin.

I should've known Zeke would get queasy over broken things.

"You two figure it out," he said, and chucked the bundle at Fawn's feet in surrender. We both lunged for it, but my sister was ready. As soon as her fingers closed around the parcel, she broke into a sprint toward the bathroom, the only other door in our loft with a working lock.

"This is your fault," I said to Zeke.

"She was aiming for your head."

"So what? She missed."

With Peanut Butter trailing behind, we crunched over glass to the bathroom door and waited with ears pressed close as Fawn struggled and grunted against the bundle's lump weight. Plastic squealed open. She released a sharp breath. All went quiet.

Zeke and I looked at each other and shrugged.

"Fawn," Zeke said carefully, as if talking down a man on a ledge. "Fawn, listen to me. We should take it to the police. It could be dangerous, okay? Maybe somebody could be looking for it." He tried the knob. "It could be anthrax."

"You are so obsessed with anthrax," I said.

The lock twitched and Peanut Butter reared toward the opening. Zeke snatched his collar and told him to sit, but Peanut Butter didn't know any commands.

Fawn's eye appeared in the gap. "You can come in," she said. "Leave the dog."

Of course, I could not have known what was coming, that I was inside the last moment of before and after. The ripped bundle was on the lid of the toilet. It leered there, shredded and still. Peanut Butter barked from the other side of the door and I touched a finger to the bland mass revealed inside the flaps of plastic.

"Look at it," Fawn said. "Tell me if it's real."

"What is it?" I asked, but she did not answer. It looked the way a hunk of meat looks, not unlike something from the butcher, a picnic cut. Mostly bloodless and waxen like a prop.

A severed foot, up to the ankle and sheared of toes.

"It is real, isn't it?" Fawn said. The air in the little bathroom was ripe. Zeke was swaying behind me, breathing down my neck. There was the frailest gasp in my ear. Then, he fainted.

When he came to, Zeke was the one who thought to call the cops.

Men in rubber gloves whisked the bundle away to someplace official and asked us to lock Peanut Butter in the bedroom while they combed the house and the rest of Geronimo Street. Zeke's mother, Nance, went with Fawn to show the police the spot where she'd found it.

"It was the dog," Fawn kept telling anyone who would listen. "The dog is new. I didn't even see what was in its mouth."

I tried to call my mother where she was staying in Manhattan, but I was forwarded to a chipper answering machine message. We had been trained to keep a respectful distance when she took off for the city. We were told never to jump to conclusions. While those in charge milled around and managed, I took the broom and swept away the glass of broken heads and tails and torsos across the floor of Fawn's bedroom. Nance insisted we spend the night, but I lied an easy lie and said our mother was already on her way. I pulled departure and arrival times out of thin air, because that was usually enough to keep prying adults at bay—the promise that someone else would soon arrive to manage the fuss. Fawn said nothing during this exchange. We preferred to watch ourselves.

That night, we slept on the couch with the windows open and the TV puttering into the wee hours of infomercials and televangelism, Peanut Butter piled between us. I dreamt of the butcher and duffel bags overflowing with entrails, of speeding trains. It was the next morning, home and alone, that the news van arrived.

Out popped the woman from the local news in her same shade of coral lipstick, the same pressed lapel. She held out her hand and introduced herself. I whispered my name as she turned to Fawn. "And who is this little one?"

"I'm the one who found it," she said.

The reporter snapped her fingers and from inside the news van, a man emerged, hauling a camera on his shoulder. He rammed his eye into the viewfinder and a red light blinked on.

"Would you mind walking us through the events?" the reporter asked Fawn. "Please, tell us what you saw."

"Well," Fawn began, and took a sobering breath. "It was, I guess, like a nightmare." My sister came alive on camera. She was easy to believe, and it would always be so. "I had bad, bad dreams last night." Fawn stayed very still as she spoke. She stared into the lens as it dilated, choking back tears. "I hope they catch the bad guy. I don't want anybody else to get hurt."

The reporter was positively vibrating, surely splicing footage together in her head. Her grip on the microphone tightened. "And how about you?" She angled the mic toward me for the cherry on top. "Do you think the police are doing enough to catch the killer out there?"

"What?"

"Are the police doing enough? Are you frightened?"

"Oh," I said and squinted against a light that wasn't there. I was very dizzy all of a sudden. I pictured the person responsible, still at large and now retracing his steps, polishing the blade that had done the job. It was an eerie serendipity: a stranger killed, body partitioned, carried off, tossed away—only to be uncovered by another stranger, an unusual little girl. There could not have been a recipient more game than she.

I remember a sneeze coming on. I was sweating profusely, the reek from the van's exhaust pipe toxic. My sister looked at me expectantly, embarrassed for the both of us. She knew what needed to be said, and I was letting it all leak away. I heard myself apologize, and apologize again. I remember that—the regret—just before I hit the pavement.

When the segment aired that night, Fawn and I were ready with a blank tape and the VCR. Our mother had left a message that she'd caught a return train, but that was hours before, and we hadn't seen or heard from her.

"She's going to miss it," Fawn said.

"We'll get it on tape."

"It's not the same. It's not *live*."

"It's better if she doesn't see. It's better if we can explain everything ourselves."

"Quiet," Fawn said. "It's me."

She was perfectly symmetrical onscreen. Blue eyes, blond hair nearly sheer, skin like the white of a candle, my opposite in every way. She was talking about Peanut Butter, her trusty pup, and I was standing there beside her blinking at half-speed. I tried to imagine how I read to viewers at home, like some soft-skulled interloper who had wandered into the frame, struck dumb. "How do I look?" Fawn asked.

"You look fine. A little pink."

"Better than you," she said. "I sound good. I sound pretty good."

The camera veered to my face, round and pasty like I'd been hot-dipped in wax. The reporter asked her questions, and I watched as my eyes crossed before the microphone, then retracted and rolled back inside my head. Lights out. The camera scrambled and panned to the sidewalk where I was strewn. It almost looked like I was faking it.

"Oh dear," the reporter said offscreen. "It's okay. You're okay. Up you go. All right."

The clip cut back to the newsroom, where the anchors shook their heads and shuffled papers as they tried to stifle their amusement. "What brave little girls," they agreed, as the next chyron trumpeted onscreen.

I never thought Fawn cared about TV, or even contemplated how she might appear on camera, let alone to others. It was others, their prying eyes and unseemly habits, their expectations of reciprocity, that always seemed to weary her. I was ready for the whole ordeal to fizzle out, to lock the doors until our mother returned— but once she did, she hardly patted our heads before squirreling away inside her master bedroom, satisfied that we were alive and at least where we were supposed to be, at the same neutral location where we'd been left. I knew she was in the middle of another heartbreak. She needed me to be steady.

Only a few days of quiet passed before I woke one morning to Fawn by the front door, pulling on my old sneakers and leashing up the dog. She asked if I wanted to come along. When I asked her where, she tipped her head in invitation.

"Out there," she said. "We're going hunting." For more parts and parcels. For her prime-time segment. For the next fixation to bleed dry.

Fawn cruised on a high from her TV debut for weeks while our mother shuttled back and forth from the city as though nothing out of the ordinary had occurred. This was how she became herself again and again, in transit, while Fawn spent her days outdoors, and the dog began acting strange.

Over the phone, Zeke and I rehashed our twin fainting spells, but he did not want to relive the gore of what had been, until that point, the pinnacle of our summer vacation.

"I can't stand her like this," I whispered to him over the line. "She thinks she's famous. She's trying to teach Peanut how to be *on camera*. To do tricks. Like they'd care about some dog who can play dead."

Zeke told me to ignore her. He said that in time Fawn would return to normal. He promised that everything would. Violence elsewhere was roiling the world. Nearby, New York was subsumed by Ground Zero, tracked in sound bites and headlines and incendiary footage on repeat as the rest of the country watched the closed experiment drag on and leach into the general supply. Sometimes I could hear Fawn talking animatedly in her room or in the shower, or I'd see her stall in front of a mirror, smile and gesture with her hands like a royal, waving. She was conversing with herself. Perfecting a routine until the cameras found her ready.

Always, my mother warned me to go easy on her. She said Fawn was on the brink. I thought this meant the brink of puberty, but it was the brink of something else. For as long as I could remember, my sister excelled at nothing in particular and yet everyone gave her the wide berth reserved for savants. I tried to find some new angle by which to see her, or I tried to bite my tongue. Meanwhile, my mother went on believing her youngest possessed an uncommon sensitivity, that Fawn was the vessel unto a rare, inherent seed sure someday, in spectacular fashion, to bloom.

When the Juvenile Transportation Services come for you in the night in a preordained kidnapping, complete with an unmarked van and husky guardsmen you can't outmatch, you have been sold for a promise. It's all there on the brochure. The Veld Center specializes in emotional preparation for the outside world. A structured environment combining therapy, physical rigor, and self-interrogation. It's hard to believe any witting adult could fall for a pitch so vaguely aspirational, but when you are desperate, the mere suggestion of hope is enough.

After they've got you in the van, they may take you to an airport or a train. Maybe they will drive you through the night to wherever it is you're going. You might end up in the swamps of Florida, or the blown-up ranges of Appalachian coal country, or in the remote wilds of Idaho, Arizona, Kentucky. Wherever you go, you will stay there for at least a month, but probably longer. Alongside other troublemakers, you will learn to set up camp and cook with fire and trek for miles and miles until civilization becomes a feeling you dreamt of once, a flinching muscle memory. If you are sent to Veld, you must begin in exile.

They took me to Maine.

It was a long drive, eight hours north of Deerie, and the sedatives hardly made a dent. I remember lying on my back in the rear seat of an otherwise empty sixteen-passenger van, looking up through the window as highway lights glazed by. My mother had floated the idea of Veld a few weeks earlier, but she floated all kinds of ideas that never took. I had been on a downward spiral, that was true. Zeke had died a few months before. I kept running at the wall full-speed thinking I'd hit it, that the impact and injury would stop me, but I just kept barreling through. Later, I would dub this the *Supermarket Sweep* era of my life. An abundance of time was no longer a promise. I felt I should seize all stimuli from the shelves, devour and run, say yes to everything offered. My mother didn't know what else to do with me.

We arrived at dawn. Camp was a vision through the trees, boxed in by red pines, their long throats bared on all sides. To see the sky, I had to crane my neck, and the view made me dizzy, like I was inside a tunnel narrowing into darkness instead of opening to light. I thought I'd smell the ocean, but we were nowhere near the coast. I said I needed to sit down. Suddenly there were new faces herding me this way and that, ordering me to change my clothes, gather my pack, wolf down a bowl of cold oatmeal, submit to a search so no contraband remained in my possession. I had nothing to surrender. I had been asleep when they took me. I was arranged at the end of a line of girls, our counselor in the lead, another bringing up the rear, six bad seeds between them.

They call this banishment a pre-enrollment program. Wilderness Commitment. It's meant to strip away bad habits and reactivate a dormant respect for the natural world's grand hierarchy. More than this, it is meant to break you the way a horse is broken. Ranks are whittled down to those most inclined for success on Veld's formal campus, a hundred-acre compound in Virginia. When you are on Commitment, the round-the-clock surveillance and extreme topography are meant to keep you in place for the duration of the healing process, but plenty of campers make a break for it only to be tracked down days later, miles adrift in the snow or heat, food gone, defenses at their weakest.

My first day on the mountain, we hiked ten miles and the cold climbed with us. High winds speared the stitches of my outerwear and the soles of my boots felt frozen like two discs of ice I skated upon. I imagined us girls on the map, our location as the head of a pin in a great, mottled expanse the color of camo. Ghosts up here. Feathers in the wind. Every breath was a raw wheeze, and just when I thought my heart would fail inside my chest, our pack leader held up his fist at the front of the line and called it a day.

"Make camp," he commanded. He had named himself Shine.

One time only, he showed me how to string up my tarp for shelter and hoist my pack out of reach of wildlife. He told me I'd have to dig a hole to bury my boots in, that I should sleep on top of it so they didn't petrify in a night freeze. Then, he handed me a letter from my mother. A Veld rite of passage. Before the bad apples are spirited away, parents are told to pour their hearts out. Outline grievances. Be specific. And because contact with the outside world is prohibited for the first three months of treatment, the letter is both tell-all and send-off. I held the thick envelope and pictured my mother at her desk, face in the lamplight, left hand on a tear as she downed wine and read aloud her progress.

I stuffed the letter into the pocket of my cargos. I wanted to keep it there, sealed, potent as long as it remained unread. Shine told me it was my job to dig the latrine, an inaugural honor I undertook with a pint-sized shovel. With every thrust of dirt, the letter pulsed. Someone got the fire going. If it was too wet for a fire, someone soaked the rice in water so it was soft enough to eat. I kept thinking about the preposterousness of it all. The day before, I'd been strolling home high. I had watched every treetop like a great creature might swoop down and snatch me up, and I wanted that. I wanted to be on the wing of something—and now I was. There one day, gone the next. And Fawn had watched, face utterly blank as the men carted me through the living room by my arms and ankles. My mother was crying, apologizing, promising it was all for the best. She begged me to go with dignity. I screamed obscenities while trying to reduce my body to dead weight.

When dinner was done, it was time for Share. I stared into the faces of the girls around me, all bleached out and bloated, some completely chinless—the side effects of extreme exposure and happy pills. They stared off with the absent eyes of the regularly harangued. How long had they been out here? What had the wilderness driven into or out of them? And what did they make of me?

Shine drew himself into a lotus position, brought his fingertips together, and pointed them at me. "Okay. We're ready."

"For what?"

He smiled like I was trying to trick him. "Tell us why you're here. Okay?"

"My mother put me here."

Somewhere in the trees, an owl hooted. For a second, I thought one of the girls made the noise as a joke.

Shine turned to the girl on his right. "What's Share all about, Gia?"

"Sharing," Gia said.

"That's right. That's why we're here. To share the load. Cooking. Hauling. Making camp. We each take turns lugging the sled with the week's supply. Even digging the latrine." Shine winked. "It's not always easy, but it is necessary, and mandatory. So, let's collaborate."

"What am I supposed to share?"

"You can start at the beginning," he said. "Or, you can start with an event you regret. With the real reason you're here."

On one hand, it was a relief to be commanded, and on the other, it felt more invasive than the strip search. I thought of all the stories I might trot out, what strategic choice to make knowing nothing of where I was or who I was with. I could intimidate Gia and the rest, or stay mum and position myself above vulnerability, or else turn supplicant before the grand jury in a bid for my freedom. What were our afflictions? Diagnoses were darts thrown in the dark. Conduct disorder with callous traits. Conduct disorder displaying oppositional defiance. Conduct disorder characterized by deceitfulness, or theft. Your disorder can be hot-blooded. Your disorder can be cold-blooded. Your threat-detection instinct may be erratic, causing you to become swift to fear, anger, and impulsive violence. Or perhaps you watch and wait, patience your virtue until provoked. By then, you will be ready.

After a few false starts, I chose a place in time that felt true as any other. I told the faces I was never one of those needy children. I never wanted the dog. The garishness of teeth and tongues and muzzles gave me pause, as did their messes, their oils, the obsessive panting. I took it for granted, how he accompanied me room to room and stayed vigilant on our behalf. When our warehouse trembled in the night, when drunks rabbled in the alley, broke glass and retched, when mice dashed around the loft and there was no one but me to scoop them into a cup, free them in the gutter— I took comfort in his shadow at my back. That first night, I told the girls that eventually I came to envision Peanut Butter's place firmly rooted in our lives, like the final credit of a family sitcom opening: Peanut Butter played by Peanut Butter. The dog had been unlucky in that regard.

Wednesday nights at eight, there was a show I watched religiously called *MAYDAY*.

The eponymous May, sixteen years old, works part-time at her family's dockside diner in a little salt-flecked village on the coast of the Pacific Northwest. In secret and mostly for fun, May hosts her own amateur radio hour in an ad hoc studio in the diner's basement, and these broadcasts narrate each episode in voiceover. May spins records for no one, dispenses advice to imaginary callers. At the close of every show she salutes her father, lost at sea years before but whose fate May cannot accept. All the while, she juggles two brooding boys: the tackle shop manager's bookish son, and the ne'er-do-well rich boy who zips through the marina in his speedboat. It was a sort of rip-off of *Frequency*, with more girl power and Fair Isle sweaters and juvenile heavy-petting. I was hooked. If May ever learned her lesson, it would all be over.

The summer the body parts arrived, *MAYDAY* had just completed its third season. It was the Fourth of July and I was eating a Pop-Tart, rewatching the most recent finale. I had seen this episode countless times already, having spent years recording new episodes on VHS tapes I would study during the summer hiatus. There was always something more to see. Also, I had fallen in love for the first time, and every episode was like a message. Antonia.

She was dating Zeke's older brother Kent and living in their basement. Her mother was a nasty gambling addict with a propensity for smoking and vacuuming late into the night, and Nance couldn't help but take in strays. Seeing Antonia on a regular basis was too torturous, my adoration too revealing. It felt as if my every twitch were being broadcast via jumbotron, a tight shot as I watched Kent's fingers close on her bare leg, or saw a frill of lace spilling from her gym bag, the gum tumbling inside her mouth. It had stopped being exciting and was mostly painful. I wanted love the way May had it, at her disposal.

That day, there was no avoiding her. The Heller boys had been balling melons since dawn. I was supposed to dress in red, white, and blue. There was a party to attend.

"What is it, May? Please. You can trust me."

In the penultimate scene of the finale, May and her primary love interest—tackle-shop boy—are at odds. Her father has inexplicably resurfaced, but will only reveal himself to his daughter.

Though there was no shipwreck, no broadcasts received, May cannot escape her choice: family loyalty, or love.

A tear coasts down her perfect cheek and bursts onto the dock underfoot. "Reed," she begs, "I'm not doing this to hurt you, I swear."

This was my favorite part. He pulls her close and kisses her to shut her up good. In the next scene, she will choose her father's confidence over Reed's devotion, but before she says goodbye, he will try one last time to keep her. He was supposed to say, *"There's nothing you could ever do that would make me stop loving you,"* but the tape cut out. The screen emptied to blue.

I dropped my Pop-Tart. The VCR was old, so I tried not to panic. The tape had been used and reused to record years of Olympic games and Academy Awards ceremonies and *60 Minutes* exposés. There was the season Fawn was obsessed with *Hollywood Squares*. I took the tape out, blew dust from its reels and inside the flap of the VCR. Only blue.

"You should keep watching."

Fawn was in the doorway of her bedroom in pajamas, a Minnie Mouse shirt that went past her knees. "Don't worry," she said. "You'll like it."

"What did you do?"

"Watch and see."

The tape jumped to life again, the scorched blond of an African savanna filling the screen. A lion with a scarred face gnawed at a baby gazelle in his clutches. The gazelle still had its fluff, and its doe eyes bulged as it tried to free itself from the lion's jaws. It was a useless instinct. With another chomp, the calf went limp as a chew toy and the screen went blue again.

"What is this?" A flash from *MAYDAY*. The lighthouse and the bluffs. Another cut: this time, the jungle.

A fleet of chimpanzees screeched through the treetops while an austere British voice narrated. *"The red colobus monkey is a favorite meal of the chimpanzee,"* he said, as a colobus female dashed toward the canopy, an infant clutching her underside. *"The vitamin-rich organs of the colobus, particularly the fatty liver and brains of their young, provide chimpanzees a wealth of nutrition to supplement their diet of fruit and insects."*

The mother colobus and her infant were alone on a high tree limb, seemingly out of harm's way. A drumbeat persisted. The tape went blue again and cut crudely to an advanced frame. Now the chimpanzee was center, holding the flaccid body of the colobus mother in one hand, her baby in the other. He slurped at its broken head like an egg. The jungle screamed.

If I wasn't so disgusted, I might've been impressed. It was a trick that required effort, timing, patience.

"What is wrong with you?" I said. "You're sick. You are a sick individual."

"I knew that would get you."

"Get me for what?"

"For what?" Fawn said, impatience flaring. "Because you stole it from me. Don't play dumb."

"You have nothing I could possibly want."

"You know what I'm talking about. I'm not falling for it again."

She pointed at the dog.

Peanut Butter was in the shape of sleep beside me, but his eyes were open and watching. It was true that he had taken up residence in my room as of late, but I had not invited this. I assumed Fawn had reached the end of her interest in the idea of a pet, a predictable conclusion.

". . . A baby water buffalo is no match for a pack of hungry hyenas."

I punched the power button on the TV.

"I have the rest of your tapes," she said, "but you are never going to find them."

I yanked her clothes from drawers, junk from the closet. I kicked through her pile of stuffed animals, tore the blankets from the bed. Fawn watched the flurry in silence, her satisfaction more palpable as my search went on.

"You really think I would hide them in here?" she said. Peanut Butter was yapping at her door, teetering and tapping at the threshold as if it were impenetrable. "Shut up. Shut up, shut up, shut up!" she said, but this only made him louder. He began to yowl, the racket amplifying off the brick walls of our warehouse home. "It only likes you because you feed it," she shouted over him. "Now it won't go on walks anymore. It just stops at the end of the street and sits there like it's broken."

"Him," I said. "You keep saying *it,* but it's *him.*"

"Him."

When I hit her, I was most amazed by the perfect smack, like I'd practiced it before. Her face was a wide open range. I stared at my palm and admired the tingle of contact, just as the bolts on the front door began to turn. The dog skittered toward the entrance.

"My god. It is absolutely brutal out there. Where is everybody?"

In the perfect second it took for our mother to pass through the door, an armful of groceries obscuring her face, Fawn swung back with her palm and caught me near the chin.

"I've got bags here. A little help would be nice. Girls?"

I stood there stunned, a swarm of blood under the skin. Fawn leveled her shoulders, kinked her neck like an athlete loosening up on the starting block. "Coming," she chirped, and trotted to the door to greet our mother.

While she unpacked, Fawn and I staked out opposite corners of the kitchen. There might've been a handprint seared upon my cheek, and I wondered if my mother would detect the puff of flesh across Fawn's. The dog was circling my mother, tripping her as she opened and shut cabinets. She had been gone three weeks. Safe inside her circle of fair-weather friends, she planned to fling herself into a fugue state. Her ex-boyfriend Billy had gotten married that spring to the very tidy woman from Connecticut. Out of all the boy-friends, his personality had at least been most detectable. I almost missed him.

"Now I can tell you both some juicy neighborhood gossip," she said, oblivious. "Actually, it's awful news. I don't know why I said that. That was crass."

She made tea and sat us down at our long wooden table as if no time had passed. There were never any intervening comments, no notice of how our hair had grown, if we'd gotten bigger or smaller from the bevy of canned and boxed goods on which we subsisted.

"The rest of the groceries can wait. I want you girls to think about this, what I'm going to describe to you right now." She flapped her hands around, indicating air, transience, a bubble of nothing. "It's our job, or else it's just nowhere. Forgotten."

She told us to imagine ourselves in a Cessna Skyhawk.

A Sunday afternoon and the skies are clear. Father is at the pilot's yoke. Mother sits beside him. Her hair is tamped down by a flowered handkerchief she wears on windy days. In the rear seat, flat farmland scrolls past, tidy as a book of stamps. It's not every day Father invites the family along for an outing in the friendly skies. It is spring. We coast high above a field lit with tulips, and when the rattle of the propeller cuts out, we are alert to the stillness.

In the cockpit, Father wrestles the yoke in his hands and jabs at the control panel while Mother clings to his shoulder. The nose of the Cessna lists, a balloon rises in my stomach. The plane is Father's favorite thing. There are pictures of it in his office. As the equator tilts, it is like we are being dumped out of the sky, too fast to sense a cloud as we pass through it. The roads below are dilating. I can see the color of the houses, people driving in their cars, their faces staring into the blue. I catch a whiff of blazing humidity, like a pot set to boil, just before the end.

This was the story our mother brought. News of the neighbors. The Wepplers. Their son.

When she relayed to us what happened—a prop plane downed at an airfield near Deerie; the Weppler family, all lost—the whole scene projected onto the front wall of my brain, wobbly like home movie footage, and as intimate. Whether it was mechanics or human error, my mother could not say, and the accident had actually occurred a few months earlier while she was out of town. I must have walked by the house a dozen times since then, none the wiser that their Cape Cod style was sitting bereft, sprinklers fizzing on each morning, porchlight faithful through the night. No one survived them. The estate was in limbo.

Theirs was my favorite house on Arden Avenue. All those mature trees bowing in the yard made the perfect frame. I liked to imagine myself in the bedroom on the second floor, the one tucked under the eaves with its lone window over the street. That was the room I would've chosen. I remember walking by once on the way back from Zeke's. It was on the verge of evening, and the lights in the Wepplers' backyard were switched on. I was going at a good clip, enough to see through the slats in the fence posts in a quick-moving image, like a flipbook. Mrs. Weppler was wearing her flowered handkerchief. She was in house shoes, raking leaves. She looked up at the sound of my footsteps and held still until I passed. It was a plotless kind of memory, but set in amber all the same.

I thought of the Wepplers' house as a favorite bit of b-roll in my own life. In that way, it felt like it belonged to me, mine enough to give away.

While my mother prattled on, switching to city gossip and observations from the train, I touched a finger to the tender spot on my chin. Let them have their Fourth of July, I thought. My mother and Fawn could climb up to the roof and watch the whole valley spew fireworks, drink sparkling cider from the inherited champagne coupes. I had no desire to endure the latest round of homecoming tales, and more than that, I didn't want to spend the night with Fawn, my mother's most fulsome audience.

Before I left for Zeke's, I saw the look on my mother's face—that washed expression she deployed when she was working very hard to respect my autonomy.

"If you have to go, then take the dog," she said. "Give him some exercise, will you?"

I said I didn't want him and slipped out the door alone.

The ride to Zeke's was a ritual. At about the halfway point, there was a particular house, abandoned since before I was born. I tracked it over the years as a ravenous shrub swallowed the structure square foot by square foot. It had the building by the throat now. A bristled plume of greenery stretched like a barrel of smoke from the flower bed into the second story window, where it climbed inside.

I pedaled past the brick signage of Zeke's subdivision, The Gables. Paint colors and exterior embellishments shuffled house to house, but all the structures were variations on the same proto-types. After every fifth house, the pattern regenerated. Most of the trees had been clear-cut the summer before, when an exotic fungus claimed most every oak and maple. That was the summer of the Red X, every trunk spray-painted. I was waiting for someone to do the same to the rest of Deerie. To be crossed out. To be marked for demolition.

As I was coming up on the last curve before Zeke's Colonial, a rickety Dodge Caravan went by.

Its brake lights flared. The van reversed decisively. I slowed and shielded my eyes as the power windows lowered. There was a glare off the metallic trim.

"Hot one," a man said behind the wheel. He eased off the brake to roll beside me.

"Hot one," I batted back, and did not stop moving.

"I live around the corner. I was going to see if you needed a ride out of this heat." He squinted into the sky to divine the weather. "My boys are out of town. They're down the shore for the Fourth with their mother, but you know how the beach gets. You step off the boardwalk and have to sit right down. That's what I told them. But hey, kids never listen." He knocked on his temple. "Listen to your parents. That's my advice."

I was straddling my bike, and I saw him eye the seat where it pressed into me. "My friend lives just there," I said. "They're having a big party for the neighborhood."

"I'm the neighborhood." He looked past me to the house, a virulent old green. "You sure you don't want a ride? I know you think this is a nice neighborhood, but I live here, I should know. You should stay alert." Sweat was gathering in the folds of his neck and the bramble of chest hair extruding from his shirt. I turned abruptly onto the Hellers' front lawn and ignored him as he asked my name, and again where I was going, if someone was expecting me. Only when I knocked on the front door did he veer off, the man in the van with his arm dangling, a wet glimmer gone.

I told all this to Antonia while she puffed a cigarette and blew the smoke from the Hellers' upstairs window, draped with a blue tarp. There was exposed subfloor and loose wiring all around. The master bath was mid-renovation. She was sitting on a decommissioned toilet.

"Mom's renovating ours too," she told me. "Buyers love modern tile. Didn't I tell you? We're trying to sell."

She was wearing a khaki bandana around her neck. I couldn't guess from where she'd stolen an affectation like that. It reminded me of Jane Goodall. A week before, I'd taken down the hardcover of *In the Shadow of Man* from my mother's tallest shelf and found my father's name scribbled inside the front cover.

"In my dream kitchen, I'll have one of those built-in breakfast nooks under a big window where you can read the paper or craft or whatever. I want a place I can entertain. Eight burners and an ice machine." I was going to explain what I wanted in my dream kitchen, but Antonia remembered the man in the van again. "God, I hate predators," she said. "Predators are vermin."

"I'm not really sure what he was trying to do."

"Men shouldn't live alone like that. Not by themselves."

I hadn't said anything about living alone. It was possible she really cared one way or another, but more likely she was thinking of her father in their old house back in Bayonne, where none of the phones ever seemed to be working.

"Don't you have a little sister? Isn't she already messed up from the thing? The foot? And now this? If I were you, I would be very concerned. He can't just go around telling girls to get in his van. We should do something."

"You're right," I lied. "We should do something."

Antonia peeked past the tarped window. Outside, Zeke and his older brother, Kent, were dumping ice into coolers while Nance fluffed the patriotic tricolor table settings. She burst into tears every time she heard the national anthem. Indiscriminate marching band music had been blasting for hours. Three renditions of "76 Trombones" had already gone by.

Antonia waved a cloud of smoke toward the open window. There were flecks of ash in the folds of her bandana, and above her head, three test swatches of blue paint going light to lighter, labeled in pencil. *Robin's Breath. Sunday Celebrity. Middle Distance.*

I liked Sunday Celebrity best. Antonia exhaled again and followed my eyes.

"Robin's Breath," she said. "Definitely."

"Definitely."

"Can I tell you something?"

"Of course." The moment I had been waiting for. An aberrant

spigot was jutting into my hip where I leaned against the wall and I pretended not to notice.

"I might break up with Kent," she said. "I feel horrible just saying that out loud."

"Did you have a fight?"

"It's more than that. Nance hates me."

"How can you tell?"

Antonia scoffed. "It's in her body language. I know she's going to kick me out, and anyways—fuck her. Every time someone flushes the toilet here, I hear shit surfing by my head. And Kent? Mostly I want to punch him in the face." She stubbed her cigarette out on the lid of a paint can and twirled the filter in her fingers. "In the *face*. Why is my life so complicated?"

"Complicated," I echoed. "Always."

She nudged my thigh with the tip of her sneaker. "It's good I have you around or else I'd be trapped here pretending I'm in love with everything."

Like Kent. "Like what?"

"Of course they're doing me a big favor, but I have to show off being grateful for every little thing, but I've gained five pounds eating Nance's cheap food. The drains are clogged with cum. The soap is covered in pubes. But I do the dance, even if everything here smells like raw beef. I am the guest. Guest for life." The tarp flapped. Two of the innumerable Heller boys were lighting firecrackers in the yard and sending them flying with badminton rackets. "I'm not always like this," Antonia said. "It's the heat. I'm usually upbeat."

"Is it really so bad that you can't just go home?"

"That's cute. It's cute that you don't get it."

The screen door downstairs swung open and sneakers pounded across the kitchen tile. I could sense the moment closing up before me. Antonia sighed and inspected the ends of her hair.

"Well, if you know any other places to crash, I'm looking. I'm always looking," she said.

Kent couldn't appreciate her, I thought. She and I were more alike. Fathers gone, mothers absent. It occurred to me that I could offer what he could not, and so I moved without thinking.

The spigot left a dent in my hip and I rubbed the skin under my T-shirt. Slowly, carefully as possible, I touched the tip of my finger to every fleck of ash in her bandana, collecting each, letting each dissolve into my prints, disappear. Who was I in that moment? I can't recall. I knew just what to do.

I thought of the Wepplers' house on Arden Avenue left empty, the little room upstairs I had never entered but felt I could offer as my own. All the other pieces would sort themselves. I believed that.

I told her I knew a place she could go.

3

I discovered the love of my life after walking one night in a daze down Geronimo Street. Nothing was as I remembered. All the patchwork lots and cratered side streets and hungry storefronts of my childhood had been dusted off, reinvented for some new era. It was the earnest start of winter, just after Thanksgiving, and I found myself on a bustling thoroughfare aglow with the season. People were staying out later and drinking more.

I had left the city on a lark.

Earlier that night, on the train back to my apartment, I received an email from a spokesperson at the Veld Center. She was writing to inform me that my sister had been released. It was possible she might try to get in touch with me. Warm wishes for the holidays, and a Happy New Year. The subject line might've read: *Don't Say We Didn't Warn You.*

I had forgotten Fawn's eighteenth birthday. She was a newly minted woman unto herself, and now she was free. It was six o'clock in the evening and she might've been anywhere—hat in hand on my doorstep, or watching from across the train car as my face turned to stone.

When we lurched forward again, a kind of portal opened before me. Inside it, I saw my roommate toiling away at our outer-borough roach palace, unwashed and energized by his next big project. I saw the scab of rust on the shower floor, the yellow light of the refrigerator suffused throughout the whole apartment, everything cast the color of drawn butter, everything sticky and past its prime. If my sister was waiting for me there, then all the more reason to do what I do best.

I allowed myself to be shuttled an hour north. I got off in Deerie and lingered there on the platform. A few miles ahead, the raised interstate cut through town. The elevated belt of highway was a streak of light, an eight-lane channel curving northeast, upstate and out of sight. There was the impulse to call someone, someone to come and get me and begin the next phase of my spontaneous evening. There was no one, so I began to walk.

The interstate extension was funded in the eighties, back when Deerie was going the way of other mill towns. My mother was living in New York then, unencumbered and splitting scant square footage with the aspiring artist types she claimed as friends. Together, they were always weighing the merits of buying land upstate. When the train broke down, or pests procreated in the cupboards, or the sewer line exploded in the alley, the dream of a kinder, simpler life was potent. It hardly mattered that logistics never materialized. No town was ever named precisely. My mother and her friends were content to refine their illusory lives, adding and subtracting amenities as they pleased, and it would've gone on in that half-baked way until a natural current lifted everyone apart, into their separate, parallel lives. Only, my mother went and did it. She poured her fresh inheritance into a dilapidated three-story warehouse on the edge of Deerie's industrial downtown, on our Geronimo Street. She and her chosen brood would mastermind a mini utopia just a train ride away from the heart of things. Art would become their lives, and their lives would become art. It was a dream they could share.

Of course, no one followed. Her friends caravanned to unload her earthly possessions and admire the massive structure she'd acquired. So much potential, they marveled, and went back to their lives.

It began to snow. The wind was hurtling in all directions, flakes vibrating and suspended midair. I thought of turning back for the train, but was suddenly sure that every passing car was driven by someone I once knew. I wondered what I looked like to them, hulking through half-frozen snow pile rutted with gravel and petrified dog shit and trash. Every time a car caught me in its headlights, I tried to arrange my face into what I thought was a lucid expression, as if I might reassure passing drivers of my dignity. Like them, I too had a destination.

When I reached the underbelly of the interstate, the traffic surged overhead in a wave that never crested. Husks of creeping vines rattled from rafters where webs and nests had proliferated in a complex colony of suspended vermin, and I counted the support pillars rammed deep into the earth, going on in pairs for miles until I couldn't count them anymore. Eventually, my walk dead-ended on Geronimo Street. Thirtysomethings flitted in and out of storefronts and bars, twinkling restaurants—all new additions. The warehouse had been partitioned into high-end condos, and giant ten-foot letterforms were painted across the building's broad side. THE GERONIMO LOFTS. At the end of the street, before the avenue bears toward the woods and high-tension towers, I saw Rochelle for the first time. She was standing in Fawn's old bedroom.

There was a service alley across the street, threaded between an old YMCA and a former foundry. I bummed a cigarette off someone passing and tried to make it last while I watched her in the window. The curtains were pulled back, and she was standing close enough that her nose seemed to brush the glass. She was looking out at something. A candle burned. I saw its orange flicker wavering under her chin. Occasionally she tilted her head as if puzzled by the view.

Once I started living with Rochelle, I realized she did this sort of gazing all the time. She might stop short, like someone on the street had called her name. As she gravitated toward the windows, I'd watch from the kitchen, or the living room, or the dining nook— wherever I was, trying to earn my keep by pulsing smoothies or fluffing pillows or otherwise showboating productivity. By evening, the loft's windows were translucent and the lamplight doubled itself inside the dark sheet of glass. That was why Rochelle was posed there that first night and so many nights thereafter. She was taken in by her own reflection.

I never asked her to keep me. Did I make sure we met the morning after, on the street where she lived, two hands reaching for the same blood orange at the corner of Geronimo and Vine? Yes. And did I take her on a date the day after that, pepper her with questions designed to endear, that flexed livelier lobes of my personality usually left on the blink? Yes, that's true. But Rochelle was the one who invited me back to her place. And Rochelle didn't balk when I slept in the morning after. She encouraged me to run a bath, to pocket the spare keys on the hook by the door, to make myself at home while I was in town on business. Was I in town on business?

I never travel for business. That would require a real job, one with stakes high enough to strap employees into planes and blast them toward consequential meetings. I get by on remote freelance, drafting property descriptions that lure families on the hunt for dream homes. It doesn't pay well.

Rochelle is more than a decade older and has entered the phase of wealth that's all about refinement and escalation. She pays someone to dress her and exercise her and decorate her life. I'm always discovering tasteful selections I've overlooked, like the strategically placed glass baubles purchased from museum catalogues, all amorphous, all weightless as tree ornaments. A week into living here I woke up alone and noticed the oil painting above the bed for the first time. Stretched on thick, fragrant canvas, the composition is no more than a royal blue scuff on a sea of bone white. I stare at it every morning believing I will soon feel differently, that one day I will possess an answer to its question.

Despite our obvious differences in age and carriage, I know Rochelle is someone's total package. And not just someone, but someone in particular. Someone who is probably wondering where Rochelle is, and why they haven't found her yet—if she even exists. And here I am, just keeping them apart. It's not as if I could've known she was single and looking, or that she would even be interested in another woman, that I might fall inside the strike zone of her personal predilections. I have since tried to interrogate myself for some ulterior motive, some specific scheme I was lusting to unleash on a heart unsuspecting, but I returned north to Deerie for the same reason birds venture south. I never imagined I would stay.

Now, on weekend mornings, Rochelle and I jog the perimeter of town that borders the woods. Where there used to be a chain-link fence, there is a paved pedestrian path crowded with baby buggies and zealous cyclists. Rochelle has shown me new ways to optimize my life. She orders vitamins online in bulk and has arranged an exacting regimen just for me. I take them every morning with coffee and she ruffles my hair when I do. Dinner awaits when she arrives home from her high-stakes city job. I rub her shoulders at night. We floss side by side. If she ever wonders where I came from, how such a pliant partner arrived out of the blue and into her arms, she has yet to show it.

And who's to say this new life can't be mine? That my future hasn't been waiting exactly where I left it? After all, I was the one who spotted Rochelle from the sidewalk that first night. I was the one who looked up and watched her move inside the yellow square of a midnight window, watched her until that light went out. Now it's as if I have stepped inside a giant set piece, wheeled before me preassembled and perfectly lit, complete with a live-in girlfriend who subsidizes my days and asks no questions. That was what

Rochelle claimed to want when she traded her Manhattan studio for the airy loft and up-and-coming zip code: the sort of balance you can buy into. Two months have congealed. Christmas came and went. There's been no word from my sister. No word from my surviving family. I should relish the shape my life has taken. I should sleep soundly.

I haven't told Rochelle I used to live here, and sometimes I let myself forget.

Lately though, there seems to be a kind of leak behind the walls. The warehouse settles into itself at night, creaking just the way it used to, and there are phantom smells and sounds where my mother's kitchen used to be—a clatter of silver, an absentminded hum. Most alarming is the music. All those familiar songs adrift in other rooms, murmurs belonging to the dead or gone. The moment I strain closer to listen for my name inside the static, the record skips a beat. The sound disappears completely.

Do I love her? The friends I have left in New York always want to know. I catch up with them over drinks when I take the train in to check the mail and pay rent on my old place. They're really asking if Rochelle is worth it. The age difference. The bedroom community. The wrong end of a short leash. Does it all add up to a sum I can live with, or should they be worried?

They are asking the wrong questions.

A year after I moved to the city, having left the Veld Center and my family behind, I went out with a few friends who mostly turned out to be temporary, and I learned a little something about my personal history.

I was trying on a few lifestyles back then while I made money at a mid-tier restaurant flanked by galleries and music venues that opened well after dark. My shift was almost over, and a few cooks and waiters were headed to a fancy party down the block at a penthouse loft owned by someone famous. I hadn't been at the restaurant long, but this worked in my favor. People hadn't made their minds up about me yet, and they invited me along.

The penthouse looked like the set of a game show. Everything was the same shade of luminescent pearl, and all that white gave off an oiled sheen, like disco footage. Upon our entry, a doorman gathered our phones in a basket. We spread out into the party where a cornucopia of booze and powders and pills and smokes awaited.

"Who's supposed to own this place?" I asked one of the servers I worked with.

Her name was Steph. We were in the crowded kitchen and she was prying open the white refrigerator, which was spotlessly empty, as were all the cabinets and drawers and counters.

"Some rapper," she said. "No, actually. I think it's a producer. No. An executive."

Out of thin air, a heavy-bottomed mirror the size and shape of a dinner plate appeared between us. A hand beyond my line of sight proffered a rolled-up bill.

"Party favors," Steph cooed. She snorted two neat lines and shivered. "*Et toi?*"

"I don't think it works right for me," I said. "Last time I ended up texting my landlord these really long, intense messages about nothing, for like an hour."

I thought I liked Steph. I had heard she dated girls in the past, one of whom had worked my spot at the restaurant before quitting. A dishwasher told me it had been messy. Drama, he said. Though this was the same dishwasher who told me that was why girls shouldn't be with other girls. The woman makes a mess, he said, so the man can clean it up. If you have two girls, you have two messes. What kind of math was that?

I wanted to find someone to spend the winter with. It wouldn't even be so bad if things didn't work out forever. I could carve out a humble place inside her social circle, learn how the city worked, which places mattered. Steph wanted to be an actress. Everyone at the restaurant loved her.

Steph's eyes drifted to see if someone more interesting might be standing behind me.

"I'm going to try and find him," she said.

"Who?"

"The guy who owns this place."

"And then what?"

She did a twirl, delighted by the way her skirt fanned out around her. She ran her hands over the fabric. "I need to meet him," she said, and was gone.

I had to last until two A.M. That was the deal I made with myself.

I wandered the loft, looking for faces I knew. On the balcony, an oversized bottle of Veuve burst when an amateur tried to saber it with a samurai sword. I thought security would come to whisk away the offender, but a new bottle appeared before they'd mopped up the suds and glass from the last. Like in a dream, I went down a long white hallway where all the doors were locked, except one.

Inside was a plush little enclave, a massive window unto the city as its fourth wall. Every surface was carpeted, dark but for the glow of traffic and skyscrapers and the little blue square of a digital display. An audio system was built into the walls in a sleek architecture of glass and chrome. As soon as the door closed behind me with its hydraulic wheeze, I realized the room was soundproof. I couldn't hear the party anymore, but there was still music, quieter fare, breathing close on all sides. An eerie choice, with all the revelry down the hall. Elvis Costello was singing "Almost Blue." Around me, the room lifted into a dull red glow.

"Welcome," a voice said. There was a man lounging in the corner on a leather settee.

"Oh," I said. "I thought this was the bathroom."

He sat up to make room beside him. "Come in. Come sit with me."

I moved past his invitation and went to the wide window. I tapped the glass.

"How many birds have bitten the dust on this thing, you think?"

"I can't say. I haven't lived here terribly long."

I was surprised the party had an actual human host. He was in his forties maybe, dressed in a cardigan and a wrinkled button-up, some chinos and sharp-toed boots that were all wrong. At least he had a decent haircut. "Great party," I told him, and tried to think of a reason to leave.

"Wait," he said. "Let me show you something."

He told me to call him Rod. For the next half hour, Rod walked me through all the components of his sound room: the programmable lights, the recessed locations of the speakers and subwoofers, little black saucers the size of my palm. He tapped a button and a blackout shade rolled over the window, plunging the room into airtight darkness. He asked if I was ready for the pièce de résistance.

He led me to the far corner near the settee and felt around the padded wall until he seemed to find what he was looking for. He pressed both his forefingers into the lining just so, and a concealed panel popped out. It was a polished wooden nook. Illuminated and on display were a handful of plastic-wrapped records, aligned in a row. "These are the really special items."

"Are they rare?" I asked.

"A few. A few are quite rare. Others have supreme sentimental value, and in that way, they're rare too."

I recognized a few of the albums. There was David Bowie's *Diamond Dogs*, just as forward and beguiling a cover as I remembered from my mother's collection. I said I'd seen that one before.

"I doubt you've seen this one precisely," he said. "Look closer. It had a limited initial run that included the dog's genitals, in rather explicit fashion. The label balked and had the offending bits airbrushed. Those in the know kept the originals." He turned over the cover to show me.

"I love it," I said.

"Me too."

We went down the line and Rod gave me a brief education, each record more coveted than the last. "There are only a handful of these available in the wild," he said, "but I'm a hunter. I know what's worth it, and where to look." He tapped the face of another record, the one farthest from me. "This one is different from the others. Its value is in its story."

"May I?"

"Please."

He handed me the album, preserved inside a plastic sleeve. I held it gently, as if it were made of ash. I hadn't seen it, let alone held it, heard it, in years. I knew this album. I knew the image as intimately as a family photograph, because it was.

On the cover, six young men postured on a city street corner. They mugged for the camera, some stone-faced, others goofing off, the lot of them in grayscale. They wore a ragtag uniform of black leather jackets and driving gloves, knuckles bared. The band was called Playa Mala. Bad Beach. The name of the album was *Vieques*. In the album's far left corner, the letter *V* glowed electric red, almost three-dimensional. I traced the letterform with my fingertip and my father looked up at me from the group photo.

"I always do extra digging on the buildings I acquire, not simply for the due diligence, but because I'm naturally curious. Actually, I believe my curiosity is one of the reasons I've enjoyed so much success in my life. That's why I keep this particular record in my collection. As a sort of party trick."

"A trick?"

My father was the one leaning on the lamppost, wearing a black newsboy cap with buttons pinned along the brim, their text a blur. He was tallest. He brooded best. It wounded me to see him so young and alive, locked up in this cupboard.

"I started with the building's architect, as one does, then dove into contractors, suppliers, all the period details and local color. There used to be a neon studio in the basement. Quite prolific in its heyday. It produced some wonderful signs, some of which you can still spot around the city, if you know where to look." He pointed out a blurry street marker on the edge of the album art, then flipped the cover to the liner notes, delighted by my interest. "See here? *Recorded in the Banquet Building.* That's where we are. That's what my building was called before its gutting. A fellow collector friend of mine pointed out the provenance. Of course, it was a different time and different neighborhood then. This group recorded their only record right here. More of a gang than a group, really. A trained ear can hear the difference. A little out of tune, out of time. Another speed bump in city history."

I understood then why I had been compelled down the long hallway, even if Rod's facts were incomplete. My father had been here. The basement neon studio had doubled as his residence. He apprenticed, learned to blow and bend the glass tubes, to conjure colored gas and trap it there. Later, he would tell me of the studio's unsettling quiet. There was only the breath of flame on the burner, the cranial buzz of charged neon when all the signs were switched on. He traded his labor for a place to live, a cousin of a cousin of a cousin was his host. In one corner of the workshop, he hung a curtain, slept on a cot, bought a hot plate, made a life.

"I'll never leave New York," Rod mused. "I admire it too much. It is the opposite of boredom."

I'd moved to this neighborhood on purpose, had taken the job at the restaurant because of its location. I wanted to live where my father had lived, and for once I'd pursued the correct instinct. The proof was in my hands. The relay was in motion again.

Track 1: "Perla"

Track 2: "Girl with the Nickels and Dimes"

Track 3: "Los Rateros"

Track 4: "Bombs Away"

When I was little, I liked Track 2 best. The song is about a new-lywed couple gone broke. The woman keeps the books and the man does the shopping. He comes home from the market with all the wrong items, but they turn their lean circumstances into a game, inventing recipes on the fly. That's why the chorus is a list of ingre-dients. It wasn't just a hook. The couple stayed together, thick and thin. For as long as the song played, it was true.

Rod collected the record from me and arranged it back in its row. "At least they're in good hands now," he said. He was prepared to wax on some more, but a crew of partygoers stumbled through the door, and on their heels, a gust of pandemonium. Steph was with them, smiling ear to ear.

"I don't think you belong in here," Rod said to the group, but no one listened. They had already dispersed, noses to the window and stereo wall. One cranked a dial at random and Stevie Won-der's "Superstition" shook the room. Everyone clutched their ears. I could feel the notes of the clavinet wobbling inside my chest.

"Stop," Rod said, and the music cut out. The lights came up. He opened the door to the party and jabbed a thumb over his shoulder. "Out. All of you."

I tried to make eye contact with Steph as the troupe stifled giggles and lined up dutifully for the door. She was too ebullient, too hammered, to take notice. She looked ready to rush onstage. Another server I recognized from the restaurant was towing her by the wrist. "C'mon," she told Steph. "Time to go bye-bye."

Rod stepped in front of the last few intruders, all women. "You three can stay. You're cool," he said. "Hey, girls, let me show you something." And his tour began anew.

I hung back in the low light, pretending to inspect the grain of the carpet. Rod and the girls lined up along the window to absorb the view above it all. I was no longer of interest, but my earlier attentiveness had bought me enough latitude to linger. The panel of the record compartment was slightly ajar, and there was a sliver of light where it hadn't fully latched.

While Rod fiddled with the blackout curtain, the girls babbled about the first time they came to New York, if they'd driven or flown or taken a bus from Florida. Hadn't they ever seen a skyline before? I felt a heave of disdain, even for Steph. In a year's time, we would get together and fall apart. She would say I was no good for her. She would say she wished we never met.

Steph looped arms with the other server from the restaurant and pouted, said she was hungry. The other girls agreed. Just then Rod got the blackout curtain working, and the room was like an elevator cab descending. He told them it was an experiment in sensory deprivation. That's how you could hear the music best.

Just before the ambient light squeezed out completely, I found Steph's face. I watched as Rod took her elbow, tried to turn her toward the settee, the other waitress from the restaurant feeling around for her in the dark.

It was after two A.M. I had made it. It was time to go.

On Monday mornings, Rochelle leaves early for the city. She's in some kind of market research with a tech bent. There are modular desks and a company-wide message stream. Rochelle believes everyone in her office is a born idiot, groomed to disrupt her workflow and commit grave derelictions of duty. I am her listening ear, on call.

What she doesn't know is that I board the train after her. She takes the 7:10 and I follow on the 7:28. An early team meeting drains her morning, so she'll be playing catch-up for the day, which makes Mondays my vacation from the life we've built. Mostly, I do everything I used to do. Sleep a lot. Order takeout and make myself sick. There is too much of Rochelle's exactitude on display at the loft to make this sort of slovenliness enjoyable. And in Queens, there is Victor.

Our building has long been on the outs, foundation grinding away to chalk. Various pests and feuds migrate floor to floor, and the maintenance man who lives in the basement is always shouting into his phone and pumping a dumbbell. The deterioration is both gradual and certain, which turns the squalor into something of a consolation. What worse thing could happen here?

I hold open the front door to my building and let a woman bound in a Moncler puffer pass by. I know the look because it is the same one Rochelle owns in three mute colors.

Up the steps to the second floor and my roommate, Victor, is at the kitchen table. He is dressed in fresh-pressed business casual from the waist up, volleying with his laptop.

"Funny you should mention it," he says. "I've visualized some compelling next steps."

He has been without a steady job for almost a year, but he is always setting up informational interviews to pick the brains of mid-level execs who trade their time for lunch and an ego boost. Victor says he is waiting for the right thing to come along and that he'll know it when it finds him. He gives me a pointed look from behind his laptop while the person onscreen spouts jargon, facts, figures. Victor looks amped. I can see he has a little dried toothpaste at the edge of his mouth. I bow out and head to my bedroom, a time capsule from two months ago.

Before I left, I'd dumped out a drawer in search of something I can no longer remember. A book remains open on the floor by my bed. I have visited here since, but I prefer to keep the room intact. Evidence of a previous life, in case I'd ever like to resume it.

If I had to guess, I'd say Rochelle considers me a benevolent freeloader, unaware that her little luxuries—the stocked pantry, the sublime bath products, the wardrobe she has curated just for me—are only perks, not the reason why I've stayed. I think of myself in love, or in hiding, or both, one is always taking the lead. Each time I hop on the return train and face Rochelle's front door, I fear my set of keys are decoys, that someone has swooped in to change the locks. I undergo the same moment of truth: test the knob and wait for my good fortune to expire. The door always opens.

It has been years since my sister and I spoke. For a long while, she sent me letters from Veld, pages and pages in the most exacting cursive, like a tracing. I would read through each letter once to be sure nothing had changed. I knew from my own experience at Veld that all communications were vetted—originals run through the copier, and another copy made of the redacted or otherwise altered version. They're collated, dated, set aside in labeled folders. At some point it occurred to me. It wasn't at all about what was in the letters. Fawn was sending them as a physical act, an insistent link. A jab in the side so as not to be forgotten.

While Victor marathons corporate calls, I settle in under unwashed sheets, and when I wake again, I've forgotten where I am, in which time, in whose bed. The weather outside has shifted overcast, fudging the hour. It takes a moment before I see it, or don't. The shelf above my desk looks almost innocent with its tidy row of books, the parched spider plant, the light over the desk craned just so. And then, the blank spot. What I do not see.

I slide into the kitchen in my socks and wave at Victor.

"I will absolutely shoot you an email. Absolutely. Amazing." He maneuvers one hand out of frame and firmly motions at me for one more second, grinning like a politician as he flips me off. When he closes the laptop, he lets out a long breath.

"I sincerely hate myself." He heads for the fridge and fishes a spear from the pickle jar.

"Something's missing," I say. "The album I had framed, over my desk?"

"When you leave, I pretend your room doesn't exist."

"It's worth some money. A little bit of money."

He pours himself a generous helping of cereal, but the milk is low so he runs the gallon under the tap for a few seconds. Meanwhile, I start upturning pillows and digging through piles of expired mail, but the effort is perfunctory. I know it's not here.

"Thanks for asking about my interview, by the way," Victor says. "It was very educational and worth my time."

"Can't you see I'm in crisis?"

Victor chews slowly. "Have you checked under your bed?"

To him, there is nothing suspicious about my loss. Victor believes I'm an only child. He believes I'm in love. He believes what I lead him to believe.

"Okay. All right." I try to strike a casual, appreciative sort of pose. "I'm listening. Tell me. Tell me how your day was. Let's catch up," I say. "Has anyone new been here?"

"You don't have to humor me. It's pitiful."

"Don't be like that."

"Like what? It wasn't a real interview or anything. It's just talking."

When I dropped off the radar in Deerie, I didn't return Victor's calls or texts for a week. I didn't know how to tell him I had gone home, when home wasn't there and I was pretending to be someone else. He was ready to report me missing when I finally admitted I'd fallen in love, was on the wing of fate, so on and so forth. It was not a good time to leave him to his own devices. Some days he's like a machine, guzzling coffee and Coke while monitors blink around his head. Other days he holes up in his room, plays videogames for hours, sometimes until dawn. I would wake up to the sounds of mortar blasts, gunfire, battalion commandants shouting orders. I can practically see his fingers itching for the controller.

"Come on, Vic," I say. "Tell me. I want to know. Then you can help me look."

"Fine." That's all it ever takes. "Some regional manager for Enterprise thinks he's a visionary because he flipped a rowhome in outer Brooklyn. Usually, that's enough to piss me off, but it's not even the worst part of my day."

I am thinking that somehow, she got past two locked doors and my roommate. She found what she wanted, but didn't bother to stick around for me. Victor clears his throat.

"Right," I say. "That's crazy. What happened?"

"I'm getting to that." He scrapes his bowl. "I had this A.M. networking thing with this girl I met at Press. Well, not met. She spilled her iced coffee on me, and you know, we got to talking. She knew somebody who knew somebody else at this firm that does tech for tech companies. She said we should collaborate, and when she gave me her number, I thought—" He sighs, scratches his chin. "I don't know what I thought. She had that look, you know? Like she knew what she was doing."

"What was her name?"

"My brother owns two rentals in Jersey and he's thirty-two. He goes on vacations. I could do what he does. I know the interest rates."

"I know you do."

"She said to be in touch, but I don't know if it's worth it."

"Who?"

"The girl. From Press? Hello?" Victor fiddles with the magnetic tiles on the fridge. "You know, this conversation isn't really making me feel any better. If you think I stole your shit because I'm hard up, you're paranoid. And this girl didn't look like she'd get her hands dirty."

"She was here?"

"You just missed her."

The woman in Moncler.

She had smelled clean and expensive, fresh from the salon. Her feathered hood was up. I had been batting at the phone, keeping Rochelle at bay. I held open the door for her.

"Victor, what was her name?"

"She's a princess, okay? Nobody wants your hipster collectibles."

"Victor."

"May," he says. "Are you happy now? Her name was May."

Somehow this answer is worse than I feared.

Had I taken the album from Rod's little cave because I felt it belonged with me? It was reckless, but I had never regretted it until now. I would rather it have remain sealed inside Rod's soundproof mausoleum than find its way into my sister's hands.

"As usual, you know everything there is to know," Victor says. "We're caught up. You can run back to your girlfriend's palace and I'll see you same time next week."

"Who said I was leaving?"

"You don't have to baby me anymore, okay? You're off the hook." He smiles wide, every tooth accounted for. "See? See this face? I'm the best I've ever been."

He turns away and busies himself with the crumbs on the counter. I wait for him to look at me, to relent so that I know we'll be fine like always, the bounce-back duo, but he is already sealing up inside himself. For now, the safest route is retreat. To leave is the kindest thing I can do for him.

"I may be gone a little longer than usual this time," I say, and grab my keys. "I'll make sure the rent comes."

"Oh, how mysterious. How will I ever go on without you?"

"Just lock the door behind me, okay? Eat something. Wear a shirt."

"Uh-huh," Victor says, and heads for his bedroom. "Thanks for stopping by."

On the train back to Deerie, I picture the last version of Fawn I can remember.

We were in West Virginia, living with our father then. Fawn was holding his hand, which she never did, and they were waving goodbye to me from the top of his long gravel driveway. I was headed back to Veld for my second stint, courtesy of Fawn and my father, a newly allied force. She squeezed her eyes and tears coursed down her cheeks in a shrewd performance. A part of me understood this display meant nothing. Another part of me beyond my control held out some sad hope that this was just another bruising battle in a long war of sibling rivalry, and the trouble between us could be understood as a natural dynamic of sorts, one that would ultimately smooth over or become dormant in adulthood, in spite of the scars acquired along the way.

Plenty of troubled teens mellow out, or get medicated, or find some outlet that siphons away their hostility toward the softer human world—via motorcycle racing, extreme fitness, meditation, watercolors. A lid for every boiling pot. One girl from Veld used to terrorize the staff and students so obscenely they locked her away on the solitary floor, and we only saw her for special assemblies, or through the window when they let her out for solo walks along the grounds. Eventually, she was fed the right cocktail of medications, paired with a counselor she liked, and unearthed a passion for ceramics. Now she works for a substance abuse hotline in the city. We met for drinks when I first moved there, and she looked well. She reflected on her years at Veld with fondness.

"It was really touch-and-go for a long while," she said, "but they helped me pull through."

Did a light inside toggle on and off? And if so, who controlled the switch? I felt at the mercy of some cellular agenda. I didn't think there was anything wrong with me, but what if some exercise or therapeutic session or trauma tripped a wire and suddenly I became a waking nightmare. Or, worse even, I became well when I thought I already was.

Fawn is still young, I think, and scan the train car for girls who could be her. Just another teenager trying to get lost in the city. She could be starting her spring semester at college. She could have a boyfriend or girlfriend, any friend would do. By now, she would have a personal style, a budding history of heartbreak. Maybe she would follow in our parents' footsteps—become a connector of artists, movers and shakers, a social butterfly like our mother. Or, a rebel in an imported rock band, a woman of science, a veterinarian—as our father was. She has the aptitude and imagination. After all, the album is a pointed object to make disappear. The drama of it all is both absurd and entirely her signature—a psychological heist, a sprinkle of cinematic flair. A message. She knows what can move me, how best to make me follow.

What had Victor said about her?

She looked like she knew what she was doing.

4

A freak blizzard bears down in March. Rochelle and I sleep in, make omelets, have French press coffee, and marvel at the highway, transformed overnight into a sheath of white. In boots fresh from their boxes, we walk the unplowed pedestrian path at the edge of town, where the woods are snow-tipped and all heavy boughs. We pass a few grueling joggers and spot tracks from cross-country skiers who have come and gone, but otherwise the world is one bleached vista.

Rochelle and I never spend much contemplative time together. She prefers a steady diet of anecdotes, especially stories of someone else's misfortune. Once, I mentioned an old friend who'd been fired from his job because he did not internalize company values. A disturbing diagnosis. That's what the boss at Victor's start-up told him in their exit interview. Rochelle had listened respectfully and then decided that he probably deserved it. It was like natural selection. "If you can't help yourself, you're missing the winner's gene." She said I should've told my friend to be grateful for the lesson.

As a rule, Rochelle says one *thank you* per encounter. Working at the restaurant, I said thank you so many times a day it became a tic. Sidestepping someone on the street, I said thank you instead of excuse me. At the bar, a drunk spilled gin down my back, and when he slurred some acknowledgment, not even a real apology, I said thank you—twice. I dropped a dollar in the open hat of an old woman puppeteering in the park. She said thank you. I said thank you. We chirped the phrase back and forth like two cockatiels until I forced myself to walk away.

Rochelle and I arrive along a straight flat stretch beside the densest patch of forest. There, a fence line once split Deerie proper from the telecom company's land, its infinite high-tension towers connecting the world on a string. Rochelle is going on about winters in Michigan, ice-fishing, flannel, and I nod vigorously. Though the whole earth is clean and new and near-odorless but for the scent of refrigeration—all I can smell is iron.

As we walk, I keep thinking we've hit the spot: the precise latitude and longitude where Zeke had ceased to be. There it is—empty, anonymous, and now behind us. We walk ten yards more and I realize I'm wrong. This is really the place. No, this spot. This few feet of nothing. I think I can tell by the way the grass pokes up through the snow, like this patch of ground is more nourished than the rest. It would have taken at least two minutes for Zeke to go into cardiac arrest from blood loss. He had been trying to show me something, had been trying for weeks, but I could hardly face him by then. He died on an unusually brisk summer night. Fog lifted from streets that'd cooked all day and condensation turned the metal fence line slick. He scaled it easily but fumbled at the crossing. As he struggled, in terrible shock, femoral artery pierced by the sharpest spoke of galvanized steel, I laughed. I couldn't see the life draining out of him. I didn't understand what occurred until the sound distilled. No more metal scrabble, only the animal commotion of the woods, the inhuman traffic off and away, and then that fainter sound. The zipper on Zeke's jacket as it brushed the chain-link, the softest tinkling of a bell.

All that wreckage has since been cleared away and beautified, but somehow it is more disturbing. There are no indications of what was. Mothers and fathers and children circle the loop none the wiser, the chain-link fence sold for scrap or dumped. Fibers and trace DNA and young blood lost to rust and rot, one spoke no more traitorous than the next.

I squeeze these thoughts to vapor, into clouds behind my eyes. I smile like I want for nothing as Rochelle pries into personal territory for the first time.

She is asking about my family, which means she is talking about hers. She launches again into the saga of her three younger sisters, all married with children, all back home in Michigan with their parents. "I won't get on a plane if they won't," she is saying. "Why should I?"

Eventually, it is my turn. "You can't be an orphan," Rochelle segues. "You can't always be so mum." Her cheeks are rosy. She looks like she is trying, but I am prepared for this.

"Well, my father passed away a few years ago." True.

"From natural causes." A lie.

"And I never really knew my mother." Lie. Mostly.

"And I'm an only child. The holidays are always quiet. I'm simple."

Rochelle frowns. "How could you not know your own mother?"

"We weren't close," I say, and see she is pacified by this correction. Better to have relationships run cold than carry baggage. She returns to talk of nemeses and sisters, how lucky I am that I can never understand.

That night we drink too much of Rochelle's best wine. We make a nest of pillows and blankets before the fireplace. Shadows waver over her face, gather in the roots of her dyed hair. With the tip of my finger, I trace her lips and try to soothe all future curiosities. I believe myself that powerful.

"You know, in the spirit of today's revelations," she says, "I realized I have never asked, but I see it, like now, in the right light. You look—" She takes my chin and turns my head. "You have this look about you sometimes. It's like you're from someplace else."

"I am from someplace else. I grew up in the suburbs."

"That's not it." Rochelle clacks her glass down on the concrete hearth. "I've got it. Okay. I had a friend in elementary school. I always thought she looked completely average, and then one day I go over for a playdate, and her mother is a nice blond, blue-eyed woman from Bergen County, but her father is, really, the darkest of the dark. He came over from the U.K., but he wasn't quite from there either. Do you understand?"

"I think so."

"I just find it funny when someone turns their chin and suddenly, you see it. A clue that's been there all along." Rochelle touches the rim of her glass. "I have nothing against it."

"I think I have some French Canadian blood."

She squints, as if the proof is written across my nose. I knew this would intrigue her. It is the sort of exotic she can trot out like another party trick and otherwise forget. The truth is more memorable. There was romance. There was blood. My mother and father smacked into each other face-first on a city street corner. Both considered themselves escapees in their own right. My father of the island, of Vieques, where American bombs doused the shore. My mother a blue-ribbon WASP with an ancestral estate called White Hall. It was out of their unlikely and abridged cross-cultural union that we arrived, half-batch babies, mixed up in more ways than one.

"French Canadian," Rochelle muses. "Like from Quebec?"

We brush our teeth and spit swill from the red wine. The vanity bulbs in the marbled bath are blinding, like they will pop at any moment, and they smear into a single powerful beam I stare inside. I call to mind the former blueprint and the space that used to be lifts forward like a hologram. The bathroom replaced our library. If I reach high enough, if I strain for the upper right corner, I will find the shelf where my mother kept books she did not open, but could not give away. Cowboy Westerns and detective novels in Spanish and English, the next page translating the last. Anatomy tomes diagramming the ligatures of a quarter horse. A guide to herbal remedies. A biography of Bob Dylan. Books that belonged to my father.

A few jagged notes seize my left eardrum, like feedback from an amplifier. The pain is real. The sound feels real. Music zaps inside the walls like loose electricity and Rochelle is leaning heavily on the vanity, toothbrush wedged between her molars. For the first time, I long for Queens, the version of myself left in limbo. Nothing came easy, but it was mine.

Rochelle slips against the vanity and nearly nails her chin on the marble. Time for bed. I feed her a glass of water and three ibuprofens and leave her snoring under the covers. I chew up one of her sleeping pills and uncork a new bottle, repressing the urge to call someone. I think of that night on the platform in Deerie, the impulse to dial. I wander, massaging the walls, listening. I try to recite my father's record straight through. Once, I knew every line. I used to scribble the lyrics like rabid tally marks in the margins of everything, but all the words are missing from me. I go to the window and watch a few lonely semis on the road, no time to waste. I am wishing for someone on the other side of the glass, someone vigilant in the alley, someone looking up from the sidewalk or else watching from the highway through a pair of high-powered binoculars. Not everyone gets so lucky, I think. Not everyone has someone like me.

A few nights later, Rochelle's nemesis from work arrives for dinner. They've been paired together for an upcoming project and Rochelle wants the upper hand.

"Smart move," I tell Rochelle, but she already knew that.

I make branzino, and everyone loves it. I am in Rochelle's corner, performing above class. Conversation flows and she squeezes my thigh under the table. We get to talking about town.

"We miss you in the city, Rochelle," her nemesis says. Her name is JoAnn. There is the tiniest sprig of parsley between her teeth, but I only catch a glimpse when she says words that move her lips a certain way—like *seriously* and *feeling*. As in, "I *seriously* can't believe you decided to up and move to this quaint little village, Rochelle. I can't imagine the *feeling* that must've come over you. Won't you ever come back to the city with the rest of us?"

Rochelle says she'll always be a small-town girl at heart. We clink glasses and laugh.

I know there are real reasons why she did it. She was hoping to meet someone. A smaller pond with thirtysomethings swimming everywhere, squeezing juice and hiking and opening antiques shops that sell the same style credenza until it's extinct. It was utopic, in its modern way. Dating in the city took killer instinct. Everyone was holding out for something better.

Conversation begins to die, and JoAnn admires the loft. The old rutted floorboards have been replaced by poured concrete, and even the exposed wooden beams have been freshened. Old load-bearing columns nudge the space into a workable floor plan. The kitchen is marble. The fixtures are gold. The rooms are wired for sound.

"What I'd give for a kitchen like that," JoAnn says, "but I hardly bother to cook. There are so many places I want to try. Look at all that space. Rochelle, have you learned to cook yet?" JoAnn has asked only a few cordial questions of me, but arrives now at a new one. "And you? What do you think of it here?"

"It's lovely. Plenty to love here."

Rochelle smooths a wrinkle in the tablecloth. What a catch, JoAnn must be thinking. How lucky for Rochelle to find someone so young and yet so erudite. The perfect kind of handsome a pretty girl should be. She might've wanted one of me for herself. To incite jealousy, Rochelle says, is the ultimate revenge.

"Does it feel like home?" JoAnn asks.

To distract from my own discomfort, I launch into what I think will be a fun, mindless anecdote about our new hometown—a story I pretend to have picked up from the butcher around the corner. I tell them about an oddball case back in the early 2000s. A mob man's flunky took a joy ride north out of the city, towing a pickup truck full of body parts. He got loaded on pills and booze and unloaded his cargo off the side of the highway, the very highway JoAnn can see over her shoulder.

"This idiot is flying upstate tossing pieces left and right, thinking it's marshland down here," I say, "because he can't see the lights. They blend together. And he's seeing stars anyway, completely zoinked. He goes home happy, thinking he's done a good job. Then it's lights out."

I am thinking this is a great story, something to shock and amuse, a true crime morsel, but no one is laughing with me. Instead of moving on, I force my way through.

"Some bits were so decomposed they couldn't tell what was what. Did this guy even have a face left? Not likely." More details spew out—which body parts were found, in which order, down to the sternum that surfaced in a nearby retention pond. "They never found his genitals, not ever," I say, unsure why I've chosen this as my euphemism of choice, though this is less important than the fact that I've brought it up in the first place. Rochelle pours for herself and JoAnn. The angle is extreme and the bottle makes a *glug, glug, glug* as it decants rapidly. Some sloshes onto her good tablecloth and I think I'm being kind, distracting from her error by staying animated, by telling them about the little girl who found a foot with no toes, took it home, and tried to keep it safe.

Someone tries to change the subject, and I see how far I've

overshot the landing. I clear my throat, stay smiling, go to pour more wine though there is little room in their glasses. I ask questions in quick succession, like a timer is about to go off. "Tell me about work," I quiz JoAnn. Tell me about your boss. Your commute. Your fitness regimen. Your hairstylist. Your car. We get up from the table and Rochelle whisks my glass away when our guest turns her back. I offer to do the dishes and am mercifully released.

After JoAnn has caught the train back into the city, Rochelle retreats to the lux chaise in the corner of her room, sifting through documents for work. She stays there for hours while I return the loft to its untouched state. When it is coming on midnight, I go to her.

The painting above her bed is more black than blue at this hour. The bedroom smells like fish from dinner. I wait for her critique, but she does not look up from her fan of manila folders. I go into the master bath, shut the door, and tell the story again. I whisper it into the mirror glass, trying to match my earlier inflections and detect which notes were out of tune. I am ashamed it's so obvious. Too much detail, too much excitement. When I get to the part about the foot and the little girl who finds it—another mistake. JoAnn had asked what happened to her.

"Who cares?" I had said, flippant as a ticket-taker. "Her life is probably over." I moved on to tell the bit about the other rancid elbow found that August. A summer crime spree. I put my palms flat on the vanity and watch my teeth and tongue as I tell it better, this time streamlined, with softer words and no embellishments, safer gore, no little girl.

When I peek into the bedroom again, Rochelle is sitting there shadowed by lamplight. She puts down her papers and stares back.

"Bedtime," she says.

"Just a sec."

I close the door and dawdle with the potions and serums and

sprays arranged inside the medicine cabinet. There are a dozen orange pill bottles, but none bear names or labels. I pop a lid and look inside at capsules the size of dimes and flat as discs. Whatever gift they give should be powerful, though I can't say I've noticed a shift. Rochelle calls them supplements. To supplement myself. To account for the missing. If they worked, if they corrected what they were meant to correct, how had the night gone so wrong?

The lights are off when I slip into bed beside her.

"On the table," she mumbles into her pillow. "There, for you."

I feel around for what she's left and find more vitamins, potent as seeds.

"More?" I ask.

"It's the New Year now. It's good to begin on the right foot." If she's making a joke at my expense, I can't tell. I scoop all four of the capsules into my palm and toss them back.

"I love you," I say to the dark, to the ceiling, to the room that used to be mine.

Rochelle sighs into the custom foam pillow bought on special order. One for her, and one for me. "Go to sleep now," she says, and tells me good night.

5

Has your teen exhibited destructive behavior toward property and/or the possessions of others?

Does your teen rebuff consequences through negotiation, blame-shifting, and/or manipulation?

Do you find yourself choosing your words carefully when conversing with your teen?

Does your teen appear withdrawn?

Does your teen engage in risky social conduct, such as promiscuity, substance abuse, and/or association with unsavory peers?

Is your teen unwilling to accept the reality of his/her actions?

It took weeks on the trail before I was trusted to sleep alone. New recruits are reactive, Shine explained. Girls don't understand the elements, or their limitations. "Down the mountain isn't down," he said. "Not like you think." What looks like the faint thread of a country road is no exit, but a winding rivulet iced over in shades of tar. Do not attempt to follow gravity or the moon. No descent is linear. You will not remember the crooked tree with the burr and right your path accordingly. He said, "You will end up in a bog."

The first night I was left to sleep unsupervised, the wind was relentless. The tarp siding of my shelter bowed and caught like a sail with each gust, and with each shudder came swipes of fresh ice, the yips of nocturne creatures, of girls laughing after hours. I hadn't strung it tight enough. Shine was stationed with the latest recruit and was no longer close by to correct me. It was the first time I'd been alone since the Juvenile Transportation Services hauled me out of bed and set me on a course for Maine. In my hands, I held the letter my mother had written to me. I counted twelve pages, front and back.

No one had ever written me a letter before. My headlamp was a third eye fixed to my forehead. My plan was to read each page one side at a time, rationed over the course of our trek. The longer it took to reach the last words, the longer I could entertain the possibility of an alternate ending, one in which I would be returned to Deerie and our warehouse, to Antonia, to whatever remained of my unsurveilled adolescence. I thought I knew what her letter held— grievances and rhetorical questions and disappointments. Those could only weigh me down.

On the first page, my mother excerpted Veld's admissions questionnaire. She rewrote these inquiries apparently for my benefit, as if to prove she'd only been following the rules, and that signing me away was just the qualitative outcome of a test she'd taken, like those flowchart quizzes in magazines that pinpoint your dream career, or celebrity beau, or the most flattering style of jeans for your body type. I thought the questions were manipulatively broad, but I knew she had answered them honestly. I was guilty of everything.

It was tempting to read on, but I folded the letter and tucked it away in my pack for the following night. After a grueling Share Circle dominated by one of the veterans with a propensity for faking seizures, I returned to my solo shelter and the pocket was empty. The letter was gone. It could've fluttered away anywhere along our route, and there was no going back, no one to complain to, no way to ask for another. For hours, I tossed inside my sleeping bag, but by dawn I woke within a placid state of acceptance. Now, I was really alone.

For two more months we trekked. It did not get easier or more predictable. The best days were bright and windless, or when Shine got an itch to go at a quicker clip and went ahead by a half-mile. This meant we were allowed to talk, or sit down.

The worst days were wettest because it was tedious to get a fire going, or else when someone new was added to the ranks and could not process their banishment privately. One morning, I passed by a new girl's tarp on the way to the fire and heard crying. Though it was against the rules, I peeked behind her curtain, and there she was with a rock in her hand. She was holding it high above her head, her bare foot outstretched before her and raw with cold. The rock was heavy, and her arms were shaking from the effort of keeping it poised there.

"I'm not going one more fucking mile so help me God," she said.

We had just finished the last long haul before resupply, when we covered the most ground no matter the weather or terrain. It was always a grueling march, and for dinner we threw all remaining food into a pot. Rice, peanut butter, oatmeal, garlic, rotting bananas. Everyone smelled their worst and the snow kept falling.

"If I break just one, they'll send me down," she said. The rock was trembling in her grip.

"Harlow, how will you get down if you break all your toes?"

"I'll go for the little one."

"They're not going to care."

"Then I'll go for the big one. It'll be broken. They can't make me." And down came the rock.

But they did make her. Shine fashioned a rudimentary splint and we pushed up a steep ridge followed by a muddy descent to ground level, one graceless slip-and-slide that had Harlow crying out. We were told to ignore her. Onward was the only imperative. We resupplied and Harlow was given a loop of medical tape to make do. The march went on. We went back up.

Eventually, when the mountain thawed and there came the pleasurable stink of mud and riverbeds regurgitating, us girls put the pieces together that our time on the mountain and with Shine was coming to an end. The only question was where each of us was headed next. There were three options: another wilderness tour, an advance to Veld's campus, or home. It was possible a new counselor would come to replace Shine, or else the trek would resume in some other biome near or far. I thought I wanted to be done with the walking, but that was only because I didn't know the direction I was already pointed in.

Gia was one of the veterans. She had advanced to campus before. She told us that the grounds had first belonged to the heir of a Virginia tobacco fortune, the last son of the Veld family. When his business went bust, he took a shotgun to his wife, his son, their cook, and then himself. I doubted any of this was true. After the alleged triple-murder-suicide tragedy, the property was snapped up by the state, sold eventually to its present owners, a corporation out of Cincinnati that owns a roster of other therapeutic schools. There were stories about those places too. Girls reported on various sites like safety dispatches from distant but interlocked planets. Some campuses were coed, and when the girls passed the boys in common areas, a counselor held up a tarp between them, sacred as a temple veil. Other schools were built like juvenile detention centers, all chain-link, standard-issue sweats, and dirt yards. They stripped down their so-called students and searched every cavity, gave them badges with identification numbers. There was gossip about a school in Arizona that trekked their students so long and hard across a flat of broiling desert that a boy died from exposure. As he suffered, slowed, and curled into a soiled ball, the trek leaders berated him for his dramatics.

"They find these people anywhere," Gia said of the staff. "They hire hippies who work at climbing gyms, or high school dropouts running the register at REI. They want people who look like they know something, but are too dumb to do anything."

Almost no one went home after Commitment. That was not how the program was sold. It came down to Shine's judgment, who he thought was ready. I had often wondered during those many rootless hours on top of the world, staring at the back of his head, how much he'd been told of his charges. Didn't he ever worry? Surely something could be done to him, if we all acted as one. That was how little he thought of us. Or perhaps he drew his confidence from the buck knife on his belt.

The day came when our trek was unceremoniously over and we were returned to sea level again. The next season waxed in that noncommittal climate, and the squat lodge at the base of the mountain looked witchy and quaint with chimney smoke rising overhead in the clearing. There was a white van waiting. Shine was talking with the driver while the rest of us took a knee. Plucked from our lives and reeling, we'd gone round and round like windup toys for months, and now we had come to the end.

"Leave the packs," Shine said. "Someone will come to sort through everything."

Before we drove off, he hovered in the van's double doors, haggard and proud.

"Girls. I see it on each of your faces. You won't forget what we've accomplished. I've taught you everything I know. The rest is up to you."

There was a pause where Shine seemed to expect a thank-you. I could strike flint, braid the sinew of tree bark for rope, translate tracks, read the sun's dial. My body moved differently. I had ground away a certain idleness from my gait. We knew now we could survive without the basic conveniences, but I could not yet perceive what it was supposed to mean to me.

On the ride from Maine to Virginia, we were given power bars and stopped only once for the bathroom. The smell in the van was suffocating, and everyone was anesthetized in their own way. Harlow was snoring. Gia was staring hard out the window, probably hatching an escape plan. One of the girls was in the front seat next to the driver, who'd been babbling for hours. He was telling her about watching the news on 9/11, how he'd been in bed and didn't know what to do, so he put the TV on mute and went back to sleep. The girl, Beanie, kept her hands folded in her lap. I couldn't tell if she was listening until she asked politely if he was married. Alone in the rear seat, I could not stop talking.

I listened to myself speak softly against the window, the fog of each syllable fanning out and shrinking in. I could not be sure how much of what I heard in my head was reaching the air, if my id was gushing like a fire hydrant. I don't even know who I was talking to. The dry heat of the van and the speed with which it carried us was disturbing. For whatever reason—the return to altitude, the wash of time, the rudimentary carbs coating my insides—I had finally broken. I asked several times to call my mother. I wanted to set the record straight, to hear her side and be rid of all secrecy between us. I thought I had found the answer to the dilemma of my present, simple as the exchange of a token. Exhume your discretions, arrange them in order, pair them with repentances, and then be free. I had forgotten one of the first rules of survival. I had been warned. Down the mountain isn't down.

Rise at dawn. Fifteen minutes for personal hygiene. Post. This is how the days go at Veld.

I head down to the kitchens to prep and serve breakfast, and after breakfast we have our first session, an abbreviated meeting wherein we journal and speak aloud the day's intention.

"I intend to be a positive force," I might say. "My intention is to uplift the will of others."

Staff and students alike are our accountability wardens. They keep a sharp eye out to be sure I remain in accordance. After the pretense of simplified core classes like Math and Reading, we split into Share Circles, one-on-ones, or some other variety of confessional healing. As with anything, there are trends. At one point it was rumored Veld was shipping in cows. Some center in Utah was doing it. Their most violent students had been pacified by a big-eyed Betsy and the chore of milking. Everyone would be assigned a baby heifer. Muck the stalls, give them names. For a week it was all anyone could talk about, but the cows never came. I believed this was for the best.

There's dead hour and dinner hour and before that it's Physical Education. Some days we do Movement, a kind of freewheeling modern dance meets yoga plus call-and-response. Other days it's jumping jacks on the front lawn. Forever planks. Wall-sits against the broad side of the shed. The key is to reinvigorate the primordial self. What began on the mountain is refined on campus. Brochures tout a high rate of college matriculation, applying SAT prep to snuff out behavioral pyrotechnics. So goes the pitch, but few make it that far. Those who go home often wind back again with more scars to lay bare in Group. Rare poster children reassimilate in the world, but somewhere along the line our rate of survival bottlenecks. Veld girls go on to slam their cars into concrete pylons and oncoming traffic, or overdose on weekend jaunts to Vermont or Miami, or otherwise kill themselves, accident or not, in any which way you can think of. It is impossible to extrapolate this fate from years of bad behavior versus all those hours spent reliving it, performing for an audience that demands encore after encore.

I am placed in Group with six others. We have surprisingly little in common. Our sins are diverse and ages range from twelve to nineteen. We come from everywhere, as far away as Panama. In a circle of metal folding chairs, we convene.

The hall is grand and high-ceilinged. A compact stage with a proscenium arch anchors the far end of the room, and a row of windows frames the lone road that leads to and from campus, fed a steady diet of delivery trucks, state cops, pickups toting bumpkins, and far-flung visitors to our therapeutic compound. Bowen, a hamlet of about two thousand, is the closest speck of civilization. There are rumors of escape, fables of a Greyhound station and the Black Cat bar where Veld staffers spill secrets to pervish locals who will one day track us down.

"It's all sheep-fuckers out here," Gia warned us once.

Despite our time together on the mountain, many of the girls first write me off as a Helicopter Case. This is what we call those sent to Veld by hyper-surveilling parents who caught them in some pathetic offense: heavy-petting with the girl down the block, video-game addiction, a C in Pre-Calc. We should pity them, but they are pariahs, amateurs, teachers' pets all. Lurking at the other end of the spectrum are the dangerously deranged. Molesters, cat killers, sex nuts, and those with overt bloodlust are to be avoided, if you can see them coming. They always relish the chance to have the floor. In one of our first sessions, a redheaded girl went on about the house cat she'd been caught squeezing too tightly as a child. She hauled it into a closet, sat among the discarded shoes and held fast until the animal gave up squirming. She sounded very matter-of-fact, like she was reading stage directions. Though the cat lived, addled for the rest of its sad life, her family pointed often to this episode as unequivocal evidence of her miswiring. This she could not comprehend. She said she was never allowed to be a curious child. She made one memorable mistake, and this cast all minor mistakes to follow as lingering symptoms of the first.

"I liked her to feel me doing it," she had said, "but I didn't like her to see me doing it."

At least a dozen like her roam the halls. When I catch their flat eyes like leaded glass, I think of Fawn and wonder.

As for the rest of us, our problem is saying no. This affliction is subcategorized as substance abuse, anger issues, compulsive lying, toxic relationships, narcissism, or the euphemistic catchall: risky behavior. Our guardians hope this stint will be the one that finally does the trick. We'll go back to being the children they swear we are underneath it all. Our fates are marked TBD. In the meantime, all we ever talk about is the worst things we've ever done.

That's what I deliver to Dr. John, my counselor, during a one-on-one session. A memorable mistake. It is why I am sitting across from him, why he taps a finger to the leathered armrest of his chair, keeping time like a metronome. I am brought to confess. I speak and he absorbs the magnitude of my rebellion, charts it on his secret scale.

This session, I tell him about the first time Antonia and I break into the Weppler house.

We find a window in back that's unlocked, above the sink in the kitchen. I am careful to slide it open quietly like a real intruder might, then remember I am one. I brace for some stench to come uncorked, but there's none. Everything inside is tidy, if not cramped by the accoutrements of the living. There are stacks of mail, all addressed to Dr. Gene Weppler, Mrs. Fiona Weppler, or Mr. Gene Weppler, Jr. The letters are unopened, and will stay that way.

Antonia races up the steps to claim a bedroom. I've only ever glimpsed the living room from the sidewalk. The TV is huge and empty. The couch bows where an audience sat, the remote wedged between the cushions.

"This place smells like shit," Antonia yells from upstairs. "I kind of love it."

I think it smells fine. I think it smells like real people. Like cereal boxes and dryer sheets, ash in the dormant fireplace. I turn on the TV and it zaps alive to the cooking channel, the last thing the Wepplers ever watched. A woman with a constrictive ponytail is making calzones. I go upstairs to find Antonia, who has moved into the master bedroom with its sizable en suite. Secretly, I'm happy she has not chosen the little bedroom under the eaves. The room I always wanted. While Antonia digs through Mrs. Weppler's armoire for valuables, I run my hands along the walls of Gene Jr.'s bedroom. The wallpaper print is ominous in death, but fitting. Prop planes. Three of them soar through cloudy skies before the pattern repeats. Red plane, green plane, blue, like a message from beyond, from Gene Jr. to me.

At this point in my story, Dr. John—not an MD, but a PhD in Poetry, of all things—stops me. "What do you believe Gene Jr. was trying to communicate?" he asks. This is a trick question. There is a right and wrong answer.

"Oh, I don't know." I slide down in my chair and look purposefully over Dr. John's salt-and-pepper head. "Maybe that we're all hardwired, and our fates are coded from the start like a videogame. And the cruel trick of life is that the warning signs are everywhere, all the time, obvious as the wallpaper you woke up to every day of your life. All those pieces you gathered to nest a personality of your own, to make you feel invested in the life you're living, the happy things, all yours—you know, actually wind up killing you in the end."

Dr. John crosses and uncrosses his legs.

"Is that how you really feel?" he asks.

"Not really."

"Specificity, please."

"Specifically," I say, "I believe in entropy." I had learned this word recently.

"Ah, an original idea."

"You didn't say it had to be original."

Through the window, I spot a trio of Veld girls kneeling in the garden, squabbling with the dirt. There had been a late season frost that morning.

"I don't have an answer to whatever it is that's brought you here," Dr. John is saying. "Believe it or not, I am not in the business of answers. I can offer strategies, tools you can use, but they're no good if you don't know how to wield them."

"I don't even know what that means."

"It means, you have to commit. That is the essential element. From there, it's only a matter of progress, of building upon that progress a day at a time."

"Yes. A day at a time. I will definitely mull that over."

I can feel Dr. John willing me to resume eye contact, to be taken in by his straight-talking tenor. I stare out the window. I want him to know I will not be mulling anything over. The traitorous desire to speak, the one that wracked me all down the drive to Veld, has snaked back inside, coiled deep into a tight, airless knot. What will they do with what I tell them?

He taps the blunt tip of his nose, a tell.

"In all our reminiscing," he says, "I'm surprised you haven't mentioned your terrible loss. Your friend. Zeke."

We go round this cul-de-sac all the time, always returning the way we came. The further the incident recedes, the more it changes. A popular refrain at Veld is to *live in it,* it being the interior well of darkness we are supposedly attempting to outwit or outrun with our wayward choices. Live in the hurt, they say. The only way out is through.

The trouble is, I lived with it all the time, and nothing moved. I could feel Zeke's accident hardening into something else, a place I could go to, a kind of worry stone. I vowed to keep it unarticulated, and in that way, preserved, safe from the platitudes, the moral pageantry, the voyeurism of my new setting. It was the only thing that was still mine.

"It doesn't have to be talking," Dr. John says. "It could be drawing. It could be writing."

"No," I say. "No thanks."

"All right then." Dr. John looks at his watch. "Let's do pages."

I hand him my journal. Our next session is emotional inventory day. We'll review my interior musings and graph them, commit them to a personal file that quantifies my well-being like the volatile stock it is. To upset this method I often doodle angry, crosshatched little vignettes in the margins, conscious of the Rorschach interpretations to follow. My reticence is never left untreated. Soon I will be called to the solitary floor for forced contemplation, or else to Physical Education, in case the exertion can shake something loose.

Outside, the girls are leaving the garden on the hour, chatting as they slouch back to the main building. The faintest drizzle must've begun, because they all stop at the same moment and look skyward. One of the girls holds out her tongue.

As I go for the door, Dr. John tips an invisible hat to me. "Progress," he always says at the end of our sessions, a bell he rings no matter how poorly our talks go. He returns my file to his stack of many. "This is what we call progress. Another day in the life."

6

There are a few more hours until it will be dark enough for fireworks. The troop of us have set out on our vigilante mission—
Antonia and Kent, Zeke and me—in order to track down the man
in the van. The night's animus begins here in The Gables but ends
on Geronimo Street.

We stalk down blacktops and drift toward the curb when cars
roll by. Prepubescents slurping Big Gulps on BMX bikes join our
party and depart, bored by our resolve and intent on Popsicles back
home. Zeke's neighborhood is draped in banners. The Gables is an
endless network of loops, cul-de-sacs, tree-lined dead ends where a
third of the properties are FOR SALE, FOR RENT, or abandoned. The
frozen faces of real estate agents bare their teeth as we pass.

Sensing a lull in our allegiance, Antonia says we should spread
out.

"Chop, chop," Kent says. "The sluts die first." He turns on the
two of us. "Off you go."

Antonia rolls her eyes in my direction and says, *"Men."*

What a world, I think. A world crawling with men.

Kent had no idea how quickly Antonia would discard him, or

how poorly he'd take it. Soon he'd be ambushing her with long, confessional emails stuffed with song lyrics, not even good ones. She would do dramatic readings of them for me from the Wepplers' couch. She said assholes love email. She said Kent looked like a monkfish when he came.

"I want a hot dog," Zeke says. "I want air-conditioning."

Antonia nudges my arm. "Where is he?"

"Who?"

"Who do you think? The man in the van."

It goes on like this for another hour. Each time a car approaches and is deemed innocent, Antonia's displeasure intensifies, a dial turning the wrong direction. Kent fiddles with the button on her jean shorts and pouts. When it finally does happen, it's like a glitch. There is something familiar about the sound arriving in waves down the block. Some loose belt clicking, a musical puff of engine exhaust. The minivan gliding toward us has one busted headlight, like a wink.

Though it is why we set out in the first place, I am hoping that somehow no one will notice. I am hoping we will feed back into the party at the Heller house, cool off with a cold beverage. Let the man in the van go.

Antonia puts her hand on Kent's chest to slow him down.

"Is this the one?" she asks me.

The van decelerates as it draws closer. Antonia moves from the side of the street to the center, holding out her arms until the van creaks to a halt. There is a long moment when nothing happens. Antonia keeps her arms steady and calls to me.

"Is it him?"

"I don't know," I say. "It could be."

"Well, do something, Kent," she says, and Kent suddenly takes off fast and on foot, slipping between houses before vanishing. "Where the fuck is he going?"

Zeke is standing on the curb beside me, waiting for orders.

"That's the guy, isn't it? I can tell by your face." He shakes his head like he has let me down. "Don't worry," he says. "I'm memorizing his plates."

The man in the van is staring straight ahead, hands at ten and two. He does not edge around Antonia, nor does he roll down the window to see what the fuss is about. Perhaps he has been expecting a stop such as this. He is prepared to wait it out rather than make the first move.

"Hello?" Antonia says to us. "Tell him to open up before he decides to run me over."

Zeke steps off the curb.

"Wait." As always, he allows me to take the lead. I go to the driver's window and rap on the glass. "Do you remember me?" I ask the man.

He looks different, pale and motley like oatmeal. A firecracker explodes a block over and nobody moves. Antonia is blocking the van, but authority belongs to no one.

"He recognizes you, doesn't he?" she says. "It's him."

"Yes. It's him."

The man hits the gas, screeching past us by inches as he takes off down the block toward The Gables' main artery. "Hey!" Antonia shouts as his bumper rounds the bend. The throttle of one engine fades and it is swiftly replaced by another. Mr. Heller's corporate sedan revs up the block from the opposite direction with Kent behind the wheel. He leans across the console to open the passenger door for Antonia and yells for her to get in. It is all very dramatic. I am aware of our optics, how many of the prepubescents and losers unattended in front yards wish to be us or among us, with a vendetta and a getaway car. It is much better than TV.

Off we go in hot pursuit, taking the curves at top speeds to catch up, and quickly we do.

"Slow down," Antonia warns Kent. "I said go slow." He eases off the pedal as the van takes a right onto Coronet Court. "Stop here. Let's watch where he goes."

"I don't think we should get out of the car," Zeke says. "Mom would be pissed."

Antonia is disgusted by this invocation. "Don't you have a spine? This is a public service." Kent pulls over and tells everyone to shut up so he can think.

Zeke makes a show of getting comfortable. "Have fun. I'm not going anywhere."

The van has turned into the driveway of a Ranch-style home, fourth in the masterplan's pattern, between Dutch Colonial and Tudor Revival.

Antonia turns to me. "You're coming, aren't you? This is your chance."

I feel his eyes, but I do not look back at Zeke as I get out of the car and follow. We are whittled down to three, creeping down Coronet in broad daylight.

"I'll kill him," Antonia says between her teeth.

"Calm down," Kent says. "We're just going to scare the guy."

The Ranch-style is unadorned, modest brown, landscaping evergreen. The Dodge cools in the driveway. From behind the pre-formatted scrim of the screen door, the man stares. His face looks like a composite of many faces.

"This is my property," he says to us as we hover on the sidewalk.

"This is a free country," Antonia shouts back. "We can stand here as long as we want."

On my walk to the Hellers', the man had put up a suitable show of fatherliness, neighborliness, of easy summertime concern, but no more.

"Do not make me tell you twice." He closes the door behind him, the turn of the dead bolt like a brute safe latching shut.

"Let's go around back," Antonia says.

Kent laughs. "I am not doing that."

"You and your brother are pussies, the both of you." She takes my arm and starts marching. "Come on. He can't hide out in his shithole forever."

Antonia is a natural-born stalker. Light on her feet and unrelenting. I imagine her on the prowl, circling her old home in Bayonne while her father sits in his recliner, dragged into the center of an otherwise vacant living room.

"He just asked if I wanted a ride," I whisper. We post up by the hedges in the backyard, the ones boxing in the AC unit.

"Don't be naive. Here." She hands me a landscaping rock the size of a golf ball. "Aim there." She points to the sliding glass doors, venetian blinds blocking the view inside. She palms one of her own, double in size. "We toss, and we run."

"Are you joking?"

"Does it look like I'm joking?" It seems there are only two chutes away from the present—to give her what she wants or withhold it. It's the type of power I dreamed of having.

"You first," she says, but my first throw is half-hearted and misses, bouncing off the vinyl siding.

Antonia hands me another, the size of a fat apple. "Again. Harder."

This is what she wants. This time, the weight in my hand is determinative. This time, I do not miss. The cause and effect are straightforward, and the entire sheet of glass shatters. A thousand ridged diamonds spray the wooden deck.

"Yes," Antonia says. "Good girl."

There's swearing from inside the house. The man steps through his crude new portal and onto the deck. My fingers have closed around another rock. This one I have picked out myself, bigger than the last, enough to do damage, if I make my aim true.

I pull back my arm and Antonia asks what I'm doing. The man spots us and freezes.

"Fuck it. Go, go," Antonia says, and drops her rock at our feet.

She says my name and the man repeats it.

"I've got you," he says.

We charge past Kent, who is on the street demanding to know what the fuck we've done. The three of us take off down Coronet. There are shouts behind us, but they are lost on the wind at our heels and we are halfway to long gone.

Antonia sets the pace and I match it, barely. Kent lags breath-lessly behind. I can't remember the last time I've surged into a full sprint. I can feel the air on my teeth, adrenaline a shot in the ass as I dodge divots. I will not look back. I do not look back. I am proud of what I've done.

It is in this vein that the second half of my night unfolds. I am a primed pump, inclined toward distrust and remedial action. The getaway ride back to the Hellers' is short and sweet. I tell Zeke I've got to go, and he does not question why. He looks like he might faint again. He is busy flexing and unflexing his fists in the Hellers' festive backyard, reclaiming his level head as his mother pours punch and sings the Pledge of Allegiance like a folk song. Kent is stalking around for someone to punch. He grips Antonia's hip, draws her roughly to his lips. She pulls back, swipes at his chest. There is somewhere else I'm meant to be. I picture Fawn and my mother on the rooftop, heads thrown back in laughter, gleeful at my absence. Entwined in Kent's arms, Antonia reaches past him, to me.

"You got an arm on you," she says. "Call me and we'll check out that spot of yours."

"What spot?" Kent asks, but I am already waving goodbye.

On Geronimo Street, black smoke pumps from an open window in the warehouse's upper floor. I take the concrete steps by threes and when I burst in, it's all smiles. From his end of the long table, Billy the ex-boyfriend waves. Beside him, the tidy woman from Connecticut.

My mother is flapping a dishcloth toward the window. "Sorry," she says. "Wee accident with a roast chicken."

I haven't seen Billy since he and my mother broke up months ago. When he moved out, I brought down the last box to his hatchback while my mother pretended to sort the newly liberated closets. I had been rooting for him. I planned to absorb the full magnitude of his exit and watch him drive off into the sunset, but he stalled behind a parallel parker and then hit a stoplight so I just went inside.

Now he is back at his customary spot, and he's brought company.

For starters, Billy is smiling too much. The woman from Connecticut introduces herself. Everyone keeps glancing toward the kitchen, waiting for my mother to intervene, but she is darting around chopping this and that. The happy couple had been traveling upstate. Friendly well-wishes were sent a few days before. The route lined up, so did the timing. Someone insisted. *Voilà*. That's what Billy says. That and, "It's good to see you, kid."

This was why my mother had come back from the city unannounced, with her overflowing grocery bags and renewed show of stamina. For him.

When Billy and I get to catching up, my mother decides to speak. "The dog got out again. Your sister's looking for him out back." She is referring to the vacant lot the warehouse borders, our de facto yard. She prattles on about the eye-opening experiences of pet ownership, as if she has ever picked up his shit or seen how grateful the dog is when he eats, how he can sigh the way a human sometimes sighs.

Billy's new wife has pulled her body in close, making herself as tiny as possible. I realize there is a swarm of ants overrunning the cheese board before her.

"Soon we'll head up to the roof with the beer and champagne and wine and gin and put it all on ice so the heat doesn't get to it. We'll forget about the chicken. We've got the best view in town, don't we? Billy loves this view. Go see what you can do about the dog and your sister," she says. "And be back for fireworks. I've got crudités but what's the point if we miss the show?"

In a few years, Billy will be a father of two, back in the currency trading game, the owner of a mid-century renovation in Greenwich to be showcased in *Architectural Digest*. We will become an aberrant blip in the trajectory of his otherwise merciful, straitlaced life.

I find Fawn easily. She is standing at the edge of the back lot, a clearing made of concrete, hedged by an old dumpster and a few tangled trees wild with neglect. I call her name and she jumps, squints across the lot, waves. "I found something," she calls, and I go to her.

It is a headless goose, no feather out of place. Each frond is oiled and glossy. I almost expect the animal to stir as I draw close, to peek out from between its scapulars and shudder its wings in preflight, having overslept as its flock took to the river. That's how clean the decapitation is. The shape of its body is so perfect that I want to take it in my arms, like a bread boule, or the hull of a tiny boat.

"What happened to it?" I ask.

"I was looking for Peanut and saw it." She points her toe at its body. "Look."

"I see it. Do you think he got to it?"

"No. Peanut wouldn't."

The goose's feathers ripple in the breeze, the plumage of his chest like a silk ascot.

"Is Billy still there?" she asks.

"Still there."

The way our mother comes and goes, fluttering noisily in and out of our lives and loft, is enough to make us feel unreal, like dolls that only come alive when held. Even when she is here, it is hard to guess where she is. Fawn and I agree that Billy loved her once. He should know better than to have come.

"I don't want to look at this anymore," I say. "I'm supposed to bring you back."

All that ire from earlier in the day has gone soft in my stomach. I try to get it back by conjuring apex predators snapping nurslings in two, the feel of my hand striking Fawn's cheek, her smaller one reciprocating, glass going to pieces, finishing what I started.

Fawn looks over her shoulder where the warehouse looms rectangular. The spill of concrete between us appears liquid, and impassable.

"Are you still mad?" she asks.

I look down at her, expecting her best show of penitence, but she is only asking because she is curious, not because she is hoping for a certain answer.

"I don't know. Not as much as before, I guess."

"They play reruns."

"That's not the point. Obviously."

"But that's why you're mad. Because you can't watch anymore."

"Are you going to give the tapes back? Are we even now?"

"I lost them."

"Liar."

"I did. I put them out here in a secret spot and now I can't remember where it is."

"Stop trying to get back at me. Stop touching my stuff."

"Stop being mad at me. Care about me more than you care about the dog."

Only we can speak to each other like this, in lists of commands. I wait for the anger to rev up. I am prepared to hold tightly to its edges, just as my hand held the rock before I let it fly.

"Let's go," I say. "Let's get this over with."

In a softer voice Fawn asks, "Can we look for Peanut first?"

"Who's we?"

"Just five more minutes?"

"Don't you want to see the fireworks?"

"He's going to get scared out here. Please?" she says, a word she hardly ever uses.

"Fine," I say. "Five more minutes and I'm done."

We walk downtown together. The sun is on the outs, but bursts of last light shoot through alleys and the evacuated plots between buildings. Halo light flushes all the ancient cornices, friezes, mansard roofs. A few firecrackers rebound off the long plane of abandoned buildings, all those boarded windows and doors. We call out, "Peanut! Peanut Butter!" and I think of what Zeke said once, to never name a pet something you don't want to go around screaming at night.

"Look over there," Fawn says as two cats groom each other on an old stoop, but the house it led to has been demolished. I could walk up the steps and right off the edge. Life goes on, I think. It could all be made handsome again, or at least habitable, if we were the sort of people who knew what to do with it. I whistle and make kissy noises. I call out for him with renewed enthusiasm. The dog has disappeared before, but he usually comes galumphing down the alley eventually. I realize how much of my night has been devoted to search parties, of rooting out beings that would rather be left alone.

"Let's go up," I say as we arrive at the warehouse's double doors. "If you want, we can make fancy drinks." Coca-Cola in highball glasses, filled to the brim with crushed ice and lemon slices. "I'll make popcorn, and we can bring up a blanket. We don't have to watch with them." Another firework whistles up into the sky, raining down like gunfire. "I bet you're right. Peanut is just freaked out by all the noise. He's probably just hiding for now."

"Yeah," Fawn says and brightens. "I want fancy drinks."

"Don't worry. He always comes back."

"He's getting old anyway."

"He's not that old."

"Maybe he found his family, from before." She shrugs and blows her bangs out of her face. "I'm ready to go inside now. I'll be okay."

"Are you sure?"

"I'm sure," she says, and disappears through the doors.

It's dark enough now. The show will start any minute. I take a deep breath to brace myself for the spectacle inside. I want to go into my room with my magazines. I want to read telling interviews with the stars. I wish I had never left The Gables. I wish I had thrown that last rock.

My hand is on the door when down Geronimo, where the corner meets Vine, a pair of floodlights blink on.

The lights are motion-triggered, arranged to illuminate the bay of an old ice depot. There is the same overgrowth, the same flamboyant litter piled high at the base of the brick building. After an unremarkable moment, the floodlights blink off again with a dull *tink*. I do not know what compels me closer. Chop, chop, I think. The slut dies first.

As I near the bay, the floodlight snaps on again and I find myself at the edge of the beam. That is when I see the dog among the rubble.

I notice him because his tail moves, and a slick spot on his fur catches the light like tinsel.

I can't tell if he has been buried in the trash on purpose, or if he has burrowed there for cover, a place to die. He does not lift his head when I kneel beside him. Instead, his long side ripples as if to displace water. I say his name so he knows it's me. I go to touch him and he shows his teeth. Lights out.

I wave a hand over my head to trigger the lights again, and I soothe Peanut Butter's head with the other. I can't tell what's wrong with him. There is no obvious wound of entry or exit. He starts to gag, and his gums are gray as he heaves, bile curdling in his lips, the smell like burnt milk.

I shout down the street for help, but a series of fireworks explodes and the boom triples down the block. The far-off pomp and circumstance of "America the Beautiful" strikes up, blasting over a loudspeaker at the high school baseball field. My hands hover over his body for some unknown length of time, detonations compounding.

I am useless, but the dog licks at my palm, my knuckles, the space between my fingers and up my wrists, giving the tiniest nibbles from his flat front teeth, a ravenous little suckle of desperation. I ask what's wrong with him. I press around his belly like I've seen doctors do and he whines. I have nothing to offer, no comfort or plan. I think—I could walk away right now, absolve myself, and who could know what I've seen? He is an animal. Another species. We don't belong to each other. Lights out.

I thought it would be obvious, that I would sense the life leach from the tips of his fur, the warmth of his scruff going cold, but everything feels just the same. His breathing stops. A rat scuttles by unbothered and the lights flick on again.

When the song is over, there is great applause in the distance. People will be packing up. The cars will bottleneck in the parking lot. I can hear my mother and my sister, our nervous guests on the rooftop. I sit with the dead dog in my lap and listen to the patter of their voices. Everyone is in good spirits, because the ordeal of the evening will soon be over for them. They joke about something, and no one asks where I am.

Lights out.

II

THE PIÑATA CLUB

7

When I was deemed fit for reentry into the world, I went where everyone else was going. The city was obvious. A parent had been felled, funds bequeathed. Money burned a hole in my pocket and I was keenly aware that I'd arrived at the same crossroads my parents had at my age. I told myself to make sound decisions as a tribute to my father. He labored nonstop to amass his modest fortune, but had been struck from the earth before he could fully enjoy the spoils.

I rented a streamlined one-bedroom in his old neighborhood. What was once considered blight was now considered character, like the two-screen movie theater with its busted seats, the bodega called BATTERIES CIGARETTES HOT DOGS ATM with its obese black cat. Even the pocket park had its own scuffed-up allure, shaded by a giantess photinia shrub in which rats scrabbled and birthed. To these wayward charms I was not immune. I saw myself waging a scenic life, a life in montage. I was part of something. Like weather, the neighborhood happened to all of us.

I was fresh from Veld then and had been hammered into certain habits. I fought the duplicitous itch to journal, to garden, to report to the kitchen for my post, but this new freedom was full of trip wires, Pavlovian lunges toward self-improvement and public vulnerability. Some mornings I'd wake up with no idea whether I was indoors or out. I dreamt of deep ravines that beckoned, their deceiving sunken centers jagged with rocks and splintered trunks. I had seen a girl go rolling headfirst into one while she was still strapped into her thirty-pound pack. The sound, the rattle of camp cutlery and carabiners as she bounced down, haunted me. I dreamt often of the unjust angle of her leg as she slammed into the ground and went still, but even when I woke there was no relief, sure as I was that two goons were coming to bust through my door, cart me back against my will, make me earn my way out again. I became obsessed with the rituals of security. From above, I watched the streets fill and empty on repeat. Everything had to be shut, sealed, and checked twice, or else some nefarious caller might break down the door, or scale four floors and climb into my window—discover me in my bed and make me pay.

I took the job at the restaurant to meet people. My kitchen work detail at Veld had been educational, and prep work whittled down my thinking. I watched in wonder as my hands moved in symmetry and produced nourishment. I liked the feel of a knife in my grip. I appreciated the efficiency expressed by a sharp edge. I was hardly good enough for a city kitchen, but I could wait tables, at least. Finito was an upscale but discreet neighborhood spot a few blocks away, with thick velvet curtains and a front door goldleafed with a loping letter *F*. I practiced the route to work twice before my first shift. I clicked through reviews of the restaurant, then clicked through to the profiles of reviewers and went down an endless chute of tangential impressions I edited into my own. I could hardly wait to take orders. I believed it was the beginning of the rest of my life.

After the party at Rod's loft, I took up smoking again so Steph and I could banter during breaks in the service alley. I started buying her brand and kept a pack ready. To be near her, I went to parties that left me mirthless by night's end, but it was important I become believable, someone Steph would reasonably consider a romantic outlet when viewed in the right light. I used the cash reserves bequeathed to me by my father's estate to buy monochromatic clothes and European sneakers. I was given the right haircut, the right finishing cream. I cut and pasted model rooms together until my apartment looked like a photo of an apartment. Step by step, I saw my adult self emerging in patchwork. I had never considered myself capable of projecting an image, but I understood and liked what snap judgment I might elicit.

Steph and I started seeing each other because everyone said we should. When the restaurant crew went out for drinks after close, she and I would get lumped together in a booth, bow our heads like conspirators, and wait for others to implicate us. I lured her from a group setting by dangling elite dinner reservations, and money moved the meter in miraculous fashion. We ate where everyone important was eating. We sampled from every course, drank with every plate. I listened better than any boyfriend she ever had, and in this way it was easy to surpass them. Steph was an ideal counterpart. She understood exactly the scene she was in and how best to play it. Her pupils would flare as the bill arrived and I'd slide my credit card toward the server without a glance at the astronomical total. This was foreplay. Walking home, we'd sidle close, toss our heads back and laugh, eyeing the sidewalk to see who might be coveting our moment.

I still thought about Antonia sometimes. It was easy to locate her online, though her pictures and missives broadcasted only what everyone's did—that she was, allegedly, seizing the day. It was possible to navigate a digital map to the Wepplers' coordinates, or rather, the coordinates of the lot on which their house once stood. Giving Antonia the Wepplers' house had been strategic, and I'd had little else to offer then. Now, I had New York. I didn't know anything about money or the way it would make me feel. I clicked around until I found a missing piece, whatever it was, and I did this over and over until my fledgling savings were gone and my credit cards were in the red.

It was in those final weeks of impending financial doom that things between us fell apart. Steph and I had been together a year. Twelve months pockmarked by her various infidelities and my various hang-ups, manifested as brief but prolific denotations of paranoia. When she cheated, it was always with men. This should not have hurt me as it did, but I'd set fire to a small fortune, acquired a kingdom of specialty goods, and still she sought something I could never hope to give. That was how I thought of it, at least. Becoming a victim of love did not taste bittersweet as I'd dreamed. It was solitary. Other people only cared about pain they could feel.

Steph started booking more jobs and soon struck gold with a national commercial spot for fast-food fried chicken, followed by an ad campaign for a coworking company. There came more networking, more sponsored happenings, more auditions and mid-tier gigs, more handsome costars she ran lines with through the night. Perhaps she sensed this new life waiting for her. As she pulled away, I clung all the more. I became lyrical in my praise. I showered her with gifts I could not afford. I waited for her after work even if my shift was long over, and I canvassed her social media feeds, descending down a dark tunnel populated by friends of friends and D-list faces and comments that could be interpreted any which way my mind devised.

One night, she canceled our dinner plans, and I allowed forty-five minutes to pass exactly before I went to her block. I watched her window go from light to dark. I texted her and pressed my phone to my chest so I wouldn't miss the vibration when it came. Inside her apartment, I imagined an epic orgy involving every man she had ever slept with. I pictured her pausing, mid-fellatio, just to reject my call. I didn't realize it was already over.

The days after, however many there were, melted into a singular scape of brutal daylight. It was summer and the weather was unseasonably hot. A dry wind twisted down sidewalks, blowing trash and the fine powder of a city disintegrating en masse. The floorboards in my apartment were warm to the touch. My credit cards' projected completion dates were sixteen years in the future, and I began selling everything. I worked and worked and stunk like shrimp scampi, while Steph's auditions escalated, or so I heard through the grapevine at Finito. We weren't speaking, no matter the methods I tried. I left voicemails, a dozen daily text messages in all hues of disinterest or desperation, A/B testing the right tonal combination that might win a reply. I tried to schedule my shifts around hers, but her hours shrunk, and soon she wasn't coming in at all. I sent a text saying I had two coveted tickets for an off-Broadway show I knew she was dying to see. Though she never responded, I waited outside the theater and sat through the first act. I would not admit that I actually hated her, that it had become a matter of brute dignity, that the good times had come and gone.

A few weeks after her radio silence sunk in, I waited for Steph outside her building.

Her window had been dark for hours, and when someone emerged I caught the door, relishing the AC and familiar smells, the late-night sounds of neighbors pulsing inside their human vaults. The walls shone with moisture. It felt natural to fish around the top of her doorframe and come away with the spare key. If we could only speak face-to-face, one last time, I would have done everything within my power, and then I could rest.

Her apartment was empty. Like Goldilocks, I climbed inside her bed. I let her scent soothe me into my first sleep in days. I dreamt of all the glorious plans I'd sketched for us: the brownstone, flashbulbs at film premieres, a book tour for me. These visions were so alive, so true to real time they were like premonitions, proof my loyalty would pay off if I kept the faith. Then, the reel slipped.

Technicolor bled from the life I sought as I turned beneath cool sheets. The footage caught fire, the future ablaze, and climbing through the toasted celluloid was my sister.

In the dream, I was following Fawn through the woods around our father's property. She was dashing behind tree trunks, vanishing into rock gullies, only to emerge breathless along the path ahead. The woods refracted and morphed like a kaleidoscope. The sky above was the true surface, a mirror image of Steph's apartment where I slept. I tried to keep up with her. I knew where she was taking me.

When I woke, Steph was standing over me with a frying pan in her grip. Even in my disorientation, caught red-handed in her bed, the first thing I felt was betrayal.

I put my hands up between us, one reaching for her and the other guarding my head. There was a tug at both my ankles and I realized we were not alone.

I was dragged to the end of the bed and tossed onto the ground.

"Get the fuck up," a handsome, angry face shouted, but when I tried to find my feet, he kicked me over with the tip of his boot. "I said get up."

Steph was half-shouting and working her phone at the same time. It was probable she was calling the cops, but it seemed equally probable she was ticking through messages.

"This isn't cool," she was saying loudly at her screen. "Seriously."

The handsome face picked me up by the collar and brought me to my feet. I thought of the T-shirt I was wearing—eighty-eight dollars, a basic white, now irrevocably misshapen. I wouldn't be able to get any money for it now. His fist connected with my right eye and I knew by the sting of it that he was wearing a ring, a shiny, sporty number I saw glimmering at me through the blood coursing from my brow.

"What are you doing?" Steph shrieked at one of us.

"I'm sorry," I said, fumbling in the direction of the door.

"Oh shit," the handsome face said. "It's a girl."

He twisted the ring around his finger. "Sorry, ma'am," he said, his voice an octave higher. "I don't hit women."

"I'm calling the police," Steph said.

"Babe," the handsome face said. "Don't."

"I didn't mean to," I said. "This is a misunderstanding."

"Please leave," Steph said. "Now. Please leave now. I'm asking nicely."

"Listen, ma'am," the handsome face said. "You better do as she says."

"Just tell me what I did wrong. What did I do? What happened?" I clutched my eye and felt for the knob on the door behind me. There was the urge to make a mad grab for some souvenir, evidence I'd ever been inside.

"I can't think with you bleeding all over, okay?" she said. "It just would be so much easier if we had never met."

It was the last time she ever saw me.

I went home a wreck. I opened the window in the living room and sat at its ledge for hours. I chain-smoked Steph's old cigarettes until the pack was gone and tossed it out the window. I played the same song over and over, because it made crying involuntary. Track 4 from the Playa Mala record: "Bombs Away."

My father said they wanted to be the Beatles. Their three-part harmonies and chugalug Telecasters united in a convincing off-brand imitation. *I looked up and saw/ the writing on the wall/ sky the shade of candy blue/ Down they cruised/ Guided angels, devils, all/ Bombs away/ to You.* I gazed out across the rooftops and the same hot wind dissolved each tear. I carried on like this for hours, until the roaches streamed from the sewers and the shadows stretched, until the cool-off, when a milder breeze fanned from the river block by block. My maiden voyage to New York had run aground. There was no money left to throw at this equation, no lover to target with my attentions, no friends to keep me honest, no vision of the future. It was time to start over again, though I'd hardly just begun.

Soon I'd sell all my collections and finest things to move into Victor's spare room. With his help, I'd create a profile on a freelance board, invent areas of expertise and testimonials from satisfied clients. I'd list him as a reference, but no one really cared about that. All business was conducted through keystrokes. What mattered most was that the work read as believable, if someone out there would convert. I knew how to hook. Beginnings came easier.

Almost a year later, I saw Steph on my TV screen. She had landed a pilot on a teen network, though she was pushing thirty by then. It was strangely soothing to lower the volume of her voice, or raise it. Turn her on, or off. I could rewind her. I could pause her mid-sentence, leave her hovering indefinitely. I watched her cry, again and again. The show survived a single season, and there were no breakout stars, no spin-offs. It went quietly, the world within it shelved. Steph was destined to be lost in L.A.

So long, I thought, and sipped my second cup of coffee, looking out into morning, bright and newborn. I touched my brow and felt the scab there, brought my fingers to my lips and tasted the old blood. Goodbye to all that, I'd read. Good riddance to bad rubbish. What else was there? A dozen aphorisms from Veld and elsewhere wound on my tongue. In the fire, let me be cleansed.

In the months after my relationship with Steph imploded, I found myself returning to the few details I knew of my parents' doomed-to-fail romance, in an effort to conduct my own postmortem. I was not in love anymore, and I was proud that my yearning had largely been quashed to sadness, which was easier to bear. I did not return to the same fantasies or obsessive behaviors. I had put the past behind me, and yet. If Steph were to call in the middle of the night,

I knew I would go to her without question. How could both things be true? I thought I could cure myself of this, the longing to be consumed.

When I was younger, I tried all the time to trap my mother into telling me the story. Leading questions were met with a dozen manic shrugs. To explain away the era of her life that accounted for a marriage, the warehouse, and her offspring, my mother used many metaphors, but they all boiled down to the same amorphous grievance. They had never seen eye to eye. This gave the impression that a certain contortion was necessary to remain interlocked in love. The challenge was in how things were always shifting unbeknownst to you. It was all about alignment. You must remain flexible, or else alone.

He left when my mother was pregnant with Fawn. I was about five years old. There was room to remember more of my father, but all I had were orphaned sequences from the early years when it was just us three. These vignettes were highly specific and yet absent of context, like the opening credits of a sitcom. There was me: strapped into a car seat in a coat that's too tight, an icy glare through the perforated baby shade as we go down Geronimo Street, curving the potholes. Cut to my mother standing at a slab of cutting board, dusted with flour, lipstick on, inexplicably executing a fine chiffonade. Cut to my father. Strapped into a tool belt. He wears a flannel shirt with two pockets on the chest and a pencil between his teeth. He swings a hammer. B-roll lingers on the warehouse, the ragged town, the new baby, hijinks of a life under construction.

The whole warehouse was in disrepair then. There was no view but scaffolding, no scent but for sawdust, fumes of primer, candle soot. The highway had not yet come, but there was a cavity blasted into the earth where it would surely go, its skeleton erected piecemeal over the coming decade. In the floor of my improvised bedroom, there was a perfect hole the size of a baseball. I would get on my knees and put my eye to the open knot, peer down to where my father was pounding nails on the first floor. Sometimes he arranged his hands to frame a right angle, and he'd scrunch his face at the wall like a door might appear before him, an escape. To save money, we ate peanut butter and jelly sandwiches, endless pots of rice and beans. He had sworn off my mother's family money, and they were beginning to worry that it was all too grandiose. A gallery on the first floor. Living quarters on the second. Studios on the top level to house my father's music, my mother's hypothetical art, a place where all their friends might come and produce. The roof would hold a chicken coop and a garden to feed us all. One day, the site would be credited as fertile ground for household names. You might have to apply to get in. The list was always growing. They were as young as I am now.

After he left, so many details dissolved. I was too little to cherish anything. The purpose of his existence retreated, and it wasn't until I was older, when Fawn could mostly take care of herself and my mother was free to wander, that I went looking for the signs he'd been there. His handiwork was evident in the unfinished spaces around the warehouse, or in artifacts left behind, as mundane as the artifacts in a museum, all those functional mechanisms, pottery, and tools. When I started paying attention, I saw these relics everywhere. Winter gloves at the bottom of an old basket. A can of Barbasol under the sink. A stately suit rack in the junk closet, like the drawn outline of a stout little man. I could tell whose music was whose, because the albums on the top shelf were the ones that got played. They were my mother's favorites, and I knew them up and down. What was left on the bottom shelf, the far-right corner, went unplayed. That was where I found it. An anonymous white sleeve, track listings in pencil. An original.

The first time I played it, I knew it was my father's voice. The memory had stowed away in case a moment such as this might occur, the timbre of his song rushing back even after years having gone without. I played the record straight through, body locked in place before the altar of the turntable. On the second listen, I took a paper and pen and wrote down every word I could decipher, playing songs at half-speed to catch each phrase for the lyric book I'd assemble and refine over the years, shown to no one, the first true object of my personal archive. At four tracks, the record was a spare source document, but each arrangement was a time capsule. I might hold it side by side with the present day like a book of translation. I wanted to believe that its discovery meant something.

One day after school, I played the record for Zeke. We were in seventh grade, sitting on the floor of my bedroom where I'd hauled the turntable and the speakers in an ad hoc audiophile setup while my mother was in the city another night. We were eating microwaved soft pretzels. It was early spring and I'd thrown open the windows; all the goose shit was beginning to thaw. I watched Zeke's face out of the corner of my eye, waiting for the aha moment. I could tell he was trying to produce one, but he had never been a very good actor.

"You can tell me," I said. "I don't care."

"I like it."

"Really. You can say."

He munched thoughtfully. A coming growth spurt would give him six inches, but I could still wrap my fingers all the way around his elbow. He was drowning in hand-me-downs from Kent. "It's not that I don't like it. It's just I don't know what it means."

"Well, yeah. Half is in Spanish."

"This supposed to be like, rock and roll?"

It sounded so one-dimensional the way he said it. Rock and roll.

"You have the worst taste," I said. "What do you even like? Who is even your favorite?"

"You said you didn't care."

"Obviously I care."

"Maybe you have to know the person to understand what's happening. I bet your mom loves this stuff. I feel like it would be on one of her radio stations."

"What radio stations?"

"I don't know, okay? You're putting all this pressure on me. What about Fawn?"

"What about her?"

"Hasn't she heard it?"

"You're the only person I showed. Anyway, she wouldn't get it. She's too little. She doesn't have taste. I would never play it for her."

"I don't get it."

"You have nine billion brothers and stepbrothers and cousins. You don't know what it's like to live with her. To have it just be us." Mr. and Mrs. Heller had each been married twice, and each marriage had produced no fewer than three bouncing babies, all boys. There were always tussles and insults and wrestling matches rampaging around the house, but there was too a sense that the family unit, hybridized as it was, came first.

"What do my brothers have to do with anything?" Zeke said. "I don't even have my own clothes, or room. You're allowed to do whatever you want."

"I shouldn't have shown anyone," I said, and stopped the record spinning.

"You should show her." I couldn't tell if he was saying it because it was the right thing to do or because he meant it. "Don't you think she would want to hear?"

I fiddled with a long cable and did not look up until he sighed.

"Okay," he said, and rubbed the pretzel salt from his fingertips onto his jeans. "Play it again. I'll listen harder this time."

Whatever alchemy was meant to occur upon Fawn's and my first meeting, or even after our initial adjustment period was over, according to the baby books—the result of exposure, normalization, affection, complacency, acceptance—never happened for us.

When she was brought to me in her pink bundle and settled into my lap, when I was told, "This is your baby sister. You're a big sister now," I remember thinking—who is this supposed to be?

There was only one season, one autumnal window in time, when I thought an alternative was possible. I thought it was an evolution in our relationship. It was the era in which I became Fawn's great fixation. Her interest in me at first expressed itself through mimicry. She followed me around the house, hovered in the doorway while I hung out on my bed. She repeated phrases I said, assumed the same opinions. She pretended to scribble notes about me like she was doing reconnaissance. Sometimes, I spoke at length about whatever I felt like and she recorded my every word in her own personal shorthand, nodding like a journalist with the scoop. Most notably, I became the intermediary for all communication with our mother. She was recovering from another bad breakup and was haunting the loft more than usual. Heartbreak made her loose-lipped and she talked a lot, which crowded the natural rhythms of the loft. For a while, I enjoyed playing Fawn's telepathic representative regarding grievances big and small. If she wanted to go to the movies on a weeknight, or cut her hair like mine, or have more syrup on her pancakes, these demands had to come through me.

"She needs to see you do it," I would tell my mother.

"I put it on already. It's right there. See? Syrup."

Fawn looked at me and shook her head.

"She needs to see you do it again," I said, "or she won't eat it."

I even helped her lobby for a dog.

My mother's skepticism of this new alliance was palpable, but how could she argue? We were finally getting along.

I was the last to notice when Fawn's devotion began to wane. She became impatient with me, critical of the pace and tone of my negotiations on her behalf. Sometimes when I spoke at length, I'd look over at her to bask in the doting concentration I'd come to take for granted, but I could now see I was boring her. It didn't matter that her pattern of obsession followed by rejection was not novel, because I was now the one exposed at its center. I tried to jostle her into reverence again, float an activity I thought would reinvigorate her. She could watch me pick out an outfit. She could listen to me sing along to the radio and grade my vocal performance. If I could unveil a side of me, a talent or taste that she'd never seen or might wish to emulate, she couldn't run through me like she had the rest of her doomed fixations, but it was not up to me.

Fawn took over her own negotiations, and she was better at it. She closed the door to her bedroom. We bumped around the bathroom vanity, ignored each other, sniped. I realized the only way I could stand her was when I was most needed, or else when she was most like me.

Soon enough this abbreviated era of peace was lost to all the ambient tensions of the loft, our mother's comings and goings, the interloping mystery men, the carousel of pet projects, the rigors of puberty. Fawn and I went back to our corners and slept soundly, without a single dream of the other, at least for a long time.

What never left was the bite of déjà vu. For years after, even now, if an Antonia or a Steph or whoever else, romantic or not, nods idly at something I say and turns from me, whenever I feel the room go cold—I wonder. What had my sister first identified in me worth wanting, and where had it gone?

8

From the Fourth Floor of the Residence, we watched from the windows as beams of light swept the grounds of Veld. The grounds crew was looking for something or someone. The world was otherwise an inkblot.

"Where the fuck are they going?" said Gia, the conspiracy theorist in our midst, and my reluctant roommate.

Electricity had been elusive since an afternoon thunderstorm barreled through, and though the rain had passed, campus oaks writhed in the wind and shed their droplets in clashes against the roof and windows.

"Is that rain or not rain?" said Beanie, the airhead.

Gia tapped the glass. "It's a trick. The lights work just fine. This is a test."

"A test on what?"

"I feel faint," said Harlow, the diva. "I will faint right here if I don't eat something."

After cracking the bone in her big toe and hiking on it for a week, she had developed a slight but graceful limp, dignified like a veteran.

"You're just going to puke it up later," Gia said. "Conserve your energy."

"You're a real bitch, you know that?" Harlow said, but she didn't sound offended.

"I do know that," Gia said.

There were four of us in the Piñata Club. Membership was compulsory and preassigned by counselors. There was Seedling Club, Cosmo Club, and the coveted Love Club. Gardening, astronomy, and tennis. Girls wanted Love Club because the instructor they imported from town was handsome and wore very thin athletic shorts. The appeal was lost on some of us, but the tennis court neighbored the utility shed, a preferred blind spot for smoking, fucking around, or whatever else you wanted to do in private. They gave Love Club to the good girls.

As Veld's party-planning committee, it was the Piñata Club's duty to mind birthdays. We were given preselected Hallmark cards and sent floor to floor at the Residence requesting signatures. This was chief among our oversight. No crude comments allowed. When someone scribbled, EAT SHIT AND DIE we tweaked it to EAT SWEETS AND PIE. You could hardly tell the difference. After that, our duties ceased to be until the next Veld girl completed her revolution around the sun.

From the darkened doorway, our floor leader growled.

"You two." She was talking to Harlow and Beanie. "Back to your room."

"Jesus. You scared the shit out of me," Harlow said.

"Watch your mouth. Don't be an ignoramus."

"Okay, we'll go," Harlow said. "I'm just here because I have a question. For Science."

"About what?"

"Photosynthesis," Beanie supplied. Sometimes she was quicker than she looked.

There was a dark, blank pause from our floor leader, and then, "Two minutes."

A moment later, Gia released a long breath. "What a cow."

"Think that's funny?" our floor leader said inside the dark.

"Oh. I thought you left."

And then she had, but none of the Piñata Club adhered. Our floor leader had been at Veld longer than any of us, a kind of pitiable hybrid between student and staff.

"My blood sugar is nil," Harlow said.

"What do they think they're doing?" I said. "They're just standing there."

Out on the lawn, the grounds crew had reassembled in a tight circle, flashlights in concentric arrangement, as if they might burst into a synchronized routine.

"*Why?*" Gia asked. "That is the question. To what *end*."

"I can't take it anymore." Harlow went for the door and a ghostish moon turned her profile silver. I could see her perfect hair bounce at her shoulders. "I'm going down to the kitchen."

"That's a violation," Beanie said.

Harlow made a shadow of a gesture in my direction. "Can you deal with her, please?"

In Group, Beanie told us she used to be smart. The summer before high school, her older sister was driving them home from a house party and took a back road slick with mud. When she rounded the bend at a frivolous speed the car flipped and careened into a ditch. Her sister was fine, but Beanie was in the hospital for the next six months with a brain injury. She spent two years hypnotized by prescription pain-killers. Two years of petty theft, truancy, dastardly highs wherein she stole her mother's car and crashed it, tried to sell herself to an under-cover cop, began and ended an affair with her lecherous guidance counselor, suffered a miscarriage, and ruined her cousin's wedding. She told us, "People think I'm dumb, but I still know how to have fun."

The lights on the Fourth Floor flickered on again. None of us moved. We touched our faces and tamped down our hair, waiting to see if it would hold.

"Is this the test?" Beanie asked.

Gia held up her hand. "Wait for it."

A moment later the lights died. I didn't need to see her smirk to know it was there.

"Well?" Harlow said. "Is anyone listening to me? Am I going alone, or do you fat asses care to join me?"

It was my say-so she was waiting for. The airhead, the conspiracy theorist, the diva, and me. The ringleader. "Fine," I told them. "Follow my voice."

There were four flights down. Three to the main level, and one more to the basement kitchen where I reported for work detail. A few telltale steps were known for squealing, so we slid along the edges of the baseboards with our toes and descended with bated breath. It was not the first time we had skipped out at night. It should have been more of a thrill, all things considered, but our days were occupied in total. It was exhausting, trying to be healed. Every hour was chock full of opportunities for contrition, and my shift in the kitchen required real attention. My work was nothing like Gia's mindless photocopying in the admin office or Beanie and Harlow's cleaning crew. I had learned to dice an onion, to make bread. I figured I would be given a dull instrument for safety reasons, but the blade gave no resistance. The duller the blade, the more dangerous, I was told. A honed edge was easiest to control.

That night, there were no lights inside and no lights out. Bowen might as well have been a thousand miles away, and Deerie a mote upon a distant planet. When we slipped inside the kitchen, I told the girls to be quick. "I'm not doing laps for Harlow's snack."

She was wearing our lone headlamp. She went to the pantry and returned with a jar of Skippy. Steel appliances and the long planes of prep tables glinted like sheets of ice. The room smelled like beef stroganoff from dinner. She scooted onto a counter and started mawing.

"Can't you take that to go?" Gia asked. "I can hear you chomping."

"That's how you eat it," Harlow said.

"You could use a spoon."

"How about my middle finger?"

"Wait," Beanie said, and we all froze. "Do you hear that?"

There was only the pressure of wind against the hopper windows. Harlow crunched slowly through another mouthful.

"You know," Gia said, "I knew a girl who ate a peanut butter sandwich and then made out with her boyfriend who was deathly allergic. He died on the spot."

"Everybody knew a girl like that," I said, and the rest of us agreed.

On the trail, Gia and I butted heads over everything. Inside the great white void, her conspiracies had nothing to latch on to but the rest of us. Because I was the newest in our march, I brought with me a fresh gust from the outside world, and Gia took every opportunity to put me in my place. Once, when I failed to eat the entirety of my allotted half-cup of peanut butter at dinner, Gia tapped Shine on the shoulder.

"Show me the jar," he said. "You can't ration it. You must be calorically satisfied."

"I'm not going to eat it in one sitting like this," I said. "It's disgusting."

"Then scoop out what's left. Get rid of it."

"Take it," I said, offering the jar to Gia, who was watching a few steps behind him. "Have it. I don't care."

"No splitting," Shine said. "Eat it or chuck it."

"Why should it go to waste?"

He put his hands on his hips. "You're asking a lot of questions."

I scooped two fingerfuls and wiped them on the side of a log.

Gia thought I was a spy. She told me I looked old enough to be Shine's girlfriend, which was two digs in one. Her personal assessment was that I had split personalities. She interpreted mentions of my sister as some volatile subset of my psyche, which could make me liable to melee everyone in their sleep. When she was caught whittling a stick into a shiv using the sharp end of a rock, Shine sent her on solo as punishment. She had to camp a mile out from the rest of us during a long night of snow. We were not permitted to speak to her or go to her, but that night I thought I heard her calling through the woods. Sound carried on the mountain, toyed with the senses. A fox on his kill shrieked like a woman possessed. Wind in the high trees, a brook gorging on snowmelt, even soft rains roaming the face of the mountain—anything could sound like something else. The next morning, I asked Gia if she'd been scared.

"Greatness doesn't get scared," she had said, which was how she sometimes referred to herself. "I did see a bear though." Beanie had looked over and rolled her eyes.

Now, we were comparing abduction stories.

"Mine was very civilized," Harlow said. "I got home from my boyfriend's and my mom said I had guests upstairs, and I thought—who the fuck? I go up and guess who's hanging out in my room but Reggie and Don, two bald mall cops who shake my hand and ask how my night's going before they take me to a van, then a plane, then another van, and then to Maine."

"Did you not freak?" Beanie asked.

Harlow shook her head and the headlamp swept the kitchen. "I was out of my mind. I mean, swimming. Right before the plane, Reggie and Don go—you can take this pill to get relaxed or else we'll have to stick you. I was at Transformations in Utah before this, and I did a three-week in Hawaii, which you'd think was paradise except for the prehistoric bugs. So, I knew the drill. I told them hand it over. If it's goodbye, it's goodbye. Plus, I hate flying."

"So what?" Gia said. "One place I went had lockdowns every day. If you heard the bell, it was nose to floor. They'd put a knee on your back and grind your bones until you submitted. That's the kind of place you do not want. That's when you're in a jam, because there's no way out, no matter how you play it. This last time, they had to stake me out for days before I'd let them come get me. I knew too much. I required strategy."

"You are not that important," Harlow said, "but okay."

Gia scooted onto her own prep table. We all faced one another in the steady beam of Harlow's headlamp. "This is what happens when the goons come," Gia said. "Maybe a week went by before they let themselves be seen, but I knew they were there. My mother was acting strange. Poking around, asking philosophical-type questions. Where do you see yourself in the next few years, Gia? What do you want out of life, Gia? I knew something was, as they say, amiss. And it wasn't the first time I got gooned either, but then I got cocky and they came for me while I was sleeping, when my defenses were weak. They rip me out of bed, this one guy and a humongous lady, maybe six-three, six-four. Tremendous muscle tone, like an ox on steroids. They drive me up from Boston in the middle of the night. I tell them I have to pee and can they pull over at a gas station. I try and make a break through one of the windows in the bathroom because this had worked for me once before, on the way to Connection Point in New Mexico, but this isn't the humongous lady's first rodeo and she's posted outside. She sees me trying to wiggle out and shoves me back in by my forehead, starts screaming her head off. Code Red! Like she's FBI. Of course, it's all downhill from there because then they get the straps."

"The straps?" Beanie asked.

"They didn't use them on you?" Gia shook her head. "You must've gone willingly. The Big Hug. They strap you inside the van, all tied up and down. Goons only get paid if they deliver, so what do they care? I said it was kidnapping and they laughed their asses off. They farted the whole way there just to torture me. I was on the mountain longer than any of you people. It was the beginning of spring. Baby buds everywhere."

"That's more than a year," I said.

"That's not supposed to be allowed," Beanie said.

Gia accepted the jar of Skippy and ran her finger inside the rim, brought it to her lips, and let it hover. "*Allowed* is for the brochures. I can tell you with God's certainty, they'll keep you here until you'll admit to anything, and as soon as you do, they've got you. They tell your people, Gia's finally crying out for help, the program is working, it's best if she stays a little longer. Oh, and can you please send us a big fat check? Or else, she'll probably start breaking down again." She sucked the peanut butter from her fingertip. "Me? I have never been broken. I won't give them the satisfaction. That's why Dr. John hates me."

The ceiling above creaked at the invocation.

"Dr. John is a doctor," Beanie said.

"Yeah? A doctor of what?"

Beanie shrugged. "You can't deny that he's a good listener."

"And?" Harlow said. "What if I don't want to be listened to?"

"*And,*" Gia supplied, "Beanie just wants to fuck him, like her last counselor."

"*And,*" Beanie said, "maybe I do. Maybe I will."

Harlow snorted. "You're sick," she said. "I like this side of you."

"Enjoy his thousand-year-old balls," Gia said. "You picked a fine place to be a slut."

"Are you jealous?" Beanie said. I had never seen her like this. I could tell she was pleased having Gia on the run.

"There's nothing in this whole place, not one person, not one thing, that I would ever be jealous of," Gia said. "You people don't see the long game like I do. It's pathetic."

Beanie shrugged and let her legs dangle. "Let's go back upstairs. I can't stand the smell of peanut butter anymore."

The day's theme was Regrets.

In Group, it was good to crack open an anecdote to feed the staff once in a while, wave a past indiscretion under their noses so they could catch the scent of your rotten core. They would scribble notes of progress on clipboards, move down the line to examine each little hen. Otherwise, there were the closets on the Fifth Floor, ISO, used liberally for in-school isolation and carpeted floor to ceiling in shag green, like a wall of moss.

Harlow was sharing an egregious tale about her propensity for blind rages. She and her mother had roof-raising brawls. During the most recent row, Harlow threw a knife at her. Not to hurt her, she said. She didn't even remember doing it. She could only recall resurfacing days later in a hospital bed, naked but for a paper gown and a pair of handcuffs linked to the rail.

"I must've gone on a wild ride," she told us, but could not even be sure if substances were to blame. "I was probably fucked up. Most likely. But when I'm angry, when I'm truly angry, it's like my brain is in my throat. I'm like a live animal. I just go off." She had been so delirious, she couldn't even tell the nurses her own name, let alone where the blood had come from. Her clothes were streaked with it, yet she was totally intact. "And that's my regret. That I'll never know whose blood it was. It really bothers me that I don't know."

"Very good," Dr. John said. He looked at Beanie on his left and raised his eyebrows.

"You're welcome," Harlow said.

Before Harlow's accounting, Gia had shared another paranoid gem from her life pre-Veld, and Beanie had recounted a regrettable shoplifting episode that ended in a chase, not of her but by her. Now, it was my turn to drum something up of equal or greater value.

"She's boring," one of the sadist girls said.

"Respect?" Dr. John said. "Everyone?"

I said Harlow was a hard act to follow, but no one laughed. The sadist girl tapped her toe and stared. I cleared my throat and looked toward the empty stage at the end of the hall, deciding which error to unravel.

"It's not a competition," Dr. John prodded.

"I was just kidding before."

"If you'd like, we can find a quiet place for you to gather your thoughts, circle back when you feel ready."

"I'm ready," I said, considering the felted walls of Fifth Floor ISO. I had just been thinking that while I was here reliving the same loop, everyone else in my story was barreling forward unscathed. The room was mine. This is what I told the girls.

When I make it to the Weppler house that afternoon, the back door is wide open. Inside, the TV is blaring QVC and a pot of water is at a rolling boil on the stove. A trio of hornets bump along the kitchen ceiling. I call upstairs to no answer.

It is difficult not to assume something despicable has occurred when trespassing in the house of the dead. Murder, I think. Kidnapping. Suicide. Poison. I run down the list of possibilities and the gruesome images shutter by like slides in a View-Master. There had been an episode of *MAYDAY* when the diner almost exploded after a gas leak. It was Reed, the faithful paramour, who saved the day.

I kill the burner on the Wepplers' stove top. Upstairs, movement. A fumbling along the floorboards. In the living room, the woman on the television is hawking a magic mop, designed to erase every mess imaginable. "Think of it," she says as I mount the first step. "No more stains, no more solvents, no more oopsie-daisy moments."

There's music, a canned beat, a ripple in the eardrum. The door to the master bedroom is half-shut, but I call Antonia's name. I rarely say her name out loud. I can hear my own tenderness in the way I say it. As I pass Gene Jr.'s room, the wallpaper undulates in light and shadow.

"I'm here," she says from inside the suite. She is not alone.

Kent is sprawled on the bed in white boxers. They are

wrinkle-free, I notice, which makes me think of his mother holding a hot iron.

I say sorry and turn away. Kent's eyes are all marble, aimed at his brain.

"Oh, hello," Antonia says in a voice like Snow White. "You scared us."

Kent's mouth lolls, fights its way into a blissful grin, lolls again. Supposedly, she'd dumped him a week before, but he was nothing if not resilient. She told me they went to Olive Garden because she thought a public place would be best. I listened to her, talked her down when she got cold feet, but while she and Kent were supposedly breaking up over bottomless breadsticks, they were likely fucking in my dead neighbors' bed—and I had given them the keys.

I look around the bedroom transformed by Antonia's personal touches. A scatter of weed nuggets on the armoire, half-empty glasses everywhere. All the photos of the Wepplers and their kin are facedown. This seems like bad luck, but it's too late for that. On the bed, Antonia is pinching her face, kneading it as if it is an oozing foreign substance in her hands.

"You left the water on," I say, but she doesn't seem to hear me. "Are you on drugs?"

Then I take a handful of whatever she gives me.

To the girls in Share there is no mention of hopeless love or the lengths I am willing to go. By the time the mix of uppers and downers begins to weigh my brain like a stone to the ocean floor, Kent and Antonia have begun making out on the bed in an uncoordinated tangle of partial thrusts and pornographic grunts. I don't know how long I sit in the corner waiting for some rising tide to claim me, wondering if she always looked that way, if he always sounded that way, if I have always been sitting right here. I'm not even sure if they know I'm in the room.

Eventually, I lift my own chin with two hands to keep my head on straight and scoot down the stairs on my ass. In the kitchen, the pot on the stove top is still steaming and smells of astringent, artificial perfume—essence of car freshener. It was supposed to be our place, I think. I had given the Weppler house as a gift.

The bass upstairs rattles the good china. Do the neighbors perk up their ears and listen? The woman on TV is a talking head, skating around the polished studio floor with her magic mop. I laugh like a studio audience and go to the basement door.

The compulsion to descend is familiar. The steps before me lead into darkness, like a dream I've had a dozen times. In it, the stairway goes on and on with only the next step lower illuminated—the rest is a matte abyss, miles down into the earth's interior. This will be the last stairwell, I think. After this, there are no more. I'll know what is at the bottom.

One of the sadist girls nods knowingly. Trips gone wrong are an established genre. They are less than ideal because counselors are careful not to glamorize perceived substance abuse, but behavior cannot be split from its influences. I decline to share that it was my first time. There's no point in delineating anyway, because plenty of people have first times that don't end the way mine did.

"Is that where you found their bodies?" Gia asks.

"What? No."

Gia shrugs.

From the top of the steps, I watch the basement swim in shades of chartreuse. The bass line pounding from the second floor sounds less like a party and more like a demonic battering ram. I grip the railing, prepare to scale Everest in reverse. I am hyper-focused on the work of my feet. At the bottom, to be sure I am seeing what I am seeing, I reach out and touch.

My fingertips brush the cool glass of aquarium tanks.

There are at least two dozen, stacked wall to wall and floor to ceiling, a ratty swivel recliner at the center of it all. Each tank is brightly lit, filled to the brim with dominating blooms of algae. Left unchecked, the bacterial tank inhabitants have proliferated. Watery forests of scum scale every glass wall and drift along the brackish surface. A crust marks the dwindling water levels, like stone strata. The smell is horrendous. I press a palm to the largest tank, ten feet long. Its filter spins with a hollow, plastic racket, but there are no fish to be seen, in this tank or the others. In my altered state, I receive this as a riddle. Antonia had looked into my eyes when she handed me the pills. "You are your compass," she said. "Whatever you see, don't look away."

I don't know how long I'm down there before it happens. The sensation crests the way a roller coaster crests, lead car tipping. I press my nose to a tank and a few ghostly wisps of matter brush the gravel. Fins. Tips orange and black, attached to nothing. Made for the current, they skate across the tank floor in search of amputees. Vacant bellies that drift like wet paper. In another tank, a sunken skiff lurks in the filth, its hull gaping and indecent. Every ten seconds, a water feature blows open a hatch and a toy diver bubbles to the surface. I watch this scene for what feels like hours, until the basement becomes one giant fetid tank I float inside, the ripple of music two floors up like news from the shore.

I imagine an apex amphibian prowling the depths. How long did it take for her to devour the little ones, and how long until she was the last? I brim with tears to think of her, ravenous and solitary, nosing around for the barest sustenance, aquarium bulbs bleaching her scales white.

I curl up in the recliner and bury my nose in the polyester, breathe in a dead man's oils. I think of Peanut Butter's body evacuated of spirit, no better than the wild deer and skunks and possums that smack Deerie pavement after a highway hit-and-run. Ever since the Fourth of July, Zeke had been pressing me. I hadn't told him about our new clubhouse. Antonia and I had agreed to keep it under wraps, purely functional, so she didn't have to sleep in Kent's basement anymore. I stopped venturing to The Gables. I stopped answering Zeke's calls. He kept leaving messages with Fawn and my mother. He dropped by, but I was never home. I gave him no hint as to what ailed me, and if he dared to ask directly, I turned even colder.

Antonia said not to waste my time with him anymore. She said it was natural to grow apart. Paging through a magazine on the Weppler couch, she said, "He's either sexless, gay, or stupid. Maybe all three."

No one but me knew what happened the night of the fireworks. My mother had been quick to accept Peanut Butter as a runaway, and of course this theory was easily conceivable to her. Fawn had lost interest in the idea of the dog entirely. She stopped looking after that night.

When I was sure he was dead, I lifted Peanut Butter into my arms amidst the aftershocks and bangs and whistles downtown. I propped up my elbow so his head didn't loll. I walked with him a long while, past an old residential pocket gone dormant, past a gravel lot crowded with dumpsters like freighters afloat on a slate sea. I walked into a thick copse of trees that went on longer than I planned. My back ached. I took one step after another, until the lights receded. I laid the dog down at the base of the biggest tree and wiped my dirty palms on the bark.

After that, I had walked to the Wepplers' house. I let myself in the backyard gate and found the hose. I washed myself down and sat on one of the deck chairs, shivering as I waited to dry. I woke up when the automatic sprinklers chugged on. It was hardly dawn. I walked home in a daze through my city of ruin as I had done and would do many times more. Geronimo Street was pitted and empty. A woodpecker rapped his beak against a stripped telephone pole and stared me down as I went. I thought someone might be waiting, that my mother would stir when the utility door to the loft swung open and shut. There was no skitter of paws to greet me, no nose at my knees, no trace of Billy or his tidy wife. If it weren't for the cheese board specked with ant bodies, I might've wondered if the whole holiday had been one long trick of the heat.

I look around the circle and all the girls are staring expectantly.

Dr. John looks like he's doing long division in his head. "We have ten minutes," he says. "Are you ready to proceed?"

I don't know how long I've been sitting there, saying nothing. I look at Gia.

"The pot on the stove," she says.

"What?"

"That's where this is going."

"Gia—" Dr. John starts.

"It's okay," I say. "She's right." The only way out is through.

Down in the basement, I watch the diver in the tank synced inside his forever loop. When the idea comes to me, it's like he knows it too, and the beady eyes inside his rubber mask make clear he is no innocent. As Antonia instructed, I do not turn away. I let my compass spin.

Whatever liquid was roiling inside the pot on the stove has distilled to vapor, and the vessel steams so furiously it looks like it might launch. I load pots on every burner, crank the heat on each one. Flames lick the iron grates as I drop a dish towel inside a pot and instantly the smoke thickens to black and billows. A handful of mail follows the towel, then a comic book, the TV remote, a family photo stuck to the fridge, snapped on some cruise liner in a diamond sea. In goes the diver in his painted neoprene suit, melting so fast that a spit of flame singes the peach fuzz of my cheek. I uncork a souvenir bottle of olive oil tied neatly with twine, let it gurgle out freely and overwhelm the pot's molten brew. The impulse to cut the burners is to be expected, and so is readily refused. I have to see it for myself, the moment the inferno takes over. If the timing isn't right, it will all be for nothing.

With one hand gripping the knob of the back door, I take in the final frame. Smoke chugs toward the ceiling and eats itself, multiplies, no place to go but along the limiting plane of the ceiling, a dark ivy with creeping fingers. The TV is on.

Outside, the backyard is an untouched idyll. A butterfly glints in the air. Each flapping leaf pulsates from its branch, each vein fully realized, pure and sweet, a voice in a chorus of many whispering voices. A brisk wisp of smoke escapes below the back door. Too early and I'll be alarmist, but too late will guarantee disaster. I grit my teeth, do a circle in place, absorb the Weppler yard for all its overgrowth and sundials and plastic furniture. When I can't stand it anymore I take a step toward the back door, but behind me, a voice.

"I wouldn't do that if I were you."

Fawn comes to stand at my side in the Weppler jungle. I expect her expression will read as pure delight, lusty for carnage—or perhaps even filled with a kind of fraternal pride, now that she knows we are one and the same, but the look on her face is grave.

"Aren't you going to call someone?" she asks. "Call someone."

"Did you follow me?"

"I don't have to follow you to know where you'll be."

It's as if the house has begun to swell, the slatted siding inhaling. I go for the back door, but the knob rattles in my fist. I can't tell if it's warm from the blaze inside or the direct sunbeam chipping the brass. I rattle it again, but it's locked.

"I told you," Fawn says. "You don't want to go in that way."

"I have to go in," I say, as if the knob will concede. "We've got to go in."

"We?" she asks. "There's a hatch window round the side that's busted."

"How do you know that?"

"I've been down there before. I don't bother you guys upstairs, I just hang."

"Hang?"

"I could go in for you," Fawn offers casually, as if we're switching shifts. "I'm the faster one, so maybe. I'm not sure you will fit through the window."

"That won't work."

"I can do it, if you want me to."

"Do what?"

She shrugs. "Whatever you were you going to do with them."

I look up to the second level, but all the shades are drawn. The sky above the roof is cloudless but for the jet streams arcing north. It is just another day in August. The sound of summer is a single, psychedelic orchestra chaired by lawnmowers and AC units and ecstatic sparrows and grass prying through the topsoil and flower bulbs stiffening.

"I'm fine," I say to myself. "I'll be okay."

"You don't look okay," Fawn says.

There's a smack of water against glass. I peel open one eye and Fawn is training the garden hose toward the back window where smoke is siphoning through the vinyl lining.

"Hold this," she says, "and I'll go through the basement window."

"It has to be me."

"You won't fit."

"I'll go through the kitchen window."

"The window is on fire."

When the plan had revealed itself to me inside the watery basement, it appeared logical and complete. Not only would there be no more love shack for Antonia and Kent to burrow inside together, but I would be the one who acted when sudden tragedy struck.

Step 1: Set fire.

Step 2: Rescue.

Step 3: Transform into charismatic hero with a spot on the evening news.

I stand on the rear AC unit and peek inside. Flames have engulfed the cabinetry. The living room is in a thick haze and a new woman on the TV gestures to her co-host.

"Stay here," I tell Fawn. "I'm going to get someone."

I sprint to the nearest neighbor and ram the doorbell a dozen times before I realize no one has been home for a very long time. Across the street, the same story. When I return to the yard, Fawn is nowhere to be seen.

What follows is a quick series of poor choices. I punch through the glass of the back-door window, and there's blood. I make a single attempt to throw water at the flames while cradling my cut hand, but the fire is fueled by grease, oils, the stuff of cupboards. The water hisses on impact and the blaze lunges. I call out for Antonia, Fawn, Kent. I hear Fawn yell back from the second story, but the room before me is now impassable. A spire of smoke funnels through a widening scar in the ceiling, where the subfloor above has charred away. After a moment, it is clear that I am not brave enough to leap faithfully through the veil of fire and smoke to execute my plan as envisioned. My head is pounding, the hairs on my arm are alive to the heat. I back out of the broken kitchen door and go wait on the sidewalk with the neighbors to watch what will happen next.

A fire truck and ambulance duet in the distance as the roof belches black clouds, tar fire, sparks like Roman candles as the wiring and insulation sizzle. Though it is high summer, onlookers clutch themselves and one another as though an arctic breeze is blowing.

"Stand back," they tell me, and do not notice the cuts on my hands.

As the men in helmets reach the threshold, the front door bursts open from the inside. Figures emerge, hunched silhouettes holding each other. Kent and Antonia. A little girl appears a few steps behind. She reaches out as if to propel them forward into safety. Some old neighbor jostles me out of the way and points toward Fawn.

"The little girl," he shouts. "Make sure she's okay."

Antonia and Kent are on their hands and knees, coughing. Kent is still in his boxers, though they are the color of dishwater now, wrinkled and bunched like an old diaper. She is in her bra, eyes primal, hair mussed unmistakably, her makeup on the run. She looks ten years older. She turns to Kent, and they bow their heads together as two figures in a baroque painting. I shout my sister's name but the roof is seared, collapsing beam by beam, firemen and their radios holler, no one hears me. I could be any onlooker.

When I step onto the lawn, a neighbor grabs my arm. "Give them room to breathe," he says, as an EMT sprints over in latex gloves.

The three of them sink their faces into oxygen masks and hold hands. Kent is crying, which makes him look like Zeke—and what will Zeke say, when he finds out? What sequence of lies could work to pacify the one who knows me best?

A news van pulls up to the curb and a neighbor shakes his head. "Quick, aren't they?"

"I was in there," I say, to anyone. "I was in the house."

As the roof blows away in chunks, I think of the basement crypt, slowly filling with silt and hose water. A summer wind has swept the streets. Sidewalk spectators murmur about the safety of adjacent structures, but so many homes are empty now. Whoever is left will soon be leaving, and they console themselves with this. The dark clouds will be seen for miles.

On the Wepplers' front lawn, Fawn is shivering like a street rat, and Antonia pulls her in close, soothes her hair the same way she must have been soothed once. My sister's eyes are all the bluer for the soot that coats her face and neck, is streaked across her upturned nose. A cameraman pivots on the trio, his spotlight a second sun. Fawn finds my face in the crowd. Inside Antonia's arms, she waves to me, though it is impossible to tell if she is waving me closer or waving goodbye.

———

We were five minutes late for lunch by then. All the girls around the circle were getting antsy and gathering their things. Dr. John nodded at me, allowing room if I wanted to say more, but his was an expectant sort of courtesy, and I said nothing. Sometimes there came the initial thrill of new information being poured into our circle, but few things were shocking anymore.

Beanie squeezed my arm on our way out the door, but I brushed past her. It was happening again. That rev of adrenaline I had in the back of the van, on our way to campus the first time. If I opened my mouth, I knew I wouldn't be able to stop. I remember the flush of it, the lunge to get away, reject the certainty of where I was, but this urge would pass.

I would revisit the event and others countless times more through repetition, writing, abstract expression. Sometimes new details emerged. I painted once a flaming building, cartoonish except for the windows, which I was good at—thin splinters of whitish-gray to denote the glass where it met in four panes. If it was not this scene it was some other from that time. They all became edgeless after a while, overly remembered. I drew from the same series of defining events, the time between catastrophes like efficient runways. Everyone official insisted that progress was being made and now, years later, by Veld's sacred estimations, I am thriving.

I am alive in the big city. I've spent more time out than in. A record of my existence has been filed with utility companies, subscription services, payroll. Any substance-based revelry rarely outlives the weekend. I possess a few friends, a promising paramour, a nonvolatile relationship with the world at large. In Veld-speak, I have learned to stay on task. I have turned down the dial on my life. I am living in it.

9

Rochelle is a connoisseur of spreadsheets. Each grid she tends like a garden, always admiring, always pruning.

Sometimes when she is at her desk, inside the beam of her computer screen, I watch her while she works. I used to wonder what it sounded like, the siren's call that lured this woman to a life in marketing. So content. So rapt with the numerical feedback of the Fortune 500 that has enlisted her services in tapping the gene pool and divining taste. But off the clock and on, she has been charting herself: a one-woman focus group, every moment of her life sliced and diced, stats stretched into a graph taut as a tanned hide. A data set for every outfit she assembles, every train taken, every cup of coffee she drinks, every morsel that passes her lips. A record not only for what has been consumed, but also how long it took to prepare, to nibble, to succumb to her next snack.

At first, I am delightfully horrified by these inventories. I have been handed the technical instructions to the woman of the house, but this illicit thrill is soon eclipsed by the discovery of more esoteric spreadsheets, ones that tell too much. Bowel movements.

Times we've had sex. Times she has had sex with others. If she orgasmed, how many times.

Our first night together, under NOTES, she wrote: *Conversation natural. Attraction good. Room for improvement in the bedroom— confidence required.*

It is unclear to whom the requirement for confidence is referring.

I discover her cache while snooping around her computer for solutions. The nosedive with JoAnn the coworker has left Rochelle and me at an imbalance. I am overly affectionate, overly complimentary. I can sense that my trial period is coming swiftly to an end.

The folder of spreadsheets on her desktop is titled INVENTORY. The first folder I click on is labeled SKINCARE. There are inputs for everything. Each product's ingredients, directions, intended effects, when it is applied, how often, how much—even if only a colloquial approximation that operates on its own personal metric scale: *Dollop, Swipe, and Dab.* There is a column for miscellaneous observations, further dissected into seasons/months, and other extenuating factors that might affect the pH balance of her skin and its reception to said product (i.e., menstruation, ovulation, change in diet, illness, heightened stress, countervailing weather).

Every item in her possession has been entered into this mainframe too. Our special-order pillows, purchased at Christmas, the oil painting above the bed—acquired from an East Village gallery in 2007. According to Rochelle's records, the oldest archived item in her bedroom is her alarm clock, a nineties-era behemoth the size of a shoebox, with faux woodgrain and a fuzzy red digital display. She has arranged it inside every domicile beginning in Egan, Michigan, and off to Macalester College, to Ann Arbor for grad school and then New York, and now at the Geronimo Lofts. Unlike the rest of her bedroom entries, the alarm clock's date of purchase is unknown. This anomaly is symbolized by a rare *?* in the entry field. I picture her face pinching as she keys in the single offending symbol.

Almost anything I want to know about Rochelle is documented

and at my fingertips. If this glut of information wasn't so repulsive in its detail, I might relish the new power it affords. I could model myself into the perfect girlfriend. I might never have to leave.

The last folder I click on is labeled SUPPLEMENTS.

For months now, I've submitted to Rochelle's wellness routine. There are eight vitamins in total. Some stink of seaweed, others taste of earth. One vitamin is completely odorless, flavorless, a bit of cloud inside my palm. Another rebalances fight-or-flight reflex. Another bolsters cognitive resilience. Another is a natural remedy, a primordial root synthesized in a gel capsule, meant to impart a powerful relaxation effect. I am like a locked door, secured by many bolts. Each vitamin undoes a latch until my true potential is free to pass through.

Perhaps it is too soon to tell if Rochelle's pills will make any difference, or if they have already. I don't blame her for her impulse to enhance. Her whole life is an ode to smart selection, so it is only natural I undergo the same process of enrichment before she is able to fold me in.

At Veld, they ordered their own regimens, prescribed by some off-site physician who visited campus a few times a quarter. They'd line us up at the infirmary doors and after a glancing consultation with some octogenarian in a stethoscope, off we went to test the bolts, hoping this time they'd open for good.

During my first round, I entered an endless night through which I slept for weeks. I dreamt I was at the bottom of a stagnant pond, blinking up through gelatinous waters. I watched the glittering surface beyond with no interest in pursuing it. I closed my eyes and eliminated myself from the face of the earth. The light of day, the dark of night, all became a faceless clock. It was a relief, in a way. I was the thinnest I'd ever been. "Cut your hair short," Harlow told me. "Now you have cheekbones."

When they stopped the meds I zapped awake like a lightbulb. Gia had been relishing the newfound quiet of our room and took my hibernation as an opportunity to rearrange the furniture. I was given a new combination of pills to pop and soon I could detect the electricity within the walls. I heard zaps and fuses and dull thunks of disconnects all around me, in a massive invisible infrastructure to which only my ears were privy. I'd stay awake all night in a perpetually adrenalized state, locked inside the agony of the present moment. It took Herculean effort to shift focus from one crack in the ceiling to the neighboring crack in the ceiling, sure as I was that the whole roof would collapse and bury me in the rubble. Survival was of little interest. If the end was near and inevitable, I only wanted to be aware.

After that, I took nothing. I tongued the pills they gave me. The orderlies had us swish water around in our mouths to be sure we weren't trading or stockpiling or going without, but it was easy enough to tuck a pill behind my last upper molar. It was a trick Gia taught us. She was infamous for remaining unmedicated. I'd pass inspection and then spit the pills into the toilet, flush away the reconditioning for the fish to consume.

After the discovery of Rochelle's data mine, I go on as if nothing has changed between us. She hands over my morning supplements, but there are too many to keep tucked behind my teeth. I swallow them as usual, receive my pat on the head, and send her off to work. Once the door is closed, I wait ten minutes to be sure she won't come back and empty my stomach before the pills can disintegrate inside me. I wait for some indication I am returning to normal, but nothing yet feels changed. There is no falter, no gap between before, during, and after.

It is through her own meticulous accounting that I learn Rochelle has booked the communal rooftop of the loft for a party, the progress of which I've been monitoring with great interest. I had penned a dozen Hallmark cards, baked a dozen cookies during my reign as head of the Piñata Club, but no one has ever thrown me a surprise party before.

It's in moments like these that I can see myself really loving Rochelle one day. It's important to go through the motions sometimes and exhibit some fanfare. To appreciate the value of a gesture.

I wonder how she has built the guest list, given that I've introduced her to no one. Of course, there is a tab for that. I scroll through the names of my associates listed. I have only let slip his name once, in error, and still I find him. Victor. Nestled in his appropriate alphabetical rank.

I thought Rochelle preferred my anonymity. I don't have to make room in my life for her because there is already plenty of space. Sometimes I catch myself languishing in it, my vacuous history, cavernous and so unthreatening, no interrupting episode to serve as an unsightly smudge upon the walls. I haven't spoken to Victor in weeks. He texts every few days with a link, or a slew of question marks in an accusatory row.

It feels safer inside the loft. Like I am out of danger even if on display, like a ship in a bottle. Ever since Fawn's birthday release, it feels as though I haven't been living my life alone. I dress and speak with premeditated nonchalance. I self-edit. I pose in various states of mundanity. It is not a script I'm following so much as I am living my life as I wish it might be interpreted, my life as I want her to see it.

On a Friday night, Rochelle and I go out to dinner in the city. She has heard about a new place from JoAnn the coworker, and mention of her name has already set an unstable tone. The aftermath has been more telling than the incident itself. We are both determined to act normally, but every comment does double duty, no gesture is benign.

The restaurant is in my old neighborhood, which has risen considerably in stature since my father's tenure here, and even more so since I left it. The lights inside the brasserie are so low that

Rochelle uses her cellphone's flashlight to peruse the wine list. She motions for the waiter, and as she lifts her arm I see Rod, the man from the white party years ago who had held my father's record hostage. He is sitting saintly by candlelight, just a few tables over.

Rochelle begins squinting into the darkness, in search of our waiter.

"Shall we split a bottle?" she asks.

"Sure. Why not?"

Rochelle lifts an eyebrow above her menu. "If you wish," she says, as if it was my idea.

All I can see of Rod's companion is a sheet of blond hair, naked shoulders. He looks thinner. Impossibly, he has chiseled away a jawline. He wears a signet ring.

"I do see some things I like here," Rochelle says.

"Anything is fine," I say. "I'll follow your lead."

New York is not so big that you don't run into people. This was something Victor tried to work out constantly because he had unusual odds. We couldn't make it two blocks without running into someone he knew. I'd stand off on the curb while he caught up with a high school basketball teammate, the two of them having the time of their lives—both then in their glory days, and now again, in the present moment of their reunion. As soon as his long-lost friend turned the corner, Victor would rub his temples like he was receiving a vision. "I hate that guy," he'd say.

The pacing of our meal is impeccable, and Rod's table carries on course for course. Rochelle appears energized and orders a second bottle. Meanwhile, the blonde at Rod's table tosses her head this way and that. I feel a strange sense of righteousness, knowing what I've liberated from him, like I am one in a long tradition. Track 3 of the Record: "Los Rateros"—is all about pickpocketing. Playa Mala. Bad Beach. The hunting grounds. The U.S. military bombed the hell out of Vieques, the little island nine miles off Puerto Rico from which my father comes, but they helpfully identified their test sites. It was all target practice. Red Beach. Green Beach. Blue. In my father's song, military pilots to mess hall workers and anyone with anything worth stealing is a target of choice. There were encounters in the little barrios, at bars, with women, with a grandmother I never knew. My father and his homegrown gang ran rampant through sandy streets, aimed their thumb and pointer fingers at the sky like a downed soldier marooned with his sidearm. They watched the planes drum past, explosions marking the hours. Shrapnel and incendiary residue isolated the beaches, turned them stark and wild. Stealing was a small, useful revenge.

Rings, watches, Lincolns, lockets. Right out from under your nose.

"What have you been staring at all night?" Rochelle asks. She takes a very long sip of wine and watches curiously as I shift in my seat.

"I thought I saw someone I knew," I say, "but I don't think it's them."

"An old girlfriend?" Rochelle looks over her shoulder. I almost reach out to stop her, but she wouldn't know Rod's face anyway, or what it means to me. "Who is she?" Her mouth is in her wineglass, so the question sounds loosed from a bubble.

"No one. An old friend is all. Are those our entrees?"

I reach for the bottle of wine between us and find it empty. Rochelle twists in her chair, ogling every table. "My god it is dark in here. It is like a cave." Rod's face looms in chiaroscuro as Rochelle lifts the bottle in the air. "Another," she announces to the dim room.

"Are you sure?" I ask. "You don't seem like yourself."

"I am perfectly myself," she says, "and I suggest you recall who is footing the bill."

We make it through the dinner course quietly, though Rochelle is unusually voracious. The pappardelle doesn't stand a chance. Meanwhile, Rod is carving his way through a N.Y. strip, while his companion is still as a mannequin, a plate of leaves arranged before her. Rochelle has lost all pretense of sobriety and slumps back in her chair when her plate is cleared.

"No more," she says. "I couldn't possibly withstand another bite."

We order dessert. Rod's date stands and wobbles toward the ladies' room, leaving their table exposed. Rod is a man who seems like he'd be good with faces. A sleight of hand and a slip out the door. He must've known who was responsible. When things were good between us, I had asked Steph what happened the rest of that night, but to her it was all a blur.

Instead of telling Rochelle there is cream on her nose, I go numb as Rod folds his napkin and moves toward our table.

"Hello there," he says to us, perched like a waiter with the specials.

Rochelle gasps. "Rodney," she says. "Oh my god, Rodney."

"I thought that was you," he says. "Radiant as ever."

"Am I?" Rochelle asks, and Rod nods. "Have you been here this whole time?"

"I'm seated just there, with an old friend."

At the mention of old friends, Rochelle is reminded of my presence. I watch the teeny dollop of cream cresting the tip of her nose as it turns on me. "Introductions, of course."

I shake Rod's hand quickly and bow my head into my wineglass.

Rod frowns. "Have we met before?"

"No," Rochelle answers for me. "I found this one a few months ago. Out of town." She swallows a hiccup and Rod glances around in case someone elite is tallying who is winning their interaction. "Just out for a bit of celebratory dinner, us two. A pre-birthday dinner," she says. "*Twenty-three*. An auspicious age, remember?"

"Happy birthday," Rod says and hardly looks at me. "Mine is powdering her nose, of course. Twenty-two. Auspicious in its own right."

As they exchange personal stats, Rod's blonde emerges from the bathroom and casts around, finding him otherwise engaged at a table of two women. Her face remains totally intact as she slumps back to her seat and whips out her phone, a halogen puddle she peers into. I feel a tender rage begin to mount. I will her to look in my direction so that we might unite.

Rod and Rochelle are reminiscing over a forgotten summer in the Hamptons. An absurd lunch at Sardi's. Suddenly it is not all that surprising that they run in similar circles.

"You know," I interject. "Maybe we have met before."

The two cast their eyes toward me, the meddlesome child.

"Sorry?" Rochelle asks.

I look at Rod. "You seem familiar. Like we've met. I'm almost sure of it."

"Perhaps in passing," Rod suggests. "Perhaps."

"You live in a loft on a corner nearby, no? Top floor."

Rod glances to his date. Maybe she is feeding me information somehow. Maybe we met in the bathroom and exchanged tips. "I do," he says with a laugh. "You've caught me."

"Why do you know that?" Rochelle asks.

"Everything is white," I say, and Rod's eyes narrow, "and there's a long stone terrace. There's a room in back with a huge stereo system. I remember it all being very impressive."

"Stop that," Rochelle says, and tacks on a laugh so as not to put the mood on ice.

"Is this a party trick? It's uncanny." Rod smiles graciously. "I suspect you've been to one of my gatherings. Forgive me, but those evenings are so often a sea of faces."

"Yes. Quite the sea. You'll have to forgive me too."

The memory unravels in his eyes—the blackout curtain, the record shelf, the girls parading in and out. Steph and a chaise lounge. Lights out. "I remember your face," he says.

I turn to Rochelle, relishing the reins of the conversation in my grip. "We met at a party once," I say, to throw her a bone. Rochelle is looking back and forth between us, feeling around for her wineglass. Rod takes a step toward me, but remembers where he is. "Rod showed me and some friends around his music room, all these amazing records. You must remember Steph at least, don't you?"

"I don't recall."

"The actress? Big head of curls. You were a raving fan."

"Honestly, it is dark as night in here," Rochelle says. "I want to leave. Is this meant to be an experience of some kind? Rodney, it was a delight to see you, or what I *can* see of you." She taps a fingernail on the tablecloth. "I don't understand your generation. This inane obsession with ambience. You all have some explaining to do."

Silence courses through our trio. Without speaking, we all decide to abandon the mounting tension and return to the controlled environs in which the night began.

Rod pats my shoulder. "I can see it was a mistake to have forgotten you. Happy birthday, indeed. And," he says, finger wagging, "before I return to my lovely companion and marvel at how small our fair city is—you must tell. Please, do. How was it that you two met?"

The only seats left on the train back to Deerie are in the quiet car, which is not the mood Rochelle is in. Inside the slosh of wine, she sensed the intonation in Rod's voice, the dig and the allusion to what she does not know. The intensity of tonight's mood has found its target.

In a whisper Rochelle says, "You remember how we met, don't you?"

"How could I forget?"

"The bodega."

"Blood oranges."

"Funny that you knew him," she muses. "Funny coincidence that was."

An elderly woman in a beaded shawl cranes her neck at us purposefully and Rochelle stares her down until the woman returns to her paperback.

"You're always saying how small the city is," I say.

"I do say that."

"Hadn't we read about that restaurant somewhere?"

Rochelle looks out the window, though the dark only reproduces her image. Towns and riverscapes and industrial tracts pass almost undetected, a shudder in the moonlight. Rochelle squints and makes a face like the one from the night we met. What does her gaze snag on?

"You sure have a silver tongue," she says. "An answer for everything."

When she looks back at me, she is smiling.

"I do, don't I?" I say, to test the waters.

"You're a flirt, and a nuisance. I keep you around for the entertainment."

"And because you'd be bored without me."

"Of course. I'd put myself to sleep."

I was feeling it again, that pleasant feeling of forgetfulness. For some, true love happened on a street corner. For others, within the decisive passage of time. For us, it could be a concerted, brokered partnership. I didn't see why there had to be a better reason than that.

"Thank you for a wonderful pre-birthday dinner," I say. "I can't imagine what the real thing is going to look like. I hope this is all. This was enough."

Rochelle ignores this modesty and rests her head on my shoulder. "Rod is an old toad."

"A prehistoric toad."

"And I'm old." Rochelle sighs. "Though not as old as he, at least."

The train rattles over a curve and I pull Rochelle close, smell the perfume she had requested and received. Eventually, the loft will become our loft. The years I will spend there as an adult will outnumber the years spent there as a child. In this way, it will become mine.

"We should move in together," I say, and the woman in the beaded shawl looks up from her book.

Rochelle's mouth opens and closes. "That's an interesting idea."

"What's interesting about it?"

"Aren't we already? Living together."

I slide back to my side of the vinyl seat.

"I just want to understand what more you are looking for," she says.

"Sorry I asked."

"Technically, you didn't ask, but my question is sincere. Where do you see this"—she trails her finger through the air as if punctuating an ellipsis, dot-dot-dot—"ultimately going?"

"I'm happy for now," I say, backpedaling. "I don't mean to throw a wrench in our plans."

"What plans?"

"I just meant—you know, dinner. Forget I said anything. As you were."

It's not until the cab ride from the station that Rochelle has decided.

Remarkable that the roads had been paved so evenly, I am thinking. We take the curves as smooth as a yacht slicing through the chop. When I was little, I earned a scar on my shin from tanking my bike in a pothole. I probably could've used stitches, but my mother and father ripped up an old T-shirt and wrapped it tight around the gash. They sat with me in front of the TV, and during commercials, when I'd point out toys I wanted, or movies I longed to see, they said yes to everything.

"Move in," Rochelle says. "In fact, I'll do you one better. I think we should finalize the position we're in. We live well together; we've established that by now. And, in our way, we understand one another. Isn't that the most important factor, after all?"

"How romantic. To finalize our position."

"As if your pronouncement on the train was some kind of what—an ode? The matter of you and I has always been a practical one, if nothing else."

The cabdriver glances into the rearview mirror. As if from above, I feel the fine adjustment knob of a microscope edge closer to our position as we beetle over the map. He touches his ear where a Bluetooth is nestled. I can't tell if he is pausing his conversation or returning to it. I try to keep my face in cold neutral while I mentally scroll through the spreadsheets I know exist. I am wondering if there is one master spreadsheet I have failed to uncover. What numbers has Rochelle crunched between the train and the cab? Which scenarios has she run to inspire her change of heart, or has this moment already been statistically foreseen?

"I know it's your birthday, but I refuse to treat you like a child," Rochelle says. "I took your offer of moving in, and I counteroffered with marriage. If you want time to think over the terms, then say so. Don't feign obliviousness and paint me as improper."

"Dinner upset you, didn't it?"

She shakes her head vigorously. "Hardly."

"But a little then."

"You're always so technical." We pass the tavern, the trattoria, the soap shop, the roastery, new sights and smells rewriting all the old ones.

"Fine," I say. "Let's do it. I vote yes."

She looks up at me cautiously, but I can see in Rochelle some excitable version of herself, a younger, distant iteration unencumbered by prevailing data. "Shall we?"

"Yes," I say. "We shall."

The cabdriver turns down Geronimo and shouts, "Okay! Yes!"

"Thank you, sir. Thank you so much." Rochelle pulls out her wallet as we idle at the curb. "How kind of you. It's so refreshing to share a warm moment with a stranger."

The driver turns around and looks at us.

"Excuse me," he says. "I'm on the phone."

10

"If you could go anywhere, anywhere at all—where would it be? Who would be waiting for you there? What's the weather like?"

It was Boulder Day, and the Piñata Club was crouched in a row on the gym floor. Our Movement coach drove in from Richmond once a month and was prominently featured on the brochures. I didn't mind Movement, but Gia found all the body bending demeaning.

"Choose a place that grounds you," our coach commanded from the front. "A place where you feel the gravity of the earth at its most profound."

I thought of the loft, envisioned the warehouse in its perfect brick rectangle, like a naturally formed plateau, clouds rolling overhead in epic time-lapse.

"Send me to the Fifth Floor. Please, put me in ISO." Gia was attempting to work herself into the shape of an oval.

"Alone time is the last thing you need," our coach called back. "Shall I come give you an adjustment?"

"Yes!" Harlow called back. "She says she needs one bad!"

One of the sadist girls moaned a few rows away. "If you break my concentration, I will end you."

"Eat my ass," Gia shouted.

The counselor did not like this talk at all.

"Do less, ladies," she commanded. "What are boulders if not immovable? And, most important, silent."

Beanie's interpretation of a boulder looked more like a statue. She was standing stick straight, chin bowed to chest, arms limp at her sides. From my rounded position on the floor, I asked her what she was supposed to be and cracked an eyelid open.

"I'm Stonehenge. I am a very sturdy column."

"Be conscious of the wind, wherever you find yourself," our coach called. "Be conscious of the earth's pressure, from above and from below."

"From below?" Harlow said. "Pretty sure that's hell."

Beanie said she was in an open field. There were many open fields to choose from back in Pennsylvania, out near Dutch country where she was from. She said the wind there was cool because it was autumn, and she could hear the clap of horse hooves on the road.

"I'm on a beach," Harlow told our row. "I'm on a beach in Tahiti."

"You've never even been to Tahiti," Gia said.

"I'm drinking a daiquiri and talking on the phone."

"Who's on the phone?" I asked her.

"My attorney. He's giving me the good news."

"You're all just picking calendar prints," Gia said. "Consider security. That's where I get my peace of mind."

"What kind of rock are you supposed to be, Gia?" Beanie said. "You look like a fat troll."

"You think that's funny?" Gia turned on me, though I had said nothing. I was trying very hard to be silent and immovable.

"Please," the sadist girl said. "Tell them there's no talking."

"Inhabit the stationary," said our coach. "Push your center of gravity into a tight ball."

"Technically," Harlow said, "what we're doing right now is the opposite of Movement."

"Okay," our coach said. "Okay, thank you."

Our coach drifted away to attend to the Helicopter Cases, who were always eager to perform.

"Tonight," Gia whispered to us. "A field trip."

"Not again, Gia," I said. She was obsessed with the idea of raiding the admin office.

"Fine. Then you'll miss out."

"On what?" Beanie asked.

Gia shook her head. "Just bring your coats, whores. I'll find you at midnight."

Because there was one lone road in or out, and because campus was buffeted by old woods rampant with kudzu and unruly bramble and moldering logs and ancient bear traps, and because the nearest blight of a town could offer nothing in terms of relief or exit, security in the Residence was simple as lock and key.

We ventured beyond the kitchen service entrance and left a Dutch oven as a doorstop. There was a valley of mown grass between the Residence and the woods, and we stuck to the tree-lined walk that wove toward the tennis courts and field hockey pitch, though there was no field hockey team to speak of. The sticks were blunt instruments, unfit for our leisure. I assumed we were headed to the shed to find a stash of liquor, or weed, or pills rattling in their vessels, cigarettes even, Hostess cupcakes—anything that might impart a rare thrill. Gia picked up a rock, and though it took three tries, the padlock gave. We pried open the cobwebbed doors and found something even better.

"Does it really work?" Harlow asked.

Gia rapped her knuckles against the plastic top of an old TV set. "It will."

"Did you do this?" I asked.

"Who has the time? I was just a passive observer. A dot connector."

Harlow felt around the shed for a remote and came away with more cobwebs. The shed looked like a cluttered bait shop. All broken things. Instead of tools and lures, there was badminton netting knotted to hell, a loop of dull-toothed metal from an old band saw, deflated volleyballs like dented heads. All was past its prime, used elsewhere and by others more deserving. There were boxes everywhere, taped shut so tight a whole roll had likely been expended for each, and they were all labeled. CLOTHES. TOYS. BOOKS. I wondered if it was the beginning of some kind of donation program, or a sad rummage sale. Was this where all those aspirational oil paintings of foamy beaches and sunset cliffsides originated? In the back shed. In the dark. I asked what it was all doing here.

"The tennis coach?" Harlow asked.

"No," Gia said, "his girls just want cigarettes. That's breakfast, lunch, and dinner for them. All we need is a good place to put it. A power outlet, some batteries for the remote."

Beanie was hovering at the shed doors, glaring at the drapery of cobwebs. She had, conspicuously, offered nothing in the way of encouragement or complaint.

"There's no way we can keep this," I said.

"Well, not with that attitude. All I ask is an ounce of positivity, for once." Gia circled the shed to wind up her pitch. "Don't let those Love Club sluts think they're special. We can't let this gift go to waste. Use your imagination. We'll have something real. Something to last us. Unless," Gia said, "you have a better idea for all this stuff, Beanie."

Beanie shook her head quickly.

"No?" Gia circled the stash. "No ideas? Cat got your tongue?"

I had a soft spot for Beanie. She was not without her flaws, or her allegiances to a system I did not believe in, but she was not like the rest of us. We deserved to be here. Unlike hers, our mistakes had been within our control.

"Are we supposed to cart this thing inside?" I asked. "And stash it where? For when?"

Gia rolled her eyes. "Name a better time than now. Call it a perk of our organization. It's something we can all enjoy, isn't it? And maybe, one day, you all do a favor for me."

"You sound like a mobster."

"I am not a monster."

"I said *mobster*."

"In that case, thank you." Gia pawed a dented volleyball and brushed past Beanie in the doorway, punted it into darkness.

"Fore!" she called out in a stage whisper, and turned back to us, giddy. "You guys don't even know the best part yet. Don't you want to share the good news, Beanie?" She threw her arm over Beanie's shoulders, but Beanie had yet to cross the threshold. She swung slowly with the hinge.

"I'll take that as my cue then," Gia said. "For our happy return to prime time, we must thank Beanie here, and our beloved Dr. John."

I was the only one who didn't appear to comprehend the joke. I touched the edge of a cardboard box and watched Harlow as she laughed into her fist.

"What?" I asked.

"I'm impressed," she said. "I bow down. Honestly, I should've seen it coming."

"Should've seen what coming? Beanie, what's she saying?"

I looked between the three of them. I could tell Gia was very pleased with herself because she was biting her tongue to bask in it.

"Finally, something we can teach you," Gia said to me. "A proper education."

Beanie turned on her heel and started walking. One purposeful stride after another, out of the shed and toward the woods.

"Oh, here we go," Harlow said. She took her time getting to her feet.

"Where is she going? Beanie?" I hurried after her with only a glance back at the main building, its windows lifeless. Beanie did not answer nor pause at the tree line. Through the spectral overgrowth and over the crumbled stone wall, she moved as if compelled, and I stood stuck there at its edges. A few yards more and there was no sign of her, no noise but the forest's unrest and me.

Gia said to keep my voice down. "They'll hear you."

"Who? There's no one out here."

"Are you really that idiotic?"

"Jesus Christ—you think there are fucking paratroopers up there or something?"

Harlow had joined us at the edge of the woods, along with the smell of smoke. She lit a cigarette and took a long, luxurious drag. "Found this in the shed. You guys want?"

"You did this," I told Gia. "You go and get her."

"You're still giving orders. You really think your stupid title and clever little birthday cards mean anything? Out here?" Gia accepted the cigarette, took a long inhale, and closed her eyes. "Oh yeah. This is good. You know what? Get it out of your system. Get it all out in the open."

"I'm going after her."

Gia grabbed my wrist, careful not to squeeze too hard. "You don't want to follow her. You think you want to, but you don't. Use your head."

On the trail, we learned to move by moonlight, relax our eyes to the curve of shadow. That was when I felt most dangerous, knowing how possible it was to vanish. Shine told us that with a flashlight you can see only a few feet ahead, but the whole forest can see you.

Harlow said we'd want to be in bed for checks before they realized who was gone. I called out again for Beanie, and Gia elbowed me in the side, hard enough that the wind rushed through me.

"Why?" I wheezed.

Harlow shook her head and kept smoking. I knew she was trying to be gentle. "You already know. If you just think about it, you already know."

Gia was closing up the shed behind us, replacing the broken padlock in its slot.

"You don't have to worry about Beanie anymore, okay?" Gia said. "Relax. Take a breath. Good. Unlike you, she can take care of herself. It's what she's been doing since the beginning."

It sounded fabulous and terrible, which was Gia's favorite combination.

The affair had been going on for months. Everyone mistook Dr. John as gay, and this was the perfect cover for his perversion, according to Gia. Beanie was nineteen. She could do what she pleased, in a technical sense. Dr. John had promised her things. She was given top privileges. She could sign herself out at any time, call a cab to visit the outlets an hour away. She could even call home, if she wanted. This was a freedom not bestowed until a certain amount of fealty had been demonstrated. If you wanted to step off the paved pathways that circuited through campus, you had to ask permission. Grass that showed signs of disturbance was investigated.

Some nights, Dr. John whisked her off campus to his bookish farmhouse. He had a few acres and a flaccid pond on the edge of Bowen, a horse in a stable. As the two of them lay in his four-poster bed, her head on his chest, the moonlight spilt upon the lake's surface—he'd recount every confession ever received, and together they ranked them, tragic to most tragic. It explained the shed, the TV, the hidden goodies. It was a stockpile of bribes, Gia said. Beanie would get her own private room on Fifth. A phone line. An internet connection.

"She plays dumb," Gia said, "but she sees everything."

Veld operated like a network of spies. Every student was an envoy of her own country, the country of herself. Staff maintained the world order, and the only way to curry favor or avoid persecution was stepping on the necks of your neighbors. Every club had a

mole, and Beanie was ours. Gia told me I could not see the forest
through the trees.

"You know what happened to her," I said. "She doesn't think like
that."

"So she's got a few dead bulbs up there, that's just as good a
cover as any. Around here, you can't spit on the sidewalk without
someone hearing about it."

She said that hidden away in the admin office, on some
password-protected computer, each girl was dissected in an elabo-
rate spreadsheet. Our names filled one bubble, and all the other
bubbles below were populated by our various offenses and the
probability that we might harm ourselves or others. Adjacent columns tallied the money being poured into the endeavor of returning us reshuffled in the right combination. A month at Veld might
cost five thousand dollars or more. Like religion, it was possible to
pay your way to the top.

The last column outlined our chances of recovery. There was a
point system attributed to this, the result of some mysterious algo-
rithm. Our scores were partially derived from all the surveillance.
Every tape-recorded session, journal entry, letter to a parent or lost
friend—all passed through the same sieve of authority, tabulating
every infraction or glimmer of hope. This score, Gia said, was written at the top of your permanent record.

"That's not real," I said.

"What would your permanent record say?" Gia mused. "Hoards
her meds. Peeks at girls in the shower. Does not abide by the two-
towel rule."

"Very funny."

"You think things aren't too bad right now, but that's because
you haven't been here long enough. Above your head are a bunch of
neon dollar signs. Why would they let you go?"

It was nearly morning. It seemed no one had noticed Beanie's
absence yet. We were in our beds, and Harlow was back in her

half-empty room. The only thing left to do was wait for sunrise and the next loop to commence. A drizzle was coming down. I thought of Beanie, unequipped, exposed, however many miles off by now. She had been hearty on the trail. What was at the end of the woods, if she kept walking? Dr. John's petite farmhouse. Bowen and a drink at the Black Cat.

"The world is held up by a series of strings." Gia was riffing now.

"I'm not interested in this. Whatever you're saying right now."

She sighed. I heard her turn over and punch her pillow a few times. On the trail we'd learned to sleep the sleep of itinerants, deep and wary. It would be no time at all until she was snoring.

"Fine," she said, and settled. "You always want to learn the hard way."

The next day, Group Share carried on the same as usual, minus Beanie.

I watched Dr. John's face for clues as to his mood. Usually when one of the sadist girls spoke, he was all ears. It was clear he found their breed particularly interesting from a research standpoint, but he only twiddled his thumbs and offered a canned idiom.

"That's it?" the sadist girl asked. "That's all?" Eventually, she'd go to prison for taking a baseball bat to the slumlord that booted her from her place in Reno. Beforehand, she texted everyone she knew saying she was going to do it. In this way, she was not very complicated.

"Progress." Dr. John nodded, and moved on to the next.

No one made mention of Beanie's absence. I expected little from Gia, but even Harlow didn't seem concerned, though it was difficult to detect any of her emotions besides displeasure.

I asked around in the kitchens during work detail, but no one knew anything or cared. Girls often came and went, were picked up by family, expelled, or moved to ISO. I thought of slipping out onto the lawn, calling for Beanie at the wood's edge like a lost cat—but for what? I thought of my score, my marks dwindling, chances of release reduced to zero. Family Day was coming. Everyone and their visitors would be arranged in circles in the main hall. Kin would have the chance to air their grievances. Though I'd been given no letter or phone privileges, I had been informed of my mother and Fawn's intent to appear. If I had one chance to make my case, to free myself from my present trappings, Family Day was it. I thought I cared about what happened to Beanie, but if I had to choose between myself or her, the calculation was obvious.

At dinner that night, I was half-listening to Gia's latest mono-logue on mind control via fluoridated water, how the pills they gave us contained distillates of the same substance the government used in chemtrails. I reminded myself that soon, I wouldn't have to know people like Gia anymore. Harlow was giving me eyes over her fruit cup, trying to get a rise out of me, which she knew would get a rise out of Gia. I was in no mood. I was going to tell her so, dump my tray, and go start on dishes as a distraction when Beanie sat down in the chair next to me.

There was a slash above her eyebrow, already in the beginning stages of scabbing over. The cut altered her face enough to suggest a kind of savagery, and I was going to ask where she'd been, how it was she'd gotten hurt, where she'd come from, but Gia kicked my shin under the table and mouthed, *Ignore her.*

"Hi, guys," Beanie said. "I'm back."

Harlow chewed very slowly and stared her down. Beanie was a mole, I reminded myself. The only difference between her and the sadist girls on the prowl was a carefully constructed artifice. Beanie operated at Veld's behest, one of Dr. John's minions, his favorite plaything. At least the sadist girls only served themselves. There was some logic in that.

"Don't you want to know where I've been? Don't you want to know how I got back?" Beanie tapped the cut on her eyebrow. "If you're wondering, yes, it does hurt."

Above us, the lights in the dining hall flickered. There were no storm clouds on the horizon, no break in the blue sky.

"Typical," Gia said.

Beanie looked between us and up at the lights. "What is?"

Gia shook her head and addressed me pointedly.

"Omens," she said.

Though it was clear to her a rift had occurred, Beanie trailed us to all the same spots, lingered in the door to our room, and swiped her signature on a birthday card we delivered to the Second Floor. Harlow stayed mum, but Gia was overt.

"Can't you see you're not wanted?" she would say anytime Beanie was hovering.

The more torment Beanie endured, the more she persisted. She saved us her dessert brownie, split it into equal thirds, and delivered it to us during dead hour. She worked double-time on cleaning crew so Harlow wouldn't have to do the toilets or bins, and she delivered to Gia an old map of the grounds, a campus key designed invitingly for some former institution that had already come and gone. An ideal Veld, an academy envisioned for the elite. Gia looked it over. I could tell she was committing it to memory, though she tore it down the middle and let it flutter at Beanie's feet. She didn't ask where she got it, because she already knew the answer.

I tried to fortify my own ire with moving images of Beanie and Dr. John rolling around in bed as moorland winds swirled over fields, drinks clinked at the Black Cat, cherry neon near the highway ramp. I could not help but wonder, if I had the same chance to manipulate my odds—would I have taken it?

One morning after breakfast, I was in the bathroom scrubbing my hands, trying to get the stink of garlic out from under my fingernails, and Beanie followed me in.

"What do I have to do to make you like me again?" she asked plainly. "I'll do it."

"I like you fine."

"I'm not that kind of dumb."

"Then you wouldn't bother cornering me."

"I have something for you." She held out an envelope. I recognized the handwriting on its face immediately. All the pages were there, including the first, the only one I'd been able to read on the trail before my mother's message had vanished. I took the letter from her and inspected it.

"Where did you get this?"

"I don't know why you trust Gia more than me, but maybe this will prove it to you."

"Where?"

"Gia keeps a stash in the back of the utility closet. You know how she is. I found it a few days ago, but since you won't pay any attention to me, I haven't been able to explain."

"Did you read it?"

"Of course not. Who do you think I am?"

Gia banged through the door to the bathroom. I turned back to the sink quickly and shoved the envelope into the front of my work pants. "Ladies," she said.

"I was just leaving," Beanie said.

"No, no. Please. Stay." Gia strode past us to relieve herself in the far toilet. There were no doors or stalls. That sort of privacy was a privilege reserved for staff. While Gia peed, Beanie stepped to the sink next to me and pressed the bags under her eyes. She touched the wound healing on her brow. It would leave a small, intriguing scar.

She waited for Gia to flush and whispered the word *midnight,* and slipped out the door.

Gia zipped up, washed her hands. She came to stand beside me and stared in the mirror.

"It's best if you two aren't left alone together," she said.

"I'm not worried about it."

"She's a spy."

"Says you."

Gia turned to face me. "I'm looking out for you. As a roommate."

"Oh, as a roommate."

"Your attitude is very tiresome. Not at all consistent with your daily intention, so maybe someone should hear about that. Help you chill out in ISO."

"Now who's the spy?"

Gia pinched the skin of her forehead and cheeks.

"This place ages me," she said. "It has a way of doing that, you know. Even after you leave. People forget how to walk straight." Even under the fluorescents, there was something dim about her, a dearth of internal light. I wondered how many mountains Gia had been forced to climb.

"You're the smart girl," she said. "I'm sure you'll make it through just fine without any help or advice or people looking out for you. Me? I've been down this road so many times, it's like sleep. It's like being unconscious. Lights out. I just don't know what I might do."

11

After the fire at the Wepplers', many blistering days transpired. The concept of punishment was repellent to my mother, but this did not stop her from stalking my bedroom door, bursting at the seams with rhetorical questions. Instead of being grounded or sent to a shrink or otherwise made to account for my involvement, I was steamrolled into long, circuitous conversations about the nature of autonomy and adulthood, the evolving poles of a moral compass, and how this act of demolition would scar my record. She kept reminding me she had been young once. She said she knew all the tricks. I could see she was experimenting with tones that were by turns authoritarian or conspiratorial, but she never found the right thing to say, let alone the right voice to say it in.

Zeke kept calling. He called so often my mother sometimes unplugged the phone. Once, I picked up and yelled into the receiver before he could start talking. "You're either sexless, gay, or stupid," I recited, just as Antonia had. "Don't call here again."

My mother suspected a kind of breakup between us, or perhaps that one of us had confessed our love and ruined everything. Something had been ruined. I let the phone ring.

Unlike my mother, Zeke would not be pacified by denial or excuses, and the truth was too knotted together. If I told him one thing, it would tug on the rest. How the Wepplers' had become our clubhouse led to how I felt about Antonia. The fire's point of origin led to my botched plans of heroic rescue. Meanwhile, I had done my own research. To determine the root of a fire, investigators read the damage like a map—char patterns, heat shadows, the direction of melt. Zeke had a nose for the truth, and I knew that's what he would do. Follow the wreckage. He would trace this silence to the man in the van, the Fourth of July, and, eventually, to what I suspected Fawn had done to the dog.

There were bottles of pills left haphazard in the bathroom cabinet above the sink, old prescriptions my mother let linger for years. There was rat poison, roach bait, the skin of onions gathered for dye she'd never assemble. In limited search terms I scoured the internet for the combination of symptoms I'd seen in Peanut Butter. I added and subtracted, trying to test my memory and what was real. Natural causes were possible. Accidents occurred, sure. No website could spit back the truth as I knew it. I had seen her face. The absence of grief. No anguish. Only the impatience to spring upon the next fixation as it crossed her.

As far as I knew, Fawn had told no one the truth of how the blaze began, and by keeping each other's secrets, it felt somehow that we were finally even, or else locked in a stalemate.

One morning, I woke up very early and went into the living room. It must've been the sound of the TV that stirred me. Fawn was sitting on the rug with a blanket over her shoulders. I didn't ask what she was doing because I was doing the same thing—watching her onscreen.

My mother's home movies weren't just thrown together composites of candid family leisure. She liked to stage scenes, create a focus.

The loft looked different on camera. All that clutter appeared as a cinematic tableau, little colonies of ephemera she had assembled over a lifetime. We had a crescent moon made of layered vellum strung up in the rafters, and it spun the light as it swayed, its sad singular eye bemoaning the underworld to which it was now tethered.

In the video, Fawn was sitting in a chair by the window. She was reading aloud from a book of island fables, a gift given to us by our mother, the sort of flimflam brought back from an airport gift shop, no doubt an attempt to get us in touch with our history. The story was "El Perro de Piedra."

As Fawn read, the camera's eye floated over shelves and end tables and window ledges crammed with favorite rocks, foreign coins, tufts of dried moss.

"Amigo was the company mascot, loved and cherished by all."

A Spanish colonial soldier found a puppy in the gutter and took him back to his barracks. The company fed him scraps and let him nip their heels as they trooped the cobblestone streets of San Juan and reported to their post at Castillo de San Gerónimo.

"Suddenly," Fawn read, "the company was called away to another colony where there was a battle going on. The soldier hugged Amigo and promised to come back soon. He knew the other soldiers would take good care of him." I could hear my mother breathing behind the camera. The lens dissolved in and out of focus. "When the soldier's ship sailed away, Amigo leapt over the fortress walls and splashed down into the water. He swam as hard as he could to a shelf of coral, just beyond the breakers." She looked into the camera. "Should I keep going?"

The camera nodded. Fawn closed the book and continued on from memory.

"Amigo waited and waited. Every day, from sunup to sundown, he sat on his rock and looked out to sea, yearning for his master to return. Far, far away, a sea battle raged. Cannons fired. The soldier's ship, and everyone on it, went down to their watery graves."

She allowed a dramatic pause, during which she looked out the window, daring the camera to catch her in longing profile.

"The other soldiers at the fortress discussed the tragedy and mourned. In his way, Amigo understood what had happened, but he does not give up. Every morning, he paddles out to his coral shelf. He sits and stares into the sea. He waits with fear, and hope."

I know what happens next, what follows fear and hope.

Hundreds of days pass. The shoreline ruptures and gives way to the peaks of luxury hotels and condo towers, their façades a series of balconies from which a hundred faces stare in the same direction. Jets rifle overhead. Cruise liners tear through the vista and idle on the horizon. Though the elements have altered him, he waits. Bitter nights and salt-spray like buckshot scar the animal to stone. El Perro de Piedra. The Stone Dog. Forever faithful.

The tape ends in a jumble as my mother fiddles for the right button on the camera. The floor and the ceiling and my sister's imploring face streak by. I hear Fawn offscreen, asking if she got it all, if she should start from the beginning and do it differently this time.

Fawn turned away from her performance onscreen and regarded me.

"Well? What do you think?"

I stood there in my sleep shirt. It was like a dream. "What's it for?"

"It's for anything. I was just telling the story."

"When did you guys film this?"

"After the Fourth," she said and lowered her voice to a whisper. "I think you were out. You know? At our spot?"

I thought of all the time I'd spent at the Wepplers' with Antonia, watching her lips move, ecstatic at her proximity. How many of those golden afternoons streaked by with Fawn just one floor below us? I imagined her slithering through the hopper window to the basement, twirling in the recliner as the tanks clouded and the fish went belly-up. The food pellets had been sitting right there.

"Why didn't you feed them?" I asked her suddenly. "If you were down there, if you were just hanging out all the time, underneath us. Why not say anything? Why did you let them die?"

"Let what die?"

"The fish. In the basement."

She looked at me dully.

"At our spot," I said.

"Oh." Fawn turned to the TV and pressed rewind. "I guess I didn't want to get in the way. What was I supposed to do?"

I watched the story of the stone dog skim by in reverse, the light rippling in time-lapse.

"I know that story," I said. "Was it Mom's idea to read that one?"

Fawn frowned. "Why does it have to be her idea? I was reading it for Peanut. To remember him."

I returned to my room and lay very still. I spent a lot of my days like that, those last summer days. Worlds were overlapping. I dreamt of the Wepplers' house often, and when I did, I sensed my waking self, my real self, standing at the edge of my bed, watching my sleeping body. My nightmares never had fire in them. They never made things more horrific than the reality of what had happened. It was the opposite. I dreamt of Antonia and me in bed together. I dreamt the basement in a spectrum of blues, flush with life. Even absent of violence, these dreams taunted, the punch line arriving when I woke.

At a certain point in our stalemate, my mother cracked. I knew how to withstand her laissez-faire parenting style, and she refused to diminish herself by trying other, more traditional methods of discipline. Her friend was staging a play in the city and insights were needed. It was as good a reason as any to retreat. Now, I was going out for the first time in what felt like forever.

Zeke had given up on calling. Fawn was spending all her time outdoors. Antonia and Kent had been briefly reunited by their shared trauma only to break up all over again. I was needed. The Weppler house was rubble, and I had been summoned to Antonia's pink house on the edge of town. On my way out the door, I saw Fawn in our mother's bedroom.

She was sprawled on her belly, across the bed. The room was rich with perfume, and I peeked in at the sound of her sneeze.

"You know you're not supposed to spray that," I told her.

"Spray what?"

"You're being obvious." I picked up the cut crystal bottle of Dior perfume on the dresser. My mother used to dab some behind her ears on her birthday, or when we all went into the city for a show. I asked her once why she kept it only for special occasions. It had been a wedding gift, and she wanted it to last. She said they didn't make it anymore.

Fawn turned onto her back and stared up at the wooden rafters, the patchwork of metal piping. My mother's room was smallest. The bed crowded everything out.

"What are you doing in here anyway?" I asked. "I'm about to leave for the night."

"Summer's over."

"Okay."

"Basically over." That was a new word she'd been trying on lately. *Basically.*

"And?"

"And I don't want to go back. I don't want to go to school every single day. They never stop talking and I hate fractions and there's so much chewing. I basically hate listening to everybody chew."

"You'll see your friends."

"Sure," she said. I couldn't conjure a face or name. She never threw birthday parties. She never went swimming in anyone's pool.

Fawn bounced to her feet and began peeking into drawers. She pulled out a pair of our mother's underwear and swung it around her finger before flinging it at me. I dodged it, and she took the bottle of Dior from the dresser and brought it to her nose.

"Have some," she said. "I bet your friend will think it's fancy."

I dropped my backpack. She spritzed, I strutted. We sniffed vigorously at our wrists, the hairs on our arms, our collars, the cuffs of our sleeves—until the scent became almost common. I tried to preserve it in my mind. Warm velvet. Something like the height of a season. Through the window, the afternoon sun starched a frill of curtain. The smell was everywhere but suddenly impossible to recall.

"When is she coming back this time?" Fawn asked.

"Who?" I said, but I knew. "I don't know." I had trained myself to stop wondering.

Fawn inspected the bottle of Dior like it was the first time she'd ever seen it. "When she does come back," she said, "you should tell her."

"Tell her what?"

"About what you did to Peanut Butter. Kind of like what you were going to do to your friends. She might understand now. She might know what to do."

"You know what happened at the Wepplers' was an accident."

"Do I know that?"

"And what do you think happened to Peanut?"

"Well, he isn't living with some other family." She tossed the bottle of Dior high in the air and caught it underhand, like a softball. "I have the best reflexes. I'm a stud."

"Don't do that."

"It's not like you ever wanted the dog anyway. You should tell Mom the truth."

"You know what happened to him."

"It's a mystery."

"Someone gave him something. He ate something poisonous. He was really sick."

"You told everyone he ran away." Fawn spritzed her neck, fluttered her eyelids like an old screen star. "I guess that was a lie."

"Who do you think would do something like that to an animal? Put that bottle down."

Fawn held out the perfume, and when I reached for it, she snatched it back, held it close over her heart. "So, what will you say to her?"

She smiled and extended the bottle again.

"You can try to put words in my mouth, but you aren't smarter than me."

"I was just trying to help." She sighed. "Remember the fire? I was the one who saved us. I just don't think it's fair if both of us get in trouble for something you did. Peanut Butter didn't deserve that."

"Stop it."

"Here." She waved the bottle at me. "Really. Take it this time."

I knew what would happen, and yet I reached for it anyway. My fingertips hardly brushed the glass before she released it, and it dropped to the floor.

The instant thud, the sound of the nozzle skittering off under the bed. I lunged to retrieve the bottle, and though the glass appeared intact, the thin, cold solution it held streamed through my hands, so fragrant I could taste it. There was no putting it back in.

"What did you do? There's no more of this. She can't get it anywhere," I said.

Fawn was careful to sidestep the puddle as she went to the door. My hands clutched the egg of glass. The little room was poisonous with the smell.

"You were supposed to be watching me," Fawn said, "and now look. It's all over you."

———

The Italian Renaissance Revival was all cream columns and pink plaster, like an iced cake. The state of the yard reflected the tension indoors. Antonia said when her mother and father weren't fighting, he paid for the landscapers, but when they were on the outs, the yard became a jungle. Antonia's room had a window seat that overlooked an oblong retention pond adjacent to the property. A twitching, mint-green skin coated the surface, but the walls in Antonia's bedroom were the color of a healthy pink tongue.

She had a desktop computer to herself, a high-speed connection. She was taking a quiz online. *Which Leading Man Is Your Prince Charming?*

Downstairs, her mother had been vacuuming for hours. Her mother smoked while she did this, because she was never not smoking. When ash fluttered onto the high-pile rug she rammed the vacuum over it instantly. Tomorrow, she was leaving for Atlantic City and taking Antonia. When she played at the Borgata, she got a champagne suite. She said it was as good as Vegas.

"Doesn't your mom ever wonder?" I asked. "All those nights you were sleeping in Kent's basement, and then at the Wepplers'."

"I say I'm busy with school. We're studying. Something like that. If she thinks it's for school, she doesn't have to worry."

"But, it's summer."

"I have to come up with something, don't I? When she's not in AC, she's here all the time. What are you telling your mom?" I realized I never really had to tell her anything. She always said autonomy was a gift she gave us, that we were supposed to use it to become our own masterpieces. "You know," Antonia said, "now that I think about it, my mom gets all our money from my dad. Usually she takes it to AC and it's gone pretty fast, but eventually he sends more. Who gives your mom money? Does she even have a job?"

"She just attracts money when she needs it. I guess that's like her job."

"She should play the slots." Antonia selected a new quiz on her browser. This one was about matching your personal style to a season. "My mom thinks she's going to be a motivational speaker one day. I can't wait to move out."

"I bet you'll go to New York."

"Maybe," she said, "but I don't want to be a cliché."

"Will you go back to Bayonne?"

"I wouldn't give my father the satisfaction."

I was leaning over her shoulder, watching her click around, selecting bubbles without a moment's hesitation.

"Zeke always talks about wanting to go away for school," I said. "Someplace across the country. California, I don't know. He wants to surf, but he's scared of sharks."

"And you're going with him?"

"I was just saying."

"You only do something like that if you don't want to come back."

"Why wouldn't he come back?"

She sighed. "It's too hard to go back and forth. You end up picking a place, and of course you pick the place you already are."

"My mom said she almost lived in California once."

"She probably would have been better off."

Antonia clicked out of her quiz, which told her she was a Summer—not surprising. She swiveled around and we were face-to-face, inches between us.

"What is that?" she asked. She closed the distance with the tip of her nose, brushing my neck in a warm puff of air. "It's you."

"Oh. It's Dior." I told myself not to move, and I didn't. Downstairs, the vacuum had ceased its droning. The vents were blowing full blast, a processed, acrid breeze. Antonia swiveled away and stood. I asked where her mother was now.

"Probably asleep on the couch. Casino Dreams."

She flopped onto her bed. She had tanned far darker than I had that summer, one of the benefits of her residency at the Heller house. Their kidney bean pool was always rank with bloated field mice, but they whipped the dead ones into the shrubs and dumped in more chlorine. Antonia said her parents' old place in Bayonne had a saltwater pool. The saltwater was softer, like a micro-exfoliant. "Lie down next to me," she said, and I did as I was told.

I could tell she was waiting for me to ask about Kent. She talked through things by starting at square one, and it often took her an hour to rechart the course of their stormy relationship, and their most recent breakup. It was during these marathons I proved my endurance.

"He's embarrassed me at the mall at least three to five times," she was saying. "But I guess we went through something together. We have a history. It's all so complicated."

"It happened to all of us. All of us have history."

"Yeah, but you act like it was this big exciting thing, when it was probably the worst experience on drugs I'll ever have." She rolled away from me. "Maybe I'll just stay in Atlantic City forever this time. My mom lets me order room service. I wish you could come."

I touched my hand to her hip and without hesitation she pulled it over her body and tucked it under her chin so that I had to draw close, spoon her, my face tucked into her neck.

"Maybe I can," I whispered.

"Do you promise you'll come with me?"

"Do you want me to?"

She nodded.

"What else do you want me to do?" I asked. "I'll do it."

This is love, I thought. Yes, I've got it now. It was a choice like any other, a consequence of bravery.

By the bed, Antonia's private phone line rang. She was on her feet in a second. She looked wide-eyed at the door as she clutched the receiver. The vacuum started up again. Now it was in the upstairs hallway. Antonia nodded into the phone. "He's there right now?" she said. It was nearly midnight. The vacuum banged against the doorframe, its miniature headlights glowing in the gap. "What's he saying? You know what, never mind. Just meet us."

She hung up and looked at me. "We're leaving."

"Who was that?"

"Your Mr. California," she said. "I'll explain on the way."

She towed me down the spiral staircase, right past her mother at the top of the steps. Her mother said nothing as we went, and she would continue to say nothing no matter how many times we would soon meet in the middle of the night, coming and going.

Outside, the weather had turned. On the back of a vaporous fog, August dissolved to October, though the trees were full as ever and massive as they clashed in the high, chill winds as we hurried toward The Gables. We were on our bikes, tires spinning. Through the haze, a lost seagull cawed. I closed my eyes along a smooth stretch of asphalt and on the air, I tasted salt water. Town looked different at this hour, in this weather, like it was a domed tableau we moved through as if on a track. I listened for the suction of boats bobbing at their moorings, the growl of motors over water, the sounds of MAYDAY. To someone, somewhere, those sounds were real.

Once we pedaled past The Gables' crumbling brick signage, I skidded to a halt before the Heller house, but Antonia kept pedaling. I took one look at the darkened windows, at Zeke and Kent's shared bedroom on the second floor. I knew where we were headed.

Coronet Court looked like every other street. There were the same FOR SALE signs belonging to competing brokerages stuck into yards around the cul-de-sac. We stopped in front of a familiar house and a set of headlights blinked on, blinding us.

Antonia braked before the sedan out front. It was Mr. Heller's corporate car. Zeke was in the passenger seat, and Kent was behind the wheel.

Antonia banged the hood twice and Kent killed the lights.

"Get in," Antonia said to me. "This will be quick."

The inside of the sedan smelled heady and thick, like a locker room. Antonia kicked Zeke to the back, and he and I sat shoulder to shoulder and pretended not to hear the conversation in front of us as Kent cried softly. I tried to imagine myself in his shoes. I pictured the tiles of the mall where their most recent breakup happened, the atrium full of dusty potted palms, Antonia and Kent by the fountain as she broke the news. It was almost possible to pity him. When we looked at her, we both wanted the same things.

"Why won't he stop crying?" I whispered to Zeke. "Why is he like this?" Kent was gripping Antonia's hands, moaning promises about becoming a man. The week before, he'd been fired from Sunglass Hut.

The engine turned over with a spike of a backfire and a house light flicked on.

"Well, you made us come all this way," Antonia was saying. "You better go and do it. Go on. Go and get him. Be the man. Bring him back here to me. I'm waiting."

Kent wiped his nose and looked at us in the backseat, remembering we were there.

"Shut up," he said, though we hadn't said anything. "You and you. Get out."

"I'm not leaving without her," I said, but Zeke was already grabbing my elbow and towing us out onto the sidewalk. "Wait. I'm not leaving her."

A shadow moved inside the house, the house that belonged to the man in the van. The front door of the Ranch style opened, and he stepped out in a robe, holding a putter.

"Who's out there?" he shouted. "Show yourselves."

"Get the bikes," Zeke said.

The man took a step off his stoop. "You," he said. "I know you."

"She's not going to just leave us here," I said, as Kent cranked the sedan into drive and screeched forward. "Wait. Antonia, wait."

I caught a glimpse of her face in the passenger window, but she did not wave or give some signal, or even throw up her hands at her powerlessness, mouth to me a sorry or goodbye. She did not even look back.

The man was wearing slippers, but there was nothing under his robe but ragged white underwear. The putter in his hand glinted in the porch light.

"Sorry," Zeke called out to him. "We're leaving now."

"Don't apologize to him," I said.

"This is trespassing," the man said. "You're going to wait inside while I call the police."

"No, thank you," Zeke called back, trying to right both bikes by himself. I couldn't move. "Get over here. Grab the handle."

"Help," the man yelled. "Someone help me. I know your faces."

A few lights in neighboring houses blinked on. The man pointed at us and began crossing the lawn. "I know your faces," he shouted again.

Zeke said my name. "Wake up. We're leaving."

We mounted the bikes and aimed them toward the main thoroughfare. I looked over my shoulder as I pedaled, watching the flaps of the man's robe as he trotted after us, his silhouette losing definition as we picked up speed. I almost lost my balance staring back.

Once we were far enough from the scene, we coasted and caught our breath. Antonia's bike was too small for Zeke, and his knees jutted up against the handlebars.

"We can switch, if you want," I said.

"Do I look uncomfortable?"

"You look like a giant." I complained that Kent had a death wish. That he couldn't just drive off like that with Antonia as a hostage. "Let's go back to your house. We can regroup."

"She's not going to be there," Zeke said.

"Who?"

He gave me a look.

"Well, where else would they go? They're over."

"Over?" He laughed. "Where do you think she's sleeping every night?"

"Whatever was happening before isn't happening now."

"This isn't the first time Kent's gone to that guy's house to start something. And it's not the first time I had to call Antonia to come and get him. This is what they do. They love to pretend there's something big keeping them apart so they can always end up back together."

We had reached the end of The Gables. I tried to smile and couldn't. I was embarrassed, emptied of excuses. Of course Zeke knew the truth of Antonia before I did. Standing there together, it seemed so possible all of a sudden that I could confess to him everything else.

"It's okay to cry," he said.

I blinked and a single tear squeezed out, a marvel. So much had happened that summer that all the amputated gore of June felt unreal. I thought of Peanut Butter, his fur, the coolness of the clearing where I laid him down the last time. A stone dog rooted there, as endless suns rose and set. Zeke and I let the mist pass us by.

"I don't know why I care," I said. "I guess I should just go home."

"Don't go yet. Not yet. There's something else."

Now he had me, and my defenses were weak. I could tell he had practiced what he was going to say, because he never talked like that, never posed the truth like a riddle.

He said, "I need to show you something. When you see it for yourself, you'll understand."

"Understand what?" I asked, though I required no answer. I was already following him.

12

Once I had my mother's letter back in hand, I wouldn't let it out of my sight. The notion that Gia would steal for her own archive of blackmail did not surprise me, and I could not be sure when she'd next sweep our room for new collectibles. I kept the letter tucked in my waistband. During an exercise that evening, counselors killed the lights of the main hall, blasted the air-conditioning, and pretended we were all crewmen on a failing ship, forced to decide who in our ranks would be tossed overboard to save the rest. Most everyone agreed that it should be Gia, but I was belligerently uncooperative. I said a sinking boat would sink no matter who we abandoned, it was just a matter of how soon.

This was an easy ticket to ISO on the Fifth Floor, the only place I could guarantee extended privacy.

I settled into my carpeted closet and waited in case any counselors came to check on my welfare, but this was unlikely. The envelope was stained with dirt and fingerprints. It had clearly been opened and folded and paged through many times, though Gia had somehow managed to remain mum about its contents, which was unlike her. Now that I'd been given a second chance to hold it in my hands, whatever anger or distrust I felt for Beanie washed itself to pity. I reread the first page of grievances and hours looped by inside my mother's alphabet.

She was writing about 1974 like it was supposed to mean something to me. It was the year she dropped out of college to hitchhike across the country. My grandmother, who I never met, was the one who let her off at the highway ramp, but this was not a show of support. Along a jagged route, she thumbed her way south. She often wondered how her parents were keeping up appearances. Their only child was diving dumpsters behind grocery stores, slurping cold marinara from expired jars. Instead of bringing a boyfriend home for holiday ham, she cowered in ditches as rural men stalked the roadside. They stood in beds of slow-rolling pickups and fired guns into the brush. Hippie Hunting. She took the graveyard shift at a greasy spoon and when a coked-up trucker refused to pay his bill, she pulled a butter knife on him. He punched her in the face and left. It was a lesson in big ideas. What she needed was money, but she had burned her bridges and there was only one number she was not too proud to call. Her roommate from freshman year, her rescue, who happened to pick up the phone. Candace.

I remembered Candace. Her name and voice sprung forward in my mind and with it all the messages I'd taken down over the landline in the loft, that and our brief but fateful meeting years before. Candace, ever waiting in the wings, always with a caveat. She had family money from the nuts and bolts business. They were from Ohio. My mother thought this explained a lot.

If my mother agreed to call from each stop, Candace would send along a cash injection. She was greedy for my mother's stories of the drivers who picked her up, the places she slept, the poor choices she made.

"I can't wait until you get back here," Candace said, but my mother had no plans to return.

She had a pocket knife for protection, the blade no more than a few inches and dull as the lip of a pan. It was a good luck charm at least. She found a tarnished chain and hung the knife around her neck, hidden under her shirt and within reach. Later, she would tell Fawn and me how to determine if you were in the presence of a dangerous person. First check their shoes, and then their eyes. Sometimes danger was obvious, sometimes undercover. "It can be hard to tell the difference," she explained, "but undercover is worse. You might not notice until it's too late."

She had her own man in the van. He picked her up on the way to San Francisco in his VW Westfalia, gleaming new. They stopped for dinner and he bought her anything she wanted. She ordered a cup of soup, a hamburger with a runny egg on it, a chocolate milkshake, peach pie. She treaded lightly in case he was floating this friendliness in exchange for something she was not willing to give, but he asked questions, and he was kind to the waitress. They talked about what California was going to do for them. He was an ex-Realtor, but like her he was trying on a new life. As his first order of business, he was going to get himself a dog.

"Why would you go and get a dog?" my mother asked him. The responsibility of ownership, of being owned, was repellent as a matter of course. Entanglements stole the wind right out of you, no matter how loyal the bitch.

She called Candace from a rest stop in Fresno. Everything stunk like dirt and shit, but that was nothing new. She gave Candace instructions as to where to send her latest payout. When my mother mentioned her new friend, Candace cleared her throat. "Who is this guy?"

"Oh, you see all kinds of faces out here." My mother looked across the lot. The man was stretching his calf against his bumper and doing jumping jacks. He looked like a townie, though from where she couldn't say. He caught her eye and waved. "He's not my type," she said.

"I thought you said you didn't have a type."

"Who doesn't have a type? Candace, I've got to go."

"Already?"

"Well, what're you doing over there? Aren't you busy?"

She sighed. "I'm supposed to be studying, but what's the point? I was thinking I could come out to San Fran."

"No one calls it San Fran."

"Whatever they call it then. I thought I might see it for myself."

A few years had passed since their shoebox dorm, but my mother pictured the same eighteen-year-old Candace who rarely left their room and was always waiting up for her.

"We'll chat soon," my mother said, hoping it was the last time they'd have to speak.

My mother and the man with the van were in the last eight-hour stretch when he offered her the thin mattress in back. She tried to read his face, but the sunset was ahead of them, and the view made her trusting. When she opened her eyes again, it was his she saw. He was sprawled beside her on the mattress, one leg hooked high and tight between hers. He nudged his knee deep between her legs and covered her mouth with his hand. She let him do what he wanted for ten seconds, the time it took to maneuver her hand up her own shirt, to the pocketknife between her breasts. The flip of the blade was rote. She aimed it where she believed his heart to be.

He swore and shoved her back. The knife stuck out just below his shoulder like a bad prop. She couldn't stop herself from apologizing. She heard her own voice saying sorry while another heckling voice at the back of her brain told her to shut up. She yanked the door open and they were on an empty road, long and flat like the desert in a cartoon. She took off running across the dirt prairie, backpack hiked under her armpits. There were only supersized clusters of brambles, like tumbleweeds but rooted in place. She squatted in a small wash overnight and at dawn she walked the direction the sun said was west. Inside city limits, pounds lighter and wind-whipped, soles of her feet so tender she tiptoed the last mile—fog obscured everything. San Francisco was a walk in the clouds, but the dream only held for three months. She wrote that there were so many people just like her. She wished there was some kind of line she could stand in, a signal she could send that she was ready to begin life in earnest.

The last straw came after a night spent beneath a bushy pine in Golden Gate Park. When she woke, her hair was wet. It stunk of ammonia and burnt coffee. Piss. Though it could not have been the man with the van who'd done it, that was who she pictured. Unzipping his fly in the dark, chuckling about the local inventory as he released his hot stream and shook himself off over her face. She felt bad for herself, but worse for whatever dog he'd make his.

There was only one thing left to do. She called Candace, who picked up on the first ring.

They spent the summer together in San Francisco. My mother had never been with a woman, but Candace had her virtues. She rented them a pied-à-terre and was a world-class enthusiast when it came to my mother's fleeting ambitions. On occasion, the stars aligned, and they met in the right mood, the right angle of day. It was in those instances that my mother felt unlonely. That was how she described it. To be in exactly the right company.

Rankled by the failure of her great San Franciscan experiment, my mother considered what might make her happy. She hadn't yet made it back East to New York. The loft was still a button factory. She decided she liked best the long stretches of country, the light of the morning so immediate there, how remarkable the smallest scenes became when there was nothing but nature to entertain—a crane balancing in the water, deer haunting the mist, so elegant, so big-eyed. I knew this feeling, the meditation of footfalls, the scroll of an environment as it did the daily work of existence whether you were its witness or not. She decided to find an empty space where she could devote herself to the holiness of the quotidian. She told all this to Candace over lunch in Nob Hill, and to her surprise, Candace bit.

My mother wrote, *I lost interest in the whole idea the instant she agreed to go along.*

Some decade and change later, that was how we got to Nova Scotia, as part of my mother's tour of contrition. She needed Candace to put her back on track again. It was where the seed of Fawn's dark bloom began to break through. I thought this was the direction my mother's letter was finally headed, and if we both understood the truth about my sister, however delayed our revelations, my own freedom could not be far behind. I began pacing the solitary closet, now too tiny to contain what was in my hands, forgetting that months had passed since the letter's loss and no one had come for me. The little green closet shrunk and shrunk and I was the one who locked myself in.

The Chip had three decks: the bottom for cars, the top for people, and the middle for slot machines. It was my dream to pull the lever, but I was only thirteen.

We were taking the ferry to a Canadian island I didn't know existed. Before Veld, the farthest I'd ever been was Philadelphia's Main Line, when my mother took us to see our grandfather on his deathbed. I thought he looked like Frank Sinatra. For weeks after, I listened to "One for My Baby (One for the Road)" on repeat. I had been to the ocean, but never on it.

Fawn and I were out on the observation deck, watching the sea chop past. She was so little then. Her light hair had been cut only a few times her entire life, and it mousetailed down her back in tangles. She stood on the metal railing and teetered over the edge for the best view of the water as she spat into it. "Would I die if I fell?" she asked.

"You'd probably get sucked under by the propellers, like *Titanic.*"

"I can swim. I can do a running dive."

"It's not the same as a pool."

"Would you jump in to save me?"

"What good would that do?"

We were visiting my mother's college roommate, who lived in a primitive inland cabin with her two children. I asked if we would have our own rooms and my mother scoffed. "That's not the way they live," she said.

Through the speckled windows of the ferry's main compartment, my mother was reading a dime-store romance novel. She and Billy had met a few weeks ago for the first time. Love was on the brain. After *The Chip* docked in Yarmouth we drove the Volvo another hour on a lonely road, on which heavy-duty trucks revved thirty miles above the speed limit and passed us even if it meant breaking the double-yellow of the two-lane. We were coasting by a whole lot of empty. The woods on either side were so dense it was like a curtain pulled closed. There was no telling what was in there, or how deep it went. What did I know about the world outdoors? Veld existed, but not to me. I hadn't climbed mountains or toed ridges. It was all bugs and mud. That's what nature looked like. And though she spent a year hitchhiking cross-country, eschewing her good breeding to live rough, my mother felt the same about the world alfresco. Dirty.

Since leaving Deerie, my mother had nibbled her fingernails to the quick. When I fooled with the radio, she batted my hand away. I didn't understand why we were going north. I'd been forcibly introduced to dozens of my mother's friends, but we never traveled for anyone. I had never heard of Candace and I asked my mother if they were close.

"I've known her for years," she said.

"Is she nice?"

"She's a very competent woman."

"Do you like her?"

"You know, I used to be very different. I had a very strange idea of fun, I'll tell you that."

"Mom."

She glanced into the rearview mirror. Fawn was dead asleep in the backseat. A running engine always knocked her out. It was one of the few things about her I found reliable.

"Candace is not my favorite, but so what," my mother said. "Also, I think she might be in love with me, but you know not to repeat that." She jabbed the radio button and static blared, fumbling with the dial until she found a station playing Tammy Wynette. "Obviously."

One of Fawn's longer-running fixations was that our mother had a secret family somewhere and didn't even know it. The requirements of conception were lost on her. She imagined babies popping up like weeds anywhere a flake of skin fell, as if you might slough off sons and daughters and leave them behind like all that human dust. I was thinking of this theory as we snaked down Candace's private drive, the car rounding boulders and petrified trunks left where they fell. At the end of the perilous drive, the cabin was dark, seemingly empty. This could be our house, I thought. This could be our long-lost family.

"This is scary." Fawn was awake in the backseat, now alert. "I like it."

We dug through our luggage for sweatshirts while our mother circled the house for signs of life. There were rocking chairs on the front porch. Fawn and I sat and swung in them as we waited to be told what to do. She sniffed the air and said she could smell the ocean.

"We're not even near the ocean."

"We're on an island."

"Who even lives here? What sort of air is this?" The house was closed in by towering woodland. There were no neighbors for miles.

"Did you see that?" I asked. There, a flicker in the trees. I stopped Fawn's rocker, mid-swing. "Is that them?"

"Is it bears?"

"Bears don't have flashlights, stupid."

"I don't know what bears do."

Our mother circled to the front of the house and called out to the woods.

"Yoo-hoo. Hello? Is that Candace?" And it was.

On the porch, we got acquainted. Candace and her handsome twins. She looked much older than my mother, but far healthier somehow. She had the look of a woman who could gallop away on horseback. "So sorry to have missed your arrival," she said. "We were taking a moonlit stroll. It's something we do around here. Let our senses be our guide."

I thought this sounded insane, but my mother clapped her hands. "Delightful."

The twins were a little younger than Fawn. A boy and a girl. They looked like catalogue models for an expensive coastal brand, dressed in seersucker and white linen and denim jumpers with oversized buttons, like slightly feral Scandinavian dolls. Inside, the structure was rough-hewn, with an open layout and two exposed sleeping lofts accessed by ladder. That was a detail Fawn could appreciate. "Like a pirate ship," she said. *Treasure Island* and all things swashbuckling were her most recent fixations.

It was over breakfast the next morning that the twins asked if we wanted to play a game.

Fawn and I looked at each other as they scurried up a ladder into their little lofted area.

"Come, come," they said from above.

"You first," Fawn told me.

The game was called Crackers. Its rules were indecipherable and blended the glass tiles of Mancala and the play money from Monopoly. New rules and objectives sprung up with every roll of the dice, of which there were three. I rolled a three, a six, and a two.

"I don't think I get how to play," I said.

"That means you both go to jail," the boy said. Fawn and I were on a team.

"But you rolled that before," Fawn said, "and you got an extra roll and a hundred dollars, so I should get an extra roll and a hundred dollars."

"*We* should get another roll," I said. "*We* should get a hundred dollars."

"Well, this time you get jail," the girl said. "Those are our rules."

That was how the whole stay at Candace's cabin went. Our twin chaperones towed us around, inventing parameters on the fly. We were not allowed to speak each other's names. Guests don't have names, they said. Names were privileges bestowed by hosts. They took us to their lean-to fort tucked in the woods, but to earn entry, we had to complete a series of arbitrary and demeaning tasks. Fawn was especially taken with the fort, but each time she tried to step foot inside, the boy put a hand on her chest and pushed her back, ready with another demand in a never-ending list she could not hope to satisfy. And because there were no walls inside the A-frame, I could never find a moment private enough to run our issues up the flagpole. My mother and Candace ping-ponged around the kitchenette while keeping a polite, choreographed distance, batting back and forth empty remarks. I got the sense it was an us versus them situation—three on three. The balance would keep shifting until the final second of our stay, and then the winning side would be revealed.

As advertised, we set out for a moonlit ramble beneath the stars on our last evening on the island. The mothers' flashlights meandered as they launched a deep dive into the past. I feared spiders were scaling my jeans, burrowing in my ear canal to birth a thousand more. I confused the sound of my footfalls for some interloper. A man on the lam, armed and dangerous.

"And what does *he* have to say about all this?" Candace was asking my mother at the rear of our pack. "Let me guess. *He's* got you right where *he* wants you."

My mother was running out of money. I'd heard snippets of

conversation all week. Bits about my father, the woes of getting in touch, his meticulous accounting. He called maybe once every few months, but it was always at a precise interval, on the dot, and my mother would be waiting to snatch the phone from its cradle. After these calls, the cupboards were restocked, my mother resumed monthly train passes, and the mood inside the loft loosened, at least until her accounts were in the red again.

While my mother played the meek patient, Candace opined on the virtues of a self-sufficient lifestyle. No grid. No TV that told you what to think. No men. The trail split before us and I called back to the mothers to ask which way.

"This way," the boy said. He had been keeping a cautious distance. Up ahead, his sister was babbling to herself about the constellations, while Fawn dragged a long stick in the dirt behind her. She was looking up through the treetops, sidestepping every tree root and divot without ever looking down.

"Communication," Candace said. "That is the problem in a nutshell."

"I'm backed into a corner now," my mother said. "I've got nothing left."

"That's why you came to me. And here I am."

Candace's words were my last landmark. I fell into my own rhythm after that, muscles warm, anticipating my footwork. My ears were like satellites receiving the screech of the woods in stereo. My mind had left my head. I blinked and we were back at the tree line, the cabin dark as the night we first arrived.

It was Candace who sensed it first.

She called the boy's name and did a few circles in place, shining the light along the path. She drifted toward the house, my mother forgotten, while the girl danced off toward the porch, a carousel in motion inside her blond head.

"Well, that was fun, wasn't it?" my mother said, bumping my shoulder. "I liked that."

They weren't in the house. They weren't in the vegetable patch. They weren't in the shed by the creek. My mother hadn't even noticed Candace's mounting concern, or that her own youngest was gone. Inside the lean-to in the bramble-hidden hollow, inside another envelope of darkness. That's where Fawn and the boy were now.

My mother and Candace told me and the girl to wait in the cabin while they went out looking. That way, if Fawn and the boy returned on their own, someone would be there. An hour had passed. The girl was waiting by the front window, her hair swishing as she scanned the tree line. I knew the girl did not want to be alone with her worry. I could feel her watchfulness radiating, but I picked a book from the shelf and brought it up to the loft.

Once, I'd seen a show about twin-sense. It was on one of those channels in the high-forties that played wonkier fare you had to be in the mood for. Unsolved murders, medical marvels, special features on the Bermuda Triangle. A twin could hear the other's thoughts, the episode claimed. They could sense each other's feelings from afar. Joy and shock and hurt. Like a nail driven up through the sole of a shoe, one twin was pierced by the extreme feeling of the other. But this phenomenon was not without its glitches. The episode featured two sets of twins. The first pair were from England. Two otherwise staid women broke from reality simultaneously and dove headlong into a thirty-six-hour rampage. They set fire to trash cans, punched unsuspecting strangers in the crotch and the face. Eventually, they were kicked off a public bus for spitting on passengers. When the police arrived, the women sprinted into the busy road, found the path of a semitruck, and flung themselves before its grill, dying instantly. The second set of twins were brothers separated at birth who led parallel lives. Both married women named Betty, then divorced their wives for women named Jennifer. Both served in the Coast Guard and became police lieutenants. Both joined the Elks. Both preferred hockey to football. Both drank Budweiser,

King of Beers, and nothing else. It didn't matter if the twins grew up drooling over the same blocks, wearing matching onesies. It didn't matter if they'd been pried apart as infants, set on distant courses, opposite coasts. They were a closed loop.

I wondered if the boy's aura was emitting some distress signal only his twin could receive. Perhaps the girl could only sense that something wasn't right. This might've been worse—the suggestion of pain but no clues as to its source or extent. I looked out the window and practiced an expression of grave concern. I thought of Fawn shivering, lost in darkness. There was a flit of anxiety at my throat, but I pulled away from the image and the turmoil dispersed. I went back to my book. It was called *Begin to Keep Bees*.

> Between inspections, you will probably be watching the activities of the bees at the hive entrance nearly every day. You will find it fascinating and relaxing, so pull up a lawn chair and enjoy it. As the season progresses, some hive activities will begin to occur that may cause you concern and may lead you to the conclusion that your bees are about to swarm.

When I woke again, my mother was brushing hair from my face. "I let you sleep in a little," she said, "but now it's time to go."

"Where is everyone?"

"Downstairs having breakfast. You must be hungry, huh?"

I sat up on my elbows. I was alone in bed. The other sleeping loft across the way was empty too. "What happened?" I asked.

"We found them."

Candace only kept muesli in the cupboards, so I pretended I wasn't hungry. I watched Fawn and the twins bantering at the table while the mothers got everything packed by the car. It felt as though I'd slept through an important truce.

"Where did you guys go last night?" I asked. "What happened?"

"We got lost," Fawn said. "We stepped off the path and got turned around."

The boy nodded. "We got lost," he said. "I stepped off the path."

"That's right," Fawn said. "It was really dark out. All the woods look the same, right?"

"Right," the boy said. His twin did not seem disturbed.

"So, you were both just wandering around until they found you?" I asked.

The boy looked to Fawn, his cereal spoon hovering.

"Yep," she supplied. "They found us, but it was scary."

"It was scary," the boy said.

"It was," Fawn said.

This was the move she learned in Nova Scotia, the private power within the folds of nature, the lean-to situated off the beaten path.

Next to me, the girl was humming through a mouthful of muesli. All was well.

"Have you ever gotten lost before?" I asked her.

"No," the girl said. "We've never gotten lost."

"It was an accident," Fawn said.

"It was an accident," the boy said. The girl looked at him oddly and set down her spoon.

"Stop saying what she's saying," the girl said. "You're not being funny."

Fawn dropped her own spoon with a clatter. Everyone looked on as she picked it up again and scooped a mound of cereal. "This is delicious. I love every bite."

The boy looked at Fawn for direction that didn't come. "It was an accident," he said again, like a glitch. He picked up his orange juice. He put it back down. He glanced at his sister.

Fawn smiled. "Let's everyone play a game. Let's go upstairs and play Crackers again." She took the boy by the elbow and stood him up, pushed him toward the ladder. "We'll all play one more game and then it'll be time to go home. Just give us one minute to set everything up perfect."

The girl and I waited to be summoned. Upstairs, she rolled first. A two, a six, a four.

"Okay, that means you have to do laps," Fawn said. "Six of them."

"Laps?"

"All the way around the house. All the way. Quick, quick, before your next turn."

The girl looked to her brother to rekindle their alliance, but he'd been silent since the game began. At least we were leaving soon. That was what the girl must've been thinking. That was why she listened and climbed carefully back down the ladder.

When the front door closed behind her, Fawn put the dice in the boy's hand. Crackers was her game now.

A one. A two. A three. Neat in a line, like it was meant to be.

"What does it mean?" he asked.

"Stand up," Fawn said, and he stood. "Now spin in a circle for ten seconds."

"I don't know if I want to."

Fawn laughed. "Why does everyone want to forget the rules all of a sudden? When it was your turn, we played by the rules." She turned to me then. "It's our turn now, right?"

"Just do it," I told the boy. "Get it over with."

He took a steadying breath like he might cry, and Fawn got very close to him, her forehead nearly against his.

"You want to play with me, don't you?"

The boy nodded.

"Okay," she said. "Spin."

He held his arms out straight like propeller blades. The boy was being very careful, watching his feet. Fawn counted out like a choreographer as he made measured revolutions, and I saw the girl dash by on one of her laps, hair flying behind her. All it took was a little nudge. Strength was not required, only timing. Fawn's hand found his chest at the precise interval. She drove him back with the proper ratio of force to will.

What had I seen? The boy: pushed. The boy: one foot slipping and the body following behind, like someone jerked his pant leg and down he'd gone.

I'll never forget the sound of it. Body to floor. A smack to the eardrum, like a sack of flour let drop.

It was possible I was dreaming. There was an eerie silence as Fawn scuttled quickly down the ladder to the ground floor, and when I peeked out over the edge, she was by his side.

The boy was gasping on the floor, eyes wide like a ghost was descending from the ceiling.

"We won," Fawn said, looking up at me. "We win the game."

Things happened quickly after that. The girl appeared in the doorway and screamed, which made the mothers come running. The girl dropped down at her twin's side. "What happened? What hurts?" she was saying. Everyone was out of breath. My mother appeared and looked up to the loft to where I was watching. Fawn had been alert enough to go to the boy. I knew what I looked like, the eldest, my head poking over the edge to survey the damage.

"He fell," Fawn said. "It was an accident."

The boy reached for his head, touched the back of it gingerly. When he touched his collar, the front of his T-shirt, he left behind a smear of blood.

"Oh no," Fawn said. "He's hurt."

The boy's tiny family hovered over him like doting birds, pecking around for any sign of grievous injury, but it was shut up inside his head, leaking out.

Candace swept the boy into the backseat of her double-cab truck. She told the girl to hold him steady. The girl was not crying, but there was an absence in her face. She was someplace else, within the static eye of shock, the same kind the boy was in. Candace cranked the engine. I realized how bright and clear it was outside, how perfect the weather.

"Should we wait here?" my mother said. "Or, we could go with you?"

"I don't know. I can't think right now," Candace said. "Actually, I do know. Come with me. Please." She lowered her voice. "I don't want to do this alone."

"Oh," my mother said. "But, the kids. Maybe I shouldn't. We have the ferry. But if you want, then we could. If you need me to."

Candace looked past my mother, to Fawn and me. I smiled though I don't know why. It was just what I did when adults went searching for me.

"Mommy," the girl said in the backseat. She eyed us like we might rush the doors and rip them from their seats. To her, we were the moody heathens who crashed their little birdhouse, hypnotized their mother, dropped her other half from great heights. Candace shifted into drive.

"We're going, sweetie." She swept a hand through her hair and looked at my mother a last time. "Do what you want," she said. "That's what you do best."

Good for her, I remember thinking.

"Hey," my mother said, but gravel was already kicking up behind the truck as they roared toward the main road. We watched the dust settle, and then it was just us. It was as if the woods zipped up behind them, and behind us too once we closed the cabin door and went, wondering aloud if it was all right to leave things unlocked, if we should keep a light on, leave a note saying goodbye. It was not until the ferry pulled away from its moorings and slid back into the current, like a hunk of continent sloughed off and set adrift, that my mother dared to ask the question.

———

She found me in line for the snack bar. I was going to get a hot dog. I felt I deserved something after the whole ordeal. Fawn was guarding our seats and luggage in the far corner by the trash cans. I watched her eyeball each face in the crowd in search of ours. My dollar bill was in hand. I was next in line, but when the teenager wearing the paper cap told me to step right up, my mother took me by the arm and pulled me off to the side.

"Hey," I said. "Wait."

"I'm going to ask you something," she said in a low voice, "and no matter what, I won't be angry. As long as you tell the truth. Right here, right now."

"But—"

"If something got out of control today, if things got a little out of hand, then I need you to tell me. It's important to do the right thing, understand?"

I nodded.

"All right then." She took a deep breath. "Did you push him?"

"What? Did Candace say that?"

"Would she be right?"

I felt I might cry, but knew this would appear guilty. I grasped for the right combination of words and cadence that would demonstrate sincerity, but I hadn't touched him. It wasn't a lie.

"No. I didn't."

"I'm disappointed," my mother said. "I'm really disappointed."

"I know why we came up here. The real reason. I know it wasn't to kayak or to collect sea glass or eat lobster or any of the other things you swore we would do."

"I'm disappointed because I know you're not telling me the whole truth."

All I wanted was my hot dog. I wanted to dress it the way I liked, take it to the corner, to eat it lovingly while I studied *People* magazine. A great pall had been cast over the entire expedition, the crude accommodations, my father's specter in every whisper and sip of wine. All that dull conversation at the table. I had told the little boy to get it over with. And when Fawn announced that it was an accident, I was relieved. She was too young to mean what she'd done, and in that way it had been a type of accident.

My mother turned my body toward her and rooted me in place. "Hear what I'm saying," she said. "React to what I am telling you."

"I am. I'm hearing. Tell me what you want me to say."

"I thought we could tell each other anything."

"What made you think that?"

She laughed, and it sounded painful. I asked if I could have my hot dog now. My mother released me.

"Sure," she said. "Go ahead."

Tomorrow, we'd be back where we all belonged. Candace and the twins in their northern retreat, Fawn and I pacing the loft. I pictured my mother emerging from the burrow of Penn Station and unto the mottled city sky, ascending as she had a thousand times before.

I located Fawn over her shoulder. She had one arm flung across our herd of suitcases, and I could see she had tried to make her body bigger—wide stance, shoulders set. She was gripping my backpack to her chest, and she held it there in her tiny vise grip, as if she would go down fighting if it was what she had to do.

The last page of the letter was the opposite of the first. No grievances, just apologies, and a last request.

My mother wrote that she was sorry she hadn't acted sooner, once she knew what I had done to the boy. She could see it now, all these years later, the pattern I'd left behind. She might've been able to help me, to correct my course if she wasn't so ineffectual, or obsessed with some mythical autonomy that children, she realized too late, were not meant to possess. It was her fault that I was where I was. She couldn't blame me.

Still, she said, after this was all over and I was back at home and on track again, I would need to write a very heartfelt thank-you note. It was the least I could do, after everything. The type of care I needed did not come cheap, and she could never forgive herself if she settled for some half-rate institution. Candace understood this. Candace, in her infinite generosity, had made Veld, my second chance, possible. Candace, despite what I had done to her boy and the scar it left, had never broken her promise. I read my mother's last line and let the walls close in.

You are more loved than you know.

13

Midnight and I was wide awake, back in my room with Gia snoring close by.

I had already decided not to meet Beanie for the rendezvous she requested. After reading my mother's letter, it was clear what I had to do. Family Day would proceed free of error. I would set the record straight, go home, and write as many thank-you notes as it took until I could make my own way, hitch west if nothing else. Unlike Zeke, I could make it to California. Unlike my mother, I could survive it. I walked myself through these steps again and again like a salve to sleep, and then I got out of bed.

Out in the back fields, the busted padlock on the shed had not yet been repaired. Beanie was sitting inside next to a battery-powered lantern, another item otherwise verboten. The TV was still there, and the junk had multiplied. Now there was a lamp with a frilly shade, a fine leather trunk, an ottoman, an empty fishbowl. Stacks of teen magazines, each cover embossed with a windblown starlet.

"You're late," she said. "Good thing I waited for you."

"What's all this supposed to be?"

"Don't you know already? I'm a big slut. That's the joke."

I picked up one of the magazines. I recognized the cover star from a show that aired after *MAYDAY*'s slot. The actress had one of those plain, beautiful faces that look positively engineered, and in that way forgettable. I fanned the pages and caught scent of a perfume ad.

"Why am I here?" I said. "I shouldn't be here."

"Were you followed?"

"No."

"You're alone?"

"Yes."

"Gia isn't trailing you?"

"I don't know how to say it any better. I'm by myself."

"I need a moment to gather my thoughts," Beanie said. This was a phrase she repeated often, a mechanism imparted by one of her recuperative counselors after her accident. "Here's what I wanted to say. I wanted to talk to you about something, but I didn't want Gia in the way."

I rolled my eyes. "This has nothing to do with me, does it? The two of you deserve each other. I don't know what I was thinking." I rummaged through the stack of old magazines. "I'm taking one of these," I said. "Two of them. For my time."

"Take whatever you want."

"Where did Dr. John even get these? And why are there so many? It's so much paper. This one." I tapped the cover. "She's in rehab. Or, maybe she's out by now."

"There's more," Beanie said. She moved her lantern closer and pawed through a few issues. "My mom and dad saved every single one. They kept my room exactly the same."

"You're allowed to talk to them?"

"Twice a week."

"Of course. One of your many unique privileges."

"And the TV works, you know. I made sure they got batteries for the remote."

I leaned against an ornate bureau and admired the fine wood beneath my fingertips.

"Beanie," I said. "How could you?"

I don't know why the whole idea offended me so much. I had entertained so many offensive nights and interactions, ogles and hangovers, pharmaceutical blitzes so intense my eyelids pulled back and my jaw worked an invisible bit. I thought my capacity for shock and disappointment had been exhausted, but here we were.

Beanie opened and closed one of the bureau's drawers—a near-silent, well-oiled pull.

"Are you wondering why I chose to stay?"

"Gia said you and Dr. John, that you're, you know—fucking."

"These are my things. They were sent to me. Dr. John is just keeping them here until my room is ready. He's coordinating."

"What you said, in the kitchen. And your last counselor too."

"I didn't fuck Greg because he was my counselor, I just knew he would have a big dick."

"Okay."

"Dr. John is nice. He's romantic. My parents think I do better in a stable routine," she said, her voice smoothing over. "At home, there are a lot of bad reminders. They trigger my mind. It's better to be in a place where there are clear boundaries and structures."

"Yeah, I've heard the pitch before."

"It's different for me."

"How?"

"Because this is home now."

The lantern burned bright, and spiders rappelled from the rafters, twiddling their silver threads. She told me the staff was preparing a room for her on Fifth. They were going to convert all the solitary spaces up there to premium dorm rooms and expand the student body. Her parents had sent her things—the bedroom set, the TV. Surrounded by the trappings of her endless, stunted youth, she'd preside over every new batch of girls to come. A lifetime appointment.

"John has made everything easy," she said. "Mom and Dad trust him. I trust him. We stick to the plan."

I had never heard the story of her getting gooned because she'd come willingly.

"Were you ever going to tell us?" I asked.

"See how you're acting? Pretending I don't exist? I knew Gia would turn you all against me. You're supposed to be my best friends."

"I'm getting out of here as fast as possible. I'm not supposed to be here."

"But you are here."

On Family Day, my mother might take one look at me, the company I kept, all the unpleasantness my face had morphed around— she would think I was in the right place. With Candace bankrolling her, I might have a room of my own on Fifth if I wasn't careful.

"It's good for me here," Beanie was saying. "They'll let me have the TV for the common area. You know, I got to pick my room. I picked a room with a view. It's high up. That's how I figured out my spot. I can see it through the trees."

It was the place she'd been drawn to the night before, steady as an arrow as she cut through the trees. Far beyond the crumbling stone fence, past a wall of bramble, a crude stone cottage decomposed in the overgrowth. A hunting cabin. She had confirmed the location on the old campus map, the one offered to Gia as a peace offering. Though the structure was in ruin, it had become to Beanie a kind of solo retreat. She had always been the swiftest on the mountainside. She was fluent in the language of knots. She had been going out there for weeks without anyone but Harlow knowing. The night she disappeared, that's where she went, and come morning she reported to Dr. John's office and was reminded of the limits of their arrangement. She was sent to the infirmary to have her cut checked and left in ISO until dinner.

"I could take you there," she said, "if you wanted. You could see it for yourself."

"Why the fuck would I want to do that?"

I looked around the lightless little shed as if its four walls might fall away, expose me at the center of some extreme immersive therapy. Dr. John would be there, with Gia, Harlow, and the rest in a circle, poking at me with cruel questions until I told them everything, the worst thing. Zeke. The tinkling of the smallest bell. Clear as day, I heard it.

If I wanted to leave, I was going to have to give it up. I couldn't keep it any longer.

Beanie held the lantern out to me. "What is it?"

"Are we really friends?" I asked.

She opened her arms to show me that the answer was a given, that there was nothing she could hide. Once Beanie knew the truth, Dr. John would not be far behind, and after him, everyone else. I held a magazine, tore the cover to strips. I told myself the only way out was through.

Inside a ring of boxed mementos that did not belong to me, I told her everything as I remembered it. The girl I picture, moving through the fog that unseasonable summer evening, only bears a passing resemblance to me. Like a sibling, her face is a rearrangement of my face, one of infinite iterations possible. There's her, and then there's me watching her, and we go there together.

The moon that night was bright, but finicky. At the right angles, where it hovered inside the fog like a bull's-eye lens, the girl could make out Zeke's face, his freckles even, but he'd retract into silhouette, deeper still into shadow, and be gone. The walk from The Gables to the opposite edge of town was long, but there were few cars on the side roads to spook them, and the big-rigs droning on the highway were some consolation the world had not stopped moving.

She upped her pace a half-step to keep up with his. She finally asked what was going on.

It had started as good-natured worry. Fawn kept Zeke appraised of his best friend's suspicious comings and goings, encouraged him to report his concerns to their mother. The Wepplers' house fire had not been an accident, Fawn warned him. She was frightened for the safety of her sister and family. What else was Zeke to think? He always thought his best friend was hard on Fawn. He always thought there was some strange jealousy springing back and forth between the two sisters, a competition with nowhere to go and no end in sight.

He might've believed all this, might've acted in his best friend's interest, if only Fawn had stopped there. She kept calling. Her reportage ultra-sensational and becoming off-key. She left messages citing examples of the girl's exploits on the highway to hell. He said Fawn sometimes became breathless on the line, enraptured by her own telling, as if she'd forgotten he was there or why she had called in the first place. It made him wonder, and now he knew.

There was a place deep inside the woods. A specific place, set up just so. Zeke had followed her there. The site was wrong, an aberration of a kind, but he could not explain how without losing his words and will.

"Don't be polite. Just say it," the girl told him.

"But you won't believe me." It needed to be seen to be understood. He said to his best friend, "Soon, you'll get it." The girl asked no more questions.

As they walked, their estrangement collapsed like timber falling. Zeke would know what to do. Her mother would trust him, and he would be readily believed. Things would right themselves, the girl thought. Soon, the summer would be over and forgotten.

There was no paved path then, and the grass was folded where overgrown. The fencing curled at the edges like peeled wallpaper, and in some stretches the metal rod that ran the top of the chain-link had been knocked out, so that exposed tips of steel glimmered like the teeth of a saw. "I think this is it," Zeke told her. "Can you climb?"

There was nothing distinct about this patch of fence line except the bowed bottom of the chain-link, where something or someone tiny could fit through. On the other side of the fence was undulating woodland, punctuated by a long narrow field of tall grass where the high-tension towers had been planted. Fog hid their red bulbs blinking, but the girl knew they were there.

On her side of the fence, all the same suspicions.

"Is there a way around?" the girl asked.

He shrugged. "This is how I saw her do it. It's the way I know how to go."

"Just tell me what's there. I don't need to see it."

Zeke did not sigh, or roll his eyes. He stood beside her and said softly, "Take a minute," and they breathed together. With every inhale, a nudge—the bristle of Dior in her nose. The spill of it potent under her fingernails and on the thin, elastic skin of her wrists.

"I'll go first," he offered, "and if you decide you want to go back, we can."

A dense cloud passed over the face of the moon. As her eyes adjusted, it was difficult to see him in detail, but she sensed his movements. He hiked up his pants, zipped his jacket, tightened his shoelaces like he was on the starting block. He took the first few feet of the high fence with ease. He had always been athletic, though never interested in sports. The girl envied his uninhibitedness when it came time to use his body. She loathed the fence before her for the obvious physical challenge it presented. She was thinking this over, how she should've strategized to go first, so as not to be discouraged by his agile ascent, so that he wouldn't have to watch her struggle from the other side. She was going to say as much to him when Zeke hissed in pain. "Ow," he said, and then, more emphatically—"Shit."

There was a ringing, metallic scrabble and the girl watched his blotted silhouette struggle at the top of the fence just before he fell over, though he never hit the ground.

She remembers laughing. An insane kind of laugh, solo and half-embarrassed. Next, the tactile. Remembrances most pure. Cold, crude metal. Blood, invisible. Running down the hexagons of the chain-link in trained rivulets, how it coated her fingertips when she reached out her hand to touch his leg. She rubbed the pads of her fingertips together and they came away warm and thick. She touched one to her tongue without knowing what it meant.

"Very funny," she might've said. Or something like, "Come down from there," but he would never answer. She patted around his body and realized he was upside-down. The loss of blood was profound, and swift, given gravity's imperative, the angle as though he'd been strung.

At least, that was what her brain supplied as an abridged accounting of events.

Later, the police would say his belt loop, his pocket, his jeans— something snagged as he swung a leg over, wrenching him back down onto the exposed tip of steel. Perfect timing, perfect place-ment. The girl would imagine the blood in the grass, suspicious of what might grow there. This was the last of their private moments together. A marker she could only insert after the fact.

How long before the girl left, shell-shocked and in search of help, she could not rightly say. Blood and delirium and a ripple of sound so innocent followed her down alleys, darted from behind each brutish tree trunk. The zipper on his jacket where it brushed the fence line. A tinkling little bell, dismissal and summons. Only her ears to hear it.

The news van arrived the morning after the accident. They showed up on Geronimo Street looking for the girl. The heat had returned, the cold front an anomaly only she seemed to recall. The Hellers had refused them, and so the red-faced reporters called up to the loft. What did she have to say about her friend's tragic passing? Didn't she want his story to be told?

Her mother was on the phone in the other room, the chore all adults resorted to when an event unforeseen came home to roost.

"Aren't you going to say something to them?" Fawn asked her sister. "Aren't you going to go down there just to see? Maybe they should hear about it from you."

All that time resenting how the limelight passed her over, and suddenly she couldn't think of anything more graphic, more garish than a microphone in her face, the spool of tragic footage unraveling only to become another blip, a sad sigh in someone's living room before the turn of the channel for lighter fare, no reminders. She closed the window and pulled the curtains, though the van lingered until dusk. After that, it did not appear again. Some new tragedy had commenced. In some other town, another child would not grow up, and the TV crew raced through the streets to be first on the scene.

Two months passed between the funeral and the goons that would come for me. The *Supermarket Sweep* era. There were gatherings on the roof, populated by Antonia's friends from her new part-time job. I couldn't look anyone in the face. She and Kent stopped speaking. His grief was too toxic. She said this happened to her all the time. She'd fall out of love with a guy long before she got around to dumping him, and after being sideswiped by the news, they'd all go mad, come banging down her door at midnight, or attempt poetry for the first time in their lives. I didn't talk about Zeke, or Fawn, or anything else that might weigh heavily. I made myself easy to keep around.

We escaped into the city often, any night of the week. Once, we found a white pill on the floor of a train car and crushed it, only to fall asleep in our seats for the next five hours. We let people find us, almost exclusively men. Their faces lit up once they realized we'd talk back. They'd suggest a place and we'd go, wondering aloud to our new friends if they were going to ransom us, rape us, dump our bodies in the park. We laughed and did whatever it was they were doing, wherever it was they took us. I wondered if these were the sorts of things my mother did while she was here. What did she look like, swishing down a crowded sidewalk in a trench coat, knowing precisely where she was headed and how many blocks it would take to get there? What a tantalizing mecca it would've been for her, the life she wished she had chosen. So close and forever in motion, out of reach, not a single pause given for her absence.

More than once, we missed the last train home. Our wallets were lifted from our pockets as we slept on the terminal floor. Someone snatched our iPods and left our headphones dangling from our ears. Fun wasn't free, so I began to steal things as a matter of practicality, but eventually just for the thrill. I crashed out of Algebra II. American History. My classmates' faces lost their definition and my teachers' pity was abhorrent. I realized with indifference the amount of time I'd once devoted to self-assessment. Now I just did what I wanted without thinking.

I could tell my mother was getting restless. She was all encouragement, believing I should make the shape of my own grief, but her displays were thin enough that I could detect the resentment lurking, how she was fighting to remain subtle. Her friend, a psychiatrist in the city, suggested I take something for what we were calling my Upsetting Moods. I ingested one pill a day, and it sheared away the lip of reality, just so.

In town, Antonia and I frequented parties thrown in buildings I'd written off as abandoned or trashed, but in the midnight hour, some rowhomes were resurrected. There were nicknames for a few choice spots. I remember all those empty closets. I had the sense that the spirit of the Wepplers could follow me, passing through relic picture frames and bathroom mirrors, as if there was some network of dispossessed souls stuck in Deerie's underground. People at parties started to know me. They knew I went around with Antonia, that I'd been best friends with the dead kid, that my sister was the girl from the news. Still, sometimes people confused the facts and the two of us. They thought my name was Fawn. I was the hero who rescued Antonia from the blaze. Sure, I had that sister with the sad story, but at least I was having fun now, wasn't I?

When these mix-ups occurred, Antonia did nothing to correct them. It would only get people down. Instead, she threw her arm around me and steered me to the next new face. I went along with her. I never stopped smiling.

14

It was not as if a renewed alliance formed between Beanie and me after that night together in the shed, swapping secrets. In fact, it was the beginning of our club's true dissolution.

Gia and Beanie weren't on speaking terms, and Harlow always blew with the wind. It became easier to drift than to connect. There always lingered the question of sunk cost, how worthwhile it really was to care. Once we left, we would never meet again by choice.

I could sense Beanie's frustration. The opposite of what she wanted had come to pass, despite her efforts to avoid Gia's meddling. Our revelations were supposed to bring us closer, but I couldn't look at her straight anymore. The both of us seemed tainted, more tragic than before. Beanie would become part of Veld instead of a girl passing through, and I'd told her too much. Her face was a reminder of both.

As Family Day loomed, everyone on campus was on their worst behavior.

"The rats are out in full force," Gia said. "Mind your asses."

Everyone wanted to take everyone else down a peg. Girls were sent to ISO for minor infractions, like forgetting to cover their bare shoulders with a towel on the walk from the showers to their rooms. Beanie passed me another note, and another, always requesting that I meet her, that she had something else to show me, some reveal— but I battened down the hatches as Saturday approached. No more midnight meetings.

Staff had us spend the week dusting and scrubbing instead of attending core classes. Each club was assigned a task to soften Veld's slate aesthetics. The Piñata Club painted a wall in the main hallway with an aspirational quote that all the girls were supposed to sign with permanent marker. CHANGE THE WAY YOU LOOK AT THINGS, AND THE THINGS YOU LOOK AT WILL CHANGE.

Then came the cars with alien license plates rolling up the long gravel road. I wondered what we looked like to them, all our faces in the windows. Harlow's mother arrived in a silver Lexus firing up the drive like a bullet. There was only a murky resemblance between the two of them, since her mother had been altered by various plastic surgeries, followed by corrective surgeries to fix the shoddy handiwork of the previous slice and dice. Gia's parents arrived promptly at nine. Their flannel and fleece outfits were coordinated. They looked meek as birders, astonished by the sanctuary they'd come upon.

Harlow and Gia were giving their visitors a monitored tour of the grounds, and it was just me and Beanie at the long end of the Fourth Floor, haunting the windows, last in line.

"Yours are coming," I said. "Aren't they?"

"They want to see my new room. Look." She held out a crudely mapped blueprint of her tiny room-to-be, drafted in pencil, rectangles and squares in various sizes plotting the arrangement of her bed, her dresser, her television set. It was clear she had labored over it. There were streaks of eraser, several faint iterations that preceded this one.

"Great," I said. She folded the blueprint and tucked it away, embarrassed. I knew her charges on the Fifth Floor would give her hell.

The morning hours were reserved for a special session of Group. My mother and sister had not yet arrived, and based on how things were going, this was preferable.

From nine to noon, the gymnasium was an echo of tears and recriminations. Dr. John floated group to group, stoking fires and putting them out. He had failed as a poet, and now he was a salesman. To his credit, there seemed to be a few breakthroughs. Some circles collapsed as the two subjects, student and parent, embraced and promised better things for the other. There was light applause, but no telling how long their optimism would last.

Beanie's parents remained unaccounted for. She was usually a reliable contributor to discussion, and in that way, one of Dr. John's greatest discoursal assets, but she couldn't keep her eyes off the row of windows, through which her hideaway seemed to beckon. I saw her tug at Dr. John's sleeve more than once between rounds. She kept asking if she could save a tray of lunches for her mom and dad, if she could go and make sure her room was clean for their inspection. Gia kept saying they weren't coming, and though Beanie flinched each time, she refused to acknowledge her. This only made Gia more volatile, and now it was her turn to share.

On folding chairs, Gia and her parents were arranged face-to-face in the center of our circle. As was custom, her parents had been charged with narrating their daughter's most egregious offenses. Opportunity was lost in the unsaid, that was Dr. John's theory. It was as if the gym was gradually filling with noxious gas, every accusation a dirty bomb, every rebuttal a detonation. The chairs creaked nonstop from all the shifting.

"Gia," Dr. John began. "As you know, we've made a lot of progress this quarter. We've really pushed ourselves to dig deep. We encourage you to embrace that mindset this morning."

"Who's we?" Gia said.

"Gianna, please," her mother said, and Gia slumped in her chair.

There came the list of all of Gia's moral turpitudes. It was true she'd been sent to many schools and programs. There was even a brief stint at a military academy, but her parents pulled her out when they realized they'd given her tactical training. They recalled nights of terror when they woke up to find Gia in the basement taking a putter to the drywall. Also, she was adopted. That was important, Dr. John said.

Gia's mother wondered aloud at the luck of the draw, if Gia's aggressive temperament was somehow the fault of her sister, Gia's spinster aunt, who had always wanted a child of her own.

"Always tossing her in the air like that," she said. "No regard for fragile babies."

Gia was doing her best to project indifference. She yawned a lot, and watched the sky outside. It seemed campus never fully embraced a season. The weather was always on the verge. When the subject switched to her most recent episode, the one that returned her to Veld again, she could no longer stay quiet.

"I didn't say you could speak on this. I did not give my consent."

"They don't require your consent, Gia," Dr. John said. "They have every right to speak to their own experience. Action and consequences. Behavior is not a one-way street."

"It's my turn to have the floor."

Gia's mother jabbed a finger in her direction. "Not yet," she said.

She told us how Gia had recruited the younger neighborhood kids into a cultish brood under her thumb. They lived in a sprawling sub-development specked with playgrounds and dog runs. Like the Pied Piper, she worked one child after the other, luring new believers everywhere she went.

"Parents complained," her mother said, "but it was hard for them to articulate the problem exactly, because at that point, all the children were behaving normally."

Gia waited outside their houses, called at all hours asking if Dick or Jane could come out and play. She invited herself for dinner. She waited for the children at the bus stop. She distributed cheap walkie-talkies so they could chatter into the late-night hours. They had call signs, codes, a mysterious plan they were hatching.

"You're making it sound all wrong," Gia said. "You're ruining it."

Eventually one of the parents learned of Gia's spotted history and the gossip traveled. Gia was kept indoors. She was in between schools, so her parents gave her workbooks and counted each undisturbed day a blessing. The adults assumed the group infatuation had run its course, that Gia was just a lonely and undersocialized child—until they found one of the boys bound to a tetherball pole. He had been there for a few hours, and it was dark. The temperature dropped. They'd been calling his name through the streets like a lost pet.

"He asked us to do that to him," Gia said. "It was an inside joke."

Then she started harassing the boy's father, writing him letters and leaving messages as if they'd had an affair. When she was ignored, she liberated the family's new bichon frise from their backyard. Posters went up, but the dog was nowhere to be found. The family moved away.

"That poor man," Gia's mother said. "That poor, poor man. And his wife. Oh god, his wife. His child. The dog."

"His wife," her father echoed. "His child. The dog."

"She was blackmailing them, threatening them. Had children spying, stealing, trespassing. And that little boy strapped to the pole. My god, his pajamas. He'd wet himself, he was so frightened. It was a laundry list, all they got into."

"Shut her up," Gia said.

"There was always some rationale with her. All those empty words. And then, of course, she tried to kill herself. Her selfishness should not have surprised me."

Gia stood so quickly her chair folded onto the gym floor and her parents recoiled. Dr. John snapped his fingers at the for-hire security guards by the gym doors, but Gia put up a hand and stepped back, inhaling very slowly.

"Please excuse me," she said. "I only need the restroom."

Dr. John was grateful for the break. He told everyone to take five, but the dead time was just a different strain of awkward. There was no mingling in a place like this. The members of other circles were tear-streaked, bloated with anger, withdrawn. "Tough crowd," Harlow's mother said as she glanced around.

Dr. John was whispering with the two guards by the door. Five minutes passed, and then ten, fifteen—and Gia had not returned from the bathroom. The guards were sweating inside their nylon polos, perspiration beading on their bald heads. Gia's parents scowled. At the very least, a place like this should've been able to keep tabs on the merchandise. Dr. John disappeared with one guard and the other took up the entire doorway.

"What sort of productions do they put on here?" Harlow's mother asked Beanie. The stage at the end of the room had been outfitted with an amateurish backdrop of a moon and stars across a sheet of plywood, painted black like night. It had been erected in the last few days by one of the clubs.

Beanie shrugged. "Do you have a suggestion?"

"I don't," she said, and looked at Beanie oddly. "Or, perhaps, *Macbeth*?"

"I love *Macbeth*."

"Are you a fan of Shakespeare?"

"Oh, very much a fan."

Harlow, who had been pretending to ignore this exchange, finally looked at Beanie. "Oh yeah? What's your favorite Shakespeare then?"

"*Macbeth*," Beanie said. "Obviously."

The guard returned without Dr. John. We were to make our

way to the dining hall for lunch. If our visitors sensed any greater disturbance, they did not show it. They were too absorbed in their own familial disinterments, eager to surrender to a plan larger than themselves.

"To the left please," the guard said as we exited. He had his arm outstretched, his body blocking the view of the windows in the front hall. "Carry on," he said. "To the left please."

When I turned back, I saw Beanie and Harlow at the window. Out on the drive, at the brick rotunda before the main entrance, a Volvo.

"Who's that with Gia?" Beanie asked.

There was Gia, and there were my mother and Fawn, chatting beside the car. Dr. John was hovering at the edges of their conversation, gesticulating, smiling. I could tell he was trying to edge Gia out without creating a worrying first impression, but it was too late for that. Gia had immersed herself in the role of tour guide and was walking backward, motioning to the cornices above the main entrance. My mother was rubbing the skin behind her ear, wide-eyed, nodding at the architecture. Fawn, on the other hand, appeared deeply skeptical. She wasn't as skinny as I remembered. Her body was mid-morph and she was now a small, pudgy version of my mother, who seemed to have aged overnight, though it had been much longer than that. They were all pilled sweaters and frizz, belt buckles cinched to the last notch. The both of them shivered in late spring like exiles, though they'd been right where I left them.

It was my time in the center of the circle.

Technically, my mother was supposed to start, but she was chewing on something she could neither swallow nor spit out, and Fawn kept looking her over anxiously, then at Dr. John, and then at Gia lumped between her parents.

"Should I . . ." Fawn trailed, but no one came to her rescue.

I remember thinking how thin my mother looked. During prolonged bouts of anxiety, she had the annoying habit of resorting to tiny snack foods. Olives. Nuts. Maraschino cherries. Anything she could hold between her fingers and nibble very slowly, as a meal.

"I feel that I," my mother began and stopped. "I feel . . ."

Everyone in the circle leaned in.

"What?" I asked finally.

"No talking," Dr. John said.

Awaiting their rescue, I had been on my best behavior. I wasn't prepared for their presence to make me so agitated. I eyed Fawn, peach-fuzzy as a piglet since puberty had laid claim to her. I had a million things to say, a million arrows in my quiver to let fly. I had a vision of her fastened to her chair, an open target.

"We should just move on to somebody else," I said. "This is a waste of time."

"Why does she get to talk?" Gia said from the outskirts of the circle.

"You don't get to talk either," I said.

"Ladies," Dr. John said. "Let's create some space here. Let's distance."

No one appeared convinced of Dr. John's authority. Harlow and her mother were stoic clones with arms crossed, and Beanie's face was a lesson in expectations. She had skipped lunch to watch the windows, and there were empty folding chairs on either side of her, though Dr. John had tried to scoot them away before we started up again after lunch. Beanie would not have it. "If they do finally come," she had said, "I want them to look at these empty chairs." Now her arms were draped over either seat, palling around with her invisible loved ones.

I wondered how long Gia had my mother's and sister's ears in the parking lot. I imagined she used the time expeditiously to unleash whatever ammunition she had in store for the day. A marathon of confessions awaited us all.

Dr. John removed his suit jacket and pushed up his shirtsleeves in a demonstration of buckling down. "Okay. Let's look at this from a new angle, shall we? Might I suggest a tactic?"

"Here we go," Gia said.

"Who are all these people?" my mother blurted out. "I simply don't know these people." It was hard to watch. She couldn't last a single afternoon doing what I'd done for months.

Beanie nodded at me. "Why don't you just tell them? Tell them what you told me."

"Cross talk," Dr. John said.

"But they have loads to say to each other," Beanie said.

Fawn looked between us. My mother bent forward in her chair.

"I don't know what she's talking about," I said.

"That's a lie." Beanie clucked her tongue. "She's lying to you."

Gia could hardly suppress her delight at this turn of events, but Dr. John was unwilling to throw grease on the fire and straightened his tie roughly.

"Let's stay on task. Thank you, Beanie. That's all for now."

"Don't you know what she did? Don't you know what happens when somebody gets in her way? You were right." Beanie turned to my mother. "You were right to bring her here, and she's not ready yet. I read your letter. I know how she treats a friend."

Gia perked up at this. "What letter?"

I could feel heat venting up through my chest. I had never felt the pulse at my jugular engorge like that, as if all the blood in my body rallied with the same intent, to ram at the thin skin there and spill through. Dr. John was not pleased.

"This is not the appropriate framing for this discussion," he said, more sternly this time, but this only drove Beanie deeper.

"She laughed. Did you know that was the first thing she did?

After her best friend in the world was swinging there like a pig, she laughed. That's what I'm trying to tell you. She doesn't know what a friend is. You shouldn't take her back."

"Dr. John," I said. "Are you just going to let her talk like this?"

"She's scared of you." Beanie pointed at Fawn. "You. But you should be the one scared of her."

Dr. John snapped his fingers at the guards, but Beanie was only sitting there, body pointed and voice sharp but otherwise immobile—harmless. "This is no longer productive," Dr. John said, as a guard came to stand beside Beanie and motioned for her to rise. My mother had turned a very yellow shade of pale.

"I'm not done," Beanie said.

"This is a free country, pal," Gia said. "Let the girl speak."

"Young lady. On your feet, please."

Beanie ignored this and ran a palm tenderly over the seat of the empty chair next to her. She peered at my mother and smiled. "You knew already, didn't you?"

"I apologize," Dr. John said. "This can be a taxing exercise. There's a lot to unpack."

"I'm not going anywhere." Beanie wrapped her ankles tightly around the legs of her chair. She turned to the rest of us. "None of you are better than me. John, tell them."

My mother's lips were moving wordlessly. Her fingers itched for a kind of small nut to latch on to and nibble to death. Fawn was staring but stayed quiet. If there were no outsiders, it would have been an easy task of carting Beanie to ISO by force.

A guard made a move toward her. "Touch me," she said, "and my parents will have you canned."

"Oh yeah." Gia started clapping. "This is the good stuff." In some other circle across the gym, a sadist girl started clapping too.

"This is highly out of the ordinary," Dr. John assured my mother.

Harlow's mother then raised a finger. "Can we take five again?"

That was when she finally spoke. "No," my mother said. "I don't think so."

"Progress," Dr. John began, "is sometimes a difficult—"

"It's over," my mother said.

"Pardon?"

"Yes. I think it's time we go."

Elsewhere in the room, someone was crying over an unrelated tragedy. I could sense Dr. John trying to muster his best presentation of tranquility, but this brief window allowed enough time for my mother to collect herself, stand, and pull Fawn in close.

"Where are they going?" Beanie said, still coiled around her chair.

"Are you deaf?" Gia said. "They're leaving."

Dr. John waved his hands. "No, no. No one is leaving."

"Yes," my mother said. "We're leaving."

"Ma'am," he tried. "Miss."

"We're all leaving." My mother put her hand out to me. "Come on."

It was what I wanted, wasn't it?

I bypassed my mother's hand and we extricated ourselves from the circle, the room watching us like the dramatic production we were. My mother was muttering under her breath, holding tight to Fawn's arm, and Fawn was staring daggers over her shoulder at Beanie and Gia and the rest. Beanie would not release her desperate grip on the chair. She was chanting the words *not yet* again and again, the volume of her distress vaulting off the ceiling.

Gia saluted me as I went.

In the parking lot, Dr. John was skidding over the gravel in hot pursuit. "I think this will prove to be a harmful decision," he was saying. "This is quite disruptive to treatment. If you would just follow me to my office, I think we'd be capable of a more productive conversation."

"Those are just words!" my mother shouted into the air. It was the type of thing she'd exclaim during one of her late-night sessions at the loft. "They're just words, man."

"You'll leave here and very soon discover your wish to return. Tuition for this quarter is non-refundable. You are parting with a tremendous opportunity. I can't fathom why you would prefer to squander such progress."

My mother dug through her purse for her keys. Pricey cars in neutral tones were parked down the drive, the license plates from all over the country. I thought of bad kids everywhere, north, south, east, and west—in the streets, sneaking through windows, slithering out from the gutter in torn clothes and black eyes while someone cried for them back home. The Volvo's bumper was a worn battering ram and stuck out from the fleet. In that moment, I could not have loved an object more.

"Give it to me," I said to my mother and took her purse. I fished the keys out easily and slapped them into her palm.

"Oh, thank god," she said. "Get in."

Dr. John was in the final, desperate stages of his pitch as a crowd of faces gathered at the front windows to watch our exit. This was my triumphant moment, what every girl wished for on the eve of Family Day. I took my time rounding the back of the Volvo, relishing all the eyes upon me. I considered my things upstairs, my clothes, but nothing was really mine, not even the journal so meticulously dated, passing from my hands to Dr. John's every Thursday for inspection, not even the smooth round rock I'd picked up on the mountain and kept with me for so long. It was only a rock.

I twiddled my fingers at the group of girls in the window and tried to flash a megawatt smile, but I saw that my hands were shaking. Harlow waved back, along with a few others. Gia's face was not among the rest, though her parents looked on urgently from their vantage point inside the zoo. Beanie was crying, clinging to the window pane. It was almost embarrassing to be on the receiving end of such melodrama, after what I'd told her and what she'd done with it. I thought of her little hunting cabin in ruins, tucked among the birch trees. A guard had her by the arm and she fought his hold, pressed a palm to the glass, sobbed. Harlow pointed at her and laughed.

15

The drive into Bowen was the first car trip I'd taken since the van ride off the mountain. We passed a tractor going five miles per hour and my mother tapped the wheel impatiently.

"This place," she kept muttering. "Where *are* we?"

She might've been talking about Veld, or Bowen, or the thorny situation she'd created and was now ejecting herself from, or even the two-bit motel on the edge of town that she pulled into, to my own mild revulsion. The single-level motel was one long, shingled turd. Even the plastic lawn chairs out front did not have the decency to stand upright.

"You're staying here?"

"It's fine, Mom," Fawn said. "We're very grateful, aren't we?"

The room was little more than two dingy double beds, but there was a coin operated television, a novelty. My mother promptly disappeared into the bathroom and rammed the door in its frame until the lock engaged. It was just me and Fawn, the sound of running water. A quarter bought twenty minutes of cable.

Fawn sat back on one of the beds and arranged the pillows behind her.

"This one's been acting very unpredictable lately," she said, and cast her eyebrows toward the bathroom door. I scooted onto the opposite bed and asked if she had a quarter. She gestured to the pile of coins on the nightstand. "Channel 40 is HBO."

"HBO. Not bad for a dump."

"That bed probably has bugs," Fawn said. "And blood. People had sex on it. It's got pee."

"Didn't you miss me at all?" I asked. "Don't I look different?"

"You look fatter."

"Well, that's impossible."

She shrugged again and I wanted to hurt her, just to see what it would take.

The water in the bathroom stopped and started. The toilet flushed. We were watching a nature documentary about the Appalachian Trail, full of reverent landscape shots.

"I've been there," I said.

"Not exactly there."

"You don't even know where there is."

Fawn shrugged.

"Stop shrugging," I said.

I wanted to ask what the two of them had been up to all this time, and how the loft had made it through the winter. I wanted to ask if she had anything real to eat, if our mother had gotten rid of my things, if Antonia was in Atlantic City, if she thought I was mad at her. I wanted to ask if the Hellers ever called. I wanted to ask what we were doing in a place like this, but I was so tired of talking. Fawn took a quarter and bought another twenty minutes of peace. We watched old sitcoms and the evening news, prime-time dramas that lit up the screen with flashes of teeth, pharma commercials, until the late-night shows chattered on into the infomercial twilight and Fawn was asleep.

When I knocked on the bathroom door, the water cut off instantly.

There was a cautious silence before the latch twitched and my mother peeked through. Before I could speak, she took me by the shirtfront and tugged me into the bathroom.

It was unspeakably warm. Hot water plunged into the tub on high and spritzed the tiled walls, the toilet, the floor. My mother was sweating. Her hair had gone completely haywire, like a Cathy cartoon.

"Lock the door," she said, upper lip dewy. I could hardly hear her over the showerhead.

"What is going on?"

After my father's departure, I had learned how to wait out one of my mother's moods, or else weasel my way inside them with her, so that I could guide her back out. She began pacing the bathroom, her sneakers squeaking with each quarter turn. I leaned against the chipped tile vanity and waited.

"I think I'm feeling this way because of all that coffee at lunch." She fanned herself. "What do they put in that coffee?"

"Is this about the money? Is it Candace? Is that why you took me out?"

"You're not supposed to worry about that. I'm supposed to worry about that."

"I wasn't even sure you were coming."

"That girl, that awful girl. Did you tell her to say such a thing? Of course I was coming. That you should even wonder."

The showerhead sputtered violently, shot out a stream of rusty water, and carried on.

Alone at Veld, doing my daily jumping jacks, folding over into a rock, in moments of stillness or exertion, sleep or waking, I used to wonder what they were doing in those parallel moments. I pictured the hole in the roof of the loft widening into a sky-blue maw. I saw my mother's and sister's faces turning upward, squinting into killer daylight. I wished a force above would beam them up, abduct them as I had been abducted. More realistically, I thought of them on the couch, passing a bowl of popcorn, taping over the rest of my collection for a Lifetime movie and taking for granted their unchecked leisure. I didn't have to ask questions. In whispers, tangents, non sequiturs, and tears, my mother told a different tale.

Concerned that my sister might suffer some long-term damage from the sight of my unruly departure, my mother tried to emphasize the concept of rest. That's where I was going. A place where I could exist in tranquility. Fawn processed this development astutely. As soon I was carted away by the Juvenile Transportation Services, the first thing she wanted was a new dog.

She deserved the dog, Fawn argued, because of all she had been through. The foot. Peanut Butter. The fire. The sister. Fawn would have the dog for company, and protection. She would walk it, feed it, brush it, love it. Dog owners lived longer.

In the motel bathroom, straddling the lid of the toilet, my mother bowed her head. I squinted into the steam and glimpsed all the other motels, the long nights, the weariness of travel while my mother hit the road so many years ago. She hadn't been much older than I was.

The second dog was named PB2.

He was only a year old, with a brown-and-white dappled coat like a setter, always wiggling around for looks out the window, a constant sniffer.

"Car lover," my mother said. "Goes absolutely bonkers for cars."

She no longer had me as a de facto nanny, and her trips to the city were increasingly few. This afforded her new observation time. Every afternoon, when the school bus rumbled up Geronimo to give its hydraulic wheeze, PB2 retreated to my mother's room. Not even the rattle of his bowl could lure him. Fawn complained that he was broken, but he seemed prototypical enough, and my mother found solace in long walks with the new mutt. He chose to sleep at the foot of her bed, crossed his paws over her ankles. She narrated his thoughts while he watched her cook, taught him to play dead. Fawn asked to exchange the animal with increasing impatience. She wanted a ferret, or a chinchilla, or two white rats that could make babies. My mother imagined a pile of wriggling, hairless rodents in the corner of a glass tank, eyes mercifully sealed shut.

"I had a rare instinct," she said. "That's when I took the camera and set it up in the living room. I hit record when I heard the bus and told Fawn I was going to the store for lemons, but I only drove around the block. I couldn't say what compelled me, and then I could."

All she got on tape was Fawn yanking PB2 by the collar into her bedroom and closing the door. A few barks, a single yelp. Later, my mother could not find a mark on him.

He had been born in a dumpster, they said at the pound. He'd been found among the bodies of his dead siblings, lone whimpers heard by a busboy smoking on his break. The pound warned that the dog would require proper socializing, but he had been loyal to my mother from the start. Whenever she had to venture from the loft and leave him alone with Fawn, she returned to his look of betrayal. Animals didn't think like that, she reasoned. It was less complicated for them, duller. Any sheen in their eyes was pure projection.

The week before she arrived for Family Day, my mother went to visit Mrs. Heller.

She had only seen her once since the funeral. "I'm embarrassed I wasn't a more active friend," she said, but they had never been friends. My mother always pitied Mrs. Heller's suburban enthusiasm, and Mrs. Heller always pitied my mother everything else.

When she arrived for a glass of wine, the house was packed up into boxes. The Hellers were leaving. They would sell the house at a loss, move to Pennsylvania, settle into some land where the boys could ride ATVs. They were thinking about starting a goat farm.

"They don't know the first thing about goats," my mother said, "but I wish them peace."

She saw the kids, the whole horde of half-siblings and step-children and girlfriends and best friends who descended upon the Heller house in the wake of tragedy and had not left. They all fit together, no matter their biology, lineage, or temperaments. A sense of loyalty. I would never see any of them again.

"If it's any consolation," my mother said, "Kent seems to be doing okay. He says hello."

If it were true, he would've been the only one. My mother drove home and found PB2 whimpering in her closet. His tail was warped, bent at a painful angle. My mother marched into the living room and stood between Fawn and the screen. She demanded to know what happened, but Fawn had disposed of her favorite scapegoat. My alibi was solid.

It was an accident, Fawn said. Something about his tail and the front door.

"Can't you see it wagging?" Fawn said, and craned her neck for a better view of the screen. "It's fine. It doesn't even care."

"He's not fine," my mother said. "Why didn't you call?"

"I knew you were coming back."

My mother swaddled the dog in a towel because she thought it might be a comfort. She drove two towns over to a clinic open late. She felt unequipped, hot with adrenaline. She thought something was wrong with her, but this was how she was supposed to feel when something loved was in danger. It was natural. The vet told my mother there was a break, and nerve damage. He reset the bone and said PB2 would live to wag another day. She waited to be asked more, for the vet tech to press at the story until the cystic truth gave way, but they were free to go. Perhaps it was an accident after all.

Vacuum-eyed, my mother navigated downtown Deerie, a shamble of orange cones and floodlights and piles of upturned rock and asphalt. She felt hungover. She wanted to take the train to where the bars didn't close, but PB2 was sedate in the afterlife of intravenous drugs, curled in a ball on the passenger seat. It was possible she was overreacting. It was possible she required a broader understanding to hold the world in hand and comprehend her children. But the vet visit was not the finish line. Her youngest was waiting.

Construction was happening near the underpass. A new master plan was coming to fruition, and the site blinded half the town as the earth rumbled late into the night.

"Too little, too late," my mother said aloud to herself, idling in that long line of cars.

The construction worker holding the reversible STOP/SLOW sign on a stick was smoking a cigarette. He spied the dog in her front seat, waved, and made a kissy face. PB2, who should've been comatose, and was not supposed to get riled up, leapt brightly at the sight, totally open. That was when it occurred to her in force. The pound had been wrong about him. Though the dog had been left to suffer at the loft for hours, was carted off to the vet for an exam on cold steel, subject to the snarling of canine inmates rattling the hallways, all those clinical balms and antiseptic, iodine, enzyme-removers for piss stains and the shits—he'd even had a thermometer stuck up his butt, and still—all he wanted was to lick a stranger.

The dog was not the problem.

"Now you understand the immense pressure your absence has created," she said.

"What happened to the dog?"

My mother squeezed her eyes shut and vapor gathered in the folds of her skin.

"I drove over to The Gables. It was probably the last thing I should've done, but I thought, if a farm was where they were going—what dog wouldn't be happy there? I'd be happy there. If you could've seen them, how their faces lit up. Better with them than with us."

The shower was running cooler. I could feel the heat tipping, escaping under the door and away. My clothes stuck to me like a second skin.

"What did Fawn say?" I asked.

"Nothing," my mother said. "She hardly seemed to notice."

That's when I told her about Peanut. The Original. I had my own theories about which of the pills in her medicine cabinet made for a deadly combination when fed to an eager animal. I had done so much recitation by then it all slipped out in easy chronology. I moved through the event without even much feeling, hardly stopping, hardly breathing, and when I was through, I believed our understandings had finally aligned, superimposed upon each other.

I asked what we were going to do about Fawn.

"I'm not sure what you mean."

"Well, something is wrong with her. The older she gets, the smarter she gets—it'll be worse. You saw it for yourself, with everyone today."

"Fawn isn't like those girls."

"And I am?"

"Of course you aren't."

"I don't get it. Aren't you angry?"

"At who?"

"Her. Obviously, her. Why can't you do this one thing right?"

"Is that what you think?" She took my wrists and shook them as she spoke. "Nobody is bad. When something is wrong, that's not the end of it. You don't get rid of it."

"Then why did you make me come here?"

"Even mothers need help."

"You can help me right now. That's what I'm asking."

In the Volvo, riding away from Veld with my mother behind the wheel, I had tried to curb my optimism. Remembering Gia and Harlow and their multiple stints, that Beanie was never leaving, had all but signed away her choice in the matter—I knew not to get my hopes up. It was foolish to think the world would welcome my return. Even if progress had been made in all our talking, here in the bathroom of the Little Acorn Motel and in all those circles at Veld, the question of healing went unresolved. They were separate. Saying the truth and knowing what to do with it. Things were different now. I was different. If I could only go home to Deerie and finish what Zeke had started, to see for myself and show my mother what was in our midst, it could be a beginning, if only she would take me with her.

"I need a minute alone now. Give me a minute alone," she said, and released me.

Fawn was awake and waiting. She was flipping through a stock Bible on the bed. She said she was reading the Book of Job.

"Who wrote this?" she said. "It's awful." Over the gold-leafed cover, she eyed me. "Do you know you look like a wet rat? What took you two so long?"

The room was arctic. "Don't worry about it," I said. I realized I had no change of clothes.

"Do you have any idea what you've done?" She snapped the Bible shut and tossed it back in its drawer. "I guess I have to do everything around here. All right. Come on."

The water was running in the bathroom, ancient plumbing clanking inside the walls. There was no telling how long my mother would keep herself locked inside.

"Where are we going?" I asked my sister.

She gathered a few bills from our mother's wallet. "Follow me," she said.

We visited the change machine in the boxy lobby at the motel's edge, closest to the road. There were three vending machines there, all in a row, beautifully backlit and fully stocked. In the lot, we turned the plastic chairs upright and arranged them by the Volvo's trunk like we were tailgating, a feast across our laps. It was coming on midnight and Bowen was strangely alive. The main drag was a strip of fast-food chains and gas stations. Across the street, a flat of broken asphalt where a few cars were parked, motors running. Two of them circled the lot in unhurried loops like sharks on the prowl.

Fawn was chowing down on a bag of Famous Amos cookies, but I couldn't eat. I was waiting for her to say whatever it was she was going to say, but she knew this, and took her time. After she funneled the crumbs into her mouth, she watched the cars across the way.

"Do you want those Bugles?" she asked me.

"Fawn."

"Personally, I think your friend was right. Mom did the right thing sending you out here." She dusted the crumbs from her lap. "But that place isn't free, you know. She had to spread it out over a bunch of credit cards. I saw the bills."

"Candace paid. You remember Candace? Candace and the twins."

Fawn barked a laugh. "You've been away almost a year. Even a Candace has limits."

"I didn't ask to be put in there."

"Everything got easier when you left. We do more things. She makes breakfast every morning. We never fight."

"You even got a new dog."

She looked at me. "She's selling the loft. The whole building is on the market."

"That's not even a good lie. Where would we go?"

"We?"

"I'm serious. If she can't afford the loft, she can't afford New York. Where else is there? New Jersey?"

"Worse than that."

The answer was Canada.

It had only taken my mother something like two decades to

make good on her promise. Candace called sometimes, but I passed the phone off so quickly her existence had shrunk to nothing. I had otherwise blotted out our violent aberration of a vacation. Maybe this was my mother's plan all along. A series of liberations, first the loft and next: her children.

"What are we supposed to do up there? Where are we supposed to sleep?"

"I told you," Fawn said. "I'm not going to fucking Canada."

I would be eighteen in less than a year. I always planned on college, but that sort of experience seemed trivial now. So orderly, so chatty. Our mother threatened to sell the loft all the time. I reminded Fawn of this. There was no reason to worry.

"Except we're poor," Fawn said. "She wasted what was left on you and now she's leaving the country. She cries about it all the time."

"She told me about PB2."

Fawn shook her head and smiled. "Look where we are. Look why we're here. Why should anyone believe you?"

Across the street, a faded yellow Datsun revved its engine and flashed its headlights.

"What do you think they're doing?" Fawn asked. "Are they trying to go somewhere?"

"I'm coming home now, for good. Whatever you had going on before, it's over. Things are going to be different. You're going to watch your step from now on."

Fawn stood, eyes on the Datsun. "I'm going to ask one of those guys for a ride."

"You will not."

She started walking toward the edge of the lot. For some reason I thought it would hold her there, the threshold of the sidewalk, the gap of black street. "Come back here."

Before a teal Geo, she stopped and knocked on the hood. "Who can give me a ride?"

A passenger door opened.

"I know you're doing this to prove a point," I called. I hurried to the sidewalk, called across the chasm of the street. "She thinks she's going with you, but she's not. She's a minor."

The window of the Geo rolled down. There was the flat brim of a ball cap, a fist on the steering wheel. "How old are you?" the driver asked Fawn. "We guessed eighteen, nineteen . . ."

"Eighteen," she said.

"Thirteen," I said.

"Lady says she's eighteen," he said. "You can come too. We'll get you A to B."

"She's not coming with us," Fawn told him, and got in.

In a neat line of signals and appropriate speeds, the cars exited the lot with no hint of where they were headed. Perhaps to the edge of town and back, or down a country road to burn rubber. Soon the lot filled again with a new batch of beaters, rumbling, waiting, gassing it to nowhere.

Inside the Little Acorn, my mother was asleep, or pretending to be. Her hair was wet, the covers bunched at her nose. I whispered to her, and when she didn't answer, I let it be.

The next morning, my mother's face hovered above me, as it had innumerable mornings before. "Where am I?" I asked. The side of a mountain. In my bed at home. On the Fourth Floor with Gia snoring.

"You're here. Get dressed."

Out of habit, I did what I was told without delay. Fawn was sipping an instant coffee by the door, apparently still in one piece after her nighttime exploits. She grimaced anytime we made too much noise.

"Fun night?" I asked, and she gave me a thumbs-up. We would have to sort the rest later. If I had learned anything in exile it was patience.

Our mother had withdrawn into a wordless mood. We lingered at the car while she fussed with the room until it looked better than we found it. It was that murky hour before sunrise when long haul travel begins. Finally, she appeared in the doorway and nodded.

Fawn took the front seat, and I took the back. I was prepared to watch several states flit by in welcome silence. I wanted to hold a thought in my head and leave it there, undisturbed until it faded. The grand ordeal was over, and there was no one to tell. It surprised me, the old internal lunge for Zeke, the longing for someone who knew me before. I saw the roll of his eyes, the sly grin as he reacted to my stories the way I liked, with delighted incredulity at all I'd gotten myself into and out of. I marveled at the gap inside where he was no longer, then the instinct folded, was made vestigial. I cracked the window and a rush of air whistled through.

When we passed by the entrance to the highway, I knew something was wrong.

Our mother laid on the pedal, took two corners at a severe angle. The Volvo jerked back around the way we came.

"Did you forget something at the motel?" Fawn asked. "You're making me sick."

I knew where we were headed, because there was only one road in.

We weaved through a long sweep of trim fields, dirt shoulders, and in the distance a band of trees that marked the entrance to the woods. From the Fourth Floor, we could always spot a car coming from miles away, exposed on the road like a moving target.

My mother let me out at the top of the driveway.

The gate was open, like they knew I'd be back. If she drove me to the front doors and lingered too long, she might lose her nerve. Fawn cranked the window down in the front seat. My mother gripped the wheel.

"I don't understand," I said.

"Just a little more time," she said. "I promise."

I watched until the last low hill swallowed them up and I was alone. It was early yet. It was almost peaceful. The sky gave a low rumble and on one hand I counted all the places I could go. Maybe I'd make a break for it, I thought. Hitch my way to a distant destination. Not California, but the desert maybe, someplace arid. Wherever it was I was probably halfway there. Each path was well-articulated. I saw a version of myself waiting at the end of every avenue, like a specimen preserved in a glass jar. I was loose in the world. Around every corner, a new life. If only I started walking.

III

BOMBS AWAY

16

The party is the party of my dreams. Paper lanterns, lilacs in the wind. The rooftop is alive with visions of my glamorous adulthood, even if no face in the crowd is familiar to me.

After I perform surprise, Rochelle whispers in my ear.

"Do you like it?"

"I love it," I tell her. "I love you."

Rochelle looks at me quizzically for a long moment.

"What is it?" I ask. "Sorry."

"No, no," she says. "Happy Birthday."

JoAnn the coworker butts in with a greeting, and Rochelle describes to her the rum cocktail she curated, tugs her away to the bar. I am alone, a party of one.

In the days leading up to the festivities, I tracked Rochelle's spreadsheets daily. I watched, rapt, as each field evolved, tolls rising and falling and braiding together through my wife-to-be's expert manipulations. By the numbers, it was to be a superior evening, and now, in the thick of it, it feels right to be back. Though the street level has changed, the view above is the same. Even in the dark, the trees twinkle with flowers cupping moonlight, streetlight, an inner, fertile glow. I catch my breath with a drink in the corner and look out over the rooftops, where it is possible to detect the purple aura of the city many miles south. I have sampled every canapé, sipped many a signature cocktail, but the alcohol has had no gathering effect. Dinner sits like a stone in my stomach, and Rochelle has been gossiping with JoAnn the coworker for the past half hour. They glance over often and whisper. Perhaps Rochelle is breaking the news of our marriage. The last frontier. As I watch them, an old instinct alights. Women of the past, mine and not, cast a shrewd, collective eye upon me and smile among themselves. I'm primed to storm over, but the dance floor full of guests parts mid-sway.

"Victor," I say. I had been waiting to see if he'd show.

He looks sharper than the last time I saw him, more than two months ago. His hair is trim, his outfit tastefully coordinated. It looks like he's gotten sun. I tow us to a corner and grab two beers off a passing tray.

"For a minute there," he says, "I thought I was in the wrong place."

Hadn't I been having a wonderful evening? Until Victor's arrival, I realize it was as if I'd been experiencing everything through a thin layer of grease, a kind of runoff from the labor of Rochelle's self-conscious preparations.

"Happy Birthday," he says and hands me a gift bag overflowing with tissue paper. "I stuffed all your mail in there too. You should really change your address."

"Why bother?"

"Is it dying down? Am I late or something? I see a lot of orthopedic shoes around here."

"How dare you," I say. "That's a gross exaggeration. Keep your voice down."

"Oh, are their hearing aids turned up?"

"Get it out of your system. These will soon become our people."

"They're already your people. They're at your party."

"And so are you."

I am unspeakably happy all of a sudden, as uncontrollable and unrelenting as a tremor, though I know the easy tenor of our conversation can't last. Victor has texted relentlessly about whether or not I am staying on the lease for a new year, if he should be hunting for another roommate. I do not want to pry open the seal between one world and the other.

"So, things are good?" I ask.

"Which things do you mean?"

"Oh, you know." I try to keep an eye on Rochelle and JoAnn across the rooftop. "How's the job hunt? The neighborhood?"

"Let's not do the bullet points. I want you to have a good birthday and all, but we should talk. I came all the way up here."

"There's still the cake. You don't want to miss that."

Victor sips his drink and looks behind me at the view. "This place could be nice, if they'd done it differently."

I tell him I'm getting married and he almost spits. "To her?" he asks.

"I could be really happy here. I am happy."

Victor sets down his beer on a rooftop ledge, rubs his hands over his face. "Do you remember the night we met?" he asks.

"Not really."

"You were in the thick of it. You were sick and obsessed over some girl. Stacy. Sandy."

"Steph," I say. "Probably. I think that was her name."

"You get like this. You fix on something, and you let it ruin you."

"You don't have all the facts this time. This isn't the same."

"I don't have the facts because you disappeared. Did you just forget I existed? I honestly don't know the answer."

"Of course not."

"You remind me of her. That face you have on right now."

"I don't know who you're talking about."

"I'm talking about whoever you were back then, when we met. I felt sorry for you."

"I hardly remember," I say, trying to steer things toward a lighter tone. Sometimes this succeeds with Rochelle, but Victor is not so easy to work. I slip a finger between the tissue paper of his gift. The item inside is wrapped with clean butcher paper, a minor heft.

Glass breaks on the rooftop deck. The crowd looks around like the unthinkable has occurred. Victor's face smooths as he looks past me. "There's somebody you should meet."

It's been almost five years since I've seen my sister.

She walks across our rooftop. The crowd splits to let her through. Her face has shed all evidence of malice and distrust. Tall, willowy, straight blond hair, and eyes a familiar shade of sapphire. She holds her chin up and smiles at Victor as she walks over.

If we ran into each other on the street, I'm not sure I would recognize her. And I hadn't, that moment she brushed past me in the doorway of my own building, in transit with precious cargo and newly freed upon the world. Why hadn't she stopped me then? All those months are now behind us. Why did she let me go?

"May," Victor says, as Fawn comes to stand inside the loop of his outstretched arms. "I want you to meet the birthday girl. This is who I've been telling you about."

"Finally," she says, and throws her arms around me.

I look over her shoulder at Victor and he shrugs. He has introduced two powerful fronts and is unsure what weather will result. He has no idea how inconsequential his presence is in the grand scheme of things. What if I was living with Steph instead, would Fawn have stolen her?

Victor shoves his hands in his pockets and grins. "You can thank May for the present. She picked it out. You know I'm hopeless with that stuff."

"Isn't that something men say?" says his winsome date. "That they're hopeless at stuff they don't want to do."

Victor is so happy to witness our modicum of banter that he is unbothered by the accusation. "Just open it," he says.

"No, no," Fawn says, or May, whomever she is impersonating, to whatever end. "Let your friend enjoy her party. There'll be plenty of time for that later."

"What is it?" I ask.

May smiles. "You don't want to ruin the surprise, do you?"

"This must be the famous Victor." Now Rochelle has arrived, nose glowing, the slippery wash of liquor in her eyes.

"And you must be Rochelle. Thanks for the invite. You were right. The train in wasn't bad at all."

"That's what I love about it," she says. "That's what I absolutely love. The location."

May holds out her hand. "So close, and yet so far."

Rochelle, Victor, and the newly minted May get on like gangbusters while I hang off to the side and sulk. Down below, the sidewalk is lively with roving bodies relishing the weather, heads thrown back, plans on the move. Victor can't help giving me the side-eye, attuned to my distraction, an admonishment that makes it clear he knows I am not doing my best.

"An actress," Rochelle says, exaggerating her awe. "That is delightful. I so admire creative expression."

"Oh, I'm just starting out," May says bashfully. "I don't know anything."

"She's modest," Victor says. "She's in rehearsals for a play downtown."

"Have you always wanted to be an actress?" I ask, and collect another cocktail from a circulating tray. "Is this a new inspiration?"

"Oh, I've been passionate about performance my whole life. Acting is just the most constructive outlet," she says, and our little circle laughs.

There are so many things I'd like to know about this young woman, with her practiced hand in applying makeup, the outfit that suggests a personal aesthetic. Her age presents as timeless mid-twenties, not so young as to be embarrassing and not yet deadened by routine. Surely Veld did not impart these qualities. They could never teach her to play the role of interested girlfriend, balancing deference with detectable personality. Perhaps, I think, she is being herself. If I can't know the answer, I at least want to know the story she's in, or how it ends.

"Where are you from?" I ask.

"West Virginia. Small town."

"Day job?"

"I'm a hostess at this amazing tapas place in the neighborhood."

"Which neighborhood?"

She grins at Victor and he grins back. "Your neighborhood," she says.

"May moved in last week," Victor says. "I tried calling you, but as usual—"

"That's amazing," I say. "That is so, so amazing."

For the first time, there is the barest flit of calculation in my sister's eyes, a flicker that does not belong to May or the moment, but to us, a challenge received and countered.

"What can I say?" she says. "When you know, you know. Like you two. How did you meet? I know there must be an amazing story there."

I had forgotten Rochelle's presence, though I realize she is becoming wobbly. It is unlike her to loosen the reins in public, but it's not my job to chastise or suggest that which is obvious.

"It's a long story. Where's JoAnn?" I ask Rochelle. "Maybe you should track her down."

I'm trying to come up with a believable reason to shoo away my visitors and vacate the premises, possibly forever. No good can come of this party. The height of the rooftop now appears perilous, Geronimo Street an illusory corridor, each storefront a portal to another unwelcome remembrance. I thought I'd spent the last few months outrunning her, but she knew where I was all along. JoAnn appears at Victor's side. She wags a pill bottle like a maraca.

Rochelle tries to snatch the bottle, but JoAnn, boozed up and mischievous, and perhaps out for revenge, holds it out of reach.

"JoAnn," Rochelle says quietly. "I asked for the vintage. I left the bottle on the counter."

"Oh, I have that," JoAnn says, and glances around the rooftop, "somewhere around here. I brought these just for fun. I didn't think you'd mind sharing. I found them in the bathroom."

When the boxes of supplements arrive in the mail, Rochelle decants the capsules into unlabeled glass vials. I always thought it was an aesthetic choice. A unifying palette of wellness.

"Oh no. Rochelle. Your face. Did I do bad?" JoAnn says.

"What are you going to do with those?" I ask.

"I thought it was about the right time of night for a little boost," she says. Rochelle is smiling like a maniac. Victor and May exchange looks. "It's nothing to worry about. Something to put a little extra pep in your step and keep you smiling."

"They're homeopathic," Rochelle says. "They are all-natural."

"Derived from a rare root, isn't it?" JoAnn asks. "Or is it common, but its effects were previously unknown? I can never remember." An upper, downer, solvent, or amplifier. A vitamin for every occasion. Rochelle looks at me, mouth open to speak but nothing emerges; there is only the wordless, lipsticked maw.

"How about a tour?" Victor interjects to break the tension. While he and I are not above ingesting unknown substances, it is clear we are both performing for our better halves. He nudges me. "You can show us around your new place."

"Yes," my sister says. "This place is amazing."

"Amazing," I say.

"Amazing," JoAnn says.

"How about we switch?" Victor suggests. "Why don't you and May get to know each other, and I'll hang on to these two ladies, let them buy me a drink." It doesn't matter that the bar is open. He is hoping I will bestow my blessing, that will make it easier to disentangle our lives. I'm nearly touched that it matters. He lets a hand rest on Rochelle's shoulder and she nearly topples over. Meanwhile JoAnn is ebullient. She is rolling the pill bottle in her hand. Her mouth hangs in peculiar reverie.

"So, this is what you've been up to," my sister says.

I've shown her the new and improved loft, its marbled en suite, the shelf of baubles, the eight-burner range. We make no mention of the life preceding this one. There is hardly a need. We are standing inside of it.

"Victor said you disappeared one week out of the blue. He said it was like a spy movie or something. Amazing. This place looks brand new."

"You keep saying that," I say.

"What?"

"*Amazing.*"

She laughs. "It is amazing, at least to me. It wasn't that long ago I moved to the city. It's all so tall and loud, and everyone is so quick and beautiful. Isn't that amazing? I think so."

Whatever lightness of being I was in touch with an hour earlier has been sufficiently muddied. I see my surroundings the way Victor must, perhaps even the way Fawn does. The pomp and circumstance and prescribed décor. The many dozen white faces of a certain age, the catering staff with their thank-you smiles. The fishbowl of dollar bills on the open bar is a mockery—and I had stood by, saying nothing, when Rochelle whispered into the ear of the server to place the jar somewhere discreet.

"Whatever it is we're about to do, let's do it," I say. "Let's get it over with."

My sister sighs dreamily from inside some alternate version of our conversation, in which our problems are clean, romantic, and permissible. "I'm in love," she says. "The first time ever."

"You can't possibly be serious."

"Aren't you in love?"

"With what?"

"With who."

"Rochelle?"

She nods.

"That's none of your business."

"Victor loves you."

"Not in that way."

"Trust me, I know."

Why do I think of our mother's face in this moment? Bright eyes in the back of a van. A stranger's breath in her mouth. Dirt flying as her feet pound the desert, aimed at the mirage of safety. It was the chromosome of precognition that woke her road-worn sleep that day. Nothing else explains it. No one above was watching, and no one below knew any better. Her biology pulled a lever, and she spared herself in time. "Let's go upstairs," I tell my sister.

"I don't want to."

I know that face. May has left the building.

"You've come a long way," I say. "Tour's over, so maybe you'd like a drink."

She gestures to the hallway table. "Don't you want to open your birthday present? I brought it down for you."

"No thanks. I'm not interested."

"That's an odd answer." She retrieves the bag, and holds it out to me by its string handles. "Do you think I'm up to no good?"

When I refuse to take it from her, she pulls a perfect square from the packaging.

"It's the one you lost. Victor told me the whole story, how worried you were. Of course, it's not the original, but you can find anything online now, no problem."

Somehow, it's been sealed in fresh plastic. All wear and tear vanished. The corners are pristine, a stickered bar code in the upper left. Since she has not bothered to scratch off the price, I can see it has been purchased for a measly $24.95.

Playa Mala's *Vieques,* a newly minted mass production.

"Do you like it?" she asks, though she has no interest in my answer.

I'm in the middle of saying something else, something about reality versus fiction, the masks we wear. I'm getting poetic about it, reaching for allusion when a sequined streak drops past the window, mute. Quicker than you'd think.

"What was that?" I ask.

"You should really be more specific."

I go to the window and press my forehead against the glass, toward street level. Though I crane my neck, I can make out only the edges. A man inside the foundry-turned-brewery across the street rushes out to the curb with his hands on his head.

"Someone's coming," my sister says. There are urgent footfalls in the hallway.

"They throw all this money into making this street a haven and they can't even get the stupid gas lanterns going," I say. "What's the point? I can't see a thing."

"There you are." Victor is in the doorway. The first thing I notice are the dark circles under his armpits where sweat has soaked through. All color has departed his face.

"Babe, what is it?" The tone May favors is warmer, a well-adjusted life sheathed inside.

"Your friend," he says to me. "It happened so fast."

"My friend what?"

I had thought about it myself, the instant I saw Fawn across the rooftop, the way the crowd parted for her, the perfection of the moment she had surely planned. Three stories high. The ledges low and unlit, the ground unforgiving. It would be a lyrical gesture. To make her fall.

"Come quick," Victor says, and we go with him.

On the sidewalk, a growing crowd of partygoers and patrons from neighboring businesses have gathered around JoAnn's crumpled body. It almost looks like an installation, curated to invite introspection of our frail forms. Every third onlooker is on a phone, casting around for the cross-streets, telling whoever is on the line to hurry, that it looks bad.

Rochelle is bending over the body, saying JoAnn's name loudly. Her eyes aren't closed all the way, but they are empty. A dark slick on the sidewalk has kept respondents at a distance, but Rochelle's shoes smudge the edges and leave partial tracks. The adrenaline does not perforate her inebriation. I should go to her and hold her steady.

"What happened?" I ask. Victor's eyes dart back and forth as if he is reading bad news. We hover at the building's entrance, catching glimpses through gaps in the crowd.

"She went to have a smoke," he says. "She was leaning up against the ledge and, I don't know, she slipped, lost her balance or something. She was fucked up. She reached out to me."

"You saw?"

"I lit her cigarette."

And where has the doting May gone off to? Her arms are crossed. She is concentrating hard on the scene before her, probably to tamp down the competing stimuli of the crowd. Clusters of energy always upset Fawn. Smells were too intense, all that shuffling footwear, the accumulation of bodies.

"Let's get you some water," I say to Victor, but that won't work. "Just sit down for a second. Sit down here, okay?" I move him to the edge of a stone planter and he sinks down onto it without a fight. Fawn looks at me and then purposefully over to the epicenter of the scene, where Rochelle has begun to sidestep like a newborn animal fumbling for balance. JoAnn shows no evidence of life. I think of the parsley in her teeth, the branzino, the pills spilling from her pocket. It is my birthday. Rochelle twirls toward the crowd, probably searching for my face.

"It's okay," Fawn says. "I'll take care of him."

Sirens keen en route to Geronimo, and my sister rubs Victor's back in absent circles and murmurs. She runs her fingers through his hair.

That night, Rochelle pops three magic pills and tucks herself in. Casino Dreams. She pulls the lever and the wheels spin until morning. I think of JoAnn and cringe. I remember the horrid way she baby-talked through conversation that displeased her. What did it feel like, the weightlessness of falling? Did she catch a glimpse through our window on her way down?

Management has closed the rooftop with yellow tape, but I am not deterred. I ignore the table in the corner piled high with gifts. All the glasses left around are half-full. In a caterer's folding chair, I hold the record in one hand and a letter in the other. Stuffed between the pre-approved credit card mailers and luxury catalogues and defunct magazine subscriptions pleading for renewal—Victor has delivered a missive, from Beanie. It begins, *I hope all is well.*

There are pleasantries and recapping, mindless reminiscences like a yearbook entry. The clubs have been dissolved, extracurricular hours whittled down to work detail and A.M./P.M. calisthenics. Dr. John is gone, moved on to some facility in Nevada. Beanie dots each letter *i* with little bubbles, the curvature of all glyphs exaggerated. After all this time, I do not understand why she is writing, until I turn the page.

Fawn was sent to Fifth and became Beanie's charge. As predicted, she gave her hell. Specifics are slim, considering everything in and out is inspected by staff. I check the envelope to be sure it's real. Postmarked Bowen, Virginia, months ago. Unlike Gia, whose danger was always apparent, Beanie's subterfuge and volatility attach themselves through the guise of reciprocity. In this way, she and Fawn, May, whoever she is now, have much in common.

Beanie asks me to write back, and has included a strip of three forever stamps. She wants to know if I keep in touch with anyone. She thinks of us all the time. The good old girls, she calls us.

She writes that we always looked alike, Fawn and me, though this can scarcely be believed.

She says we have the same sense of humor. She says Fawn is a real mountaineer now.

She says, "You were all she ever talked about. You, and your father."

17

A few weeks after I'd been redelivered roadside by my mother, the Juvenile Transportation Services again came to retrieve me, and this time they weren't alone.

The shame of my return to Veld had been excruciating, as was the overtness of its meaning, that my mother couldn't withstand me even for a few measly hours. My days were spent reintegrating at the bottom of the ladder as punishment. I was removed from kitchen duty. I spent off hours in ISO, was kept from Share and group mealtimes. Gia rearranged our room again. There was no sign of Beanie, who had been sent back to some mountain for recalibration. The Piñata Club was no more.

Only the staff knew what was in the works, the arrangements my mother had phoned in. Eventually, I was delivered to the administrative office and introduced to a woman in a coordinated pantsuit. I had to ask her to explain it again, carefully, slowly, so that I could understand what I was hearing, and where they were taking us. Not just me. Fawn was waiting in the sedan out front. It took five minutes to collect my things. There were no goodbyes.

All down the interstate, our driver made promises. She was a

gentler sort, chosen by Veld and our mother to facilitate our trans-
fer. Foliage and fresh air, the power of a new beginning. These can
work wonders, she said to the rearview mirror.

We were headed south to our father and his unincorporated land.

Fawn was asleep against the window. She had been right. She
did not wind up in Canada. And I had been wrong, because the
loft was under contract, its owner a faceless series of LLCs. To the
great northern beyond, my mother had succumbed, to Candace and
her caveats. In her final act of surrender she punted us a few states
south with hopes our father might have better luck with us. Later,
Fawn insisted it was her idea. That she had invoked our father as
the closing date neared, playing his record on repeat, anything to
avoid banishment with Candace and her possibly vengeful twins.

Our driver kept offering us tiny bottles of water, and the black
county roads had taken over. Every so often, a raccoon or skunk or
possum gambled its life with a dive before the headlights. I drifted
off for however long and dreamt I was back on the trail, a stormy
night. Rainwater seeping up from the ground like the woods were
filling, a series of faucets left to run. A dry creek bed flashed with
mud and swept away my sleeping bag, fallen branches, a young
deer caught in the current, all tumbling by. I woke again as the
sedan rattled onto a gravel road. Stones spat inside the wheel-well,
and beside me Fawn was awake. A gate had come into view.

Inside the veil of dirt, the slant headlights, a figure appeared.

"Looks like he came out to meet you," our driver said. Nobody
moved. Not us, not him.

I reached for Fawn's hand and she pulled it back before I could
touch her. I wished to recede, not even as far as the loft or Deerie.
I would settle for my bed at Veld, the relative safety of routine. Our
father moved through his cloud. He pushed aside the cattle gate,
shielding his eyes as he waved us through.

———

We were shown into a stone foyer where we hung our jackets. Fawn had brought with her three large suitcases, and I had a small plastic grocery bag bulging with extra uniform sweat clothes and one of the journals I'd been working my way through.

"Hello, girls," our father said.

There was the faintest accent. His voice was octaves deeper than I remembered, but I only remembered what I'd listened to a hundred times, the reaching croon, harmonies spiraling.

He was in jeans and wool socks, curly hair, the beginnings of a mustache pronouncing itself inside the stubble. Though he looked in our direction as he spoke, it was not at us precisely. He eyed the crown of Fawn's head, or zeroed in on the switch plate over my shoulder. He asked if we wanted to see our rooms. I did not expect much from our driver or the Juvenile Transportation Services, but it was a shock how swiftly she made her three-point-turn and descended the long drive, leaving us behind with a stranger in every way but by blood.

Up the stairs, there were three bedrooms, two for guests and then the master, the only one with a lock. I understood this as a fresh development, because there were wood shavings in the carpet from where a dead bolt had been drilled. Fawn chose the corner room, and I chose the one at the end of the hall. It was long and narrow, but full of windows with fat wooden ledges. Was this my new life? Were my old things from the loft in transit? Where had the blue moon gone?

I didn't sleep the first night. Silent hours passed in half-dream, until the light lifted at dawn and I could see where I was for the first time.

There were woods as far as the eye could see. Woods clustered tight, climbing into hills, a reserve of green undulating like interminable dunes. Smoke signaled from hidden fires below the canopy. The woods followed me everywhere, or I had followed them. I sensed it even in that first tepid morning that they were not finished with me.

I went downstairs in the same clothes I arrived in. My stomach ached. The house was cold and empty but for a few chosen pieces of furniture, and there was music playing, like the celestial pluck of a harp. I followed the sound along a bank of windows that looked out onto the front of the property, where a great cleared slope abutted the tree line. A low wall of stacked rock marked the edge of my father's small civilization. After the last window in its row, a door.

There would come to be many more times like this where I'd find him hidden in his den, engulfed by books and records and files, broken things he'd tinker with, other evidence of personality. I never saw him sleep, not once. Most mornings he was gone before dawn, out on a call across the county or posted at the clinic in town. That was what he did when he escaped his life in Deerie and began a new one all his own. He became a healer. A veterinarian. He did everything he was supposed to do, only he'd done it in reverse.

His back was to me. He was hunched over his desk, scribbling ferociously, foot tapping in time to a record spinning in the corner. Whatever angelic lilt had lured me in had been replaced by the rambunctious chorus of a marching band. I knocked and my father shot out of his chair, onto his feet.

"What is it?" he asked. "What's wrong?"

"Nothing's wrong," I said. "Sorry to scare you."

"You didn't scare me, you surprised me. Is there something you want?"

I was acclimatizing to my own freedom of movement. If I wanted, I suppose I could've gone right to the fridge for food, left for a walk, slept until noon. There was no indication of what I should be doing, or when. Ever since I was shipped away, life had devolved into a series of transitions. I had to learn new ways of being, speaking, codes to live by, and as soon as I understood the parameters of my world, I was plucked away to a different one, with its own customs and assurances of its superior importance in my life.

"I might need some things," I said.

"What sorts of things?"

"Basics," I said. "I don't know. Winter boots, possibly."

"Is your sister up?"

I shrugged.

"What's that?" he asked. "What does that mean?"

"I didn't check on her or anything."

"While you're here," he said, "you two will be responsible for each other."

"Like how?"

He looked pained as the record ended. There was only the hollow spin of sound. "Often, I'll be gone," he said. "Often, I'll be out. I'll be working. My days are very long. That's why you need to be responsible for one another. I can only do so much."

He couldn't stand the silence any longer. He hurried to the corner, selected a new record, and set the needle. There were a million questions and nowhere to begin.

"I'll just go," I said.

"Okay then." He closed his eyes to the music playing, some calypso record that sputtered with age but seemed to soothe him. After a moment, he cracked open an eyelid. Wishful thinking had not worked. I was still standing there, contaminating his treasured things.

Perhaps he considered me dangerous. Perhaps that was why he'd drilled a dead bolt in his bedroom door. I'd seek retribution for all the years he'd spurned his children. I'd apply my natural talent for violence, multiply it through my exposure to other agitators, and make right how I'd been wronged. I'd come for him in his sleep. I'd have his head.

"For the record," he said, "I didn't ask your mother to send you here. You and your sister. It was a choice made out of necessity."

"It wasn't my idea either."

"It also wasn't my idea to send you to that school, if you can call it that. A waste, if you ask me. What can a place like that teach you about yourself that you don't already know?"

"Okay," I said. "You had no idea whatsoever. Got it."

"I'm not saying this to hurt you, or to excuse myself. It's only information. Information you may or may not find useful. Even though you are here now, and under my care, I never made the case that this arrangement would be for the best. I thought we should get that out of the way."

After all this time, here he was. It was nothing like the photos. Nothing like the record. No love lost, no harmony.

"The boots," my father said, and wagged a finger. "I'll take care of it."

He went to the door and swung it wide, waiting until I walked through. The lock clicked. The music amplified. The house was just as empty. He was finished with me.

The early weeks were spent in separate corners. There was nothing left to do but let parentage run its course. It was up to us now.

In private, I warned Fawn to stay close and vigilant. Our father was always out on calls when we woke up. He left a few packets of instant oatmeal on the counter for us, and we ate in silence as the dawn leavened outside the window. No matter what we hoped, we didn't know the man we were living with. I sensed our situation was tenuous. Our mother was out of the country. If not here, where else was there to go?

"I don't want any trouble," I told Fawn. "Be polite."

She rolled her eyes. "If he doesn't want to talk, then I don't want to talk. I don't think we're going to be here long anyway." At least that was one thing we agreed on. "Besides," she said, "I'm not the one who should be worried. What must he think of you?"

Calls kept our father on the road, off to different counties. And because there was no television, and barely any furniture, I busied myself with a book from the shelf and nestled into a carpeted corner. When I knew he was out or locked away upstairs, I'd sneak into his office, where a whole wall of shelves was stocked with records, books, knickknacks, framed photos. None of us. It was like the loft, in miniature. A traveling exhibit. I recognized duplicates from my mother's collection, and many more unknown to me. Though his bedroom was off-limits, his den of memorabilia was left unguarded. I tried to derive meaning from this, but nothing about his modernist home on the hill, or our circumstances, adhered to order. There was talk of starting school in the new year, but I had a feeling we'd be gone by then.

Despite the circumstances, I felt strangely encouraged by our new location. It was like a curtain had been pulled back where I thought there'd only ever be a wall. A whole other world, an inverted duplicate, was revealed to me. In a Venn diagram, each of us occupied our own bubble. I tried to identify the ways in which we overlapped and diverged, and what it meant. Whose hair was curly. Whose eyes were light. Who chewed their fingernails. Who excelled in math. I noticed my parents stocked their kitchens with the same staples. They listened to similar music, read the same books. There was in common an apparent taste, a desire for fine things arranged intentionally, in case someone of note were to stumble upon it. Of course, they were both absentees. My mother boarded a train to flee, and my father took the truck.

Fawn spent most of her daylight hours outside. First thing in the morning, she'd pull on her new boots and go kicking around the front yard. I couldn't blame her. There was not much else to do. If I trained my eyes I could discern the break between property lines, the skim of fencing or a shaved field indicating private acreage. There was nothing she could hurt out here.

There came three days straight where snow fell without stopping. Our father hadn't been out on a call in a week, a record since we arrived. Buried up on our hill, he paced his office, his bedroom, emerging only for food and water. I decided I was going to do something different. I was going to cook dinner. I had learned a thing or two and now was free to implement my understanding. We would all sit at the table for a meal, and this would lure him out of hiding.

In the kitchen, I hoisted a cast-iron skillet onto the burner and lit the pilot with a long match. I watched Fawn through the window above the sink as I stirred a risotto, a dish I'd heard discussed but had never actually eaten. What was once a slope of dead winter grass was now a slate of snow. I watched on as her explorations edged closer to the tree line. I began setting the table, glancing out the window each time I passed, and each time Fawn was closer to the stone wall. I knew she was testing the waters, or baiting me. The light was fading. There was the smell of burning, and a burst of cold from the hall as Fawn stomped into the kitchen.

"Shoes," I said, and she kicked them off. "Put them by the door," I said, and she did.

She had a placid look on her face, like she'd risen from a soothing dream. I said we were almost ready.

"That smell," she said. "What have you done?"

The three of us came to sit around the table and chewed very slowly.

"Sorry. I got a little carried away." I had tried to salvage the risotto, but the bottom had scorched, and every bite tasted smoked. "So, what did everyone do today?"

"It's too cold to do anything," Fawn said.

"You could read," our father said. "You should read like your sister."

"I don't like reading stuff that's made up."

"Why not?" he asked.

"Because when you read, you're supposed to learn something."

"You can learn from made-up things."

I knew she wanted to bat back, but she kept her eyes on her plate.

My vision for the evening had been convivial. Inexplicably, there would be wine, or at least conversation, but the rest of dinner passed in silence while we pushed food around our plates. I could tell my father was itching to go upstairs, to return to whatever he spent his time doing there. I was going to call it, accept the failure and try another course of action, when Fawn finally spoke up.

"We should get a dog."

"A dog?" our father asked. "What would we do with a dog?"

"We could teach it to do things. Like hunt, or get the mail."

"Don't listen to her," I said. "She's joking."

He leaned back in his chair. "Have you had a dog before?"

"Two," I said.

Fawn looked at me. "You weren't there for the last one."

"His name was PB2," I told our father.

"What sort of name is that?"

"Our real dog was named Peanut Butter, but it ran away," Fawn said.

Our father seemed amused. "Peanut Butter is a silly name."

"It is," Fawn said. "I named him that."

"He came with that name," I said.

"I killed a dog once," our father said. He took a bite of food and grimaced.

Fawn put her fork down. "Why did you do that?"

"It attacked me," he said through his mouthful. "I was Christmas caroling. I was a teenager. I threw it off a cliff because it bit my leg."

"Why did it bite you?" Fawn asked.

"Christmas caroling?" I said.

"How could I know why it bit me? Dogs bite."

"Was this on the island?" Fawn asked.

"Not the big island."

"Then where?"

"The little island. Like a baby sister island. Vieques."

"Where?" Fawn asked.

"The place I'm from."

"Why were you caroling?" I asked him. "Was that a tradition?"

"It was for money," he said and got up abruptly, collecting our plates, though they were mostly full. "After I got bit, I didn't carol anymore."

It had not been an entirely unsuccessful experiment. There were new, canine items to add to the Venn diagram. Still, I could sense our time with him was waning, and I was not the only one. Fawn's questions started up rapid-fire.

"What was the island like?" she asked. "Why did you come here? Why did you leave? Can we go there? Are you going back? What's it look like? Is it different?"

"What two places are the same?" he said. "Of course it's different."

"Why?" Fawn asked.

"Why," he said, bracing his arms on the counter and turning to us, "or how?"

Fawn considered this. "How."

He sighed, pained to articulate a new list.

"It's smaller than the mainland. It's warmer than here. It's an island. It's nothing like this place. Not even the hills are the same."

"How far is it?"

Our father looked in my direction to see that I was watching.

"The island is here," he said, and held a fist in the air. "It's far. And us? We're over here. We're far." He traced a line through the air that never reached a destination. "One has nothing to do with the other."

No one offered to help with the dishes. Fawn retreated to the darkened sunroom and my father to his office. Sometimes the pressure of the wind pushed upon all those glass panels that made up the house and wheezed like a sheet of ice as it thinned, made a reedy whistle where air pried through the rubber sealant. I was scrubbing the scorched pan, thoughtless, when I heard Fawn call out for our father to come quick. She had found something.

There was a rotund planter on the front deck, abutting the sunroom. It was empty of crops or soil, but it had filled with layers of snow and ice and melt. Fawn had seen a wormy tail flicking around its edges. She heard a scrabble she mistook for the wind, but through the window, hands cupped to spy into the night, she saw a little rat-nosed thing, blind eyes searching.

"What is it?" she asked our father.

We were standing on the deck, coats thrown on in haste. My father had a penlight he cast upon the scene. I looked down into the planter where the snow had liquefied and a possum was plodding in slow circles within the wash. Its nose kept bumping the edges. It had fallen in.

"What it is, is half-dead," he said. "Must've been looking for food."

"Half-dead," Fawn repeated. "Frozen?"

"You see this sometimes," he said. "Animals stuck in trash bins and dumpsters and whatnot. They can get in easy, but not out. Too icy to get a grip and they succumb to the elements."

The possum was not moving. Its body had sunk lower into the icy water of the basin, and its mouth hung open a fraction, exposing a row of dainty yellow teeth. "I don't know how far it will make it now."

"We can warm it up," Fawn said. "We can wrap it in a towel and bring it inside."

"You don't bring these things inside." He hugged his coat closer and looked down at us. "You should go in, girls. Smell that? More snow. It's going to start up again."

"I want to keep it," Fawn said. "We can just lock it in the sunroom until it's better."

"No," he said flatly, and looked to me. "Help me turn over the planter and we'll go in. The rest is out of our hands. On three, ready?"

The vessel was heavier than I thought, and frigid to the touch. A splash of ice chunks and melt coursed over the deck. The possum did not snap to its feet and skitter off, back to the woods. It lay there in a pool, inside the light my father shone upon it. I wondered if it was a boy or a girl, if there were others in its den whose existence hinged upon its survival, how it kept them warm.

"Do something," Fawn said. "Poke it. Check if it's breathing."

Our father looked at me and raised his eyebrows. *Kids, right?* he seemed to be indicating. Kids and their silly fixations. I touched Fawn's shoulder and told her to go in. She shook me off but went through the door to the sunroom anyway and hovered in the window. She did not take her eyes off the animal, not when our father slipped back upstairs and turned his dead bolt, and not when I was done with the kitchen, our mismatched meal, and turned in for the night.

The next morning, the pool of water left behind had frozen to black. The planter was where we left it, but the possum had gone.

"See, it made it after all," I said to Fawn in the kitchen.

We had a space heater pointed at our ankles. We were eating mugs of instant oatmeal. My mood was stuck somewhere between slow mornings at the loft and dawn hours on the trail. I wondered how many more chances I would be given, how many more times I'd be forced to start over.

Fawn turned her oatmeal over with her spoon. The longer we stayed, the quieter she was becoming. I asked if she'd watched all night, if she'd seen it finally gather its strength and go.

"Yes," she said, and took her breakfast to the sink. "All of a sudden, it went off into the trees. I read when they're scared like that, they play dead sometimes. Have you seen my boots?"

"Where did you read that?"

"I got a book from the office," she said, "just like he told me. I read it and he was right. In there, there's an answer for everything."

18

For once, I do everything right. It begins as an experiment.

My sister is back, and better than ever.

In the time intervening, the two of us have shed old skins, invented new presents. We were meeting as adults now, with chosen histories, predilections, names. Without trying, we had followed in each other's footsteps. What I had stolen, she had stolen. The love I made for myself, she made too. The two of us are transparencies overlaid, aligning with and thus confirming the other, but if anyone else should look on and inspect—what would they see?

After the accident, Rochelle moved us from the loft as a temporary measure, or so she has claimed. Our sublet in the city is a new construction and smells of fresh paint and laminate. It's smaller, storage-optimized, the opposite of charming, but I don't blame her for seeking distance. Though the patch of sidewalk outside the loft was power-washed not long after JoAnn's death, it was off-putting, the way the human runoff coursed into the gutter, networked toward the river, the water treatment facility, reapportioned into the general supply.

I can only wonder how long it will take for Rochelle to return to herself, and us to the loft. She has not been back to work, and this has left me little time unattended. She has thrown herself into planning our impending nuptials. She is no longer preoccupied with minimalism, detail, and order, and has instead embraced a romantic maximalism. Cultivation of her spreadsheets has ceased. Their last update is locked in time, the day of the accident. My birthday.

It is in a similar vein that Victor has gone on existing after JoAnn's great impact—dragged forward only by the changing of days, but otherwise immobile. Before, with my sister's help and in my absence, Victor had been on an upswing. He was hired at a tech company that serviced other tech companies as a third-party customer service module. When someone complained, they had to go through his port first. He dressed better. He ate better. His rougher edges—the Jersey accent and street smarts, the gruff rapport with all who crossed his path, all the things I enjoyed most about him— had been spackled over. It would have at least been risky to disentangle him from my sister while his new confidence was untested. Now, in his weakened, dependent state, it is out of the question. He had watched her tip over the ledge, caught her glassy eyes with his as she reached for him. He was the last thing she saw and he holds himself responsible. He is like Zeke in that way, internalizing all injustice as personal failing. I have to remind myself that other people have not seen injury and death as I have, up-close and reiterated ad infinitum. Now the only person he will speak to is May.

For the first time since Veld, I keep a journal. There are hundreds of pages at my disposal, an extreme sort of power. I have become adept at registering my own comings and goings, visualizing them, stirring the data until it tells me what I want to know. All unbridled thoughts and wishes live inside my notebook. When I consider the loft sitting unoccupied and am bitten by the impulse to scroll for info on squatter's rights, estate law, I halt myself. I record the offending thought like a debit in a ledger. As part of my new credo, I have stopped tempting fate. I do not assess the contents of our medicine cabinet. I erase the dots connecting Rochelle and me to the vial of vitamins in JoAnn's mashed pocket, all those capsules spilling onto Geronimo.

I do only that which is requested of me. And now that it's been a month or so, I'm beginning to reap the rewards of the newly sober. I live on a slight elevation, senses receiving the world unfettered. I swallow every vitamin and am bathed in tranquility. I am doing better. I am the best I've ever been. I am on my way to see my sister.

The theater is surprisingly cavernous, though it looks more like a lecture hall and less like a place where moody one-acts are produced. The stage is empty, so is the lobby. The building is sealed tight and gives no hint of the rumblings of the street. I imagine couples attending Sunday matinees, cellophane-wrapped flowers in hand for sisters-in-law and wayward friends. I wander, reading old programs framed on the walls, scanning the black-and-white headshots of past performers who have since gone on to do better things, though I recognize none of their names.

The current production is called *The Pragmatist,* a talky, opaquely intellectual number on the life of the philosopher John Dewey. My sister plays his sounding board, or wife. It does not surprise me that others find her a convincing actress. Since our reintroduction, I've only called her May. Her true name would be a volatile utterance, a pin that should never be pulled.

A giggle echoes up into the high ceiling of the lobby. The sound is brief, ghostly. When I turn around, there is only a wall of donor names etched in stone.

I take the stairs to the balcony level. I have to scan the rows twice before I spot a man in the corner, sitting in the farthest seat, legs spread, head tilted all the way back. There is a preposterous mustache on his face. He is looking up at the ceiling, mouth open. If it weren't for the quick rise and fall of his chest, I might think him dead. It's only when I get closer, down the steps and toward the front rows, that I see what sort of agony he's in.

I spot my sister's head between his legs, and the moment I see her, she sees me too.

There is only a flash of surprise on her face as she pulls away from him. Without taking her eyes off of mine, she clears the outline of her lips with her thumb and forefinger.

"Don't stop now," the mustache says, unaware there is company.

May runs her hands up his legs, fiddles with one of the old-timey buttons on his costume. His head tilts back and his eyes close as he relaxes. In my head, my feet are swift, I have already swung open the side door to the alley and escaped. I wonder why I haven't yet left the room.

My sister gives a little shrug in my direction, as if to say, *Now what?*

"What are you doing?" I say.

Each word is a note that carries out into the theater, like the opening salvo of a musical number. The man nearly spins in his seat. "Oh god," he stutters and tries to cover himself.

My sister gets to her feet calmly. She adjusts her woolen skirt and waits for me to chastise them. She has broken a vital part of our contract, predicated on mutual compliance. If either of us acts outside of our delineated characters, alludes to a past life incompatible with the present—a ripple breaks the surface. She must know what's coming next. It would all be over.

"Sorry," I say, and begin backing out of the theater. "I'm sorry."

I'm down the stairs as fast as my feet will carry me. On the way out, I pass a bulletin board pinned with cast headshots. There's my sister in her late 1800s regalia. Next to her, the star of the show as well as the performer on the balcony. I make it a block before she catches up. She has been shouting my name down the block, but I keep moving, slipping between couples and small clots of tourists. "Wait up," she calls, and reaches out for me, cutting me off at the corner. "I don't know what you think you saw back there, but I can explain."

My phone starts buzzing in my pocket. The thought that it could be Victor makes me queasy. "I don't need to know anything," I say and silence the call. "Don't tell me anything."

She looks sidelong. "Okay. If that's what you want."

"Of course it's not what I want." I can feel the scales tipping already, portending the end of another chapter, another forced evolution just around the corner. "How could you be so careless? You only had to do one thing."

"What thing?"

"Keep him happy. Be in love. Is that so hard?"

"That's what I should do?"

"Do you know what this would do to him if he found out?"

"I didn't mean it. Sometimes these things happen."

"Well, you ruined it. It's ruined now."

"Fine. I'll tell Victor everything, I swear. I'm so embarrassed." She shields her eyes from the strangers looking on. A passing man shoots me a dirty look. My phone buzzes again. I think of Victor helping her run lines in an unconvincing but enthusiastic monotone. It's the only thing he seems to look forward to anymore. "You don't know what it's like, all the pressure I've been under," she says.

"We can't afford mistakes if we want to keep living like this. Don't you understand?"

My sister takes a step closer. "You don't have to tell him."

"You want me to lie?"

"Don't think of it that way. It's just a thing that stays between us. He is very, very fragile right now. We don't want to hurt him."

Always the question. "Who's we?"

In the beginning, good luck came to Victor in spades. I got to know him while he still liked his life, and was good at it. He stayed one step ahead of the curve, and this quest gave him purpose, until a series of setbacks, direct and indirect, dominoed across his life. His position at the agency was eliminated. His mother developed diabetic necrosis in her left foot, and his older brother and arch-rival somehow transformed himself into the prince of home-flippers down in Matawan. His brother bought a speedboat and Victor started losing his hair. I witnessed the sad little tufts in the shower drain. It all began a few weeks after I moved in with him.

"We can't go on like this forever," Fawn says, and I know it's her, not May, who's speaking. "If it wasn't this thing, it would be some other thing. It's not like I'm going to marry him. Unless—is that what you want me to do?"

"He doesn't even know you."

"He doesn't know you either."

I grab her by the arm, push her sleeve up to the elbow, and it's there: the jagged line, her scar, puffed up, a feeble pink. "I know who you are. I haven't forgotten."

Pedestrians step around us. One bangs into my shoulder and tells me to watch it. Fawn pulls her arm away and rubs the skin there as though I've hurt her.

"We don't need to be here anymore," she says. "The loft is empty."

"Listen to yourself."

"You think I'm the same as I was when I was twelve. Were you the same after you left?"

I think of all the Veld girls who outgrew their worst mistakes, and the freer girls out in the world who were given this right as a matter of course—no mountain climb, no fortress, no group blood-letting. I wondered if the pain of innocent things was ever real to Fawn. What was she hoping to find under the skin?

My phone buzzes a third time and, fearing it might be Rochelle with some emergency, a glance at the screen shows an incoming international call.

"You should take that."

"Forget it. End it with the actor," I say. "And if Victor asks, then you have to tell him the truth—but only if he asks. That's fair."

Fawn lays a hand on my shoulder. "Let this bring us closer together."

"How? How would this do that? Just tell me, is there any part of you that loves him?"

Fawn gives me a curious look. "Of course. He's very nice. He listens to me."

"Then don't break his heart. At least not until he can survive it."

"And you love Rochelle, right?"

"Yes," I say, in a voice not my own. "Of course."

She brightens and turns a lock of hair between her fingers. "It's all happening for us. We each have somebody, and they love us so much."

"Hey," I snap. "Stay focused. Don't go getting big ideas."

"Aren't we still going for lunch?" she asks, and I give her a look before May locks back into place. "There's the most darling little lunch spot, and next to it this funky thrift store and record shop. I thought it'd be the kind of place you liked. You could take Rochelle on a date there. It isn't far from your new apartment."

"How do you know where my new apartment is?"

"We're friends," she says. "Aren't we?"

Once my sister waves goodbye, I round the corner out of sight. I linger in the doorway of a bodega for a few minutes then return the way I came.

I follow her because I know how. I've done it countless times. I am a capable predictor of her pace, where her gaze lingers. I know when something is waiting at the end of her trail.

As she makes her way through the theater lobby, I watch from the outer doors. From there, it's easy to access the mezzanine, easy to be quiet about it, to look on from the shadow of the curtain as Fawn takes center stage. There, the famous pragmatist waits for her.

"Where did you go?" he asks, and tries to sweep her into his arms. "I was worried."

She peels his hands off of her and steps back. "I've been thinking about it," she says, "and I'm quitting." She allows a stunned moment to pass and looks around the shoddy period set with mild revulsion. "Do you know if I'll still get paid for the last few weeks?"

"Are you being serious?" her acting partner asks.

"Never mind," she says. "I guess the money doesn't really matter."

It occurs to me that this actor was only a matter of convenience, our meeting and circumstances prescribed. She knew exactly what time I'd arrive, had said nothing when I walked in. Fawn wanted to be caught. She wanted to show me that her patience was running thin. Something had to change. If I didn't pull a lever, then she would.

"God, this thing is itchy." She takes off the costume jacket and drapes it neatly over the wire outline of a chair. "All right, well," she says. "I'm off."

"May," he says. "Hold on a second. This isn't right. What about the show?"

"You know, just try and forget about it," she says. "And hey, break a leg."

Rochelle insists on having our engagement photos taken in the city while all the trees are in bloom. Between flashes, I imagine what we'll look like on the refrigerators of her distant relatives. Everyone who walks by looks on as we perform our union for the camera. They assess our odds, judge our life and future in a glance, if they even care at all. The photographer tells me to angle my chin up. He says I'll fake a better smile if I pretend I'm laughing.

"Just keep your eyes open, nice and wide," he says.

After the sixth location shoot, Rochelle suggests a break. The photographer invites us for lunch, but Rochelle begs off. She hobbles to a bench, pulls off one of her shoes.

"I should've broken them in first," she says. "I don't know what I was thinking."

Both of us are in a daze from all the smiling, the posing, the blinding light. We sit next to each other and a few rollerbladers glide past, a few kids in backpacks. In all our empty silences I think of JoAnn. Not because I mourn her, but because she is a marker, a plumb line that denotes the deepening of our relationship, a mile-marker of shared trauma.

"I'm so tired," Rochelle says. "I feel like I've never been this tired."

"Is it JoAnn?"

She scoffs. "What an inane question."

"Of course," I say. "Sorry."

"It's more than that. Not everything is about her."

A smattering of old raindrops shakes loose from the leaves above. A baseball connects with its bat, a crowd cheers, an ice cream cart blasts reggae and dings a bell. It's impossible to hear just one thing at a time in this city. It's not only the birds singing, but the traffic wheezing. It's not only the jackhammers, but the scuffle of shoes on sidewalks, shop doors chiming with every open. It's the voices everywhere, the constant yammer and string of complaints. The greetings and goodbyes turned up to eleven. I'm tired too, I think. I can't remember the last time a thought wasn't urgent. I ride the train back and forth between lives so often, I feel the rumble of tracks beneath my feet even when I am still, even when I am in my bed at night.

"To be honest," Rochelle says, "I've been here twenty years. Inevitably, it all starts to blur together. You start to want more."

"That's why you're in Deerie now," I say. "To cool down. To get more."

"Right," she says, "and that helped, for a while. Of course, more square footage would be desirable, more livable outdoor space. How many times do I have to walk over that horrific stain on the sidewalk and feel responsible? Deerie is not forever. I'd like to renovate a barn."

"What?"

"A barn. Renovate it."

"Into what?"

"It wouldn't have to feel like a barn. More like an event space. Rustic, but chic. I enjoy my work, but there are limits. I don't want this role indefinitely."

"I don't know if there are a lot of barns in Deerie."

"Of course there aren't," she says. "I'm talking about Michigan."

"You want a barn in Michigan."

"I want to go home," she says. "That's what I'm trying to say."

A man with a portable speaker on blast saunters by. He nods over to us, dressed in our best, and bobs his head. "You haven't been here as long as I have," Rochelle says. "I'm tired of the stampede. I'm tired of track announcements. Randall is trying to fuck me over anyway." Her boss. "It was always my plan. Everyone goes home eventually, don't they? I love the country."

"You hate the country," I say. "You have never said any of this to me before."

"I'm sure I have. I've always felt this way, even before you. The winters here are awful."

"Worse than in Michigan?" I ask. I mentally skim every spreadsheet I've ever spied upon, every attribute ascertained from living with her for months, and there's no record of this desire. "I don't understand. You hate Michigan."

"It's very scenic, actually."

"Okay, your sisters. You hate them."

"I love each one of my sisters."

"Why did you keep this from me?"

"This isn't about you," she says, and laughs. "And why should it matter? I mean, we're getting married. Isn't it more important to live with me than to live in one specific place?"

"Yeah," I say, "a specific place like Michigan."

The photographer, who had gone to a coffee cart at the edge of the park, returns with a tray for three. Rochelle accepts her cup without so much as thanks. He's a younger guy with a slick haircut, rings on almost every finger. Rochelle stands and adjusts her outfit.

"Come on," she says. "Let's finish this, and then we can go home."

I've been in love my whole life, it seems. It's never what I think it is. With a girl on TV, with Antonia, Steph, with every woman brave enough to kiss me back. There is no planning for the hunger, or what it can become—how it can slip away from you, out from under expectation so fixed and comforting.

I look at Rochelle, the sweep of her hair, the laughter of children rounding the paved walk. I make my love aspirational. A room to fill, a home to grow into. Rochelle and I can give that to each other, and that's not so different at all from being held.

We stand below a cherry tree in bloom. People walk by and smile knowingly. They give us a thumbs-up or clutch their chests, for we are one of many pairs in a long march. Rochelle laughs and I look at her, wondering what's so funny as she waits for the next flash.

19

The sunroom was always fifteen degrees cooler than the rest of the house. The cloud cover sank over the hilltop like a cake dome, and inside the glassed box Fawn spent hours watching the inclement weather pass overhead. It was surely no coincidence that the room offered a panorama of the woods, its summoning hills and pockets, ripe for contemplation. I thought of Shine, what he said about the forest, how it is always looking back.

I was in the kitchen doing the breakfast dishes. I had taken it upon myself to manage the household, however bare. I thought if a tidying human touch was perceptible and my father took notice, he would consider our presence less of an imposition and more of an asset. Children could be useful. It wasn't all give and go.

With a soapy hand, I touched the phone on the wall in the kitchen, remembering numbers no longer in service. I recalled Antonia's and dialed, just because I could. It rang and rang.

There was a hand on my shoulder.

"What are you doing?" my father asked. "Is it your mother?"

"I was just calling a friend," I said. "Sorry."

"You don't have to be sorry."

The phone was still in my hand. The ringing had stopped. "Hello?" a distant voice called inside the earpiece. I hung up and turned back to my father. He was in his coat.

"I have to go. An emergency."

"Another one? In this weather?"

"It isn't so bad down at the road. The plow finally got to it, and Rigg is going to pick me up at the gate, take us out in his truck."

"Who's that?"

For the first time, he smiled. I knew it was the first time because it changed his face completely when he did it. "We work together."

"What's the emergency?"

"Foaling situation. When it happens, it's a problem." I had a hard time imagining the magnitude of an animal like that, or having any power to save it. "I should be back by the morning, but maybe later." He turned to go and stopped short. "Oh, and I'll call the house if I'm gone too long." He seemed proud to have thought of this gesture on his own.

I helped myself to his den as soon as a reasonable amount of time had elapsed.

Fawn appeared in the doorway with the same idea, and in silent coordination we began at separate corners and combed over all the trappings of our father's unknown life.

In some ways, it was just a bookish bachelor's room. Rows of tomes, scraps of paper with unintelligible handwriting on it, coffee rings everywhere. There was a carpeted corner where the turntable was, along with several standing shelves of albums and a six-record automatic changer. It was the only room in the house that had a distinctly human smell.

Fawn opened a drawer in his desk and removed a checkbook.

"Handy," she said, and put it back where she found it. "If he only lives in one room, why does he need a whole house? Think about that."

"And what's it doing all the way up here?" I asked.

I was combing over titles in his collection. I knew a copy of the Playa Mala album had to be somewhere. Finding its cousin here felt like a confirmative act, though what it confirmed was unclear. An item was waiting to be rescued, and its nature would unlock the location of another item, and another, and the whole office would be mine to unravel, examine at the root. I was always trying to get a prolonged look at him in our brief interactions. The years between us felt like footage I'd seen only once, in passing.

"I'm trying to remember him," I said to Fawn, "but I can't. It's all hazy. Like it's just too far back in my brain to reach it."

"You look like each other," she said.

"We do?"

She picked up a stethoscope from his desk. "Think he's missing something?"

We spent a few hours like that, Fawn and I. Sometimes a photo would root us in place, a certain book, a hat, a doodle. There were surprises, and certain objects whose presence I kept to myself. A tiny bag of pot in a carved box beside the turntable. A mug of guitar picks. A roll of undeveloped film in its plastic tube, set apart on the shelf like a prize. I opened one drawer and felt around inside, came away with a crystal bottle and put its nozzle to my nose. Dior.

We put a record on. Donny Hathaway sang about love in a place where there's no space, no time. I saw a framed picture of happy faces I didn't know. How hard would it have been to request some recent photos of us from our mother? The record kept turning.

"I don't want to listen to music anymore," Fawn said finally. "I'm tired."

"I'll turn it down. Don't go yet," I said. "We're having fun."

"I'm going to bed."

"Weren't we?" I asked. "Having fun?"

"This place is depressing. None of it has anything to do with me."

"Twenty more minutes. Ten."

The song cut out and we heard a distressed sound in the breath between tracks. The next song kicked up and Fawn waved her hands to kill the music.

A bird was trapped in the chimney. The fireplace was the center of the sunken living room, and when I opened the flue a tortured flutter of wings filled the hearth. The bird was hardly visible. Only the scrabble of its spindly feet and wingtips against brick.

"It's stuck," I said. "What should we do? Should I get the broom?"

"You don't want it flying around in here."

"He's a vet. Maybe it's hurt."

"He'll be mad," she said. "Just close the doors."

"And pretend it's not there?"

Fawn was drifting toward the stairs already. The long days outdoors took it out of her, made her more peaceable, though hardly warm. She waved over her shoulder dismissively.

"It'll be fine," she said. "They're smarter than you think."

I set a new record to play, and another after that. I angled all the receivers around me and sat down in the center of the rug. I read the backs of album covers as tracks elapsed. Hours passed until I found what I was looking for.

The best part about the Playa Mala cover, and album really, was that it was about being two places at once. The sextet was posed on a Manhattan corner, just below the sign where the street met the avenue, but the title above their heads was *Vieques*, another island, some sixteen hundred miles away. Some songs were about island life, some set in the city, some with a little of each. It was a reminder. One could leave but was never really gone.

This copy of *Vieques* was worn, but at least the packaging was complete. My mother only had the blank sleeve, the band's name and album title scrawled on the center label. She was the one with the original. As I set the needle, I wondered if this was a romantic gesture of some kind. I made it one time through the four-track EP and read along to every word, noting the lines and phrases I'd gotten wrong, how meaning hinged on the least accent, consonant, syllable. I got up to reset the needle for another go around, and saw my father in the doorway. I asked how long he had been standing there. I braced myself, but a moment passed and he did not seem angry.

He was in his coat, and melted snow had pooled at his boots. There was a hint of suspicion in his expression, but it was more investigative than wary.

"Is the horse okay?" I asked.

"Foal. And not this time."

"Sorry." The first song kicked to life and I went for the knob.

"Wait," my father said. "Do you know what this is?"

"It's you."

He took off his jacket and his boots and crossed the room in wool socks. He was wearing glasses, which was new. "It's been a long time since I heard it," he said, and sat at his desk.

"You don't listen to it sometimes?"

He shook his head. "I don't need to do that."

"I've been putting everything back how I found it."

"I've been collecting them since I was your age. They've come with me everywhere; even when it didn't make sense to cart them with me, I took them."

"I've handled records before. I've been careful."

He lifted a hand to stop me, suspended my defenses midair.

His glasses hung at his collar, and he rubbed his eyes, looked at me while his past self joined in three-part harmony.

He said, "I'm trying to tell you a story."

It was like a plug had been pulled. The record was over long before my father stopped talking. He leaned far back in his chair, gazed through the floorboards as he recounted. I did not move. I did not speak. Each story kick-started the next. Every memory on the brink of extinction he'd given a second life. Who else was there to tell? Marooned up here in snow, isolated save for animals and their anxious handlers. Maybe I could've been anyone, but this time it was me.

I tried to stay awake. I massaged my cheeks, pinched my heel, but couldn't help it. I woke up on the rug in the den, pale light rising up off the snow as the moon departed. The house was warm and smelled sweet like powdered sugar. I walked to the kitchen toward voices.

Fawn was at the table, and my father was at the griddle on the stove, flipping pancakes. I fought the urge to run. "Come in," he said. "Sit."

I didn't know if there was a code between us now, what the rules of disclosure were, and his face or mood gave no indication. He wasn't even smiling when he loaded my plate, but I thanked him and sat down. More snow had fallen, but the sky was clear and the sun direct. There was no telling how long the cover would stick.

Fawn doused her breakfast in syrup, pleased by the elevation in treatment. Our father slung a dish towel over his shoulder and joined us. He ate very slowly, watching our faces to see if we liked what he had made. Fawn nodded with her mouth full.

"It's good," she said.

"Yeah," I said.

"It is pretty good," he admitted. "I like sweet things for breakfast."

After we were through, Fawn offered to do the dishes, and my father was impressed.

"Me too," I said. "I'll help." There was something I had been meaning to tell him the night before, something I let sit in wait at the back of my mind to make way for his reminiscing.

"Great," he said and carried his plate to the sink. "I'll go throw another log on the fire."

20

I became our habit between the hours of midnight and dawn. The two of us, insomniacs. Sometimes my father found me in the den first, and other times I'd find him. I never asked him to, but he would always queue up the record to start, and after it played through once, he'd let me pick the next. We switched on and off for hours at a time. Some tracks elapsed without a word between us, but most often he narrated, as if he alone could hear and interpret what was coded underneath.

He was always gone when I woke, which made the whole thing feel illegitimate, like it didn't count. Probably Fawn knew what we were doing, but she never asked. Inquiring acknowledged the emerging fact that I had taken the lead. I should've been happy, but I also knew it was because I was the better audience. I was receptive, inquisitive, and mostly didn't mind listening. The details of island flora and fauna, of city blocks in a certain light, brands of instruments, names of clubs—his recall was impeccable, and verbose. But there was no mention made of all that dead air between then and now, the leaving or the left. He hadn't sent for us. We'd been sent. I wondered if he was surprised by how little he had to do to win me over, or if he pitied that sort of pliability, if my eagerness embarrassed him, or worse, reminded him of my mother.

Some nights I waited hours for him to show, even when I couldn't bear to listen to one more fond recollection I had no stake in. Like penance, I submitted. When was it going to happen? That feeling of coming full circle.

Fawn kept busy on small expeditions to the edge of the woods and back. She lingered there, sometimes with a stick in her hands she'd jab into the soft, mulched soil. She always seemed to be having an animated conversation with herself. It occurred to me that she had never been around so much nature before. I thought it could be good for her.

When she turned up for dinner at the end of each day, she was flush from all her activity, and there was the fixated way she tended to it, her rounds, so that when she sat down at the table, she was ravenous and totally silent, like she'd come in from a hard day's work.

TRACK 1.
"PERLA"

It happened on a street corner.

Why did anything happen? That was the theme of the evening.

This part of the city was all diagonals. It was how they connected. Smash into a meet-cute. He gripped her elbow, and she clocked him like she was fighting for her life.

She would explain to him—in the nearest diner, while he shoved paper napkins up his nose and begged the man behind the counter to let him use the phone—that it was an acquired stress response. Those were the words she used. Her time on the road made her suspicious, but he was the wary one. What ideas might the wrong person get looking at the two of them, separate hues, one bleeding, the other making a scene. He needed to call his host. He was staying with the cousin of a cousin of a cousin in the basement studio. He'd never been so cold in his life, sleeping down there, the hum of neon an earworm that would stay with him for life. It made him think of tiny flames, glass tubes melting in the hand of the first woman he fell in love with.

Not my mother, but Perla. My mother was the one shouting. Shouting and apologizing simultaneously. She insisted on buying him a new shirt, presumptuous as that sounded. He told her he was running late. He and the band were playing a gig that night and it paid. There was blood all over him. He'd have to double back to change. She was so egregiously sorry that she showed up to the gig and dropped a ten-dollar bill in the tip jar. He introduced her around afterward. The tenor of the evening dipped. His fiancée was across town and his bandmates gave him warning looks. They explained how they met, but it didn't sound like real life.

He did not yet know you could love two people at one time, for reasons of varying degrees of intensity and importance. It was also exciting. It was an excitement only he, as the spear of the love triangle, could appreciate, but exciting nonetheless. Things were happening for him in New York. It had been more than just a change of scenery. It had also been a change in carriage. It made him want more—quality and quantity. In the days of his shoeless childhood, he couldn't have dreamed of such an impulsive path. His younger brother had been passed to different families, while he too floated between those that could afford to feed him. Things were dire enough that keeping everyone together was less important than surviving. These origins taunted him. He tossed and turned on his little basement cot, gnashed his teeth and dreamt of washed-out cliffsides, unexploded bombs rigid as tombstones in the bioluminescent bay. These steered him back toward rectitude, before the nationalist meetings and brawls in Bronx alleys, the music career, his pregnant girlfriend. The daughter of the signmaker.

It wasn't even that hard to leave her. It was shameful, but true. It felt noble to follow his heart. It was proof he had come a long way. My mother's free spirit was a beacon of possibility. Her love and devotion gave him permission to dream.

Perla laughed in his face and said, "You think she can give it to you?"

And that became the chorus.

TRACK 2.
"GIRL WITH THE NICKELS AND DIMES"

My mother found something invigorating about a hard-bitten life, so went the theory. It reminded her of her time on the road, often appraised as the freest she'd ever been. My father found no romanticism in rough living, or in a house falling down, but the circumstances of the warehouse-in-progress weren't unfamiliar.

The hill houses he bounced between as a child were all without plumbing or electricity. Though the military bases dominating the coasts of Vieques hummed right along, the central, cordoned-off strip of habitable land was left in the dark. Before that, Vieques was an island of the indentured and enslaved working sugar plantations. Before that, an outpost for pirates, outlaws, and other aquatic anarchists. Before that, it was taken by enterprising conquistadors with a homicidal streak. And before that, more unbidden history. That was why he could appreciate owning something. Especially something as outsized and withstanding as a warehouse with its brutal proportions. The home they made would be an island unto itself.

My mother had done little since taking ownership. There had already been a bathroom and a makeshift kitchenette on the second level, which defaulted as her living quarters. Surveying the rubble of past occupants, the shoddy drywall, the winter moving in through the cracks, my father mistook his feeling of dread for nerves instead of what it was: a warning. To him, at least for a time, there was no way around it but through. They got to work.

It was always one project complete and two projects behind. To fix one thing, you had to tear out another thing, and to fix that, you had to buy this. They'd sworn off all funding from her frigid parents, whom he had met precisely once, inside their estate called White Hall. My father called it The Museum. Stately, trimmed, no artifact amiss. His tour began with an introduction to a walking cane that belonged to an ancient cousin who'd sunk with the *Titanic*. Rare books from an uncle who vacationed with the Lindberghs. Someone owned a railroad. Served as vice president. Threw himself off a skyscraper when the stock market went bust. Owned a Triple Crown winner. Made Knight of the Order of the Lily in France. Built a racist castle in Barbados. Went to dinners with the Kennedys. Thought Jackie O was a ditz and a snob. Each relic had been catalogued and cared for, packaged neatly for a future generation to tend. All those swords and warped tomes and oil portraits, the ships in a bottle and pocket watches suspended inside their bell jars would one day be hers, and his.

My mother knew how at odds her life must seem to him after her deft performance of a bohemian. My father clocked everything. Even their maid was white. An Irishwoman with an accent. He could never have imagined himself in such a place, and even the knowledge of such a place's existence was foreign. The history was unimpeachable. He decided in that instant he too wanted to leave a print upon the world, tangible as theirs. He would build it himself, with his own two hands, if it was what he had to do.

All the while, the band kept playing. It was harder to coordinate rehearsals. Last-minute gigs, which often paid the most, became impossible. But isolation was a different kind of boon to creativity. He read, wrote, hammered, and played music. He did calisthenics on the roof. The best and most inspiring part was that my mother was his captive audience.

She became pregnant while the loft was far from finished. She wanted to phone her parents. She wouldn't ask for money explicitly, but he knew that if they offered, she'd accept. Full of a certain kind of pride and emptied of another, he returned to the signmaker with his tail between his legs. The man had lost his wife and daughter by then when the two moved back to Yabucoa, where they were from. To save money on commuting, and to rack up as many gigs as he could, he returned to the basement. Meanwhile, my mother was pregnant and alone in a half-finished home, waiting for him on the weekends to construct the fourth wall of their bedroom. When he was present, he could at least make her laugh. It was surprising and thus funnier when he made jokes. With their discount groceries, he would make a fine Sunday feast of canned goods, rice, gizzards, beans. She counted out the money and he took it to the store. He sang to her the ingredients as he prepared them. As long as their plates were full, they could pretend the roof wasn't leaking. He cheered her. His girl with the nickels and dimes.

TRACK 3.
"LOS RATEROS"

When he was my age, my father was the serious one in his pack of friends. The same friends he went caroling with up in the hills that night. It wasn't his idea, but who would look out for the rest if he didn't go along?

My father's name was Ulises. His brother was Aurelio. They hardly knew each other, but he watched with curiosity when their respective packs bounced off each other or gathered near the beaches. He tried to work out if their names were somehow a linked message planted by their parents—both gone to the big island by then. The younger boy was weaker than the others he ran with, no older than ten, and little Aurelio still cried wet tears, threw tantrums. He had a patch of hair, white like a bunny tail, on the back of his head. When asked if it was true, that they were related, born of the same, my father denied it. It was easier to say his brother was dead.

It was dark and cooler on the hillside where they went to sing. My father's pack of teenagers jangled with every step they took, pockets full of coins for their harmonies, falsettos, and ability to take requests. They knew all the standards. They heard them on the radio and my father reverse-engineered the arrangements. Before they went caroling, he told them to clean up, to remember to smile and say thank you. What was the point of doing the work if they weren't going to get the most out of it? It was almost Christmas.

But the gangly pack of ten-year-olds that trailed them, Aurelio included, scared off the little old ladies who would otherwise open their doors. Instead, matriarchs in aprons called out through the crack in the door, "Rateros." Thieves.

A chained-up dog snarled as the boys passed a cliffside street, and roosters on the loose shook out their wings to perform their displeasure. With slingshots, the littler boys stalked parakeets and iguanas and shot rocks into the dust at the ankles of my father and his friends. When the teenagers came for them with fists raised, the boys scattered into the jungle, laughing and screaming. But Aurelio, the slowest, the dumbest, tripped over his own feet and cried.

The teenagers said to grab him, make him pay, tie his hands and roll him down the hill. And my father had every intention of adhering. There was nothing to prove. The older boys believed him when he lied. They believed he was an orphan. He had his brother by the collar when the dog came at them. My father acted with purpose. To fling the dog into the canyon, to grip it by the throat, to wrest away its teeth and riveted jaw and let the animal fly out and down into a warm, dark December night—to save the both of them, family, it came down to sensibly performed survival, the quick instincts of the boy who made it here.

The song turned over, the needle constant.

"Perla" became "Girl with the Nickels and Dimes," which became "Los Rateros," which became the last on the record, the engine and the caboose: "Bombs Away."

On the nights he didn't show, I told the stories to myself, starting at the beginning of the record, and letting it play. I pictured my mother running into my father on that street corner, her arms full of tinctures and velveteen baggies of dried herbs and books of mystical doctrine. The pedestrian current rifts. From my aerial view, I pity them. They know so little of what's to come. Fawn and I wait in the celestial wings, powerless as the wheel of our existence sets into motion as our parents trip into blood, banter, and all the usual questions. We are the last vestiges of their fateful meeting, and no one can ever know what we know.

One morning, no more remarkable than another, I woke up in the empty office with the dead record spinning. There was only the sound of it rotating in its hollow groove, and I let this rouse me, gradually, as I looked out the tall windows and watched the dawn.

I lifted the needle, docked it. As usual, there was no telling when our father would be back from his latest emergency, but the icy tracks left by his car made it clear we were alone.

Fawn and I had our own routine in the mornings. We ignited the space heater in the kitchen and ate our instant oatmeal before its altar. We sat knee to knee to absorb all the heat we could. We hardly spoke, and it was better that way. It felt like its own progress.

I was thinking of this, allowing myself the barest comfort, until I saw a shudder at the tree line. At first, it was only that, near imperceptible and just beyond the curtain. It might've been an animal, a whitetail getting bold, staying out after dawn—but it was her.

Fawn was outfitted in her new boots and our father's spare coat, hat, and gloves. By her firm gait, head down and legs pumping, it appeared to be a journey she had returned from many times before, perhaps every morning, mornings like this one. The slope dividing the house from the woods had shifted sallow as daybreak loomed on the ridge, but as the earliest rays of sunlight touched her cheeks, she stopped there in the middle of the expanse to absorb it. I thought somehow she had seen me in the window or sensed my presence watching nearby—but she believed she was alone. It was safe to close her eyes, to lift her chin, and let first light strike her.

21

As soon as I listened to her voicemail, a half-shouted and meandering non-invitation, it made perfect sense. Planned happenstance. She was coming into the city, one day only. The embedded code was clear. Our mother wanted us to meet.

I came an hour early, and now she is an hour late. I've chosen the diner for its location. Far from the apartment and far from my father's old neighborhood, the train station, and Rochelle's work. Hotspots better left unagitated. I've kept my eye on the windows to see her coming. A Jeep pulls up to the curb, two hands on the wheel, two figures in the backseat, my mother up front.

I should feel nervous, but instead I feel cold. It is like a damp chill has settled between my skin and my clothes. My mother leans over the center console to the driver, then turns to the backseat. Next she is on the sidewalk, squinting up at the skyscrapers. The devotee, returned.

The Jeep pulls away but a rear passenger peers out through an open window, eyes wide like she's on safari. The girl. The same prairie-home wonder. The twins have made it all the way to the Big

Apple, and maybe they're thinking what I was thinking after the ferry ride and inland drive. It's all a lot of nothing.

My mother enters the diner and stops just inside the threshold. Before I wave her over, I hold out a moment and watch her look for me. She's twenty pounds heavier, stronger and weathered, with a cropped haircut. She is wearing all khaki and denim and canvas, with knee-high muck boots and a holster on her belt for her cellphone. She looks nothing like my mother, but she does look a little like Candace. She refuses a menu and starts walking the booths in search for my face, a face she may or may not recognize on sight.

"Over here," I call out finally.

I stand as she sits, and then she stands as I sit. We settle and hold our mugs out as the waitress comes by with the coffeepot. "Is your sister coming?" my mother asks.

"She's supposed to."

"We agreed on eleven."

"We said ten."

"She texted. I've got it right here."

"Wonderful," I say. "I'm sure you're both right."

I haven't seen her since our father's funeral, a sparsely attended affair. Fawn was enrolled at Veld by then and given no travel privileges, considering the precarious state she was in. Neither my mother nor I pressed this matter. We stood side by side as his ashes were delivered into their tiny vault. A few townsfolk and past clients had come to the mausoleum to pay their respects. They shook our hands but said little. They knew him better than I did.

"You know," my mother says, "I forget how loud this city is. It's like a construction site. What could they possibly be building? Where is there any room?"

"You'd be surprised."

"And that smell. Has it always smelled like this?"

"What kind of smell?"

She wrinkles her nose. "Piss? Never mind."

We exchange all the usual pleasantries as we wait for Fawn to show. I ask what the twins think of New York and she demurs. It's twenty minutes past eleven, and we are running out of safe, first-layer conversation topics. If any more unstructured minutes pass, we'll be forced to discuss the real matter at hand.

"You're sure she's coming?" she asks.

"I'm not her secretary."

My mother begins ripping the edge of a paper napkin, a habit we share. Little by little, she assembles a mountain of tiny, torn edges. She probably has a hatchet in the back of the Jeep, along with a cooler full of venison, a shotgun. "Why did you call me?" I finally ask.

She begins to shape the mountain of torn edges into four piles. "I missed you. Isn't that enough?"

I laugh. "I'm not sure."

"It's the first time we'll all be in the same place again. How about that?"

"Should I just leave? If we're not going to be honest, I can go."

"Just sit, sit, sit," she says. "Right where you are. Don't get into such a huff."

"Is this about money? Because I don't have any."

"No," she says, and chews her chapped lip. "We have everything we could need."

"So you just decided to take a fourteen-hour road trip to what? See Times Square?"

She scoffs. "I would never."

"And yet, here you are."

"If you must know, I was invited."

The bell rings at the diner's doors, and Fawn spots us instantly. At the edge of our table, she stops and grins, does a spin for inspection, and throws out her arms.

"Mommy," she says.

It's the three of us, together again.

It's hard to tell if my mother's grimace stems from her acquired rural severity, or if she doesn't want to touch her own daughter. She lumbers to her feet and accepts the hug. Over Fawn's shoulder, she looks at me as if I'm supposed to feed her a line.

The Jeep rolls by again, this time idling in the middle of the street. My mother and I catch sight of it at the same time. A cab honks and the Jeep speeds off.

"You're alone?" Fawn asks as she scoots into the booth beside me. "The both of you?"

"Candace and the gang are taking in the sights for the afternoon."

"I would've said hello," Fawn says. "Is Rochelle coming?"

"Who's Rochelle?" our mother asks.

"No one," I say. "Is Victor?"

"Who's Victor?" our mother asks.

"No one," Fawn says.

We both look at our mother. Her mouth is open. She stares between the two of us.

"I can't get over it. The two of you. You're so grown up."

The rest of the day progresses in alarming accord.

We move from spot to spot around the city like tourists, all of us inhabiting the roles to which we are meant to aspire. My mother plays the seasoned tour guide, mapping train routes and cutting through sidewalk stragglers. She asks if we're hungry, if we need a rest, if we have to go to the bathroom. My sister is the child she never was, grinning ear to ear, asking impish questions, practically skipping down the street. That leaves only me. The eldest. First into the breach. The one who remembers.

We do all the things that should be done. I see pockets of the city I've never seen before. Our mother leads us through narrow neighborhoods, greets doormen and hostesses and vagabonds she knows, who know her face even now. She points out buildings, architectural flourishes, her personal history passing through them. There was once an old boyfriend there, she'd say. He had a mattress on the floor, like so many of her boyfriends, but he became a great sculptor. And in another building, a friend who'd win a Tony, another who wrote a bestseller, another whose album became a classic, another who runs a major magazine. She recounted none of this with envy, though there were traces of wistfulness, the way her eyes lingered on certain windows, her stories trailing off as the intervening years were tallied, the accumulation of decades always surprising her. Touch was lost over time, unmomentously, though all the monuments remained. She takes us to a restaurant and sits us down in a vinyl booth.

She points out a photo on the wall. "See there?" she says. "Look close."

"Who's it supposed to be?" Fawn asks and leans in to get a good look.

The photo is of a raging party hosted decades earlier, black and white. She is one of many faces in the crowd, her presence incidental. There is a flush of light at her back, like a still explosion, and she has a bottle resting in the crook of her elbow as she listens intently to some person unseen. If I didn't know her, I might miss her altogether. Front and center are all the famous faces she has warned us about, whose personal effects and images and artistic contributions have since been appraised and archived. There could only be a chosen few. The rest would scatter, become everyone else.

In FAO Schwarz, I pull Fawn into a plush corner of stuffed animals. Eyeballs of black glass gaze at us from their cubbyholes like underlings in steerage class. My mother is perusing the vintage Barbies styled as Pan Am flight attendants. She takes each down from the shelf for a closer look.

"What are we doing here?" I whisper to Fawn. "Why did you bring her?"

She cocks her head, tucks some hair behind her ear. "I'm not sure what you mean. We're having such a nice day."

"Is this supposed to be normal?"

"It can be anything you want it to be," she says. "I wish Rochelle could've made it."

Okay, I think. She's playing May. I look over her shoulder and at my mother, now occupied by a nurse Barbie dressed in World War II garb.

"I didn't invite Rochelle. Purposefully. We should leave them out of this."

"I was going to make Victor come, but I think he's planning something for our anniversary. It's nice to see him up and moving." She fiddles with the paws on a giant teddy bear. "Six months," she says, and crosses her fingers.

Like a cosmic event, I see one world pass before the other, blotting out all light.

"Did you invite Mom here because you need something? Is it money?"

"You are so obsessed with material things," she says. The Moncler coat, the latest apartment makeover—even the clothes she dresses Victor in, just like Rochelle has dressed me. The funds are coming from somewhere.

"What? Do you have some rich boyfriend stashed away?"

"I have a way of meeting people. That is not a crime."

"I'm not sure we're understanding each other anymore," I say. "I think I've made a mistake. I thought things would be neater this way, but that was wishful thinking."

"Just look at the three of us," she says. "We're back together. Soon, we'll have the loft. We can all start over. Don't worry." Fawn pats my shoulder. "You did good."

"No. I didn't do good. I didn't do anything. You're not following my lead, because there is no lead to follow. The loft doesn't belong to us. It's not mine to hand over."

"Well, that's true. It's all of ours."

"No, Fawn," I say, and she bristles at the sound of her name. "It doesn't belong to me, or you, or Mom anymore. Victor isn't yours. This is real, not a game."

"Okay, okay," she says, and laughs. "I get it. Aren't you over this place anyway? All these sticky little kids running around." She sighs and turns toward the Barbies, gestures to our mother. "Let's just show her a good time, all right? It's a happy day. We're supposed to be happy. That's what she came to see."

The day ends in Central Park. A thunderstorm brews and the long stretch beside the baseball fields is unusually barren. "I love days like this," my mother says. "I love weather."

I could pull her away into the foliage, or slip through the train doors the moment they close. There's the burden, and then there's the burden of going it alone. I remember the empty road in front of Veld. The exhaust puffing from the Volvo's tailpipe in the early morning. The shame of walking into the admin office to turn myself back in. Why couldn't I hold it all against her? All that buried past, and I could not muster hatred. I only wished she was someone else.

I ask my mother about Candace, the twins, Canada. I play the part of interested adult daughter, but she's as mum as we are. "Oh, that's all boring stuff," she says and waves away my question. "You don't want to know about that."

"How are the winters? Are they endless?"

She looks off toward the skyscrapers rising up at the edge of the park. "They're lovely," she says. "Winters there are perfectly clean."

What I really want to know is how she feels about the city now. All those years she spent longing, looking on from afar, sneaking in for her fix. Perhaps true bliss was waiting all along inside her Canadian tundra, and it only took a dramatic rewrite of her life to claim it. Perhaps there is an end to all yearning, I think, if you're willing to go far enough.

We spend our last hour circling through the springtime bramble, the wooded corners, the ponderous lake. The city's lungs, where you can be two places at once. Fawn is babbling on about the play she's no longer in. I can't guess what she'll tell Victor come opening night. I'm not sure she's even thought that far, if she even considers him sentient enough to notice.

While she walks up ahead, taking in the budding trees and the burgeoning sky like a precocious child, I slink back and my mother follows suit. The whole day has been spent wandering.

"What's the first thing you'll do when you get home?" I ask.

"That's a good question. I like that question. Let me think about that."

"You know, you look different," I say, and she turns her face away, embarrassed. "Not bad different. It's just I haven't seen you in so long."

"Well, we're very far away. Travel in and out is a whole production."

"Maybe something like that would be good for me too."

She smiles at me, looking me over for evidence of who I am underneath. "Maybe so," she says. "You're young. You could go anywhere."

"I don't know about anywhere."

"Why not? Why not anywhere? Just so long as you aren't there alone."

We say goodbye at the curb. Candace's Jeep is pulled over, hazards on. Notably, she has not stepped out to say hello.

Fawn thanks our mother for coming. "It was just what we all needed, after all this time."

There is a long embrace. A single hug that's meant to do the heavy lifting. I picture her return journey, boarding *The Chip*, being taken out to sea.

"Take care of each other," our mother says. She has come when called. She has seen us with her own two eyes. Her children, alive and something like well.

"I'm sure we'll see you soon, Mom," Fawn says. "Don't cry."

"Don't you know I love you both?" our mother says.

"Of course," Fawn says.

"Go," I say.

"Are you sure?" she asks me. Just me.

Fawn looks between us.

"Go on," I say. "We'll be fine."

Our mother begins backing down the sidewalk. Her eyes dart toward the park, like she might make a break for it. She bumps into a stranger and then another. They brush past her without stopping. Candace honks the horn and my mother surrenders.

Candace's fleeced arm hangs from the window as she signals back into traffic with Canadian plates. The twins stare out the rear window. Fawn waves as it goes and the boy turns around in his seat. I strain my eyes to spot some old knot on the back of his head, a jagged line around which all hair follicles have died, leaving only a patch of broken white scar tissue. But it's too far to see anything, and pedestrians surround us and jostle for space, and the moment is mercifully brief, the car a cruise missile speeding north into someone else's territory.

22

A foot of snow made for a trail. Morning twilight filled the pock-marks from Fawn's footsteps, and I followed her prints like stepping stones into the forest.

Muscle memory reactivated from my days on the mountain. I stepped alongside her tracks, focused on the terrain in micro and macro estimations. But there was no string of girls beside me, no governing principles. These woods could've been anywhere, were everywhere. Once I was inside, the envelope sealed behind me.

Light and temperature dipped as I moved through the trees. I came to a clearing where new tracks intersected with Fawn's. Tracks like hooves, but smaller, softer. They pattered to the base of a tree, circled the tree, crossed back the way they came, and vanished.

Even with the guidance of Fawn's footsteps, I was already unsure which way led out and how much time had passed since I entered. It was possible Fawn was already at the table with our father, newly energized by a life saved. I had brought with me some of what I thought Shine would've suggested, and with other items I had taken liberties. Water, layers, a physician's penlight nabbed from my father's desk, though it might only illuminate an abstract coin of earth at a given time. I had a mini pocketknife on me, a pharmaceutical-branded tchotchke also lifted from the house. If there was a moment to turn back, it was then.

The footsteps ahead were taunts or warnings. It was as if Fawn had left her diary wide open and unattended. It was up to me to cast my eye in its direction and read.

I moved through a dark copse of conifer trees. At times, the gaps between tree trunks shrunk too small for me to pass, and heaps of stone and frozen gulches broke my through line. I was forced off her trail for yards at a time. What was visible beyond the canopy were storm clouds, the sun banished, as if daylight had turned back.

When I finally emerged in a squat hollow, shielded by evergreen, it was the darkest section of forest yet. A humid smell flushed the little vale, of rot and cold fat and bone.

There, a crude lean-to had been assembled, anchored by a boulder and a tall pine, and there was more. All the snow had been cleared. The handiwork before me was unmistakably human. From out of the earth, a primitive home.

It began with boulders, log segments, and other natural scraps arranged into rooms, all radiating out from the central lean-to with its walls and roof of wood and pine fronds. Some rooms were framed by rock stacks, works in progress no more than a few feet high. Others had been given greater cover. Two felled trees made for a long wall, and tall branches had been aligned together tightly, burrowed into the dirt and pointed to the sky, so that they crossed overhead to make a pointed roof. There were gaps in the ramshackle walls, strategically placed like windows, looking out. From one, a flowered dish towel served as a curtain. It whipped in the breeze. One wrong gust, and the whole thing could topple, though it had surely taken hours of clandestine planning, excavation, and assembly.

It was both juvenile and meticulous—which was how I knew it was Fawn's. There was no door, but an opening, her trail disappearing inside. It was dark enough that shadows within shifted and came alive.

"It's me," I called. I looked up through the netting of branches above. I tried to hold their positions in mind like a map I could return to. I held my breath and shined the light.

A flash of teeth, a flutter of wings. The smell of expiration. I came upon the school of animals cage by cage. Makeshift enclosures—lidded pots, a shoebox, a jar that once held peanut butter, now held in place Fawn's specimens, alive and not.

First were two birds the size of a fist, one dead though suspiciously rooted upright, almost posed, the other all aflutter. Beside them, a trio of field mice, alive, trembling, and folded in a heap for warmth, or safety. After those, a squirrel outstretched on her belly, so lethargic she did not flinch when the light passed over her face, eyes two iridescent beads on this side of living, for how long it could not be said.

The lean-to was more substantial than it appeared from the outside. It was well-protected from the elements, degrees warmer. The dirt floor was hard-packed and full of prints. I shined the light toward the terminus and saw a wooden wall, a small opening in its bottom corner like an escape hatch.

I moved deeper and the odor thickened. I felt a pinch of bile at the base of my throat. On a crude slab of wood, a squirrel halved at the middle. A pristine bird body pinned to a plank like a collected monarch, wings spread. A rabbit ear, frayed on one end where it has been cut and seized from the body. In the farthest corner, the largest item in her collection, an orange tabby cat. Her fur is soft, though her appendages are stiff. There is no telling what took her, which came first. The elements, or my sister.

I'm amazed at all the bloodlessness. There is precision in her work. A series of tools, pilfered from kitchen drawers, hang on the lean-to's wall, ordered by size. If that were all, it would be enough, but the rest of the dwelling is something different.

In the farthest corner of her habitat, the last, where a makeshift roof has been erected and all light is blotted out, I shine the penlight. I uncover a mat of pine and soft mulch, a bed, a real blanket folded at its foot. In another corner, a shelf of stone, on which there are a compact mirror, a single cup, and a photo. It's us. We three on the roof back home, Fawn half-hidden under my mother's arms. Me, glowering at the camera. It was a picture taken by Billy years before, and though it was an imperfect image, it captured the full scope of the valley at our backs, the highway streak refracting like diamond light. I assumed these were the few items she thought of as necessities, but it was just as possible she was only approximating what a home should have.

I imagined her moving through her routine, inside her world within a world. How did she settle on the order of things? Setting out for a fresh catch, toiling in her workshop, retiring to her earthen bedroom. On her way back to the house, she would run her hands along the cages where her animals cowered, just before she rejoined the world of compromise.

Before I followed suit, I backtracked through the lean-to and opened the enclosures of the surviving. The field mice scattered. The squirrel did not move. The live bird hopped in place, one wing limp as it tried to gather itself in flight. I took it in my hands and it gnawed at my fingers. It didn't know the difference between my sister and me. Even as I set it down at the base of a tree beyond the clearing, it stumbled over itself, lifting up and crashing down again into the snow.

I made it back to the house using Fawn's remnant tracks. As I trudged closer, I spied my sister and father through the window at the kitchen table, chatting away. Fawn threw her head back and laughed. It had been so long since I'd seen it, the thrill on her face looked primitive.

Lone rabbit's ear. Soft as a plush coin purse.

Three bird bodies. Air-filled, light as bulbs.

The squirrel split and splayed like a cowhide rug. Shades of burgundy. Lace of capillaries.

Mindless with cold, I let myself in and watched them interact for a moment. The mood in the room was loose until they noticed me.

"Did you come from outside?" our father asked. "It's freezing."

Would he want to know what his youngest had been doing out in the woods? Would he be proud of the ways in which she'd taken after him? She had made something for herself with her own two hands.

Fawn turned in her chair to take me in. "We thought you were in your room."

"Just walking," I said, but I hadn't gone out since we first arrived.

Our father gathered the plates and whistled as he carted them to the sink. He must have thought things were progressing swimmingly. He was probably patting himself on the back for his natural ability as a caregiver, that my mother had exaggerated her woes. It wasn't so hard to keep two girls in check. All they needed was a firm hand, no nonsense, open spaces.

He pushed up his sleeves and plunged his hands into the sink. Fawn and I locked eyes. I was still in the doorway, breathing heavy inside my coat. Not a muscle moved between us. She hid nothing. There was nothing more to hide.

That night, a warm rain fell. The windows fogged and the snow pile gave. My dreams were gruesome. They had a scent like Fawn's hollow. Twice, I dreamt she was standing over me. Twice, I woke alone. I went down to the den, and my father was at his desk.

"Oh," he said. "You're up. Good."

I sat down in my usual spot in the center of the plush carpet, surrounded by speakers. When in this position, I was forced to look up at him.

"Do you want to pick something? Should we start with the usual?"

"I have a headache," I said. "Maybe we don't have to play anything."

I could tell he was disappointed. Still, he tried to make conversation. "Tomorrow, there'll be a backlog at the clinic now that the roads are clearing. I will be very busy."

I imagined all the animals lined up in a row, waiting to be removed from pain. All I could think of were Fawn's tracks. It would be hard to find her hollow again when the snow was gone, but it was like Zeke said. You needed to see it to understand. It was violent, grisly, concerning—of course. It was also something else. There was sweetness in the shape of the structure and in the labor of it. Curtains in the window. Swept floors of dirt. She was trying to re-create something, or to hold something together inside. I didn't know how to tell him this. I didn't understand it, how she chose and trapped each innocent thing and brought it there, but this same desire knew me. Every time I tried to calculate my way into love, every time I held on too tightly, I broke it.

"Did you always love animals?" I asked. "Did you always want to be a vet?"

"Absolutely not," he said. "Very long hours. It's not a very glamorous career."

"Not like music."

"That wasn't very glamorous either, and it wasn't much of a career."

"But you enjoy the animals. Enough to go to school for all that time."

"I find usefulness in what I do, but it's complicated."

"Why?"

"Because I'm not technically a veterinarian. There are levels, you see."

"Your stethoscope," I said. "Your white coat."

"I put the hours in—that's how I got down here in the first place. People seeing my potential. I apprenticed for a long time. I couldn't finish school, so I made the best of it." Over his shoulder, there was a framed diploma hanging on the wall, his name inscribed in ornamental cursive. He followed my eyes. "Don't pay attention to that. I came close enough. The kind of experience I have, you can't get in a book. It's just paper. It makes people feel better."

"If it's for other people, then why do you keep it in your office at home?"

He laughed and got to his feet. "Okay. You're bright. I knew that about you already."

"You did?"

"Sure," he said. "As soon as you could talk, you would ask me questions I didn't know how to answer. It was unnerving. I felt like I had to do my research."

He walked past me and pulled a record from the shelf. He couldn't stand to talk to me without someone else in the background. "You want another story? I've got one." He lifted his chin to remember, and his weight shifted from one foot to the other as he loosened, a performer after all.

"Your mother and me? We played music all the time. It was like a way of talking. What we picked out, when, in what order—it could be like a code, if you wanted it to be. Especially because we had different tastes. Mostly I like everything, but she had no rhythm. She could do nothing with tempo, and so some of what I like she couldn't understand. But this," he said, circling the tiny shag carpet, following a familiar tread where the high-pile had been tamped down. A moment went by as we listened. Nina Simone was singing "Stars" live. "We did better with things like this. You know, we felt real deep sitting around talking. About what even? Lyrics, life. Logistics. Eventually nothing. Bookkeeping. But toward the end, this was how we got along, pulling records while we spackled

and hammered and thought about tomorrow. Or, maybe she'd dis-
agree. I shouldn't try to speak for her."

Later, when I would see the picture of my mother in the crowd,
the fresh face in the background of a timeless photo, I thought of
who the camera hadn't caught, someone she was talking to trans-
fixed, and I wondered if that someone was him.

"How did you choose?" I asked. "How did you know what to do?"

I looked to my father and he was looking back at me, like we
had just met.

"My work?" he asked. "It's practical. It's good."

"That's not what I mean."

He huffed and gestured to the turntable. "You're missing the
best parts," he said, but he could see I wasn't budging. "Okay. All
right. Do you know what your mother's biggest complaint was?
Maybe she told you. Maybe that's all she ever told you about me."

"Never."

"I only ever learned to live for one. No one looking after me, no
one pointing me in the right direction. I pay for that still." He fiddled
with a loose thread at the end of his shirt and frowned. He looked
like a teenager, chin slumped against his chest, pitying himself as he
chose his words. "That's what's different about a job like this. It's useful. Straightforward. There's no artifice with animals. I'm better when
I'm living like that. It's why I wasn't sure about bringing you here. I
didn't want to ruin anything." He was on his feet again.

"Ruin what?" The precious projection he'd made of his life, or
the figment of him in my mind. "There's not really anything to ruin.
I don't even know you."

This caught him off guard. I could see he had considered these
nightly meetings a penance of sorts, or at least inroads, but I'd only
ever known him on his terms. I used to listen to his record spin
and thought I knew what his music was about. Like a message in a
bottle, it had found its way to me. It was my noble duty to interpret

it throughout my life, to be ready when the time came—but it was never mine.

"You're angry. I'm angry," he said. "I did my best. I didn't know my father."

"Like me."

"That expensive school you came from is not the same, I can tell you that."

"I didn't ask to go there."

"That's right. You were sent," he said. "I know all about it."

If he wanted to be of service now, after everything, it was too late for me—but he could start with his youngest. I tried to think of a segue that would move us forward to this most pressing revelation, but I hadn't earned his belief. Veld's specter had been raised. There was only one chance to say it right.

The live album ended in applause. Strangers from the past hooted and hollered and created the perfect exit for my father, who had decided no good could come from this conversation. He switched off the turntable and the record died before the encore. At the doorway, he paused, but only to cast a guilty glance at the diploma on the wall.

"What's locked up there, in your room?" I asked. "I saw the lock was new."

I pictured something sweet and tortured behind the bolt. The innermost chamber was always where the true treasure lay. Photos of us, worn at the edges. His wedding band on an altar. Instruments, polished and known to him like nothing else, hollow and arranged like tiny coffins.

"Up there?" He eyed the ceiling. He indulged me this, one last time. We would not meet again like this. I knew all the stories he would ever tell me.

"Guns," he said. "That's all."

I went to bed with a plan. I would wake before dawn and set out for Fawn's spot. I would mark a trail to bring my father along. Before he could leave for his long day of healing, I would take him to the truth. I would do what I should have done a long time ago. Even if I couldn't say everything right or explain, I could bring him there, and that might be enough.

Morning arrived in a flood of light. There were no clocks in the house but for the microwave in the kitchen, and I didn't have to see it to know I had missed my window. I skidded downstairs in my socks. Outside, the grass stood frozen on end. I had prepared myself for a standoff with Fawn for the day, but at the table, she and my father were waiting.

"Sit down," he said.

Fawn was hunched over in her chair, fine blond hair falling over her eyes. Something was wrong, but I could not tell in which direction it was wrong.

"Let's see it," he said, but Fawn didn't move. She did not even look up. "Let me see."

Fawn looked at me through the curtain of her hair. There were tears in her eyes, a sheen of snot below her nose. She whimpered a bit, surrendered, and laid her arm palm-up on the table.

There was a long, angry cut down her forearm. It went jagged where it reached her wrist, just before the bundle of veins there, bright below her skin. Her flesh was hot red at the edges of the slit. She held a wad of gauze tight against the deepest point, near the crook in her elbow.

"Now the other one," our father said.

She used her free hand to brush aside the hair in her face. There was another slice above her brow, a contusion puffing up beneath the waxen yellow of a new bruise.

My father looked at me expectantly, and I looked between him and my sister. I wanted to brush a thumb over her arm, smear away the wound like stage makeup.

"Well?" he asked. "What do you have to say for yourself?"

I reached out to take Fawn's injured arm, and my father grabbed my wrist and pushed me back into my chair.

"You don't understand," I said.

He set the pocketknife on the table. "I understand. I do."

"I would never do that." I tried to mind my words. I tried to clear my head and examine the context I was in, how best to be believed. Gia told us you should never claim to be framed. The concept was too flashy. She said it was better to herd people toward conclusions.

"Is this what you do when I'm not in this house?" my father asked.

"No."

"What is this? What is happening to you?"

Fawn was silent in her deferential sorrow—though she had left her arm draped over the table as evidence. Her hair had fallen back over her face, and I wondered if she was leering behind the curtain, or if her tears had become real, if she was frightened by what she was doing.

"Answer me when I am speaking." My father slammed his hand flat against the table and Fawn and I both jumped. She pulled her arm back, cradled it against her body.

"It hurts," she said. "Daddy."

What would dawn have looked like? I would've led the way. Through the forest, he would follow. I would need to pause sometimes to get a sense of our route, to read tracks, or so my father and I could share some water, tighten the laces on our boots. When we reached the hollow, the smell would have proven everything before my father could even look inside at the bodies. I would stand at a respectful distance until he made his assessment. The return would be slower. We would not have talked much, because what could be said? After the tree line was reached, we would stop for a moment with the picture of the house before us, Fawn inside. He might have touched my shoulder, knowing that I had done a hard thing and recognizing that more hardship was to come. At least, the gesture might've said, we would face the rest together.

"It's true," I said. "All of it. It was me."

Fawn did not look up, but I knew her well enough, am part of her even, that I too felt the lance of surprise. She was waiting for a trap, but there was none. She had won.

My father released a breath and steadied himself for his first order of business as a parent.

"You're going right back where you came from," he said, just like I knew he would.

TRACK 4.
"BOMBS AWAY"

When the record is done and pressed, he leaves us.

Ostensibly, the final song of the record is about his first and last voyage from the island of his youth. He says goodbye to no one, because there is no one left. He has crowded out his friends with dreams of the big island and the mainland, and indictments of the lives they have chosen. His long-lost brother stays long-lost. Aurelio never even got a song. In some ways, he said, his future was stream-lined. There is only himself to worry about.

Through the network of diaspora, he finds his way to Manhattan. The goal is to find footing, however he can get it. Life, he sings, is a bomb dropping. Birth is a fall from great heights, death the detonation. The fallout is what you leave behind.

It's supposed to be about Vieques, but all I hear is us.

My mother had just given birth to Fawn. She cried all the time, but the baby was eerily quiet. That's what the revolving door of city friends said. "What a placid baby." They would spend a few hours or days. They came to cook dinner, to clean the spoiled leftovers from the refrigerator, or to comb my mother's hair and do her nails, as if she were in a coma, which she nearly was.

"The hormones," her friends warned me. "Take it all with a grain of salt."

The first time I asked where my father was, my mother rounded on me as if I'd wished her dead. I thought she might hit me, but she burst into more tears. The shape of her face, how she clawed at it, the sounds she made—terrified me. I thought she was contagious, that it was only a matter of time before I contracted her affliction, and then who would care for the baby?

I used to sneak into Fawn's room and watch her, mystified. When my mother held her, fussed, fell asleep inside her room, I came unmoored. I was sure there could be only one of us.

That night I found my mother on the roof. She was standing by the ledge in the shroud of her nightgown. She was too close to the edge to mistake her intention. She looked like an apparition. My blood went cold, and I promised to never ask after him again. I said it was the hormones. I asked if she could come downstairs and make me something to eat. I told her the baby was crying. She stared off toward where the latest highway construction phase was near completion. Nocturnal crews were toiling. A crane swung across the blaze of a floodlight and cast a giant shadow over all the upturned earth. Something big was in the making. My mother told me to go to bed, and I listened, unsure if I would see her again.

I went back downstairs, to Fawn, and held her. We waited for the sun to come up.

None of it's there, in the song. The vision behind the melody is only mine. I hear one thing, and my father another. For him, there is writing on the wall, torpedoes racing toward the shore, a fleck of land usurped by ocean, but his myth was never meant for me. Either way, it's a sad way to close a record. It's a sad ending.

23

The official record denotes cause of death as catastrophic injury to the heart and major blood vessels. History repeating. This record is the only record. In the woods, my father's weapon, so carefully secured in his locked bedroom, spoken of but never seen, fires a single errant shot.

I pictured the burst of winter birds scattering, a pointed echo off tree trunks, and the body, as if it has crawled, death on his heels and creeping. It comes to rest half in the woods and half out, hand reaching toward the house, the last marker. But there is no factual accounting of the moments preceding, the day it happened, who was there or not. The cause and effect was reasonable to assume. He had guns. He liked to hunt. He was an amateur. He lived alone, almost.

I was on my second stint at Veld when I learned what happened to him. My father had coughed up the cash to put me on another tour of the mountain, another spell on campus until I was eighteen. Candace and my mother had ceded their involvement. The decision was his. I only had a few weeks left until I could walk.

My mother reported the news of his death by telephone. I had been summoned to the admin office to take the call, an occurrence rare enough that I knew something was wrong.

"Did she do it?" I asked my mother, hand cupping the mouth-piece for privacy.

"Keep questions like that to yourself."

"Where is she now?"

"She's on her way to the mountains," she said. "Candace and I talked about it. We don't know what else to do."

For months, I had kept my head down, blinders on, and now my certificate of completion was approved and stamped. I had book-marked some future date to resolve the matter of father and daugh-ter and all that was owed between us. Once my new life had been shaped into a shiny emblem, I would be ready. I would show him what he'd missed.

Fawn was fourteen and already en route to a trekking course in South Carolina. When she was ready, she'd be brought to Veld—to recover, process, be forged over. All the same ques-tions and exercises and miles and medications awaited her. They would want to talk about it. They would want to know what passed through her mind, if she internalized the accident, if she blamed herself. It was Fawn who found him in the woods. She ran back to the house for the landline, called into town for help. I pictured her running to and fro alone, from the phone to the body and back again until strangers came to take them both away. I knew what that was like.

"Will I see her?" I asked my mother on the phone.

"No, honey," she said. "Not this time."

"And you?"

"At the funeral, sure."

"And then?"

"We'll figure something out," my mother said. I thought of all the calls she made to Candace from the road, every rest stop flank-ing every town, the two of them tethered by their own endless need.

There was a shift in the receiver, and I pictured Candace standing over her shoulder, listening in. At least they had ended up together.

The apartment in Queens has undergone a notable transformation since May's auspicious arrival. The couch with its loose springs, the mottled carpet, and the plastic folding table in the kitchen—all have been replaced. In their stead, foraged standouts from designer showrooms and objects more familiar, a highlight reel of the past. Gems from the loft, my mother's signature. There is a difference between taste and tasteful. Rochelle's monochrome appointments are tasteful, can be replicated easily and anywhere, while May's swap of generic for perfectly imperfect is a demonstration of something more.

While Fawn is out for the afternoon, I knock on Victor's bedroom door. The blinds are drawn. A pressed suit on its hanger is cuffed to the top of his closet door, a hangman overseeing the body in the bed. Victor is sleeping, or pretending to. His five o'clock shadow, always on the breakthrough, has taken on a life of its own. His beard is fit for a shipwrecked castaway. That's what he is, and what he smells like. His bed is floating detritus on the ocean's surface. He dares not move, dares not upset the precarious balance of survival.

I whisper his name and his eyelids flutter. "May?" he asks, without opening them.

"No. It's me."

"Not right now."

"I went shopping. I put some food in the fridge. All you had was old milk. Has she been getting you any groceries at all?"

Victor does not answer.

I take a seat on the edge of the bed. "You don't have to get up. That's okay. We can just sit here for a while."

"I don't need company."

"What if I need company?"

"I think you have a wife for that."

"Wife-to-be," I say. "Or not."

Victor cracks an eyelid. "May will be back soon. We have to run lines."

"Right. So you're going then? To opening night, when it happens?"

Victor turns over and pulls the blanket to his chin, though the temperature outside has peaked in the high seventies and the building bakes in heat compounded floor by floor. He mumbles some non-answer and sweats.

"Do you think I should leave her?" I ask. "I'm thinking of leaving her."

Victor does not look back at me. He does not speak. After a minute, I get up to leave.

"You can sit down," he says. "If you want. I don't care."

I put a hand on his blanketed ankle in what I intend as a gesture of solidarity. "I'm sorry about everything. I'm sorry about what happened with JoAnn."

"Don't say her name," he chokes out. "I don't like to think about her name."

"Why not?"

"It's too specific. It reminds me that someone gave it to her."

"It's not your fault, you know. It was an accident. Look, in some other version of that night, you take a different train, or she drinks one less drink, or it's raining so the roof is closed."

"Or your birthday is on some other day."

"Sure," I say. "That's one example."

"Or you never up and move to that shit little town."

"All right."

"And we are never roommates, never friends, in the first place."

I eye the suit suspended on its hanger, the unoccupied outline. "You can wish that," I say.

"I think she's going to leave me," Victor whispers, and I don't know what to tell him, because she will.

He cries as if finally given the permission. I watch his face crumple and try to work it out, why it has affected him so. There is the obvious gore and shock, the proximity of a body, freshly dead—but there was everything else too. A bad year. So many expectations flat-lined. Perhaps even the fresh-pressed hurt of the absentee girl-friend, the blonde he does not believe he deserves. But it is because of both of us, Fawn and me together, that he will never be the same.

24

The series finale of *MAYDAY* goes like this.

Our characters have advanced along the board. Juvenile aspirations have been swapped for career paths, puerility replaced by efficiency. All baby faces have no more excuses. The reckoning has come.

May's father has expired, and everyone is back in town for the funeral. After seasons of teases, dream sequences, flashbacks, themed episodes, and sweeps-week flourishes, the long-lost sailor has met his end. May and tackle shop boy weigh the new reality of their relationship, now that high school is over. The boy says he'll wait for her, but they agree to part with no promises. Love is most painful when ending arbitrarily.

May goes on doing the same things she's always done. She wakes early to open the diner, turning ketchup bottles. She takes lunch on the rocky point at the harbor's edge where the bay releases. Out of habit, she surveys the water, though there is no hope to discover on the horizon. Her father is gone, and with him all mystery.

In the final scene, she issues a goodbye dispatch on her father's ham radio. Unlike the early days when he might have been tuning in beyond the breakers, stranded somewhere with a coconut and a flare gun, there is no clear audience to address—no hope to pin on apparition. She stops and starts as the camera lingers on her face. The crest of emotion is imbued with meta-finality, because we too understand that we are inside the last minutes of the last episode of the last season. In the end, she releases herself from the shackle of another. She chooses no one. The town of her childhood, borders bracketed by ocean, scenic as the felted landscape of a toy train track—will go on humming without her, even if she is the star of the show.

She throws a plastic sheet over the old broadcasting equipment and locks the door to the basement studio. She throws the key into the waves. The credits roll.

Because Rochelle decants her stash into unmarked bottles only she can comprehend, I accept what she gives me with an open hand.

Normally, I take three vitamins before bed and sleep soundly, wake in peace. In the morning, the next batch stirs me, arranges my mood, and herds me out the door come dazzling sunlight or torrential rain. The weather doesn't matter because my head is always on straight.

It was hard to go without the last month. Though I have fiddled with the regimen before, I have never felt their decline so acutely. It could be that it took time and consistency for the true properties of the pills to take effect. Or, it could be that I am changed of my own volition. Once impervious, now susceptible. Or maybe the other way around. Either way I hoard what is given to me. In secret, I grind them up or release their capsules, pound powder and granules in a mortar and pestle to create a concentration of my own design. I document my calculations and labors in my journal. I know my plan inside and out.

When Rochelle left for work this morning, I followed her to the door. I was scared to let her go. I know my leaving will set her back. The shame of being left will leave a mark on her that others can point at and press on. For this, she will never forgive me—but I have already forgiven myself. It is better for her this way. There will always be Michigan.

On Geronimo Street, white men in their mid-twenties gallivant with knees and shoulders exposed. The weather is inviting, and all the windows down the block are thrown open to receive it. I let myself into the loft and listen for an answer, but all the walls have stopped talking. I sweep a few errant crumbs from the marble counters. I make sure the trash bin is empty, but these are hollow acts, and I don't need them anymore.

In so many endings, the lead hits the lights, looks through the glass, remembers. I lock up and slide the spare key under the door. I test the knob to be sure I can't return. I bend down and peer through the gap, see the harmless spear of metal lying there, and want it back.

Behind the wheel of an old Volvo bought on the cheap and in cash, I navigate the side streets and thoroughfares. I imagine I'm in Hollywood, on a tour of celebrity homes and iconic exteriors that look nothing like their soundstage counterparts. I always wanted to see the fire escape from *Pretty Woman*. "What's your dream?" a well-placed street mystic said, passing through the final frame as the leads leaned into their forever.

All the while, I am recording. My last broadcast.

I hold my phone below my chin and release the script I've written down and memorized. I explain myself chronologically and opine. I say I should not be followed or sought, though this seems a generous estimation of myself. I talk about Zeke, and everything I know, until the timeline of his life trails into hypotheticals of what could but will never be. Other lives, unknown, echo through me. I say to Victor, "I know you will do great things," and mean it.

For the weekend, he is back in Jersey with his family. They drive him crazy, but they are safe. They all share and feast upon the same crumb of meaning, and it's enough. I remind myself of this as I take the highway ramp. They will be there to see how he turns out. No matter how hard he tries, he will never be alone.

I go to Arden Avenue first. The lot where the Wepplers' house once stood is now a tidy plot, only the old patio visible. Weeds have worked their way around the pavers, and what's left is a dissonant island of stone. From there, I take a long loop out to the edge of town where the pink Italian Renaissance Revival remains. Beautification has not reached this distant sector. There is plywood over one window on the second level, which may or may not belong to Antonia's old bedroom. Perhaps they made it to Atlantic City. The yard is wild as ever.

Finally, The Gables. Its new inhabitants have reinvented the cookie-cutter models with additions, paint jobs, eco-friendly landscaping. The Heller house is unrecognizable. The last lofty oak in the front yard has been cut, the stump dragged off, leaving behind a pustule hole beside the driveway. And when I coast by Coronet Court the same old Dodge is in the driveway. The screen door is hanging on by a hinge. The man in the van never dies.

And then the city lets me back in.

I've asked Fawn to meet me at a specific corner, all diagonals. While I wait, I squint into the basement-level windows, as if the residue of past tenants is somehow preserved.

"What is this supposed to be?" a voice asks.

Fawn has turned out to be the spitting image of our mother. Especially in her throwback threads, all seventies fringe and washed-out jeans. She blends into New York perfectly.

"Hello to you too," I say, and hand her a cup of coffee. I scan her shoes. "Those are familiar. What else have you got hidden away?"

"They were Mom's," she says. "Why? Do you want them back?"

"I guess you two have the same shoe size."

"We have the same size everything."

"Where does she keep it all? All that old junk from the loft. The paper moon."

Fawn looks sidelong at me. "You have a lot of questions today."

"Do you know where we are?"

"New York."

"It's Dad's old spot," I say. "He lived here. He recorded his album right down there." I point out a window, any window.

"There?"

"Well," I say. "Somewhere down there."

She takes a moment to look over the nondescript building. There is truly nothing special about it, except for its age. Its tenants are now high-end, its relevance subjective.

"Cool," Fawn says eventually.

"How did you do it?" I ask, picturing shiny stacks of pressed albums arranged face-out by a tablet register, bar-coded, remastered, plentiful. "How did you get the record out there?"

She throws her head back and laughs. "Oh my god," she says. "Is that what this is about? It wasn't even that hard. Everyone is buying vinyl."

"The album belongs to him."

"Belonged. What do you want me to say? It's a cute story. I met people who knew what to do with it. It's a seller. People like how it looks. It makes them feel cultured, and cool. Street kids with dingy instruments singing doo-wop rock with Spanish accents? It's perfect for this neighborhood. When someone asks what's playing, they can tell the story all over again, like they were the one who discovered it."

"That's not really how it is, or how it sounds."

"It's how it sounds to me."

Down the street, a location shoot has blocked traffic. I'm parked a few blocks away. It's time to get moving.

"Why did you bring me here?" Fawn asks. "Just to show me this? Is this about the profits? I'd give you a cut, but there's not even that much, and anyway, you owe me."

"Owe you what?"

She opens her mouth and seems surprised when the answer does not roll off her tongue.

"I just wanted you to see this place. I thought you might find it interesting. That's all."

I feel a peace come over me, unlike any fledgling comfort or vanishing future I've followed before. "That's why I asked you to meet me."

Somewhere near Harrisburg, Pennsylvania, Fawn wakes up in the backseat.

It's gloomy out, the sort of humid cold that crops up between spring and summer on off days. She had been surprised by the Volvo, but pleased that I invited her for a ride. She told me she couldn't be out too long. She was headed to Jersey to meet Victor's family. She couldn't be late, or he'd never forgive her, and that meant I would never forgive her either.

At first, she is groggy. The vitamins have never had that effect on me, but I've never consumed them in bulk. When I sprinkled their dust in her coffee cup, I watched curiously as the powder melted. Invisible little helpers, now deployed at my discretion.

It's best I keep the car moving. As she comes nearer to the surface, the drowsiness shifts to aggression. She bangs on the back of my headrest and demands to know where I'm taking her, what I've done with her phone.

"I have everything you need," I say. "We can send for whatever else."

"Pull over," she says. "Pull over or I will crash this car."

"How? Why? With you in it?"

"This is kidnapping."

I keep my eyes on the road and stifle old impulses. We are turning over a new leaf. We are taking ourselves out of circulation. "You should be thanking me," I say. "I'm the only one you have left."

We pass a sign for destinations ahead. If we go straight, there's Pittsburgh. Southeast routes us to D.C. Both anchor other lives that do not belong to us, and southwest is where we're headed. Next stop, Charleston. And after that, the end. I sharpen my tongue as I am paid to do and list the features in my head. Mid-century marvel on a scenic hillside. Double-high windows oversee a private acreage in an unincorporated community. Original fixtures. Impeccably kept.

"I know where you're taking me," Fawn says, after a prolonged silence of protest.

"It's not a secret."

I watch in the rearview as she turns her head, assessing the scenery, reserving judgment. "Are we ever going back?" she asks, and meets my eyes in the mirror.

"I think it's better if we don't."

"You never really want to know my side, do you? You never really ask the right questions, ever. Maybe you should be scared of me."

"Fine. Should I be scared of you?"

Fawn leans back in her seat and scowls.

"I think this is exactly what you want," I say.

"Tell me I'm crazy. I don't care. Go ahead and try to lock me up again."

I pull off on the shoulder and unlock the doors. "Go then. If you don't want to come, I'm not going to make you. We can go our separate ways, but I have a feeling we'll end up back where we started."

Fawn narrows her eyes. "And the plan is what—to stay forever? Two spinsters on the hill waiting to die?"

"Sure. Whatever. It's ours, completely."

A few cars fire past. She climbs over the center console into the passenger seat and fastens her seatbelt. I stare at her as the engine ticks, each speeding vehicle rocking the Volvo on its chassis. I peer into the future, whatever her face will tell me of it. After a long moment permitting me this, she turns away.

"We can try," she says, "but maybe you'll hate it."

"Me? Maybe you'll hate it."

"I don't hate anything." She scratches at a hole at the knee of her jeans. "The word is not in my vocabulary."

After a few close calls, I pull back into traffic and climb up to speed. The Volvo has pierced some kind of perimeter. An ancient engine chant fills the cabin.

"I wonder what it'll look like after all this time," Fawn muses. As always, her mood has caught on some new wind. She cracks her knuckles and lets her head loll as she gazes out the window. "I wonder if it's how he left it. Where did all that stuff go? Do we even have a key?"

Half-dreaming, she asks, "What's the first thing you'll do when we get there?"

While I come up with an answer, we go a mile a minute. Past fallow fields and tract houses, gaping cows and billboards threatening hellfire. The odometer creeps. I jab the radio. I surf for something I'll know, and when I find it, I let the song complete. There will be hours more, years, decades. We are two sides of the same coin tossed and caught, by me. I don't care about the odds. We end up together.

Picture perfect.

Acknowledgments

To my dear Kelly Linda Langone, also known as Dusty Hamilton, also known as Boss, also known as the brightest star in the sky—thank you for the gift of your stories, your laughter, and for sharing in this process. You are one of a kind. To many more adventures to come.

Boundless gratitude to Nicole Aragi for her wisdom and the Fourth of July email that altered my life. A never-ending thank-you to my teacher and coach, Brady Udall, for putting me in the game. To Joy Williams for notes, anecdotes, and dollops of advice, both scrutable and inscrutable. To Jacqui Reiko Teruya, my dreamy writing partner and hype man—I owe you a great debt and a cig. I must also thank my better half, Caitlin Sharik, for putting up with me since kindergarten and always egging me on. It's cradle to grave, you and me. And to RM, it is a fact that I couldn't have written this without you.

A massive hug to my fellow Boise State writers, especially Mary Pauline Lowry (the Texan cheerleader after my own heart), Jackie Polzin, Becca Anderson, and Natalie Disney. I will always remember Idaho.

To my family, who has known for quite some time just how weird I am, and yet still manages to love and encourage me all the same. Bendición.

Thank you to all the engines at Random House, and thank you to my editor, Andrea Walker, for shepherding this book, for your belief in its possibility. On to the next.

Certainly I can't name you all. There are so many of you.

I am very grateful.

A Conversation Between Dana Spiotta, Author of *Wayward,* and Ariel Delgado Dixon

Dana Spiotta: Your narrator's wonderfully compelling voice propels the novel: She's charismatic, funny, darkly poetic, and an astute reader of other people. Yet she isn't exactly reliable, is she? Especially about her own compulsions and her motivations. Can you tell me where that voice came from and how you think about her?

Ariel Delgado Dixon: I took many, many tries to find the right timbre for the narrator's voice. In earlier attempts, she was either too serious or too self-righteous. Once I began writing her in the present thread, especially in relation to Rochelle and Victor, I could see her more clearly as a young adult: someone wry, who had at least a little perspective on the more traumatic aspects of her childhood and could exercise some knowing self-deprecation.

That said, the narrator is still frozen in her adolescent past. Not only has she tried to run from and overwrite the tumult of her youth but she spent a formative era of her life within Veld, filtering her emotions through an institutional sieve. She's quite immature—both avoidant and impulsive, sensitive but often detached from her emotions and the consequences of her actions. Writing toward her contradictory nature set up plenty of conflicts and questions to knock down; it made her more real to me, someone I wanted to tangle with as an author.

DS: The narrator falls hard for women who don't love her back, but there is something so lonely and touching in her hopeless devotion. How is this related to her family and the way she cherishes her father's lost record?

ADD: She really is hopeless when it comes to love. It's one of the things I cherish most about her. Being in love is so often charged with the stories we tell ourselves—of intentions and future promises, how through others we can fulfill certain versions of who we want to be. Her obsession with the TV show *MAYDAY* intersects with this. What is love supposed to look like? How much suffering and sacrifice is acceptable, or even noble, to endure? How do other people make love look so good? The narrator doesn't want to give anyone a reason to let her go. If she outperforms her role as lover, then certainly she can't be discarded, right? She doesn't understand that real-life love doesn't play by TV rules. Love is a kind of chaos.

When it comes to her family, she applies similar processing mechanisms. She's thinking cinematically, filling in gaps, anticipating what the story of her life expects of her. Her father's record becomes a cipher through which she might understand her roots, the dissolution of her parents' relationship, and maybe even what is ailing her—that loneliness, that heedless devotion. She is always looking for clues: in her past, in lovers, in TV, in music. Where are the hints at how to be and how to be loved?

DS: The narrator is sent to the Veld Center, a brutal reform camp for delinquent teens. The details of detention (from the therapy doublespeak to the ISO rooms to the odd bonds between the teens) are very specific and vivid. Did you do a lot of research about such places? Does the narrator get anything good out of being there?

ADD: I have a very close friend who has done a few stints at institutions like these, and she's a wonderful observer of others, very funny, totally vivacious. We grew up together, and the idea of writing some of her observations and experiences into a novel was always discussed. There aren't any characters that mirror her exactly, but her perspective informs much of the Veld material. I also did research of my own, and what I learned was pretty disturbing. These institutions are alive and well, and they work hard to silence their detractors. It's a very damaging for-profit industry that benefits from an unconscionable lack of oversight.

I asked my friend the same question, if she believes anything good came of her experiences at places like Veld. She kind of scoffed at the idea but also admitted that the sheer physicality of being pulled out of her life, away from some toxic people, removed certain opportunities for destructive behavior. That and her intensive introduction to the outdoors—however brutal and irresponsible it was—did instill a lasting respect for the natural world. She remains a very capable survivalist. In a zombie apocalypse, I definitely want her in my gang.

DS: Why did you choose the epigraph from Susan Sontag? I wondered about the idea of the "replicate" and how it relates to repeating/replicating traumatic experiences in the novel.

ADD: While writing, I thought of the novel as operating in concentric circles. The connective tissue between sections works through common image, or recollections, or even parallel points of plot, rather than through strict chronological time. The idea of structuring the novel this way was to enhance that dark funhouse mirror sensation of replication, of inescapable patterns. For instance, falling is a recurring motif: body parts falling from overpasses, JoAnn falling from the roof, the mother considering a leap of her own. In another, more literal replication, both the narrator and her mother combat their own versions of "the man in the van."

The motivations and actions of parent and child are not always an exact match, but I wanted certain atmospheres, traumas, and challenges to echo intergenerationally. I wanted to know how parent, child, and sibling might react differently to the defining moments of their lives. Where and how is the chain of damage replicated, or severed? And, if you can break those patterns, then the promise of peace, unlocked potential, and arrival may lie beyond. At least, that's the mirage.

DS: The sister, Fawn, is the only other person who has grown up in the same neglectful circumstances as the narrator has. They both seem desperate for love while also being very different and in opposition. Fawn is frighteningly devoid of compassion and very destructive. Yet I found myself almost feeling sorry for her. What are we to make of Fawn in the end?

ADD: I also feel sorry for Fawn. Even if she can be monstrous, she's just a girl.

The narrator and Fawn share so much in common: DNA, an upbringing, their internment at Veld, their reinvention in New York, certain romantic misadventures predicated upon deception and control. And yet, they remain in fundamental opposition. I am fascinated by this. Siblings are most often born of the same stuff, the same nature and nurture, but can wind up completely different— what's more, they can love each other in spite of this difference, because of this difference, or let this difference disconnect them.

The narrator makes a choice at the end of the novel that can be read in different ways, depending on your level of cynicism. In choosing to end up together, to essentially become Fawn's caretaker and retreat to the supposed safety of isolation, is the narrator making yet another sacrifice that will come back to bite her in the ass? Or, is she being brave in breaking a cycle of abandonment, paying her penance by being present for her sister in a way their parents never were? It could be grace she's giving, or else the same misguided, almost fanatical devotion that always gets her into trouble.

These are the questions that trail the girls as they drive off into the sunset. We're all dogged by recurring patterns in our lives, familiar tugs of ennui, mistakes repeated, toxic traits we always fall for. The question is if we're capable of change. Can Fawn change? Can the narrator? And if they can—will the replicate finally be put to rest?

The sisters will spend the rest of their lives attempting to put these questions to bed, but it's meaningful that they'll be making the attempt together.

PHOTO: © JC/JONAS CASTRO

ARIEL DELGADO DIXON was born and raised in Trenton, New Jersey. Her stories have appeared in *Kenyon Review*, *The Mississippi Review*, *The Greensboro Review*, and elsewhere. She lives in Philadelphia.

arieldeldixon.com
Twitter: @arieldeldixon
Instagram: @okayariel

ABOUT THE TYPE

This book was set in Fairfield, the first typeface from the hand of the distinguished American artist and engraver Rudolph Ruzicka (1883–1978). Ruzicka was born in Bohemia (in the present-day Czech Republic) and came to America in 1894. He set up his own shop, devoted to wood engraving and printing, in New York in 1913 after a varied career working as a wood engraver, in photoengraving and banknote printing plants, and as an art director and freelance artist. He designed and illustrated many books, and was the creator of a considerable list of individual prints—wood engravings, line engravings on copper, and aquatints.